"Have you been kissed? I mean, really kissed?"

The question and the husky timbre of his voice made her twitch and feel strange inside. "I've been kissed," she said defensively, scowling at him.

He grinned. "Must have been a brave man."

"What the hell is that supposed to mean?"

"You're an intimidating woman." His gaze traveled lazily over her face and throat. "I imagine most men would back away from a challenge like you."

She blew a smoke ring toward the shadows in the corner. "Most men don't even see me. Which suits me just fine."

"If they don't see you, it's because you don't want them to. That's why you hide yourself under that shapeless poncho and wear an old hat pulled down to your ears. If you'd wear a pretty dress, you'd have men lined up to get at you, darlin'."

She stubbed out her cigar in disgust and made a face.

"If I were to kiss you, I'd start out slow. Real slow. I'd put my hands on your waist, almost on your hips. Then I'd draw you up against me. Let you feel what I was thinking."

"Shut up," she whispered.

Please turn this page for praise for Maggie Osborne and her novels . . .

W9-AAO-278

The Wives of Bowie Stone

"A beautiful romance that echoes with a fresh, unusual, and poignantly moving voice."

—*Affaire de Coeur*

"A unique, wonderful, heartwarming story that only an author with Maggie Osborne's knowledge of human nature could write. . . . Full-blown characters who steal your heart away and a story that will leave you breathless."

—**Romantic Times**

"Maggie Osborne at her best. . . . Some of the most genuinely portrayed people I've read in a long time."

—**Heartland Critiques**

"A dynamite, bittersweet story that will replay in your heart for a long time."

—*Rendezvous*

"An absolutely, positively must-read. . . . A very moving story . . . filled with characters you'll remember long after you read the final page."

—*Walden's Romantic Reader*

"A wonderful story that will steal your heart. Don't miss it."

—**Heather Graham**

BOOKS BY MAGGIE OSBORNE

Brides of Prairie Gold
The Promise of Jenny Jones
The Seduction of Samantha Kincade
The Wives of Bowie Stone

Published by
WARNER BOOKS

MAGGIE OSBORNE

The PROMISE
OF JENNY JONES

WARNER BOOKS

A Time Warner Company

To my mother. I miss you every day.

WARNER BOOKS EDITION

Copyright © 1997 by Maggie Osborne
All rights reserved.

Cover design by Diane Luger
Cover illustration by Gabriel Molano
Hand lettering by David Gatti

Warner Books, Inc.
1271 Avenue of the Americas
New York, NY 10020

Visit our Web site at
http://pathfinder.com/twep

Ⓦ A Time Warner Company

Printed in the United States of America

First Printing: April, 1997

10 9 8 7 6 5 4 3 2 1

Chapter
One

"I never heard your name before. I don't know you. I've got nothing to say to you," Jenny Jones stated, her voice cold as she turned her back on the woman the guard had allowed into her jail cell.

Turning to the window, Jenny caught a glimpse through the iron bars of the bored-looking Mexican officials rehearsing the firing squad. A light shudder tiptoed down her spine, and she wiped sweating palms against the oversize men's pants she wore.

At dawn tomorrow, she would look down the barrels of six rifles. She hoped she didn't wet herself before they killed her. She hoped she had the courage to die with a little damned dignity.

"I've come to save your life," Senora Marguarita Sanders said quietly. That caught Jenny's attention, and she turned around to watch the senora lift a lace-edged handkerchief to her aristocratic nostrils, clearly attempting to smother the stench in Jenny's cell. The elegantly dressed woman glanced at the cramped quarters and released a soft sigh, then gathered her skirts close to her body and prepared to sit on the bare mattress.

"Don't," Jenny advised, turning back to the barred window. "The mattress is infested with lice."

And so was she, but it didn't matter now. Jenny mopped her sweaty throat with a bandanna and decided the heat building in the cell and the incessant buzzing of flies was slowly driving her crazy. She watched six of the ragtag soldiers march in sloppy formation toward a bullet-pocked wall. None of them looked like crack shots. She wondered how many rounds they would have to fire before they actually killed her. The way her luck was running, they'd still be trying at midday.

"*Pardone,* did you hear what I said?" Marguarita Sanders inquired softly. She wiped grime from a low stool with her handkerchief, hesitated, then seated herself as if she intended to stay. Her silk hem billowed before settling atop the damp filth coating the cell floor.

There was no humor in Jenny's laugh. "Very dramatic. All right, I'll play along. Just how do you plan to save my life, Senora?" She turned to inspect her visitor again. "Are you going to arrange a jailbreak? Gun down the firing squad? Reverse my conviction?" She watched Senora Sanders cough into her handkerchief, glance at flecks of blood on the snowy lace, then ball the handkerchief in her gloved fist. Jenny's eyes narrowed. "You're coughing up blood." Interested, she studied Senora Sanders's pale face. "You're dying," she stated bluntly.

Death rode Marguarita Sanders's high, gaunt cheekbones, had drained the bloom from her cheeks. Her dark eyes were sunk in purplish circles, and the hair knotted beneath her stylish hat was dull and lusterless. Staring,

Jenny could see that once Senora Sanders must have been a considerable beauty. Now, her flesh had shrunk, and she probably looked a decade older than she was.

"Why aren't you resting in your own bed? Why did you come here?" Jenny asked in a gentler voice. Her grimy hand lifted to indicate the tin roof trapping the stench and the heat. "This isn't good for you. Go home."

Home was probably one of the large haciendas on a ranch beyond the village. The lace trimming the woman's handkerchief and the rich fabric of her skirt and cape proclaimed wealth. The thin blade of nose and delicate bones announced aristocratic breeding as surely as did her self-possession and quiet air of confidence. If this woman had ever performed a single act of labor, it had been no more strenuous than lifting her own fork before a servant did it for her.

Such delicate women made Jenny acutely uncomfortable. Beside them, she felt large and ungainly, about as graceful as the balky mules she drove to earn her bread and board. Women like Marguarita Sanders inhabited a different, better world than Jenny ever had, a world she could barely imagine.

Her lip curled. Senora Sanders had never worn the same dirty clothing for a month running, had never bought a vermin-ridden bed for two bits and been grateful to get it, had never picked at blisters on her palms. Jenny would have wagered half the hours remaining to her that Marguarita Sanders had never missed a meal, or prepared one for that matter. She had never worried her pretty head about anything more taxing than what gown to wear to the next fancy event.

Bending, Jenny spit the taste of envy out of her mouth,

then glanced up to see if spitting on the floor shocked her la-de-da visitor.

Senora Sanders had missed Jenny's gesture of contempt. She was coughing into her blood-flecked handkerchief again, her dark eyes closed in pain.

When the coughing spell passed, Senora Sanders's chest moved beneath a ruffled bodice, fighting for a full breath of the scorching air. "At five-thirty tomorrow morning," she said when she could speak, "Father Perez will arrive to hear your last confession."

"Tell him to sleep in. I'm not Catholic."

"He'll be wearing an ankle-length cassock and a deep hood. The guards expect him." Marguarita pressed a hand to her thin bosom and drew a shallow breath. "Only it will not be Father Perez. It will be me. You and I will exchange places." Her gaze traveled over Jenny's soiled trousers and the loose man's shirt stained by a month's accumulation of filth. "The commander, a rather stupid fellow, has been informed that you don't wish the firing squad to observe your face as you die, that you have requested a hood. The firing squad was relieved to hear this as they are not accustomed to killing a woman. It is further agreed that Father Perez will supply the hood and secure it."

Jenny stared. Her hands curled into fists at her sides. "What the hell are you suggesting? That I walk out of here pretending to be Father Perez? And you're going to die on the wall instead of me?"

Marguarita Sanders pressed her handkerchief to her pale lips, coughed, then nodded wearily. "I will die in your place."

In the hot silence Jenny heard the fat Mexican official

screaming at the firing squad. A horse trotted past the bars of her window, and a dog barked somewhere in camp. A breeze that died as quickly as it arose, curled around the scent of freshly baked tortillas and roasting chilies.

"All right. You have my attention." Leaving the window, she sat on the bare mattress. Her blue eyes burned on Marguarita Sanders. "What's the price? What do you want from me that is so important you're willing to pay for it with your life?"

Marguarita smiled, and Jenny saw a glimpse of the beauty she had been. "I was told that you are blunt and to the point."

"I didn't have the benefit of a delicate upbringing," Jenny snapped. She glanced at Marguarita's soft smooth hands, then down at her own. Heavy calluses swelled the pads of her fingers. Wind and weather had chapped the backs of her hands into a tanned semblance of old leather. She resisted an urge to hide her hands beneath her thighs and almost smiled at the impulse. She couldn't remember the last time she had displayed an ounce of feminine vanity.

"I can't think of anything I can offer in exchange for my life, but you must have something in mind. What is it?"

She stared at Marguarita, trying to guess what the cost of her life would be. The price would be huge; it had to be. Marguarita Sanders wanted something that Jenny sensed would be hard to deliver, something worth dying for.

"This is what I want in exchange for dying in your place." Marguarita returned Jenny's stare. "I want you to take my six-year-old daughter, Graciela, to her father in northern California." When Jenny started to speak, she lifted a shaking hand. "If my husband is dead, you must agree to raise Graciela as your own daughter. You are not to give her into the keeping of her grandparents, or anyone else claiming to be a relative. If you cannot, for whatever reason, place her in the safety of her father's arms, you must raise her as your own and provide for her until she chooses of her own free will to marry and establish her own household. That is the bargain I wish to make with you. That is the price I ask for giving you back your life."

Jenny's mouth dropped. She felt as if a chunk of granite had fallen on her head. "That's crazy," she finally sputtered. "If you love your daughter, and I assume you must if you're willing to die for her, then why in the name of God would you entrust her to the care of a stranger? You don't know anything about me except that I'm condemned to die for killing a soldier!"

When Marguarita's coughing fit passed and she'd caught her breath, she fanned her face with her gloves and shook her head. "I know you are honest to a fault. There were no witnesses. You could have denied killing the beast who attacked you. But you freely admitted it."

"And look where that honesty got me!" Jenny indicated the stone walls enclosing them. "No one believed a man, even a drunk soldier, would try to force himself on a woman like me."

Marguarita met her eyes calmly. "If my information is correct, you have been hauling freight into the state of Chihuahua long enough to know that the instant you admitted shooting Senor Montez, you were convicted." Curiosity flickered at the back of her gaze. "Why didn't you lie?"

Angry, Jenny strode to the window and curled her

hands around the bars, ignoring the burn of hot iron against her palms.

"Honesty is all I've got," she said finally, speaking in a low voice. "I don't have family. I don't have beauty, or a man. I don't have money, and I sure as hell don't have a future. All I've got to prop up my pride is my word." Her chin rose. "When Jenny Jones says something, you can bet your last peso that it's true."

"So I have been informed."

"If I don't have my word, then I have nothing. I *am* nothing!" She stared hard over her shoulder, watching Marguarita Sanders press the bloody handkerchief to her lips. "Everybody needs something to make them feel good about themselves, even me. Honesty is what makes me feel like I've got a right to take up space in this world. It's all I've got. No matter how bad things get, or how low my circumstance, I can always say Jenny Jones is an honest woman. It's the one and only good thing about me."

Honesty was what had placed her in a Mexican jail, a few hours away from a firing squad. "I could have lied to that mockery of a court," she said between her teeth, staring out the window at the adobe wall that enclosed the camp. "And maybe you think I'm stupid because I didn't. But telling a lie would be killing the only thing about myself that's any good." Raising a hand, she scratched at the lice in her hair. "If I don't have my word, I might as well be dead. I'd rather die with honor than live without the only thing that makes me feel like I can face another day."

It was a long speech, and it left her mouth parched. Embarrassment tinted her throat. She could have kicked herself for parading her private feelings in front of this crazy visitor.

"Your honesty," Marguarita Sanders stated softly, "is why I trust you to take Graciela to her father. I believe you will honor our bargain."

"We haven't made any bargain," Jenny said sharply. She leaned against the wall, catching a whiff of Marguarita's powdery perfume. "There's things about me that you don't know. And things about you that I don't know. Like . . ." She stared at the rich embroidery trimming Marguarita's stylish blue cape. "Why a stranger? Don't you have relatives who could take your kid up north?"

"Oh yes." Marguarita studied the blood spots on her handkerchief. When she glanced up, bitterness deadened her gaze. "Our village is filled with cousins, none of whom would shed a tear if Graciela died tomorrow." She drew a long careful breath. "My story is long and filled with tears, but I'll tell it briefly."

Curious despite herself, Jenny returned to sit on the mattress. "I'm not going anywhere. You can talk until dawn tomorrow as far as I'm concerned. But don't go crying. I can't abide weepy women."

Marguarita turned her gaze to the sunlight slanting between the iron bars. "I grew up on a rancho in California next to the one owned by Robert's parents. My father hated gringos; Robert's father hated the Spanish." She shrugged and smiled softly. "I loved Roberto." A coughing spell interrupted her story.

"You should be in bed."

"When I was sixteen, I became pregnant with Graciela. The news nearly killed my father; his shame and sorrow were so great." She looked down at the handkerchief balled in her fist. "Our parents would not permit us to marry." Now she tilted her head up to stare at the tin roof. "My father sent me here in disgrace, to my aunt. Roberto caught up to my carriage and we were married in The City of The Angels."

"So why isn't he here with you?"

"I am my father's only child. But Roberto is the older of two brothers. If he followed me into exile, he would have forfeited his inheritance."

Jenny decided she didn't like this Robert, who chose an inheritance over his young wife and child.

"Neither my father nor Roberto's parents recognize our marriage." Pain flickered behind her eyelids, followed by a flash of surprising determination. "But my father will have to acknowledge Graciela after my death. She will be his sole heir." Her gaze met Jenny's. "My father is very wealthy, Senorita Jones, and so is my aunt. But my cousins are not. If Graciela should meet an untimely end, my greedy cousins are next in line and will inherit enough money to make them *patróns* in a region this poor. Already I see them looking at Graciela and speculating: if this child should die . . ."

"I see." Jenny frowned. "When you're no longer present to protect her, you think your cousins will kill your daughter."

Marguarita flinched. "This is a terrible thing to admit. But, yes. Only one small child will stand between my cousins and a life of great ease and comfort. I cannot trust any of them to see her safely to her father."

Jenny considered the dilemma. The poverty in this area was legion. There were grand estates, and she assumed Senora Sanders resided on one of them, but clearly the cousins did not. They, like the nearby villagers, most likely lived in thatched huts and counted themselves blessed to have a single cow in the yard and a few thin chickens. Perhaps the cousins occasionally joined the bandits who roamed the countryside, hard-eyed men who would not scruple to slit a man's throat for a few precious pesos.

Jenny picked a louse from her scalp and cracked it between dirty fingernails. "What about your Roberto and his parents? Are they going to welcome Graciela with open arms?"

"I don't know," Marguarita whispered, bowing her head. She touched trembling fingertips to her forehead. "I've had only one letter from Roberto in six years. He said he would come for me when it was possible for us to be together." She closed her eyes. "Perhaps he is dead. Perhaps he despaired of our future and forgot about Graciela and me. Perhaps . . . I just don't know. I tell myself he has written many, many letters and they did not reach us because perhaps his parents intercepted them."

"If you ask me, Robert Sanders is one sorry son of a bitch," Jenny stated flatly, studying the line of dirt embedded beneath her fingernails. "You know that, don't you?"

"No!" Senora Sanders's shoulders stiffened abruptly, and fire flashed in her dark eyes. For an instant Jenny glimpsed the girl who had defied a powerful father to marry the man of her choice. "Roberto is the sweetest, gentlest man who ever drew a breath."

"Spineless, you mean."

Marguarita stumbled to her feet, coughing harshly, and flung out a hand to support her shaking body against the cell wall. "I will not listen to slanders against my husband!"

Jenny rested her elbows on her knees and watched Senora Sanders fight to draw breath. She was no expert on medical matters, but she guessed Marguarita Sanders had only days left to her. "Yeah, the guy's a real prince. Sit down and rest. And finish what you came to say," she said.

Marguarita collapsed rather than sat. Her thin chest rose and fell rapidly, struggling to find air in the fetid cell.

"I don't have much time to arrange for Graciela's safety." She raised her eyes to Jenny. "If Graciela remains in the village after I die, she will shortly follow me to the grave, a victim of an unwitnessed accident. This I fear, and this I believe. The only solution is to send her to Roberto while I still can."

"He might not want her," Jenny said brusquely. "Your sorry Roberto may have remarried years ago. Have you considered that?"

"No!" Then the fire in Marguarita's eyes died to an ember with no strength behind it. "But there may be some reason why he cannot take her. Perhaps his father will not allow it." She closed her eyes and swallowed. "That is why you must give me your solemn promise on all you hold holy that you will never abandon Graciela. If you cannot give her safely to Roberto and to Roberto only, then you must raise her as your own."

Jenny spread her hands. "Senora Sanders. I am the last person on earth you would want to have raise your daughter. I can read some, and I can write some, but I have no education to speak of."

"I see the dictionary in your back pocket. I saw the books on the guard's table among your effects."

"Just feeding myself and keeping a shirt on my back is a full-time job. And it isn't easy. In my time I've taken in wash, I've skinned buffalo carcasses, which is the worst job on this planet, I've signed on as a roustabout, and most recently, I've driven a mule team and hauled freight for the Comden outfit. Except for washing, none of those jobs is what you'd call women's work. The only reason I got hired is because I begged for the work, and I happen to be better at those jobs than most men. Course, I got paid less than a man. The point is, I can barely feed and clothe myself, let alone a kid."

"I will give you money for the journey."

"What worries me is keeping Graciela if Robert can't or won't take her. Who's going to hire me if I have a kid hanging on my pant leg? How would I support this kid if I had to? And what kind of life would it be for a kid anyway?"

Marguarita studied her. "If you let your hair grow, and cleaned yourself . . . if you put on a dress and—"

Jenny burst into laughter. "Me? And a man?" She slapped her thigh. "That's a good one." Her eyes sobered. "No man has ever looked twice at me in twenty-four years, and I doubt hanging a skirt on my waist would change a thing." She shook her head. "A man has to be blind drunk to take a grab at me."

"You have beautiful eyes," Marguarita said after a minute, sounding surprised. "And a pretty mouth."

"Forget it." Angry now, Jenny made a chopping motion with her hand. "If I have to raise your kid, it's going to be just me. And it's going to be a damned hardscrabble life for both of us. She's not going to have fancy clothes, or servants waiting on her hand and foot. She'll be lucky to have food in her belly and a pillow for her head. Is that what you want for her?"

Marguarita's head dropped and she closed her eyes. "I have no friends outside my family, no one to rely on. I have no choice, and neither does my Graciela."

"That's not the worst of it," Jenny continued, being brutally honest. "I don't like kids. Never have."

"Graciela is precocious. She's very bright. Much older and wiser than her years would indicate."

"I don't care if she's a fricking prodigy. She's six years old. That makes her a kid, and I don't like kids. I don't know how to talk to them. I don't know how to take care of a kid." Jenny threw out her hands. "Kids don't know squat about how to survive in a desert or how to gut a rabbit or do a day's work. Kids get in the way. They whine. They cry. They're only half-human."

"Why are you telling me this?" Marguarita asked softly, her eyes pleading.

"Because I want you to know exactly what kind of a person you're willing to die for. If we change places, and I get stuck with your kid, I don't want to wake up some night with me and Graciela sleeping on the dirt with empty bellies and then start feeling guilty that you died for me, and I'm letting you down."

"I am not going to die for you, Jenny Jones, make no mistake about that. I am going to die so that Graciela may live. I'll take the bullets for you only if you swear on all that you hold sacred that Graciela will not be left here to die at the hands of people she mistakenly loves! I'll stand in front of that firing squad only if you promise on your soul that you will save my daughter. I'd a thousand times rather that she be hungry than dead."

"Where does your father, the wealthy rancher, fit into all this?" Jenny snapped. The two women glared at each other. "If your precious Roberto can't or won't take Graciela, why can't I just dump her off on your father's doorstep?"

"He will never accept the child of a Sanders."

"Well, there's your answer." Jenny leaned back against the wall, stretching her feet out on the lousy mattress. "Just explain that to your greedy cousins, and the kid is saved."

And she had just talked herself out of a chance to live. For a moment she cursed herself. Then she thought about trying to support a child and decided she would almost rather face a firing squad. Things worked out the way they were supposed to work out.

"Graciela is my father's legitimate heir whether or not he accepts her. Which he will not. In his eyes, Graciela is Roberto's bastard. But when the court is presented with my certificate of marriage, which I will give to you, Graciela's claim will be secure. I have verified this."

Jenny stared at a toe poking out of her broken boot. "I've told you that I hate kids, that I can't provide well for Graciela. Hell, I don't know what the future holds. I don't even know if I can *get* to northern California." She lifted hard eyes. "But you still want this exchange?"

"You are Graciela's only hope."

"Then Graciela is in big trouble." Jenny's laugh was harsh. She thought a minute. "They may shoot me while I'm wearing a hood over my face, but they aren't going to bury me in a hood. And the minute that hood comes off, everyone around this place is going to know they shot you, not me. Have you thought about that?"

Marguarita nodded slowly. "You'll have about six hours' head start." She hesitated. "Frankly, I don't believe the soldiers will bother searching for you. They wear uniforms, but they're little better than bandits. There is no profit in wasting time chasing a penniless woman. They'll have a corpse; that will satisfy the official records."

"So what's this about a six-hour head start? A head start on who?"

Marguarita stared at her. "My cousins, all of them, but especially Luis, Chulo, and Emil. Once my body is identified, they will understand all. But they will convince themselves you have abducted their beloved little heiress. They will convince each other that it is their duty to rescue Graciela. They will try to kill you both."

"Well, son of a bitch!" Jenny pulled a hand through her hair. After a minute she glared at Marguarita. "You're sticking me with a kid, possibly for the rest of my life, and I'll have a bunch of murdering Mexicans trying to track me down and kill me. That's a heavy price."

"You will be alive," Marguarita reminded her softly, meeting Jenny's gaze. She glanced at the shadows creeping across the stone walls. "Now you must decide. If we are to make the exchange, I have much to arrange and little time."

Two minutes ticked by in the heat while Jenny thought about it. A sigh lifted her breast.

"You know I'll do it. You knew that when you bribed your way in here." She shook her head and closed her eyes.

Tears of relief glistened in Marguarita Sanders's eyes. "Let us be clear what each of us is promising. I promise to die in your place tomorrow morning. You promise to take Graciela to her father and give her to no one else. If Roberto cannot or will not take our daughter," a cloud of pain crossed her features, "then you will raise Graciela as your own child. You will try to love her."

"Oh no." Jenny's head snapped up and her eyes narrowed. "I'm not promising to love some kid I've never met and already know I won't like. I'll take her to Robert. And I'll raise her up to be a woman if I have to, but don't expect me to love her. I can't do that."

"You're a hard woman, Jenny Jones."

"You don't know the half of it! My pa beat me from the time I was old enough to walk. The only person I ever loved, Billy, my third brother, died when I was nine, and it was my fault. My ma threw me out onto the streets of Denver when I was ten. I've been making my own way ever since. Yeah, you could say I'm a hard woman."

Compassion glistened in Senora Sanders's brown eyes. "I'm sorry. This should not happen to any child."

"You're going to die tomorrow, and you're sorry for me?" Something sharp turned in Jenny's chest. "You're either a fool or a better person than I've ever met," she whispered, staring.

The terrible truth of their transaction gripped her mind in a painful squeeze. This lovely, delicate woman would die tomorrow morning. Marguarita Sanders would face the firing squad in Jenny's place because she loved her child better than whatever life was left to her. She would spend her remaining hours arranging for Jenny's escape. She would say good-bye to a child she adored. With all this facing her, she could still feel compassion for a stranger's squalid past.

"What will I tell Graciela when she asks what happened to you?" Jenny said, swallowing hard.

"She is wiser than her years. I will tell her the truth,"

Marguarita said, standing. She shook her skirts, but the filth from the floor did not fall away. "I don't want her to blame you for my death. She must understand this was my choice."

"Assuming we aren't killed by your cousins . . . and assuming that Robert is dead or something." Jenny coughed uncomfortably. "What if Graciela asks me what kind of person you were? I don't know anything about you."

Marguarita's eyes settled on the iron bars. "Tell her that I loved her and her father. Tell her that I tried to live my life with kindness and dignity." She turned her gaze on Jenny. "Then tell her to forget me and honor the woman who raised her."

They studied each other in silence. Then Jenny said softly, "You can be a hard woman, too."

"Tell her not to burden herself with the past. Tell her to live and be strong, Jenny Jones. Teach her to laugh and to love. If she does this, and if she finds happiness, then wherever I am, I will smile and be happy."

"Oh Christ." Jenny scrubbed a dirty hand across her eyes. When Jenny realized Marguarita meant to embrace her, she hastily stepped backward. "I'm dirty, and I've got lice."

Amusement twinkled in Marguarita's eyes and a hint of color bloomed on her cheeks. "Senorita Jones," she said, smiling, "the lice will not trouble me long."

She wrapped her thin arms around Jenny's waist and rested her head on Jenny's shoulder. "Thank you," she whispered. "I will pray for you, Jenny Jones."

Jenny waved her hands in the air, then, helplessly, she returned Marguarita Sander's embrace, careful not to apply too much pressure against birdlike bones. Marguarita's size and delicacy made Jenny feel huge and awkward. As graceless as a new calf.

When she stepped away, embarrassed and clumsy, she dusted her hands together and stared at Senora Sanders, memorizing her features in the fading light. "I don't know what to say. If it's possible to get Graciela to California . . . then I swear on my sacred oath, I'll do it."

"I know you will." Marguarita stepped to the bars set in the doorway and summoned her strength to call the guard. "There won't be time to say good-bye when I see you tomorrow morning. So I will say good-bye now." She smiled and pressed Jenny's big calloused hands between her small soft palms. "There are not words to express what I feel in my heart. Gratitude. Appreciation. Love. They do not touch the surface of what I feel for you. You are the salvation of my heart, which is my daughter. You are the answer to my prayers. You are the mother I give to my child."

"Some fricking mother," Jenny muttered.

Marguarita smiled and pressed Jenny's hands. "I think you will surprise yourself," she said gently. "I think you will love our Graciela. Your way will not be what mine would have been, but it will be good and strong and true. If you must, you will guide our daughter, yours and mine, into a womanhood we will both be proud of. I know this."

Jenny stared at her. The woman was dreaming. She started to say so, then stopped herself. If it comforted Marguarita to delude herself that Jenny possessed hidden reservoirs of motherly virtues, then so be it. If that thought would ease her last hours, then Jenny was not cruel enough to take that comfort away from her.

When the guard opened the door, he shoved Jenny

across the cell with a snarl, then stepped back to let Senora Sanders pass.

Jenny picked herself up off the cell floor, rushed to the door, and gripped the bars at the tiny window. "I've given my word!" she shouted into the stench of the corridor. ". . . I've given you my word!" She wanted to say something else, something more, but she couldn't think of the right words. Maybe she was saying what Marguarita wanted to hear, that was her hope.

Long into the night, she sat on the bare mattress, cracking lice in the darkness, and thinking about the woman who would die in her place when the sun rose.

And thinking about the kid, Graciela. And the murderous cousins who would come after them. And pondering with a sinking heart what she considered the very real possibility that she would be stuck with the kid for the next twelve years and maybe longer.

"I gave my word," she whispered. It was the only thing she had to trade for her life. And the only thing, really, that Marguarita wanted from her. A promise.

If she had been on speaking terms with God, she would have whispered a prayer for Marguarita Sanders. And maybe she would have tagged on a word or two for herself and the kid.

Chapter
Two

Ty Sanders was one pissed-off cowboy.

He hadn't had a decent meal in half a month, or a bath or a shave, or anything softer to sleep on than desert rocks and dirt. Twice since he'd crossed the border his horse had been stolen and he'd had to buy another at prices that made him gnash his teeth. His butt ached from twelve-hour days of hard riding, and his thumb had festered around a cactus spine.

Adding insult to injury, he didn't know where the hell he was. The map he carried was hopelessly inaccurate or outdated or a hoax to begin with, and was worse than useless. All he knew for certain was that he was two weeks into Mexico and he had yet to locate an operating railroad.

Jerking irritably at the brim of his hat, he rode down the center of the dusty street that split this mean little town into two sun-baked halves. There was no sign of a railroad depot. Only a few people in sight, none of them in uniform, thank God. Hopefully that meant the sporadic fighting that had erupted across parts of Mexico hadn't reached this area. In Ty's opinion, the Mexicans weren't happy unless they were fighting someone. If outsiders weren't available, they fought each other.

He reined up at the central plaza, which was nothing more than a weedy courtyard for a church better suited to a town ten times this size. Two old men dozed on a bench beneath the only tree between here and a low ridge of brown hills.

"You! What's the name of this place?" His Spanish had been learned in California, and his accent wasn't perfect by a long shot, but he figured the old men could understand him.

One of the men pushed a sombrero toward the back of his head, revealing a face like a wrinkled bean. His dark eyes inspected the thick dust coating Ty's boots, his hat, his saddlebags, and the lining of his scowl.

"Mexla, *Señor.*"

Ty had never heard the name. It wasn't on his map. He might be two hundred miles into Mexico, or he might have circled back toward the border. Removing his hat, he mopped the sweat off his forehead with his shirtsleeve. What he wanted most was something wet and cool to drink.

"Is there a hotel? A place where a man can get a bed and a bath?"

The old man had to think about the question, not an encouraging sign. Finally he said, *"Casa Grande."* Then he pulled the sombrero back over his eyes and folded his arms across his chest. The conversation had ended.

Ty gazed back over his shoulder. The only thing *grande* in this village was the church. That's how it was in most of Mexico, at least the Mexico that he'd seen.

Magnificent churches surrounded by shacks and poverty. Occasionally, the alcalde, if he was powerful enough, ruthless enough, had a house that might be described as *grande*. Maybe.

Turning his horse, he traveled back the way he had come, searching sagging storefronts until he spotted a sun-flaked sign announcing the *Casa Grande*. On the other side of the street was an open-faced cantina and the stables.

In the stables, he grabbed the shirt of the hombre who took his horse and pushed his face close enough to smell the man's last meal.

"If anyone touches my horse—just touches him—I'm going to carve you into pieces, Senor. You understand what I'm saying?" The man's eyes widened. "I'm in no hurry. I'll track you down, I'll kill you." He jerked his hat brim toward the stall. "That horse better be there tomorrow morning, *comprende*?"

"*Sí, Señor!*"

"*Excellente.*"

His eyes were reddened from days of squinting against the blazing desert sun, his face burned beneath a two-week beard. He was filthy, he smelled goatish, and he supposed he looked just crazy enough to lend weight to his threat. Tossing his saddlebags over his shoulder, he crossed the street and entered the *Casa Grande*.

It didn't surprise him that the clerk stood waiting with a key already on the counter. Let a stranger, especially a gringo, ride into a Mexican village, and within minutes everyone in the village knew about it and was busily scheming how to profit from the encounter.

The only thing Ty liked about the Mexican people was

their food. Even the language offended his ear. To him, Spanish sounded too soft, too feminine. You could slander a man's ancestry back to his great-grandmother, and damned if it didn't sound like you were singing a sonnet to a woman.

He slapped a handful of pesos on the counter. "A room. A bath. And something to doctor this thumb with." Taking the key, he shifted the saddlebags on his shoulder and headed toward a staircase that looked as if it wouldn't bear his weight. "Where's the nearest railroad?" he said, stopping to stare back at the clerk.

"Chapula, *Señor.*" The clerk jerked a thumb over his shoulder. "Two, maybe three days' ride that way."

Maybe. But Ty did sort of recall seeing Chapula on his map. He continued upstairs, kicked open the door to his room, and was pleasantly astounded to discover a clean blanket on the bed. The window opened over a porch roof, convenient if he had to leave in a hurry. The furniture was sparse but serviceable. The mirror wasn't too cloudy to shave by.

Twenty minutes later he was soaking in a tepid tub, happily inhaling the vilest cigar he'd ever placed between his lips, and eating tiny rolled tortillas stuffed with chicken meat and bean paste. He'd worked the cactus spine out of his thumb, and slathered it with the aloe the clerk had sent to his room.

He still wanted to kick the hell out of someone, but the urge wasn't as powerful as it had been when he rode into town. He could trust himself to go to the cantina later, have a beer, ask about the nearest railroad, and do it without starting a fight.

He had learned the hard way that unless three separate people offered the same set of directions, he didn't move.

Shifting the cigar to the other side of his mouth, he shook out his map, careful to hold it above the grimy water. "There!"

Damned if he didn't find Chapula on the first try. And it had a mark beside it, indicating a railroad. Of course, that didn't mean the railroad was functioning. He'd learned that, too. The first thing the Mexicans did when they were pissed was to blow up the nearest railroad. It didn't seem to matter who they were pissed at—the government, the local *patrón,* their dog—the way to express dissatisfaction was to blow up a railroad.

There was no way to be certain, but it appeared the tracks that passed through Chapula ran southwest to Verde Flores. Immediately, Ty's spirits rose. When he reached Verde Flores, he was only a day's ride from the no-name village he'd come all this distance to find. The first half of this lunatic journey would be ended.

Dropping the map beside the tub, he eased his head back against the rim and puffed on his cigar, scowling at the cracks in the ceiling.

In six years a hundred things could have happened to make this journey a total waste of time.

Marguarita might be dead. The child might be dead. Marguarita might have remarried. Or entered a nunnery. She might have moved or simply vanished. Maybe she had lied and there had never been a child. Maybe he was on a fool's errand.

No maybe about that, he thought, swearing silently. This was a fool's errand, and he was the fool who had agreed to undertake it.

Later that night, he received confirmation that Chapula was a three-day ride to the southwest. That, and one hell of a fight involving half of the village, improved his mood considerably. When he entered the stables at dawn and discovered his horse hadn't been stolen, he felt almost cheerful.

He had a black eye and a cracked lip when he rode out of Mexla, but he was whistling between his teeth.

"I hate you!" Graciela stamped a tiny tasseled boot on the ground. "I hate you, I hate you, I hate you!"

Jenny frowned at the kid before she pulled the priest's cassock off over her head and handed it to a grim-faced woman standing beside a better horse than any Jenny had ever ridden.

"Shut up, kid."

"I want my mother!"

"I don't want to start off by having to slap the hell out of you, so just shut up, you hear me?" She thrust her face down near Graciela's, so the kid could see the threat in her eyes. "We need to be quiet until we get away from here. I know your mama told you to mind what I say, and I'm telling you to shut your mouth. If I have to stuff a rag between your teeth, I'll do it."

"I hate you!" At least she didn't scream it this time.

Jenny reached for the clothing extended by the woman holding the reins of the horse. "This is a skirt!" she said, shaking out the top item. The woman didn't say anything. She just handed Jenny a set of petticoats. "Well, damn."

She needed to put tracks between herself and the cousins, and she was going to have to do it while carrying the kid in front of her and wearing skirts. A cussword exploded between her lips. At least Marguarita had a good eye for size. The skirt and blouse were a fair fit. The hat was laughable to begin with, and about as useful for keeping the sun off as a teacup would have been, but Marguarita hadn't forgotten to include one. And she'd had the sense to send boots that were serviceable instead of fashionable.

The finishing touches turned out to be lace gloves and a waist-length cape, both of which impressed Jenny as ridiculous. The lace gloves would be rags after two hours of riding, and she'd broil under that cape twenty minutes after full dawn. She pushed both items into the saddle-bags and her fingers brushed a pouch of heavy coins and a packet of papers. Good. Marguarita hadn't forgotten the money.

"Come on, kid. Let's *vamoose.*" She extended her arms to Graciela, intending to hoist her up on the horse, but the kid jerked backward.

"I'm not going with you! I want my mama!" She cast an imploring look at the woman standing in the shadows, then ran to her and buried a storm of sobbing in the woman's apron. "I hate her! I want to stay here with you!"

This was exactly the situation Jenny had feared. Frowning, she shifted from one foot to the other, running a dozen solutions through her mind. She could knock the kid unconscious, throw her over the horse's neck, and go. She could hog-tie the kid, stuff the gloves in her mouth, and go. She could do just about anything except leave without the kid.

The woman's dark eyes burned in the darkness, scorching Jenny's face. Marguarita had told the woman and the kid that dying was her choice, Jenny knew this, but both of them seemed to place the blame squarely on her.

Pursing her lips, she inspected the lightening sky. In minutes, the sun would drift above the horizon. She wanted to be far enough away by then that Graciela would not hear the fusillade of gunshots from the camp. Jenny didn't want to hear them either.

She stepped up to the woman and gazed into her accusing eyes. "I want to be far away before the sun comes up. Do you get my meaning?" She jerked a thumb toward Graciela.

The woman leaned to one side and spit near the hem of Jenny's skirt. She glared hard, then bent to take Graciela's shaking body in her arms. Soft crooning sounds sang in her throat.

"Remember what your mama said? Dry your tears, little one. This Americana is going to take you home to your papa."

"She killed my mama!" Sobs slurred the words, but Jenny heard them clearly enough. She ground her teeth and clenched her fists. She wanted to smack the kid for wasting time.

"No, no, little flower." The woman eased backward, smoothed a strand of silky brown hair beneath the edge of Graciela's stylish little hat. She sent a murderous glare in Jenny's direction, then managed a smile for the child. "Remember? Your mama was dying slowly. Now, she will join the angels swiftly and without pain. She will be happy as she was not happy on earth."

"She'll join those angels *very* soon," Jenny reminded the woman, giving the sky a meaningful nod. "Graciela? Get your butt over here. We're leaving. *Now.*"

The woman half led, half pulled Graciela toward the horse. "The Americana will take good care of you," she promised in a soothing tone. Her hot eyes warned that if Jenny harmed a hair on Graciela's head, she would hunt Jenny to the ends of creation and eat the heart out of her chest.

Jenny flexed her shoulders, then stared down at Graciela. She didn't know how big a kid of six was supposed to be, but the feather atop Graciela's hat reached only to Jenny's chest. To her, the kid looked like a large doll dressed in miniature adult clothing. Aside from the fashionable attire, Jenny couldn't identify much of Marguarita in her daughter.

The kid had brown hair instead of black, and her skin was a shade lighter than Marguarita's. Most startling, Graciela had not inherited her mother's large, soft brown eyes. Graciela glared hatred through eyes that were as blue-green as the sea. She had received her mother's patrician nose and cheekbones, but the rest of her face must have come from her father's side, the family of the sainted Roberto. The stubbornness, Jenny suspected, was Graciela's alone.

Feeling that something more needed to be said to get Graciela's butt on the horse, Jenny bent until her face was on a level with the kid's.

"All right, you hate me. I don't like you either. But we're stuck with each other. It isn't fair, and it isn't right, but—" How had the woman put it? "Your mama has gone to join the angels. Your daddy is all you got left, and I promised your mama that I'd take you to him. And you promised your mama that you would go. She told me so. Isn't that right?"

Tiny gloved fists scrubbed at Graciela's eyes. "I don't want to leave Maria or my great-aunt Tete or my cousins."

"Well, you have to. You'll be safe and happy with your daddy." Jenny didn't have a fricking notion if she was telling the truth or not. She hated that. "Most important, this is what your mama wanted. You and me . . . we both promised her that you'd go."

They glared at each other for a full minute, then Graciela turned and flung herself on the woman, sobbing out a long good-bye. The two of them would have been saying good-bye a week from Sunday if Jenny hadn't grabbed Graciela by the waist and tossed her up on the horse. The idiot skirt and petticoats tripped her on the first try, but she mounted on the second.

The woman tapped her on the thigh, but didn't say anything when Jenny frowned down at her. "I hear you," Jenny muttered. "I'll do the best that I can."

Then she warned the kid to hang on, and she dug the heels of her boots into the horse's side. They galloped away from the mesquite tree and the woman, away from the walled camp in the distance.

Five minutes later, Jenny heard the shots.

"Thunder," she said to Graciela, closing her eyes above the kid's head.

All right, Marguarita. You're an angel now. There's not going to be anymore pain, no more blood on your handkerchief. If there's any blood around here, it's going to be mine. If you have any influence up there, me and the kid could use a helping hand. Just keep that in mind, okay? Do what you fricking can.

They rode spit for leather, keeping away from the main roads, until midday. Jenny wouldn't have stopped then, but the kid's body pressed next to hers radiated heat like a small oven. They were both soaked in sweat when she found a trickle of water and some shade and decided to stop, hoping Maria, or whatever her name was, had remembered to pack some food in the saddlebags.

Wordless, she lifted Graciela to the ground, then walked toward the trickle, kneeled, and scooped water over her face. A long sigh lifted her chest as the water ran down her throat and soaked into her high-necked shirt-waist.

"You stink," Graciela announced, dropping down beside Jenny and cupping her hands for the water. She let the water dribble through her fingers, then patted her face delicately.

"You'd stink too if you'd just spent six weeks in a jail cell." Jenny opened her collar and poured water out of her hand down between her breasts. She released a long sigh of pleasure.

Graciela slid her a sullen look. "Were there rats in your jail cell?"

"Rats almost as big as cats." Jenny reached for the pins in her hair. "Would you know if whoever packed the saddlebags packed scissors or a knife?"

"Is that true?" Graciela said suspiciously. "As big as cats?" A shudder convulsed her shoulders.

Jenny eyed the trickle of water. She hoped to reach Verde Flores the day after tomorrow. And she hoped to board the train without attracting undue attention. That wasn't going to happen if she smelled rank enough to drop an ox. Another sigh lifted her shoulders. She hated to waste a single minute, but this might be one of those ounce-of-prevention things.

Standing, she fetched the saddlebags and opened them beneath the shade of a scrub oak at the edge of the trickle. Whoever had packed the bags had managed to cram an amazing amount inside. Jenny found a change of clothing for both of them, and nightdresses. Nightdresses! There were toilet articles including a sewing kit, and a skillet, and the money pouch, which felt satisfyingly heavy in her palm, and a thin packet of papers. She found a bar of soap at once, and another pouch that contained smaller bags of medicinal supplies.

She sniffed the bags of powders and ointments, and uttered a low sound when the pungent scent of crushed sabadilla seed made her nostrils flare. This was the remedy she had hoped to find.

Rocking back on her heels, she studied Graciela's reddened eyes. "I'm going to need your help."

"I hate you," Graciela hissed.

"I need your help anyway." Now that she could see Graciela in full sunlight, she had to concede the kid was different from Marguarita, but equally lovely. Graciela's eyes were particularly beautiful, thick-lashed and changing from blue to green, then back again. Right now those eyes were as hard as rocks. Patrician and spoiled to the core, Graciela stared at her with haughty disdain.

Jenny dug through the sewing materials and removed a small pair of scissors. "Do you know how to use these?"

"Of *course* I know how to use scissors."

"Well, how do I know what a six-year-old can or cannot do?" Jenny snapped. She pushed the scissors at Graciela, then shook out tangled skeins of matted red hair. "Cut it off."

Graciela twitched and stared.

"Lice," Jenny explained with a shrug, enjoying the horror in the kid's expression. "Keep in mind that I have to appear in public, and you'll be there with me. So cut it short, but not too close to the scalp. Leave me enough that I won't look peculiar wearing a bonnet."

"Lice! Ack! I don't want to touch them!"

"Either we get rid of them now, or in a day or two, you'll have lice, too."

Graciela's hand flew to the brown curls peeping beneath the edge of her little feathered hat. "No!"

Jenny pointed to her head, wondering at the wisdom of allowing someone who hated her, even a kid, near her head with a pair of sharp scissors.

Graciela approached with huge reluctance, as if Jenny had admitted to leprosy. She made herself lift a dirty strand between her thumb and forefinger. "Ugh!"

"Just cut it, damn it." There was a mirror among the toiletries, but it was so tiny that it only revealed an inch at a look. Otherwise, Jenny would have done the job herself. A minute later, ropy strings of red started falling around her. Jenny tried not to look at them. The one thing she was vain about was her hair. She had pretty hair, if she did say so herself. Or she might have if she had done anything with it. She stared straight ahead with a stony expression as Graciela chopped and whacked, moving around Jenny, sidestepping the mats of falling hair.

"It's done," Graciela announced, handing Jenny the scissors. She gazed at Jenny's head with a smirk.

Tight-lipped, Jenny found the scrap of mirror and held it up. Graciela had whacked her hair to earlobe length in most places, closer to the scalp in other places. Here and there a stiff tuft stuck out like the bristles on a broom.

Most women would have wept. Jenny sighed and stared into space for a long minute. It had to be done.

Standing, she pulled off her shirtwaist and skirt and tossed them toward the tree. She hadn't taken time for stockings, so the boots stuck to her feet and she had to fight them off.

Graciela spread a cloth in the shade, seated herself with enormous dignity, then unwrapped a tortilla stuffed with cold meat. First, of course, she opened a napkin across her lap. She watched Jenny undressing.

"You should have said thank you."

Jenny glared at her and said nothing. She'd be damned if she'd thank a smirking kid for deliberately chopping holes in her hair. There wasn't a doubt in her mind that Graciela had enjoyed hacking Jenny's hair into a ragged mess.

Between delicate bites of tortilla, Graciela watched Jenny step into the trickle of water and begin soaping her body. "I've never seen a grown-up without clothes before," she said, staring.

"Well, this is what one looks like," Jenny snapped. She couldn't remember being this uncomfortable in years. If anyone had seen her naked since she was a kid herself, she hadn't known about it. She tried to pretend that she didn't mind Graciela's staring at her, but she suspected her face was as red as her hacked-off hair.

"Do all grown-up women have hair between their legs, or is it only you?"

Oh God. Jenny's face caught fire. She turned her buttocks toward the kid, but hated that almost as much. "All grown-up women have hair there," she said in a choking voice.

"Why?"

"How would I know? It happens when you're about ten years old, or maybe it's twelve, I can't remember. Didn't your mother tell you about . . . ah . . . any of that?"

"My mother doesn't have a bunch of disgusting hair between her legs," the kid stated in tones of ringing superiority. She looked down her nose at Jenny.

"Yes, she does." *Did,* Jenny silently amended. "All grown-up women get hair between their legs and under their arms."

Graciela's face pinched in an appalled expression. "Well, my mama doesn't!" Her cheeks reddened, she lowered the tortilla to her lap, and her eyes filled with tears. "Mama is dead now, isn't she?" A low wail built in her chest.

Jenny paused in scrubbing her hair and looked around anxiously. She doubted there was a soul within hailing distance, but the land dipped and rolled. She couldn't be sure.

"Kid! Don't be so loud! Stop that!"

She had forgotten, if she had known it to start with, how totally, abysmally, miserable a kid could look. Tears poured out of Graciela's blue-green eyes. Her nose dripped. Her face and shoulders collapsed. Sobs racked her small body. Jenny stared at a small heap of abject anguish, and she felt as helpless as she had felt in her life.

Keeping one eye on the kid, she hastily rinsed the soap off her body and out of her hair, then she shook the crushed sabadilla seeds into a small vial of vinegar, grateful that Marguarita had included both, and scrubbed the mixture into her scalp, hoping she didn't have any sores.

Because if she did, the vinegar was going to feel like liquid fire eating into her brain.

"I'm sorry your mother is an angel now." Stepping onto the bank, she toweled off with her petticoat, then tore off a strip of hem, moistened it in the water, and bound it around her head. The sabadilla had to heat up and cook the rest of the nits. She ought to be able to drag a comb through what hair she had left by the time they boarded the train at Verde Flores.

She jerked on a cotton chemise with a small strip of lace edging, the first lace she'd ever worn.

"Kid, I know you feel bad inside. But you got to be strong."

Graciela sat hunched over as if someone had let the air out of her. Her hands hung down at her sides, limp on the ground. Tears and snot dripped off her face onto her napkin. If Jenny had seen a dog suffering like that, she would have shot the thing and put it out of its misery.

"Kid, listen. People die all the time. You have to get used to it." Words weren't helping. Jenny would not have believed one tiny body could contain so many tears or so much snot. "That woman—her name was Maria, wasn't it?—she was right. Your mama was very sick; you must have seen the blood she was coughing up. Well, she's not sick or in pain anymore."

"I want to be with her."

"Well, I know you do." Jenny pulled on her skirt and shoved in the tail of her shirtwaist. "But you can't. Now, you just have to accept that and stop sniveling. Crying doesn't solve anything."

"You're ugly and mean, and I hate you!"

"You're little and snotty, and I don't like you either." Jenny found the tortillas and bit into one. Tasty. She chewed and watched Graciela anxiously. What would

Marguarita do? What would she say in this situation? "It's time for you to shut up."

That probably was not what Marguarita would have said. The kid only cried harder and louder.

"Look. Crying isn't going to bring your mother back. Crying only makes you feel worse and makes me feel like smacking you. So stop it. I didn't carry on like that when I heard that my ma died." She finished eating, then filled the canteens and tied them to the horse. "Let's go. If we don't stop often, we can make ten miles before the light goes."

Graciela didn't move.

"Kid," Jenny said, reaching deep for patience, "believe me, I'd love to ride off and leave you here, but I can't. And you're too small and too young and too stupid to take care of yourself. So. Unless you want bandits or wolves to get you, you'd better get your butt moving and get on over here."

Graciela waited long enough to make it clear that she acted under duress. She dragged herself forward with her head down, still dripping tears and snot, her shoulders twitching. She made herself go limp and heavy when Jenny lifted her up.

Mouth grim, Jenny swung up behind her and touched her heels to the horse's flanks. Graciela sagged back against her like a kid-sized oven.

"Here's the deal," Jenny said, speaking between her teeth. "You don't talk to me, and I don't talk to you. We need a break from each other, so just shut up." She settled into the saddle for a long ride.

They rode into full darkness before she stopped to make camp for the night. Her bones ached. And she must have broken the skin when she was scratching lice because there was a spot on top of her head where the sabadilla vinegar burned like a hot spike driving into her skull.

"Can you water the horse and tether him for the night?"

Graciela stared as if Jenny had lost her mind. Jenny sighed.

"All right. Can you build a fire and get some coffee going?"

Graciela lifted an eyebrow. Six fricking years old, and she could lift one eyebrow. Jenny was twenty-four and couldn't lift one eyebrow without the other zipping up, too.

"Can't you do *anything* useful?"

"I can sew, and I can read, and I can draw pictures."

Pressing her lips together, Jenny settled the horse for the night, then laid a fire. "Pay attention, kid. Next time this is your job." She made coffee, warmed the beans and tortillas, shook out the blankets that had been tied behind the saddle. Watching Graciela yawn over her tortilla, Jenny wondered if the cousins were out there somewhere in the darkness. Or had Marguarita overestimated any threat the cousins might pose? Maybe they were back at the village, getting drunk, holding a wake for Marguarita and feeling glad to be rid of any responsibility for the kid.

Graciela stood up and politely covered a yawn. "You can undress me now. I want to go to sleep."

Jenny's mouth dropped. "Do I look like a fricking servant to you? Undress you? When I was six years old I was doing the work of an adult. You can sure as hell dress and undress yourself."

Graciela stared at her across the fire. Tears welled in her eyes, brimmed, then slipped down her cheeks. "My mama always undressed me and tucked me into bed."

"You're six years old. You're practically an adult. You can get out of those clothes and into your nightdress by your own self."

"I hate you, I hate you! And you look ugly and stupid with that rag on your head!"

Jenny smiled. "That's your blanket over there. Now you can put on your nightdress or you can sleep in your fancy little outfit. Makes no never mind to me. But I'm not going to undress you, and I'm not going to dress you in the morning. So you just figure out how those buttons work."

"I *know* how buttons work! I hate you, I hate you, I hate you!" In a fury, Graciela ran around the fire pit, kicking rocks, and shouting, her little face as red as the flames.

Jenny watched with interest. At least Graciela wasn't a perfect snotty little lady all of the time. Finally she ran out of steam and started taking off her clothing. She pinned her hat to the ground with the hatpin for safekeeping. That was an impressive bit of ingenuity; Jenny had to give her that. Then, she folded her cape, skirt, and shirtwaist, and placed them in a neat pile. She anchored the pile with a rock. Jenny nodded, then her eyes widened.

"Good Lord. You're wearing a corset."

Graciela gave her a withering look. "A true lady always wears a corset."

"You must have been miserable all day. Why didn't you say something?" She watched Graciela bending and stretching, trying to reach behind herself. Jenny sighed. "Come here. There's no way you're going to get that damned thing off alone." It laced up the back. Frowning, Jenny pulled the laces out, studied the tiny corset with abhorrence, then tossed it on the fire.

Graciela screamed, and her hands flew to her face. Horrified, she watched the corset smolder, then catch fire. "You had no right to do that!"

"I've never seen anyone cry as much as you do," Jenny said with disgust. "Where's your backbone?"

"My aunt Tete gave me that corset for my name day! It was my favorite one!"

"Look kid. As long as I'm in charge, no six-year-old is going to wear a corset. Understand? I don't wear one, and you aren't going to wear one. Corsets are unhealthy and bad for your rib bones. You can't work in them, can hardly breathe in them." She studied Graciela's sputtering face. "I know. You hate me."

Graciela kicked a volley of stones into the darkness. "I hope you die! I hope the wolves eat you up! I hope you get sores all over you like Pepe Sanchez!"

Jenny poured the last cup of coffee and grinned. She was a mule skinner, and she could cuss with the best of them. It could be said, in fact, that she was a connoisseur of cussing. Connoisseur was in her pocket dictionary, and she liked the word. Tried to use it when she could. But she doubted Graciela would understand. Nevertheless, Graciela had the makings of a cussing connoisseur herself. She wasn't using actual cusswords, but she was calling down the scourges of kid-dom. Doing pretty damned well, too.

"You finished?" Jenny asked, sipping her coffee.

Graciela sent her a murderous look, then pulled her lacy nightdress over her curls and stood on the end of her blanket, swaying with fatigue. "I'm going to say my prayers now," she said sullenly.

"So say them."

"You're supposed to kneel with me and listen."

Jenny considered. Kneeling to hear a kid's prayer wasn't going to be comfortable, but she couldn't find any harm in it. Rising reluctantly, she walked around the fire and knelt beside Graciela, who glared at the rag on Jenny's head and made a face. She folded her hands together and held them against her chest, then closed her eyes.

"Heavenly Father, please take care of my mama and Aunt Tete and Maria and Cousin Luis and Cousin Chulo and Cousin—"

"God already knows who your cousins are, skip that part and say amen."

"Thank you for all the blessings you have given us. Keep us safe and protect us. Please take care of the horse and please punish . . ." She opened one eye and looked at Jenny. "What am I supposed to call you?"

She hadn't thought about that. They stared at each other. "For the time being, just call me Jenny."

"Please punish Jenny. You could strike her dead. Amen."

Jenny blinked. "I'm no expert on this, but . . . are you supposed to pray for someone to be struck dead?"

Graciela didn't answer. She crawled in between the folds of the blanket.

"Someone who's trying to help you and take you to

your daddy? And you're asking God to strike me dead? You ungrateful little snot."

Here came the tears again. Jenny rolled her eyes.

"My mama always kissed me good night . . ."

"Well, I'll be goddamned. First you ask God to kill me dead, now you're hinting I should kiss you good night?" Jenny hated kids, she plain hated them. Kids were strange and contrary and hateful and weepy and more trouble than even she had believed.

"My mama always kissed me good night."

Jenny swore. "If that's what it'll take to shut you up and put you to sleep." She moved up the blanket and placed a quick, gingerly kiss on Graciela's smooth cheek. "What's that pin," she asked when she straightened. "And why are you wearing it on your nightgown?" She had noticed it earlier, pinned to Graciela's bodice, and it looked like a real gold heart suspended from a real gold bar. Jenny had never owned a piece of real gold jewelry in her life.

"It's a locket," Graciela said, closing her fingers over the gold heart. "Inside are pictures of my mama and my daddy. My mama gave it to me."

"You don't need to sound so defensive. I'm not going to steal it, for God's sake."

Irritated, she returned to the fire, wet down her head, and rubbed more of the vinegar of sabadilla into her aching scalp. Fire ate into her skull, and she grimaced. Damn it hurt. When she opened her eyes, Graciela was staring at her.

"Go to sleep," Jenny snapped. "Stop looking at me." Turning her back, she bound her head in the rag, then stepped to her own blanket. The temperature had dropped, and the blanket felt good around her shoulders. Graciela was going to wish she hadn't put on that skimpy nightdress.

As tired as she was, Jenny didn't fall asleep immediately. She lay with her hands behind her head, looking up at the stars and thinking about the long day. A day she shouldn't have had. She should have been in her grave by now.

"Well, Marguarita," she whispered, looking up at heaven. She picked a star and decided it was Marguarita. "All in all the first day went better than I expected." She talked to the star. "You didn't tell me what a superior little bitch your daughter is, but that's all right. I understand." Her lashes drifted shut and she forced them open again. "Marguarita? I know you didn't do it for me. You did it for the kid. But, thank you for my life. Don't you worry. I'll get her butt to California."

In the morning, Jenny discovered Graciela curled into her side like a puppy, nestled against Jenny's warmth.

Gently, she shook Graciela's shoulder. "Rise and shine, kid. Too bad for you—God didn't kill me yet. So, hustle your butt and get dressed."

Chapter Three

Ty stepped off the train, stretched, and wiped soot and smoke off his forehead. He resettled his hat, flexed the stiffness out of his shoulders and thighs.

The small Verde Flores depot was unpainted and looked like a puff of wind could knock down the haphazard weathered walls. Clusters of people waiting for the next train sweated in the heat, but they would have broiled if it hadn't been for the leafy trees bending over the platform roof.

After checking on his horse through the slats of a boxcar, and accepting that it would be a while before the animals were unloaded, Ty continued around to the side of the depot and inspected the town behind it.

A small stream divided the town into two sleepy halves. Because of the water, trees flourished in Verde Flores. Flowers nodded on windowsills, splashes of red and yellow that made the town seem almost inviting. Ty watched some women washing clothes in the stream, chattering to one another, and was glad he had arrived before everyone vanished indoors to escape the midday heat. At one o'clock, a Mexican village resembled a ghost town.

Returning to the platform, he confirmed that no one had yet opened the boxcars. He'd have to wait. As benches were scarce, filled with people waiting for luggage or the next boarding call, he leaned in the doorway to the station house and searched his pockets for a cigar.

"Pardone, Señor." A woman's husky voice spoke from immediately behind him.

"Con gusto," he said politely, stepping out of her way.

To his surprise, she wasn't Spanish. Leaving an odd medicinal smell behind her, she strode past him, then stopped suddenly as if she had forgotten something. She looked over her shoulder at her daughter. At least Ty assumed the girl lagging behind was her daughter. They both had blue eyes; they seemed to be traveling together.

Obviously, the little girl's father must be a Mex, and that disturbed him. A Spanish/Anglo marriage had torn his own family apart which was part of the reason why he couldn't help feeling some prejudice against Mexicans. The larger part of his bias had taken root as he grew up witnessing his father's intolerance, especially toward Don Antonio Barrancas who owned the ranch sharing a border with the Sanders' spread. It was hard to argue with his father, given the hostilities between the Sanders and the Barrancas family. Ty had grown up agreeing with his father's opinions and not understanding why Robert didn't feel the same level of intolerance.

Turning his thoughts back to the woman, he decided she wasn't a beauty, but she wasn't thumbs-down either. On closer inspection, her hair was peculiar, he decided, striking a match against the bottom of his boot. He lit a cigar and exhaled. Maybe she'd been ill or something, and she'd had to cut her hair. There should have been a bun at the back, but there was only a fringe of red curling up over the bottom of a hat that hadn't been designed to be worn so far back on the head.

Usually Ty wasn't drawn to tall, big-boned women who looked like they could do everything a man could do and maybe do it better. But this woman caught his attention. He guessed she was at least five feet ten or eleven, but she didn't hunch or try to pretend she was a foot shorter. She didn't affect breathless airs better left to little women, and she wasn't foolish enough to mimic daintiness. She carried herself as if height were an advantage, not the disaster women usually considered it. She moved like a real person, not like someone sandwiched between metal stays. And she looked around her with an expression that dared anyone to challenge her or get in her way.

Ty smiled, then realizing he was staring and turned his head toward the crowded benches. He hoped the woman and her daughter didn't have long to wait because there was no place for them to sit. After smoking a third of his cigar, he shoved away from the doorjamb and ambled down to check on the boxcars again. A half dozen sweating men were unloading cartons.

"You should have unloaded the horses first," he commented in disgust. The men ignored him, and after a few minutes, he swore, then returned to the platform and the shade.

The woman had taken her daughter to stand beneath the spreading branches of a large tree growing to the side of the depot. Ty leaned in the doorway again, watching them for lack of anything else to occupy his interest.

They were arguing. Too many people were coming and going on the platform, voices rattling all around him, for Ty to hear why the mother and daughter argued, but it wasn't hard to guess.

The daughter kept pointing to her hair, a sheet of silky brown rippling almost to her waist. She tried to push it up under a little hat that was more fashionable than the mother's. Without pins, her hair cascaded back to her waist.

The mother threw out her hands, her cheeks reddened, and she turned in a full circle, glaring up at the tree limbs in growing frustration. It was an odd gesture of helplessness from a woman who projected an impression of spit-in-your-eye capability.

Ty shook his head. The mother's hair was god-awful, but it didn't seem to bother her. The daughter's hair was beautiful, but she wanted it tucked away. No wonder men had difficulty understanding women.

Losing interest, he relit his cigar and shifted his attention to a hard-eyed man who galloped a lathered horse up to the depot steps and reared to a halt. He jumped from the saddle and tossed his reins to a boy who rose from a seat on the steps.

Ty watched the man stride toward the train conductor, and his eyes narrowed. There was a puffed-up thug like this one in every small town in the world. They were identifiable at a glance, angry men searching for an offense to serve as an excuse to release the fury they'd been born with.

This one was on the short side, but well muscled, covered with road dust. His hat was as black as his eyes and mustache. Rage vibrated the air around him. Conversation died and left only the sound of his spurs chinking across the boards of the platform.

The thug lowered burning black eyes to the conductor's face. "How many trains have left this station today?"

The conductor's gaze darted to a chalkboard the thug would have seen if he'd looked over his shoulder.

"The first train north leaves in an hour, *Señor*. To Chihuahua. This train departs in thirty minutes. South. Just as soon as they finish—" He nodded toward the men leading horses out of the final boxcar.

"Cousin Luis!"

Ty looked toward the mother and daughter. The daughter's face lit as if a candle glowed behind her cheeks, and she started to run forward, but the mother grabbed her arm and dragged her back. The mother's eyes narrowed into slits as she studied the thug, and her lips moved. She might have been praying, but Ty didn't think so from her expression. He flipped his cigar off the platform and straightened in the doorway. He opened his fingers wide, then curled his hands into fists.

Cousin Luis spun, and the spurs chinked across the platform, moving toward the steps. The daughter was struggling to break free from the mother. Ty could see that the mother had her hands full, trying to subdue the daughter, and shouting at Cousin Luis, who advanced with the single-minded purpose of a bullet.

What happened next caused an abrupt silence so profound that the insects in the trees sounded as loud as buzzards, and Ty heard the slap of clothing against the rocks in the stream, a sound too distance to be audible until now.

The thug swaggered up to the mother and daughter, and he backhanded the mother, knocking her to her knees. For a minute it looked as if he would strike her with his fist, but he hesitated, glanced at the people silently watching from the platform. Then he tossed the daughter up on his shoulder and started toward his horse. No one moved.

"You fricking bastard!"

The mother launched herself from the ground as if she'd been hurled from a catapult. Flying forward, she caught Cousin Luis around the knees, and he went down with a surprised and furious shout. The daughter flew out of his arms, hit her head on a rock, and went limp on the ground, dazed.

Neither the mother nor Cousin Luis noticed the daughter. The mother sprang on top of him, and started hammering away, doing her damnedest to break his nose with her fists. It was the most astonishing thing Ty had ever seen. Cousin Luis tried to buck her off of his chest, but she was stuck like a burr to his vest until he flipped on his side. Then they rolled in the dirt, slugging and kicking like two men, except the mother was hampered by her skirts and petticoats.

Ty was so thunderstruck that he didn't move until he heard the women on the platform sucking in their breath. The hissing sound galvanized him. He wasted one second looking around, then accepted that no one was going to interfere. No one was going to help the woman.

He spit on his hands with a curse of disgust. What kind of yellow-belly stood by while some puffed-up son of a bitch beat the hell out of a mother? He didn't care if

Cousin Luis was a relative or not. If someone didn't stop him, he was going to kill the red-haired woman.

By the time Ty reached them, they were both on their feet. The woman threw a right, missed the thug, and her fist glanced off Ty's jaw. Jesus. He staggered backward a step. If she'd connected squarely, she would have laid him out in the dirt. This wasn't quite the mismatch he had initially supposed.

"Behind you," she shouted, then returned to hammering at Cousin Luis.

Ty whirled in time to deflect the fist of another man, who was gut ugly and determined. He had half a second to note the man's resemblance to Cousin Luis, then they were into it.

Twenty minutes later, he pushed wearily to his feet and stood swaying over the sprawled figure of his opponent. Hoping he had enough energy left to finish Cousin Luis, he lifted his head to find the man.

The mother didn't need Ty's help. She was standing over Cousin Luis, panting and gulping air, staring hate down at his unconscious form. She had a bloody rock in her hand.

Ty stumbled toward her, sucking mouthfuls of searing midday air into his aching lungs. He prodded Cousin Luis with the toe of his boot. The man was going to sleep for a long time and wake up with the worst headache of his brutish life.

"What the hell was that all about?" he asked when he could speak. "Who *are* you?"

She'd lost her hat in the fight, and short red hair was sweat-plastered to her head. Her cape had disappeared, and her shirtwaist was dirty and pasted tight to her skin by perspiration. Ty stared. Good God. She'd been hiding an awesome figure under that cape. She wasn't small, but God had arranged her in absolutely perfect proportion. He dragged his eyes up from breathtaking breasts and studied her face. He found himself wishing he'd taken a closer look at her when she wasn't dirty and sweating and cherry-faced from fury and exertion.

"You've got a cut on your cheek," he said, staring at her. And she was going to have a black eye to remind her of Cousin Luis. "Ma'am, I have to say this. You are one hell of a fighter."

She put a hand on his chest and pushed him backward, sudden panic flaring in her blue eyes. "Graciela!"

The daughter pulled to her feet with a dazed expression. She touched the back of her head, looked around, then wobbled forward and fell to her knees. "Cousin Chulo!" Stricken eyes darted to Cousin Luis, then back, taking in the two unconscious men. She burst into tears, flung a look at the mother, and shouted, "I hate you!"

The mother nodded grimly, then lifted on her toes to look Ty square in the eyes. The experience was a new one. Not many women could look a six-foot-three man in the eyes. Maybe she was closer to six feet tall than he'd originally guessed. He forced himself to hold his gaze on her face and not let it slide down to those magnificent breasts.

She held his eyes, seemed to consider, then admitted, "We're having a goddamned family problem here."

He laughed, liking this tough woman who refused to let a man hit her without fighting back. Ty suspected old Cousin Luis would give it a second thought before he hit another woman.

"So it appears," he said, grinning at her.

"Cousin Chulo over there messed you up some," she stated, inspecting his face. Until she mentioned it, he hadn't noticed the blood dripping down his chin. He swiped at it with the back of his hand. "I'm thanking you, mister." She thrust out her hand, and he gripped it in a hard shake. "I don't know what I'd a done when the second one showed up. I'm glad you stepped in. Much obliged."

"It was my pleasure, ma'am," Ty said, meaning it. "It's a privilege to lend a hand to a fellow American." They'd moved into English about halfway through the brief conversation.

People had begun to drift off the platform, boarding the train, looking back at them over their shoulders. The woman stepped away from Ty and moved hastily around Cousin Luis and Cousin Chulo, picking up her hat, her cape, a heavy fabric traveling bag. When she had everything, she strode toward her daughter. Curious, Ty followed at a distance.

"We're leaving now. We're taking that train."

"No!" The child threw herself across Cousin Chulo's chest. "I'm not going!"

"Yeah. You are." Grim-faced and grinding her teeth, she grabbed the daughter by the arm and dragged her to the steps leading into the train. "Where's this train going?" she demanded, glaring into the conductor's eyes.

"The next stop is Hermita, *Señora.*" The conductor stepped backward as if he feared that she'd take him on next.

"Where's that?"

"Fifty miles south of here, *Señora.*"

"South?" She spit a string of cusswords that made Ty

grin. "Well, it will have to do." She scowled back at the unconscious cousins, then gave the conductor a shove. "Get out of my way."

She dragged the daughter on board the train. Two minutes later, Ty spotted them through the window as the train chugged away from the depot.

He watched until the train rocked into a curve and puffed out of sight, then he shook his head, found his hat, and dusted off his pant legs. It occurred to him that it wouldn't be a bad idea for him to follow her example and put some space between himself and the cousins.

Fifteen minutes later he cantered out of Verde Flores, heading west toward the village that would mark the halfway point of a journey he hadn't wanted to make. The second part would be the hardest, taking Marguarita and her child back to California.

Because thinking about Marguarita made him mad, he turned his thoughts back to the woman at the depot.

He guessed he had it figured out. The red-haired woman was married to a Mexican husband. That accounted for the half-Mex daughter and the cousins. She was leaving the husband, and the daughter was torn between her parents, not wanting to leave her father. That accounted for her delight at spotting Cousin Luis and fighting with the mother. For some reason the father couldn't chase after them, so he'd sent the cousins in pursuit.

It pleased him that the woman had escaped, even though she'd jumped on a train heading in a direction she plainly hadn't wanted to go. He hoped for her sake that she'd left her problems behind.

Touching his fingertips to his chin, he looked at the blood and frowned. His problems were ahead of him.

It was too bad that he'd never see the red-haired woman again. She had the best breasts he'd ever wanted to put his hands on. She was one hell of a woman.

Jenny smoothed herself up the best she could, and stared down the people looking at her. Now that the fight was over, her hands started to shake. If that cowboy hadn't leaped into the fray, the second cousin would have stolen Graciela. She'd come that close—that close!—to letting Graciela get captured. A shudder ran down her spine.

Well, it hadn't happened. And she'd learned something. Marguarita hadn't been whittling soft wood when she claimed the cousins were a threat. They wanted Graciela, all right. And after getting an eyeful of Luis and Chulo, Jenny didn't doubt that either of them could drown Graciela or shoot her in a ravine and stroll away without a qualm.

"What are you doing?" she said when she became aware of Graciela's soft murmuring.

"I'm praying that the train will wreck and kill you, then Cousin Chulo and Cousin Luis will come and take me home."

"You see this?" Jenny pointed to the scab forming on her cheek. "And this?" She leaned her eye down toward Graciela, an eye that was swelling by the second. "I got these fighting your stinking cousins so they wouldn't capture you and kill you."

Outrage and disbelief stiffened Graciela's little shoulders. "My cousins would never hurt me! They came to rescue me from you and to take me home to Aunt Tete."

Jenny's mouth dropped, and she felt her heart fall

through her body and hit the wooden seat. She knew the answer, but she asked the question anyway. "Didn't your mother tell you about your cousins?"

When Graciela just stared at her, she sighed and closed her eyes. *Marguarita, you fricking coward.*

A more generous approach would be to remember that Marguarita had been burdened with a lot of bad news to lay on the kid. Maybe she'd felt it was enough that she had to tell her child about the firing squad and that a stranger was going to take Graciela to a daddy she'd never met. Marguarita might have figured that informing a six-year-old that her nice cousins wanted to kill her was just too much. Or maybe Marguarita doubted her own assessment of the situation. Who the hell knew?

Jenny drew a breath. "All right, here's how it is. Luis and Chulo used to like you, but they don't anymore. Now they want to hurt you. It's my job to make sure they don't get you."

Tears welled in Graciela's eyes. "You are so mean to say that," she whispered. "My cousins love me. Cousin Luis brings me presents, and Cousin Chulo rides me on his horse. They would never hurt me. You're lying."

Jenny whirled on the seat and gripped Graciela's shoulders. She shook the kid until Graciela's teeth chattered. "Listen to me! I do not lie. *Not ever.* When Jenny Jones says a thing, that's how it is. Now, you don't have to like me. And you can call me any name you want to. You can pray that God strikes me down. But don't you *ever,* not *ever,* call me a liar. Do you understand that?"

Graciela shrank from Jenny's blazing eyes.

"Your mama could have picked from a dozen people to take you to your daddy. But she picked me. She picked me *because* I never lie. She didn't pick one of your son-of-a-bitch cousins because she knew they want to harm you. She told me so. Now, you just think about that for a while."

The miles rolled past, and Jenny started to calm down.

"Why would my cousins want to hurt me?" Graciela asked in a little voice. She looked up at Jenny with eyes that seemed too large for her face.

"It has to do with money, lots of money. If you're dead, your cousins get lots of money."

"My cousins would rather have money than me?"

"Your mama thought so, and it looks like she was right."

"That's a——"

Jenny just stared, until Graciela dropped her head. Tears dripped down on the hands squeezed tightly together in her lap.

Jenny watched her for a minute, waiting for the snot. "Don't you have a handkerchief?"

"I lost it."

Reaching down, Jenny tore another piece out of her petticoat and handed it to Graciela. "Wipe your nose."

"Thank you."

"Look, kid, I know it's hard right now. You've lost your mama, your cousins want to kill you, you don't know where you're going or who's on the other end, you hate me . . ." When she listed it out like that, the kid's life sounded lousy even by Jenny's standards. "Well, okay. You've been dealt a rotten hand. But that's how it is. You have to play the cards you've got. There's no use crying about it. Tears and snot aren't going to change a damned thing."

The kid didn't speak. She sat there, head down, her fingers on the gold-heart locket that was pinned to her chest.

An hour later, a man came weaving down the aisle selling greasy tortillas filled with something unidentifiable that tasted like shredded fire. The first bite made Jenny's eyes water and blistered her tongue.

"Didn't you cry when your mama died?"

Jenny had forgotten that she'd told Graciela about her ma. "Oh hell, no. I wasn't around when my ma died. But even if I had been, I wouldn't have cried. My ma was mean as a snake. Looked like one, too."

Graciela's eyes widened. "She didn't!"

Jenny laughed. "Well, she looked like a snake to me. The meanest woman who ever sucked air. I'm telling you, that woman never said a soft word to anyone in her whole life."

"Why was she so mean?"

"Why?" Jenny blinked. She'd never considered the why of it. "I guess I don't rightly know." Frowning, she turned her face to the window and sucked on her blistered tongue. "Maybe life didn't work out like she wanted it to. Maybe she didn't like living in a one-room shack at the edge of a played-out mine, trying to stretch one squirrel far enough to feed six kids." It occurred to her that things looked a little different when seen through an adult's perspective rather than through the eyes of one of those six kids. "Maybe she didn't like it that my pa hit her and kept her knocked—" She gave Graciela a long look. "Kept her with child," she finished primly.

Graciela turned the fiery tortilla between her fingers. "Did she tell you stories and give you kisses?"

"Huh? Well, I guess not! She didn't even kiss my pa. Kisses! Huh!"

"Oh." Graciela placed the tortilla on the seat beside her, then she blotted her lips with the torn piece of petticoat. She carefully tucked the piece of petticoat inside the cuff of her sleeve, then turned to Jenny and placed her small hands on top of Jenny's. She looked into Jenny's eyes. "I'm sorry you had a bad mama when you were little. She should have told you stories and given you kisses."

Jenny stared at her. Her chest suddenly hurt. "I'm sorry, too," she said in a strange voice that didn't sound like hers. She was silent for a minute, then said, "I thought you hated me."

"I do," Graciela said firmly, taking her hands away.

That was better, Jenny thought, feeling angry for no reason. It was a thousand times preferable to be hated than to have a six-year-old feeling sorry for her, for Christ's sake. She threw her tortilla out the window, then gazed at the passing landscape. She hadn't thought about her mother in years, not since she'd heard that the old lady had died. And then her first thought had been: Good riddance.

Now here she sat on a train going in the wrong direction, feeling sorry for herself because her mother hadn't looked like Marguarita, but instead had smelled like despair, and had never told her a story. Well, crud on a crust. So what? The day Jenny Jones drew aces was the day she'd fall over in a dead faint.

The heat built inside the car, and Graciela's eyes closed. She sagged against Jenny's shoulder, then slid down until her head was on Jenny's lap and her legs curled all tight and ladylike on the wooden seat.

Jenny leaned her head against the sooty windowpane, wishing it would open, and thought about the cousins. She needed a plan, because her sixth sense warned they would be on the next train after her. And next time, she wouldn't have the cowboy to help her.

Thinking of him in her sleepy state, Jenny had to admit that the cowboy had been one good-looking son of a bitch.

Usually Jenny didn't pay much mind to a man's appearance. She just didn't think about men in terms of how they looked. But the cowboy had the same kind of eyes as Graciela, blue-green like the sea and fringed with soft brown lashes. Those eyes had been something to see, startling next to sun-darkened cheeks. Idly, she wondered how he'd gotten the black eye. It had started to go yellow so it wasn't fresh. He hadn't gotten it in the fight with Cousin Chulo.

Miles rolled under the train, and her thoughts kept drifting back to him. The cowboy had the kind of tall, lanky physique that could mislead a person into thinking he might be more string than muscle. When Jenny first saw him, she'd half figured that Cousin Chulo, who was built like a beer barrel, would drop the cowboy after a couple of punches. But the cowboy's wiry form was all muscle, and he had staying power, by God. At the end, it was the cowboy who was still standing. Jenny grinned, remembering.

She wondered what the cowboy was doing this deep in Mexico. That question led to a consideration of her own situation.

Touching her fingertips to her forehead, she thought about her rig and the freight she'd been commissioned to haul back to El Paso. Undoubtedly, her rig and cargo had been stolen seconds after her arrest. Mr. Comden would charge her for losing the load of bone buttons if she ever saw him again. She had to make sure that didn't happen. Good-bye Texas, hello somewhere else. It looked like her mule-skinning days were over.

To pass the time, she tried to remember what was inside the shack she'd rented in El Paso, but couldn't recall anything she minded walking away from. A person like her didn't accumulate anything of much value. Unlike a certain prissy kid she knew, she was no fricking heiress.

Gazing out the window, Jenny watched a dry little village slip past the smoke-streaked pane. It was about as appealing as the cacti that surrounded it. Frowning, she looked down at Graciela's head in her lap and wished she could fall asleep that easily.

But her thoughts wouldn't settle down. Marguarita invaded her mind, and worries about the cousins, and the cowboy kept popping up too.

After a while, Jenny leaned to the bag at her feet, careful not to wake Graciela, and withdrew her battered dictionary. There was nothing like reading words to settle a fevered brain. Some of the definitions were like puzzles. They didn't make any more sense than the words did. She had to study them and ponder hard to work out the meaning. Many of the words she forgot almost as soon as she read them.

But other words sang to her imagination, and she said them over and over, charmed by the sound and wanting to commit them to memory.

Virile (vir-il) belonging to
Virility (vi-ril-i-ty) n. manhood.

"Virile," she said quietly. A soft word for a hard thing.
Pursing her lips, she considered, then composed a sentence using the word. "The cowboy is virile."

Heat rushed into her cheeks, surprising her. Damned if
thinking about the cowboy and virility didn't make her
blush. Embarrassed, she looked around to see if anyone
had noticed. There wasn't a soul who knew her who
would have believed she was capable of blushing, including herself.

It was a damned good thing that she wasn't going to
see that cowboy again. Yes, sir, a damned good thing. She
was happy that she and the cowboy had parted ways.
Glad that the odds of seeing him again were mighty slim.
She sure didn't want to see any son of a bitch who could
make her blush. Nosirree bob, she didn't.

He'd probably forgotten about her anyway.

That kind of man never gave a woman like Jenny Jones
a second glance.

And she was glad about that. Yes, sir, she really was.

She stared out the train window and wished that she
were tiny and beautiful, wished she could totter along on
little bitty feet and wear pretty clothes that a cowboy
might notice.

Sighing, she closed her dictionary, then her eyes, trying to decide what she would do when she and Graciela
reached Hermita. She didn't have a fricking idea.

Chapter
Four

A bloodred sunset cast coppery shadows behind Ty's horse as he rode into the village he had traveled weeks to find. The ruts curving down the main street were flanked by a few adobes; most of the dwellings were constructed of sticks and mud, roofed with tin or thatch. Scraggly patches of maize and beans rusted in the flaming light.

The village was too inconsequential to boast a church, but a small plaza intersected the road that wound up toward the Sierras. At the plaza Ty learned where he could buy a bed for the night, and he hired a boy to carry a message to Dona Theodora Barrancas y Talmas.

He preferred to speak to Marguarita immediately, but to highborn Mexicans, honor and courtesy were woven together as tightly as the strands of a rope. Arriving at the hacienda unannounced, unbathed, and unshaven, and at the dinner hour, would undoubtedly have offended. Choosing the lesser of two aggravations, he sent a message announcing his intention to call on Marguarita tomorrow.

He watched the boy climb on a burro and ride out of the village, then he rented a back room in the adobe across from the cantina and paid for a washtub and hot water. For an additional peso, his sharp-eyed landlady agreed to launder and press the clothing he would wear tomorrow when he rode to the Barrancas estate to inform Marguarita that he was taking her and her kid back to California and Robert. Thinking about it didn't improve his disposition.

He resented his Mexican sister-in-law, and had argued with Robert against bringing her back. Marguarita had caused enough problems in the Sanders family six years ago. Her return would rekindle hostilities with her father, whose lands adjoined the Sanders ranch. Moreover, Ty didn't want his pragmatic, no-nonsense mother placed in the position of having to accommodate a skittish, spoiled beauty whose knowledge of cattle was undoubtedly limited to what appeared on her dinner plate.

Because it galled him that Robert had defied their father and married Don Barrancas's daughter, he didn't refer to Marguarita as his brother's wife, not even in his thoughts. His father had often raved that Mexicans belonged in Mexico, not the United States; Ty had to agree that if Antonio Barrancas had remained south of the border, Robert wouldn't have gotten mixed up with his daughter. And Ty wouldn't be here now.

The boy still had not returned from the hacienda by the time Ty finished shaving, so he crossed the dusty lane to the cantina to have his supper and a tumbler of pulque.

The no-name village looked better by night. Deep shadow concealed the refuse in the ditches, hid the poverty. Lanterns swayed from tree limbs spreading over the tiny plaza and imparted a festive glow to the drabbest cantina he had yet observed.

The instant Ty stepped inside, the back of his neck prickled with the sudden tension of abruptly halted conversations. No matter how poor the village, there was usually music in the cantina, but not here, not tonight. And he noted the surprising presence of several respectable women. In utter silence he walked to a vacant table near the side door, aware of a dozen hostile eyes stabbing his back.

Similar situations had taught the expediency of pretending not to speak or understand the language.

"Supper," he said to a short waiter whose narrowed eyes made his resentment of this gringo all too clear. Rubbing his stomach, Ty spoke louder. "You speak American?" The waiter stared at him. "Food." He smacked his lips, thcn pantomimed drinking. "Pulque."

A low hiss of relief and contempt buzzed through the hot closeness of the night, and conversation resumed. A slender man, his upper lip concealed by a luxuriant mustache, addressed the others in a fusillade of words that he fired like bullets.

What the man said drove all thoughts of food out of Ty's head. He blinked at a savory pozole and a stack of flour tortillas, all appetite gone. After forcing himself to sample the stew, he concentrated on molding his expression into one of uncomprehending indifference.

Within minutes he understood that Marguarita Barrancas Sanders was dead. What shocked the hell out of him was to learn that she had been executed by a firing squad. Disbelief pinched his nostrils. He could sooner imagine his father rising from the grave than he could imagine Marguarita Barrancas committing a crime worthy of execution.

Old man Barrancas had sheltered Marguarita from the outside world, and Ty hadn't seen her often while they were growing up. When he did catch a glimpse, she had reminded him of a large-eyed doe, timid and poised to spring away. She had grown into a shy beauty with downcast eyes, who hid behind the curtains of her carriage or the edges of her fan. On those rare occasions when Ty had heard her speak, her voice had been low and musical and almost apologetic.

This fragile creature had died against an executioner's wall?

Highborn Mexican women were reared like hothouse flowers, protected and sheltered from life's unpleasant realities. They were guarded by hawkeyed duennas, fiercely shielded from insult by male relatives. Ty had long pondered how Robert had managed to get Marguarita alone long enough to impregnate her, and what he had seen in her to make him wish to bed her. From what Ty had observed of the aristocratic families in northern California, a patrician Mexican woman was the most boring creature in femininity. She prayed, embroidered, and gazed at the world with eloquent indifference.

What in God's name had such a woman done to merit a firing squad?

Pushing aside the platter of pozole, Ty leaned back on the legs of his chair and swallowed a long draft of pulque, letting the fiery alcohol burn down his gullet. Removing a penknife from the top of his boot, he lazily pared his fingernails, listening intently.

Gradually he culled the information that the slender man with the proud mustache was named Emil and was apparently one of Marguarita's Barrancas cousins. Fury twisted Cousin Emil's features as he shouted and exhorted those in the cantina to join him in pursuing a witch who had cast a spell on Marguarita.

"Think, Emil!" A woman stood, clutching a shawl to her breast though the night was hot. "You knew your cousin. Could the Americana have persuaded the senora to die against her will? The senora could have cried out and exposed the pretense. But she did not. What does this tell you?"

"It tells me Marguarita was bewitched." Emil gazed at the faces frowning up at him. "Are we to sit idle and allow a murderess to kill my cousin and kidnap her daughter?" He spit on the ground in disgust. "Do the men of this village have no honor?"

Until this moment Ty had not known if Robert's child was a girl or a boy. So it was a girl. He had a niece.

The woman stepped farther into the light and spoke into a swell of angry voices. "Senora Sanders was dying. Everyone knows this. I have it from the senora's own lips that it was her plan to switch places with the Americana. In return, the Americana agreed to take Graciela to her father in Norte America."

Emil flattened his palms on the table and leaned forward. His eyes glittered dangerously. "You lie. My cousin would never have trusted her daughter to a witch, to a convicted murderess. If Marguarita wanted Graciela to go north, which I am sure she did not, she would have asked me or Luis or Chulo to undertake this journey. Never would she ask a stranger."

The woman hesitated. A sharp reply hovered on her tongue, but she gazed into Emil's hot eyes and did not speak.

Emil's anger seared those around him. Spittle flew from his lips. "You all heard. Maria claims my cousin sent Graciela to her Americano father." His eyes returned to the woman and pinned her. "And where would that be?" he demanded in a voice that told everyone he knew the answer.

"The father is in California," the woman whispered. She lowered her gaze and sat on a bench against the wall.

"Then why did the witch take the train south? Explain that, Maria Torrez."

"South?" Shock clouded the woman's eyes.

"When Luis returns from the hacienda, you will hear it from his own lips. The witch abducted our little cousin for her own purposes. I say we go after the witch, kill her, and rescue Graciela. I say do not listen to a woman's prattle. My cousin would never entrust her daughter to a stranger. You know this. The honor of the Barrancas family and the honor of this village rest on saving Graciela from the witch."

Ty folded the penknife into his boot top, then drained the tumbler of pulque, letting it scald his throat. He set the tumbler down hard and stared out the side door at a swarm of gnats circling a tree lantern.

The witch business was clever nonsense. Emil played on the ignorance of superstitious villagers to refute Maria Torrez's contention that Marguarita had given her daughter to a stranger rather than family. That much Ty understood.

But there was much that he did not understand. One thing, however, was unpleasantly clear. The knot behind his rib cage told him that he had abetted in the abduction of his own niece. Now he knew the truth about the fracas at the depot in Verde Flores, and he cursed his role in it. Damn his hide, he had helped a female desperado steal Robert's daughter.

Cursing silently, he tossed some coins on the table, then stood. Cousin Luis was expected at any moment, and Cousin Luis wasn't likely to have forgotten the cowboy who came to the aid of the red-haired woman. Common sense urged Ty to step out the side door, fetch his belongings, and get the hell out of here.

Halfway to the stables, he spotted the muchacho who had carried his message to the hacienda. The boy slipped off his burro and ran forward, waving an envelope. Without breaking stride, Ty flipped the boy a coin and continued toward the lanterns hanging outside the stables.

After extracting two thin pages covered in flowing female script; he held them to the light. Dona Theodora Barrancas y Talmas begged permission to inform him that her great-niece, *Señora* Marguarita Sanders, and *Señora* Sanders's young daughter had unfortunately succumbed to the coughing disease three days since. Dona Theodora castigated her own rudeness but as much as she longed to offer her great-niece's brother-in-law the hacienda's hospitality, grief prevented her from opening her doors. She pleaded for understanding and prayed that *Señora* Sanders would forgive her for not receiving him at this desolate moment of dual tragedy.

In other words: Leave. You no longer have reason to be here.

For an instant, he considered returning to California. He could show Dona Theodora's message to Robert. Marguarita and the child were dead.

Ty crumpled the pages in his first. Frowning, he glanced back at the lights shining out of the cantina.

Inside, Cousin Emil was striving to incite the village men to rescue Graciela from a witch. Yet, Dona Theodora stated that Ty's niece had died with her mother.

The answer came in a flash. With Marguarita dead—and all parties agreed on that point—Graciela became Robert's heir. And Don Antonio Barrancas's heir.

His narrowed gaze slid down the squalid shacks flanking the main street of the village. What would Robert pay to ransom his daughter? Would he sell the cattle? The ranch? Ty didn't doubt it. He wasn't as certain about Don Antonio, as Barrancas had never accepted or acknowledged Robert and Marguarita's marriage. Still, the old man might turn sentimental when he learned his daughter was dead and this child was his only surviving family. If she survived. It occurred to Ty that the child's death would lead to an inheritance which was a less cumbersome solution than kidnaping and ransom.

The promise of a hefty inheritance or ransom would strongly appeal to villagers living in shacks built of sticks and mud. If honor didn't motivate them, Emil would eventually relinquish shares in the windfall and let greed work its persuasion.

Grim-faced, Ty saddled his horse and jerked hard on the cinch.

The Barrancas cousins didn't know it yet, but a new player had entered the game. If they thought Dona Theodora's message had duped him into returning to California without Graciela, they were in for an unpleasant surprise.

No longer was he in Mexico on a grudging errand undertaken on behalf of his brother. It was personal now. Dona Theodora had lied to him. He'd tasted Chulo's fists in Verde Flores. He doubted he was wrong about the cousins wanting Graciela for evil purposes. In the span of a few minutes, his motivations had altered.

Giving the cantina a wide berth, he rode out of the no-name village, grateful for a sliver of moon to illuminate the trail.

Near dawn, to keep himself awake, he focused his thoughts on the red-haired woman who had taken Graciela. What was her game? The people in the cantina referred to her as a murderess and implied that it was she who deserved the execution that had killed Marguarita. This didn't strike him as entirely implausible, he thought, rubbing a hand across his jaw.

However, at this point, his mind locked. Was the red-haired woman rescuing his niece? Or had she, too, seen a way to profit by kidnaping the child? Or, and this seemed extremely unlikely, had Marguarita known a woman convicted of murder well enough to entrust her daughter into the murderess's keeping? At present he lacked enough information to form a clear judgment of the situation.

As the glow of dawn revealed the low hazy silhouette of Verde Flores, Ty's lips thinned to a hard straight line. The Barrancas cousins were not going to hold his niece for ransom, and neither was the red-haired woman if that was her intention. This he swore on his father's grave. If he had to track her into the maw of hell, he would do it. He was not returning to California without his niece.

When the sun climbed out of the desert, Ty was sitting on a bench on the Verde Flores depot platform, hat pulled over his eyes, dozing while he waited for the first train south.

He no longer believed the red-haired woman had intended to go north. That had been a ruse meant to reach the cousins' ears and send them chasing in the wrong direction. She'd intended to take the southbound train all along.

He would find her.

"Crud on a crust!" Jenny was unaccustomed to indecisiveness, and she didn't handle it well. Nor was she a patient sort. Pressing her nose to the train window, she peered at cacti baking in the desert heat. "We're stopped again."

"They're fixing the track," Graciela said listlessly. She waved a torn paper fan in front of her heat red cheeks. "I haven't had a bath since I left Aunt Tete," she added in an accusing voice. "I want a bath."

"Have we been on this fricking train for two days or three days?" No wonder Jenny felt ready to explode. People weren't made to sit in one spot for three fricking days. Her tailbone hurt. The hot greasy food sold at various stops along the way was burning holes in her innards, and the heat trapped inside the car was cooking her outsides. Chickens ran loose in the aisle and left strings of stench that fouled the air. The noise of crying babies and bickering children were frazzling already frayed tempers.

"If we don't get off this hell train, I'm going to do damage to someone or something." Sweat pasted her bodice to her skin, and she pulled it away from her ribs with a grimace. She had to get off this train before she melted, and she had to figure out a plan.

None of the villages and towns they had chugged through had been large enough to hide a flea. Jenny wasn't sure if hiding out was the safest scheme anyway. Instinct insisted that she should jump on the next train headed north, but what if Luis and Chulo had mustered reinforcements and were sitting in the shade on the Verde Flores depot waiting for her to pass through again? Which she would have to do if she backtracked.

Chewing a thumbnail, she glared out the window at the heat waves shimmering above grey-brown dirt. She wished she knew what the damned cousins were doing. Were they in pursuit? Were they on a train somewhere behind this one? Or were they waiting for her to return to Verde Flores? This time there wouldn't be some foolhardy cowboy to help her. She'd be outnumbered. The cousins would grab Graciela as easily as plucking a flower out of a pot.

Right now, she thought, covering her eyes with a sooty hand, she was tempted to hand them the kid and good riddance. Graciela was driving her fricking crazy. Graciela wouldn't do what she was told, squirmed constantly in her seat, complained about everything, and if Jenny heard the word "why" one more time, she would go raving, flaming berserk.

"I want to go home," Graciela said mournfully. Accusation pulled her lips into a pout.

"Shut up. I'm trying to think."

"You have chicken manure on your shoes."

This was true. It was also a great mystery how the kid could walk to the curtained-off latrine without stepping in offal or tobacco juice but Jenny could not. Jenny scowled at the strands of heat-damp hair sticking to the sides of

Graciela's superior little smirk. She was considering slapping that smirk into next Sunday when the train lurched, belched black smoke, and crashed forward. "Thank God."

Jenny waved down the conductor. *"Por favor, Señor,* what is the next town of any size and when do we get there?" His boots, she noticed, were as frosty with chicken crap as her own were. If there was any justice, some of the conductor's chicken manure would brush off on Graciela's hem. It didn't happen.

"Buenos tardes, Señora, Señorita. We'll reach Durango on schedule," the conductor announced blandly, "around seven this evening."

"On schedule my butt," Jenny muttered in English. The train had spent more time stopped for one reason or another than in rolling forward. At this rate, the train wouldn't reach Mexico City, its final destination, until the next millennium. She would have said so except millennium was a new word, and she wasn't sure how to pronounce it in English let alone Spanish.

Frowning, she watched the conductor kick aside a rooster, then proceed down the aisle. The question was: Should she stay on the train all the way to Mexico City or get off in Durango?

"A lady does not bite her fingernails."

"Shut up."

"I hate you! My mama never told me to shut up."

That did it. Jenny could not spend another day confined with a hot cranky kid, choking on the stench of chickens and an overflowing latrine. She could not endure another night trying to sleep sitting up with Graciela sprawled across her lap. For some unfathomable reason, Graciela weighed as much as a freight wagon when she was asleep.

"We're getting off in Durango," she decided. Even her stomach rebelled at heading farther south toward Mexico City when she needed to go north. At some point she had to risk getting off this train and turning herself and Graciela around. Durango was as good a place as any to start putting things right.

"I miss my mama."

Graciela sank into another of those collapse routines, in which her bones seemed to fold in on themselves. Her shoulders drooped, her chest shrank, her hands went limp, and tears and snot flowed in copious streams.

Jenny watched and felt wild inside. She didn't know how to deal with grief because she had no experience to draw on, and as far as she was concerned, mother-daughter love was a myth. Love itself was a vast enigma. She had no idea how much time was required to recover from losing a mother you loved.

"Kid," she said helplessly, gripping Graciela's arm. "You're making me want to hit you. You've got to get over this. You have to forget about your mother and move on."

"I'll never forget." Graciela glared at her with drowning eyes. "You killed my mama."

"Damn it, we've discussed this a hundred times. You know I didn't kill your mother." Jenny shoved a hand through her hair, knocking the stupid bonnet to the back of her head. Changing the subject, maybe that would help. "Look, when we get to Durango, we'll find a place to stay, and you can have a bath. You'd like that, wouldn't you? We'll get something decent to eat, and we'll sleep in a real bed."

"Cousin Luis and Cousin Chulo are going to kill you and take me home."

"Huh! Let them try."

But after reflecting, Jenny decided that Luis probably wasn't the type to sit on the depot steps and wait. He'd chase after them. Chewing on her fingernails, which were more tasty than anything she had eaten since she'd boarded the train, Jenny focused her thoughts. She had to make up in cleverness what she lacked in strength or numbers.

Nine hours later, when the train steamed to a halt in the outskirts of Durango, Jenny had a plan. It wasn't the best plan she'd ever come up with, and risk was involved, but she felt better for having a strategy.

"I hope you can wash yourself, because I'm not going to do it for you," Jenny warned, eyeing the tub that had been delivered to their hotel room. A surly boy had brought them only enough water to fill the dented tub about eight inches and the water was tepid. Bits of grass and leaves floated on the surface.

Graciela removed her fancy little outfit and shook the dust and soot out then folded it neatly before she inspected the tub. "I'd like some rose oil, please."

"And I'd like a shiny blue carriage and a pocketful of diamonds." Jenny rolled her eyes, then tossed Graciela a cake of the soap Maria had packed. "Get in there, and hurry up. I'd like a bath, too."

"I need help." Graciela lifted her arms to be picked up, and Jenny sighed.

"You can't do anything yourself."

She picked Graciela up and placed her in the tub, then stepped back and stared. Graciela's naked skin was soft; touching her was like touching warm silk. Looking at the kid's slender, curveless body, Jenny wondered at the mysteries of nature. Somewhere inside the child, a woman bided her time, waiting to emerge. It impressed her as very clever of God to hide adults inside children.

Jenny watched Graciela picking bits of grass and leaves from the surface of the bath water, displaying the patience of a rag picker, then she turned and walked to the window overlooking a tobacco factory and the mountains beyond. The foothills of the Sierra Madres had yielded centuries of silver. Now that the silver was nearly played out, Durango's miners plundered the earth for iron ore.

After glancing at Graciela over her shoulder, she pushed up her sleeve and ran her fingers down her arm. The warmth was there, but not the silk. Stroking her arm was almost like rubbing tanned leather. *Hell.* Frowning, she opened her collar and dragged her fingertips across her breast bone where the sun hadn't baked her. *Better. But not silky.* Scowling, she decided her skin wouldn't be silky even if she bathed in a vat of fricking rose oil. Not that it mattered. No good looking cowboy was ever going to compare Jenny Jones's tanned hide to some rose scented, silky skinned woman who had never labored under a harsh sun.

Why was she thinking such foolish thoughts?

Sighing, she inhaled the smoky stench wafting from the tobacco factory, then carried a stool to the side of the tub. "Wash behind your ears." She paused. "Or is it inside your ears?"

Graciela gave her a withering glance.

"Just do it."

"Why?"

"Because that's what your mother would have wanted." Recognizing at once that it was a mistake to invoke Marguarita, she jumped to another subject. "All right, here's our plan. We're going to assume that your stinking cousins are chasing after us. Durango is large enough that we can hide from them as long as we have to, which won't be long. Every day I'll go to the depot when the southbound comes in, and I'll watch and see if Luis and Chulo get off the train. The day they do, and I'm guessing that will be tomorrow or most likely the next day, you and I will catch the next train north. While Luis and Chulo are searching for us here, we'll be heading for the border."

She had no idea if it was wise to share these plans with the kid. Since she didn't know how to relate to a kid, she spoke to Graciela as she would have spoken to an adult.

Graciela made a floating raft out of the washcloth and carefully covered it with grass and leaves. "They'll find us."

"Not if I can help it. We're going to make it plenty hard for them." A redheaded Americana accompanied by a Mexican child was certain to be remembered. Unless Jenny made some changes, the cousins would track their whereabouts in about an hour flat.

"Here's what we're going to do." She drew a breath. "I'm going back to pants and a serape and a man's hat. And I'm going to dye my hair." An unconscious sigh dropped her shoulders. It would be her hair that she cared about. She hated it that her hair was chopped ragged, and, after her bath, she'd paint it with bootblack. It would work. God.

"I'm not saying anybody is going to mistake me for a man, not after a second look, but at least I won't fit the description your rotten cousins will be using."

Graciela studied her with interest, examining Jenny's head. A tiny smile hovered on her lips.

Jenny squinted. "Wait until you hear your part before you start feeling superior. We're going to hide you by turning you into a muchacho. We cut your hair short, and we dress you in pants and a jacket and a boy's hat and boots. Then tomorrow morning we move to a different hotel. The redheaded Americana and her daughter disappear, and the trail stops here."

Horror widened Graciela's eyes, and her hands flew to her hair. "No! You can't cut my hair! No, no, no, no, no!" Thrashing and splashing she tried to climb out of the tall-sided tub, then struck blindly at Jenny when Jenny reached for her. "I won't let you, I won't let you! No, no, no!"

"Kid. Stop screaming! You hear me? Stop screaming this instant!"

Paying no attention, screaming and sobbing, Graciela splashed down on all fours, then she rocked up and flattened herself against the far wall of the tub. She wound her long hair into a dripping rope and held it as far from Jenny as possible. "No! I won't let you!"

"Kid, listen to me. Damn it, shut up. They'll think I'm killing you!"

At once Jenny understood that words were not going to

stand against the storm of a full-blown tantrum. She wanted to smack Graciela as much as she had ever wanted to hit someone in her life. She'd actually leaned over the tub and raised her hand when something in Graciela's expression reminded her of Marguarita. Scowling, she hesitated. She could not imagine Marguarita doing violence to a fly, certainly not to a kid. Jenny's hand lowered, but the effort to do as she imagined Marguarita would want her to made her clench her teeth until her jaw ached.

"All right," she said sharply.

Pressed to the side of the tub, holding the rope of hair protectively, Graciela studied her warily. Her chest heaved with suppressed sobs, but she'd stopped screaming.

"Listen, you little snot. I'm trying to save your fricking life! And mine. Why can't you get that through your head?" Jenny met the kid's glare head-on. "Now, I *am* going to cut your hair. And you *are* going to dress like a boy and pretend to be one." Graciela's mouth opened, but Jenny spoke before the next scream emerged. "But, we won't do it right now, so calm down. We'll cut your hair in the morning. You'll have all night to get used to the idea." Her eyes narrowed and glittered. "But you have to do your part, got that? We're in a tight situation here, and I can't save your butt without a little help from you."

"I hope you die! I hope Cousin Luis shoots you," Graciela said wildly. Tears trembled on her lashes, and she gripped the rope of hair like a lifeline. "You're mean and you're rude and you say bad words." Dropping her hair, she covered her face in her hands. "I want my mama, I want my mama, I want my mama." She started crying, this time softly, and this time with quiet hopelessness.

Jenny rocked back on the stool, her lips pressed in a line. Naked and sitting in eight inches of grimy water, Graciela looked tiny and lost and helpless.

"It's a real pisser to be a kid," Jenny conceded, her expression easing. "I remember how that was. I hated it, too, having to do what grown-up people made me do."

Graciela looked through her fingers. "What did they make you do?" she asked finally. A hiccup twitched her chest.

Suddenly Jenny felt Marguarita's presence again, telling her that it wasn't a good idea to relate how her pa had taken a strap to her and her brothers and sisters when they didn't work hard enough, answer quickly enough, bring him the liquor jug fast enough. She gazed into space, seeking another example to show Graciela that she understood.

"Well, once I had to go into a dark cave by myself. My pa was a miner, see, and he wanted to know if anyone else was working a certain shaft. He figured if there were men inside the shaft, they wouldn't shoot a kid, or maybe he didn't care if they did. Anyway, he made me go inside. I hated that, let me tell you. It was cold and black as a murderer's heart, and I kept hearing things moving in the dark and thinking I was going to get shot any second."

Graciela clutched the soap to her chest, her eyes wide. "Did they shoot you?"

"They were hiding outside." Jenny laughed, remembering. "They shot my pa. Didn't kill him though. Anyway, I guess I know about having to do things you don't want to do. That's how it's been all of my life. You probably won't believe this, but adults have to do things they don't want to do too. I sure don't want to smear bootblack in my hair, no sirree bob, I don't. But I'll do it because changing my appearance will help us."

This was where Graciela was supposed to say that she'd do her part, too, but she didn't. Extending an arm, she ran the soap up and down, not looking at Jenny. "Do you know my father?"

"No," Jenny said, frowning, "I don't."

"I don't know him either." She glanced up, studying Jenny's face. "You said you wouldn't cut my hair until morning."

"And I don't lie."

Graciela tilted her head, her lack of trust as evident as the bits of grass sticking to her bare skin. "I need you to help me wash my hair."

"You know the rules. I'm not going to do anything that you can do yourself."

"Why?"

"Because I'm not your fricking servant, that's why. And because you have to learn how to do things for yourself, or you'll never amount to a hill of beans."

"I can't get the soap out by myself."

Jenny considered before deciding this was probably a legitimate request. She waited until Graciela had worked the soap into a thin lather, then she unbent enough to scrub places that Graciela had missed before she lowered Graciela in the water and gently rinsed the suds out of the long soft strands.

To her immense surprise, she got a funny warm satisfaction from helping Graciela bathe. She wouldn't have believed it.

* * *

They ate supper downstairs at a table ringed by other boarders, none of whom spoke. Then they returned to their room, and Graciela sat on the edge of the bed silently watching while Jenny cursed and muttered and applied the bootblack to her whacked-off hair. The paste was lumpy, smelled bad, and was difficult to work with. "Too much beeswax and not enough syrup in it," Jenny said between her teeth.

When she finished, her fingers were blackened, the sheet around her shoulders was spotted, part of her neck was black, and her hair was stiff and waxy. She looked like hell.

"Well,"she said finally, staring mournfully into the mirror on top of the bureau. The cut on her cheek had healed, and the scab had almost flaked away. But the black eye Luis had given her flared purple and yellow. All in all, Jenny decided she looked about as hideous as a woman could look. "I've done my part." Pulling the sheet off of her shoulders, she slid a glance toward Graciela, who had gone rigid and stared at her with an appalled expression.

"You aren't going to do that to me!" she whispered.

"We're just going to cut yours like a boy's. That's all," Jenny snapped, suddenly irritated. "It's time for bed. Get out of your clothes and go to sleep."

"I have to wash my teeth and say my prayers first."

"Then do it." When Graciela was finally ready for bed, Jenny waited while the kid knelt and basically offered up the same prayer as she did every night. Jenny made a face during the blessing of the cousins, and she spoke the last words in unison with Graciela. "And strike Jenny dead, amen. We don't need to suggest ways and means, all right? We can leave the details of my demise to God. Now, go to sleep."

She sighed when Graciela lifted her cheek for a kiss. She didn't think she would ever get accustomed to death wishes being followed by a good-night kiss.

"Don't get any of the black on me," Graciela warned.

Not trusting herself to speak, Jenny brushed a hasty kiss across a silken cheek, then she blew out their candles and went to sit beside the window.

A pungent burning odor continued to drift from the tobacco factory, but the building was dark and empty now. A man wearing a mended serape and a wide hat led a burro down the deserted street toward the sound of voices and music coming from some distant place that Jenny couldn't see. The burro's hooves striking the cobblestones made a lonely sound.

When Jenny was certain that Graciela had fallen asleep, she lit a dark cigar that she'd purchased earlier from a vendor in the *mercado*. Leaning her arms on the windowsill, she gazed at the night sky, seeking the star she had assigned to Marguarita.

"I don't smoke in front of the kid," she said defensively once she located the correct star. Marguarita had not impressed her as the type to appreciate a good cigar. Not that this was an especially good cigar.

"I sure hope things are going better for you than they are for me." She drew on the cigar and exhaled. The smoke hung on the still, hot air. "I told you I wasn't a kid person. Don't say I didn't warn you." Waving a hand, she tried to clear the smoke that obscured her view of Marguarita's star. "I wanted to hit her. I came this close. So tell me. Sometimes you have to hit a kid. You just have to, right?" Jenny waited, gazing up at the star. If the star winked, that would signal agreement. The star gazed back as unmoving as a fleck of cotton on a square of black velvet. Jenny sighed heavily. "Well, I'm not a fricking saint like you are," she said sourly.

She smoked for a while, occasionally pressing down one of the waxy black tufts sticking out from her scalp. "Maybe I shouldn't have told her about our plan. Maybe I scared her, I don't know." She waved the cigar. "This would have been easier if she'd been a boy. I've been around men most of my adult life; it doesn't matter what you say to them. But see, that's part of the problem. It's not only that she's a kid, she's a girl kid. I don't know what to say to her. Can you imagine me talking about fashions? Huh! And I don't know how to fix her hair . . ."

Leaning on the sill, she earnestly appealed to the star. "Marguarita? I've got to cut her hair. You see that, don't you? It's our best chance. So you tell her that she's got to let me do it. She'll listen to you. Hell, she thinks you can do no wrong."

The odor from the tobacco factory mingled with the aroma of the cigar and the heavy scents of town. Jenny smelled grease and rotting garbage, dung and urine, smoke from a thousand cooking fires.

If she leaned far to the left, she could see a glow of light in the direction of the plaza. Otherwise, the night was dark, hot, and sultry, the kind of night that made Jenny feel restless inside, itching for a vague something that she couldn't name. Nearby, someone unseen strummed a guitar. The music was soft and achingly sad, opening a hole in Jenny's chest. At that moment, she

could believe that she and the guitarist were the only people left on earth.

When the cigar had burned to a stub, she flipped it into
the street, then eyed the bed with anticipation. It had been
a long time since she had slept on a decent mattress, between clean sheets and with a pillow for her head. After
stripping to her shimmy, she elbowed Graciela aside and
slid into bed. Pulling the top sheet to her nose, she inhaled deeply, letting the clean scents of starch and home-
made soap obliterate the stench of the night. She was
going to sleep as soundly as a dead man.

As it turned out, that's exactly how she slept. When
she awoke in the morning, Graciela was gone, and Jenny
hadn't heard a sound. Not Graciela getting dressed, not
the click of the door closing, nothing.

In two minutes flat, she was dressed and running down
the staircase, shouting Graciela's name.

Chapter
Five

Graciela had never been to a town the size of Durango, nor had she imagined that so many people could crowd into one place. Within ten minutes of slipping out of the hotel, she was hopelessly lost.

Although the prospect frightened her badly, she realized that eventually she would have to speak to a stranger, would have to ask directions, a dangerous act she had been cautioned against all of her life. Thus far she hadn't mustered the courage to approach any of the people who jostled each other in the streets as the morning progressed, but she was uncomfortably aware that she attracted attention.

Her hair hung loose like the hair of the ragged girls she saw in the streets, a condition distinctly at odds with the rich fabric and workmanship of her traveling skirt and jacket. The campesinos' daughters wore hats only on Sunday, and their hats were made of plaited straw, not fabric like Graciela's. They wore shapeless dresses, nothing fashionable or trimmed with lace and braid.

Most telling, her fine clothing signaled that she should have been accompanied by a duenna or a family member.

That a richly dressed child wandered alone made her an object of curiosity and speculation. This meant that Jenny would experience little difficulty following her. She would be remembered.

Pausing beneath the shade of a log-and-thatch overhang, Graciela observed inquisitive dark eyes sliding her way. Wringing her hands and averting her gaze, she understood that she had to do something to hide herself, and she had to ask someone for directions. Both courses of action confused and upset her.

Always before there had been adults to make the decisions, adults to protect and care for her. Never had she been on her own or imagined that she would be. She was not accustomed to or prepared to rely on herself. Therefore, no solution leaped to mind when she wondered how she might evade the eyes and memory of the vendors ranged along the street.

Troubled, she watched a wagon rumble past, watched the driver turn on the seat to look at her, and she stamped her boot in frustration.

What would her mama have done to solve this predicament? Or Aunt Tete? Unfortunately Graciela could not imagine either her gentle mother or ancient Aunt Tete ever finding herself in a situation like this.

However, she experienced no difficulty imagining that Jenny might want to hide from someone. She considered this realization. What would Jenny do? Though it galled her to rely on the person she most hated, the very person she wished to escape, thinking about Jenny revealed the first inklings of a solution. Jenny would do whatever was necessary; neither pride nor vanity would stand in Jenny's way. Jenny would . . .

Gradually Graciela comprehended that she had been staring for several minutes at a barefoot urchin on the other side of the cobblestone street. The girl appeared to be about Graciela's age, but there the similarity ended.

She wore a formless dress that once had been white but was now grey with age and heavily soiled. Rips in the skirt showed flashes of bare leg, and a torn sleeve hung from her shoulder. Her hair had not known the touch of a comb or brush in recent memory, and dirt, twigs, and odd lumps were matted in the strands as if she had used the cobbles for her pillow. The girl was very dirty.

Lifting her hem, Graciela darted across the street, dodging offal, refuse, and horses and carts. When she stood before the girl, she noticed the child held a half-eaten tamale. The scent of roasted corn and meat made her stomach grumble.

"My name is . . . Theodora," Graciela announced solemnly. The girl slid an expressionless stare up from Graciela's fashionable little boots to the ruffles trimming the throat of her jacket, but she didn't speak. Graciela glanced at the corn husks peeled back from the tamale and swallowed hard. "What's your name?"

"Maria, *Señorita*," the girl said finally. Shy before the richness of Graciela's clothing, she focused on a point somewhere above Graciela's shoulder.

Graciela clasped her gloved hands against her skirt and watched two caballeros prance down the street. One had a saddle with silver inlaid on a wide pommel. Her cousin Emil had a saddle like that one.

"This is my first visit to Durango," she said. "I rode on a train."

Awe filled Maria's eyes. "You rode on the train?" The

tamale forgotten in her hand, she stared as if Graciela had fallen from the pages of a storybook. "Where is your duenna?" she asked at last. Even a street urchin knew a personage such as Graciela was never left unattended.

"I was stolen by an evil witch," Graciela explained, watching to see if Maria believed her.

"Oh!" Maria's eyes widened, and she nodded. "The same thing happened to my sister."

"I escaped. I ran away from the witch because she wants to cut my hair to look like a boy's."

Maria did not disappoint. The girl examined the shiny hair falling nearly to Graciela's waist and horror filled her eyes. A sense of satisfaction swelled Graciela's chest. Even a child of the streets knew it was wrong to shear a female's glory.

"I have an idea," Graciela said, leaning to whisper in Maria's ear. When she finished speaking, excitement danced in Maria's dark eyes, and she nodded enthusiastically.

"Bueno." Taking Graciela's hand, she led the way into a narrow alley and ducked behind a mound of smoldering trash.

When they emerged, Maria wore Graciela's finery and Graciela wore the filthy dress with the rips and tears, her gold locket pinned inside at the waist. Also, she had what remained of the girl's tamale. She finished the tamale in four hungry bites, then dropped the corn husks on the cobbles. As she had no napkin, she hesitated, then wiped her greasy fingers against the folds of the skirt she now wore. The clothing stank.

"Thank you," she said to Maria. Her traveling outfit was small for Maria, and a seam along the waist had already begun to unravel, but Maria gazed down at herself with blazing pride shining in her eyes.

When she finally remembered Graciela, she pointed to Graciela's hair and then to her own. At once Graciela understood. Sighing, hating it, she bent to the street and filled her hands with dirt, powdery sun-baked dung, and rotting garbage. The stench made her eyes water, but she rubbed the refuse into her hair. With a weak smile and a wave, she moved away from Maria, who had lifted her new skirt to inspect the first shoes ever to grace her feet.

Before she had walked half a block, Graciela turned her attention to her own bare feet. Aside from the tenderness of unhardened soles, she felt a rush of disgust when she stepped on anything wet, anything that oozed up between her toes. Revulsion shivered down her body when her bare foot came down on something warm and soft and smelling of dog.

Shuddering, she hurried blindly forward, not pausing until Maria was lost in the maze of narrow lanes and twisting streets behind her. Only then did she stop to catch her breath and dare to lift her eyes and carefully examine the people moving around her.

No one looked at her. No one paid her the slightest attention. She had become as invisible as the wind.

A jubilant grin curved her mouth and she swallowed a shout, celebrating her own cleverness. "She will never find me," she said aloud, pleased with herself. The town was too large and teeming with people, there were too many alleys and places to hide. And now, no one would remember her.

She had triumphed over her enemy.

Not ten minutes later a hand landed heavily on her shoulder, and a man bent to examine her face. *"Hola, chica,"* he said in a hoarse voice that made her mouth go dry and her blood turn cold. If snakes could talk, they would sound like this man.

"You and me," he said, flicking his tongue at her, "we are going to be very good friends. *Sí."*

Possessive fingers tightened painfully on her shoulder.

Heart pounding, Jenny raced to the end of the block, then halted, spinning around to scowl back at the hotel entrance. Graciela might have turned left instead of right.

"Goddamn it!" She struck her thigh with her hat, then jammed it on her head and glared up and down the crowded streets.

Not since childhood had she experienced panic this gut deep and overwhelming. Her heart galloped in her chest, she couldn't breathe, her hands trembled as if she had the palsy.

Think, she commanded herself, calm yourself and think.

Graciela couldn't have gotten far. Most importantly, she would be remembered, a kid alone wearing a fancy outfit that screamed wealth and status. That was the place to start; inquire about the outfit. Striding forward, she hurried from one vendor's stall to another until she was satisfied that Graciela had not come this way. Reversing direction, she tried another street and another, her shoulders as tense as rock until she located a mestizo woman selling blankets. The woman remembered Graciela.

From that point, it was as easy as following the beads on a necklace that would circle her right up behind the little snot. When she found Graciela, she would wring the kid's neck. Getting angrier by the minute, Jenny followed the trail until finally she spotted Graciela in the middle of the next block. Breaking into a run, she closed the distance.

And stopped abruptly when she saw the girl was not Graciela. The child wore Graciela's clothing, but she was filthy and she didn't move with Graciela's ladylike prissiness and grace. At once Jenny understood what had happened, damn it to hell.

Removing her hat, she wiped the sweat from her forehead and scanned the traffic moving in the street, the women strolling toward the *mercado,* baskets slung over their arms. Her gaze swept the street children and the ubiquitous dogs darting through carts and wagons, dodging among the flow of pedestrians.

Grudgingly, she conceded that Graciela was far more clever than she had believed. And the kid was in far more danger than Jenny could bear to contemplate.

The sweat appearing on her brow had nothing to do with the sun blazing overhead. Her hands started to shake again.

Graciela could step in front of a wagon or a horse and be run down and crippled in the street. She could be dragged into an alley and raped and murdered. She could be abducted and sold to a child brothel; Jenny had heard of such places. A hundred unthinkable horrors could happen to a child alone and lost in a rough mining town of this size.

Trembling with anxiety and frustration, Jenny glared at the dirty little creature wearing Graciela's fine clothing. There was no point questioning her. The chase ended here, and Jenny knew it.

Swearing beneath her breath, she turned into a café and bought a cup of strong Mexican coffee, which she carried back to the street, sipping while she watched the rhythm of the town unfold, while she fought to control the panic boiling in her stomach.

She felt as helpless as she had felt sitting in her jail cell waiting to be executed.

Then Marguarita had appeared and calmly offered Jenny her life in exchange for a promise. Jenny had given her promise, her solemn word, and Marguarita had died; Marguarita had kept her end of the bargain.

A stream of cusswords blistered her tongue. Marguarita's part had been easy, all Marguarita had to do was die. Dying was a fricking piece of cake next to dealing with this kid.

A huge sigh lifted Jenny's chest.

If anything happened to Graciela, she might as well put a gun to her head and pull the trigger. Her life wouldn't be worth crap if her promise meant nothing, if she failed the woman who had died in her place.

Acid poured into her stomach, and she felt like throwing up. Leaning a hand against the café's adobe wall, she dropped her head and swallowed repeatedly.

All right. She knew two things. First, there was nothing she could do for the next several hours, nothing at all. Graciela was on her own, in the hands of God or whoever. Jenny had to accept that she was helpless to intervene; there was nothing she could do except hope like hell that the damned kid was lucky. Second, she knew where Graciela would be at seven o'clock tonight. That is, if Graciela continued to be as resourceful as it appeared she was, then Jenny knew where the kid was going. Please God, let the little snot be there at seven o'clock.

Straightening, she drank the rest of her coffee, then tossed the cup to a waiter. She needed food, but her stomach was cramping so badly that she doubted she could hold anything down.

Walking aimlessly, staring at each urchin she passed, she gradually settled her mind into accepting what she could not change. The best plan was to keep busy. Do the things she had planned for today before the fricking kid ran away and made her age ten years. That included buying boy's clothing for the kid, and a sidearm for herself. These chores would take about an hour.

This was going to be the longest day in her sorry life.

"Now aren't you the prettiest little thing."

Even the man's voice was hot and oily. His breath in her face smelled of chilies and cigars and something sickly-sweet that made Graciela think of liquid flame. His eyes frightened her badly.

"You're hurting me," she whispered, wiggling beneath the fingers clamping her shoulder. Darting a look toward the street, she realized that no one paid them any attention. Near the door of a leather store, a man backhanded a boy, and the boy shouted in pain. No one glanced in his direction either.

Heart thumping in her chest, she dragged her gaze back to the man kneeling in front of her, blocking her way. One hand gripped her shoulder, the other circled her ankle and slid up her bare leg to her knee.

Shock stiffened her body. No man had ever touched her

so intimately, and she knew instinctively that it was very wrong.

"Would you like to come with me, *chica?* We'll have some food, something cool to drink."

"No." Her mouth was as dry as the desert air.

"Light skin, light eyes." The man's fingers inched toward her thighs and Graciela's stomach lurched. "We'll make a fortune together." A speculative gaze dropped to her mouth and he licked his lips.

With sickening clarity Graciela understood the man meant to do something bad to her regardless of her protests. She stared at his thick neck and wide chest and black dots of fear swirled in front of her eyes.

Panicked, she tried to think what to do. What would Jenny do? Jenny wouldn't meekly give up; Jenny would not let this man put his hot hands on her.

Pretending that she was Jenny, Graciela turned her head and bit down on the man's forearm. She held on until she tasted blood. At the same time she kicked out with her free leg and felt her heel strike something soft between his thighs. He shouted, and they both fell to the ground, rolling toward the hooves of a burro. In a flash, Graciela sprang to her feet and ran as fast as she could, skidding around a corner then another corner and another until she was gasping for breath and holding her side.

Stopping to breathe, she gripped the bars of an iron gate to hold herself upright and cast a fearful glance behind to see if the man pursued. The quiet street was deserted. Here there were no noisy vendors; no wagons rattled over the cobblestones. Only the distant splash of a fountain disturbed the silence.

Thick adobe walls lined the street, overhung with leafy branches, shielding fine houses from envy and curiosity.

As her heart quieted, Graciela became aware of voices behind the walls and the iron gate, the light voices of servants gossiping and laughing as they attended to their chores.

"Please?" she called. "I need help." Gripping the iron bars, she peered inside at the statue of a saint guarding the doors to a fine house that reminded her of Aunt Tete's hacienda.

Homesickness raised tears to her eyes and made her knees go weak. "Please. Help me!"

A woman approached the gate wearing a frown and a damp apron that smelled like laundry soap. She scowled at Graciela and waved a hand in front of her nose. "Get away from here! Go!" Someone called a question, and she glanced over her shoulder. "It's only a beggar."

Pride lifted Graciela's chin. "I am not a beggar," she said swiftly. "Inform your mistress that Graciela Sanders, the great-niece of Dona Theodora Barrancas y Talmas, begs your lady's kindness and assistance. You will do this at once, *por favor.*"

The washerwoman grinned and rolled her dark eyes toward heaven. "Where did you learn such a pretty speech?" She turned her head to call over her shoulder. "Even the street trash is putting on airs now."

For the first time in her life Graciela spied no respectful recognition at the mention of her aunt's name. This woman—this servant!—laughed at her. Shock and confusion drained the color from her face.

The servant woman waved her hands in a shooing motion. "There's nothing for you here. Get away from the gate or I'll call someone. You won't welcome a beating from Jose." Frowning, not a flicker of sympathy in her gaze, she watched Graciela's shaking hands fall away from the iron bars.

Frightened, Graciela moved out of the woman's line of sight and sank to her knees, pressing her back to the high wall before she covered her face in her hands. Hot tears wet her fingers.

When she left the hotel this morning, she had anticipated a great adventure. She had not been afraid.

Now she trembled with fear. She was lost and hungry, and every stranger who looked at her made her stomach hurt. Overwhelmed by her own helplessness, she sobbed into her hands.

When no more tears would come, she wiped her eyes, hiccuped, and stared at the filth on her toes. She longed for a bath and something to eat. At this moment she would gladly have taken a pair of scissors to her hair if Jenny had appeared at the end of the quiet street.

The thought made her cringe. Forming a fist, an unladylike gesture her mother would have disapproved, she struck the adobe wall.

The hated Jenny would not have given up. And neither would she. Her small chin steadied into a stubborn angle that her mother would have recognized.

She had begun with a plan, and she would see it through. Somehow. If no more bad men grabbed her. If she was fortunate.

What choice did she have?

After a final homesick glance toward the iron gates that closed her away from the only life she knew, she turned away, dragging her bare feet over the rough cobbles toward the noise and smells of commerce and people.

She told herself that Jenny wouldn't have been afraid.

Sunlight bounced off the Rio Nazas and momentarily blinded Ty as the train chuffed across the bridge. Turning his face from the window, he consulted his pocket watch. The conductor swore they would arrive in Durango on schedule at seven o'clock, but clearly it would be later. Nothing ran on schedule in Mexico.

After returning his watch to his vest pocket, he pulled his hat down over his eyes, folded his arms across his chest, and tried to doze, but an active mind interfered with sleep.

The way he had it figured, the red-haired woman was headed for Mexico City. If he'd guessed right, then catching her bordered on hopeless, but he couldn't return to California and tell Robert that he hadn't at least tried.

Unfortunately, he'd heard there was a large Anglo population in the capital. An Americana and a Mexican child wouldn't be an anomaly there. Plus, Mexico City was huge. He'd never find the red-haired woman and his niece.

Opening his eyes, he shoved up the brim of his hat and frowned out the window past streaks of soot and oily smoke. The train had entered a fertile valley enclosed by the wrinkled arms of the Sierra Madres. Small farms appeared with increasing frequency, brave patches of green scratched out of the grey-brown earth. He spotted slag piles spilling down the face of hills thrusting up from the valley floor.

Before the train arrived at Durango, he had to decide if he would get off and give the town a cursory search just in case that was the red-haired woman's destination, although he couldn't think why it would be. He doubted she was interested in the thermal springs, and she wasn't a miner.

He stayed on the train after it stopped at the Durango station, scowling out the window, trying to decide if it was worth looking for her here or if he'd be wasting time.

The town was larger than he had expected, housing perhaps ten to fifteen thousand souls. He saw a church spire rising near the center of town, watched the sun sinking past a surprising number of trees. Losing interest in the town, he idly watched a flock of child beggars descend on the passengers stepping out of the train. When the children were certain no further prey would emerge from the cars, they ran after the people walking toward waiting carts or carriages.

Ty's gaze settled on one of the children who had remained behind. She stared at the train with utter despair, her shoulders dropped, her small body trembling on the verge of collapse. Her hair was filthy and wild, and a thin shapeless rag covered her frame. What a waste, he thought. She was going to be a beauty one day. With those eyes . . .

"What?" Abruptly, he sat up straight and his gaze sharpened. He knew those eyes as well as he knew his own. Hell, he ought to. He stared into those same blue-green eyes every morning in his shaving mirror.

Before he could recover from the shock of finding his niece so easily and in such unexpected circumstances, a man pushed away from the side wall of the depot and stormed toward her. No, not a man. A woman dressed in male trousers and a lightweight poncho that swung open at the side slits to reveal a pistol strapped to her waist.

Ty couldn't believe his eyes. She had done something to her hair, and now it was as black as roofing pitch. Stiff waxy tufts stuck out between her ears and her hat. Who-ever the hell this woman was, she didn't possess a stitch of female vanity, that was for damned certain.

It was also certain that she was furious. Although he couldn't hear what she was shouting, she started waving her arms and screaming at his niece even before she reached the girl.

Ty rose out of his seat, bending to the window while hastily gathering his belongings. With large hopeless eyes, his niece watched the raging advance of the now black-haired woman. As the woman rushed forward, her expression hardened and her arm rose as if she intended to beat Ty's niece into pulp.

His shoulders tensed. If she struck his niece, by God he would kill her.

When she was almost on top of his niece, the child stumbled forward and wrapped her arms around the now-black-haired woman's waist and sank into her. The woman stopped and the descent of her arm halted. Her expression flickered from fury to surprise to confusion to exasperation. Ty read her emotions as easily as reading words on a page. For a desperado, she was amazingly transparent.

She waved both hands in the air as if she didn't know what to do with them, all the while looking down at the child. Then she rolled her eyes toward heaven, heaved a massive sigh, and dropped to her knees on the cobblestones. She gathered the child into her arms and awkwardly patted the child's back while the child clung to her and sobbed on her neck.

She was a large woman, dressed as a man and wearing a sidearm. Ty didn't doubt that she knew how to use it. But right now, the child-stealer wore an expression of helpless confusion that would have done credit to the smallest, most feminine of creatures.

Ty had no idea what had just happened here. Frowning, he watched the woman and the child holding each other and could not imagine why either of them was dressed the way she was or what their relationship might possibly be.

A cloud of grey-white smoke belched past the window, obscuring his view, and a whistle screamed overhead. The boards lurched beneath his feet. Slinging his saddlebags over his shoulder, he strode down the aisle and out the door at the end of the car, then jumped to the ground. When he looked up, the now-black-haired woman and his niece had disappeared. They couldn't have gone far.

Before he set off to follow, he shot a glance toward the departing train. Damned if his horse wasn't on its way to Mexico City. How many horses had he lost now? Three? Cursing, he rapidly crossed the square and peered into the lengthening shadows creeping down narrow streets.

He spotted them about a block ahead, the large woman and the small girl. The woman had a protective hand on the child's shoulder. His niece rested her head against the woman's side.

Ty followed, keeping well behind them, pausing when they did. At the corner, the woman bent and lifted his niece, slinging the child over her shoulder like a sack of grain. She carried the girl another six blocks, to the entrance of a hotel that Ty would have overlooked entirely if the woman hadn't turned in at a door recessed from the street.

When he was certain that she wasn't coming out again, he walked around the block, looking for the alley, pinning the location in his mind. A thick stench of roasting tobacco leaves burned his nostrils when he passed a factory on the north side of the hotel. To the west, a man wearing an apron hung lanterns in front of a cantina. In the street to the south, vendors packed away their wares for the night. When he had circled back to the hotel entrance, he stopped across the street and lit a cigar, frowning and considering his next move.

Who the hell *was* she? He kept seeing her face in his mind. Tanned, strong features, a chiseled, stubborn jaw, blue eyes, one of them still bruised from the fight in Verde Flores. And that magnificent figure. The poncho she'd worn at the depot was no shield against his memory. A man didn't forget breasts like hers.

He almost laughed aloud. After a lifetime of chasing soft, dainty creatures no larger than dolls, it amused him to realize that no woman had riveted his interest as did the tall strange-haired woman with the wicked punch who had stolen his niece.

Shaking his head, he kicked at a horse-apple and waited for full darkness to settle.

Chapter
Six

Jenny sat by the window, hoping for a cool breeze while she watched Graciela wolf down a plate of food the manager had sent to their room. Between bites, the kid told of a harrowing day, about a man who had stroked her bare legs, about being chased by adults and street children, about falling and skinning her knee, about a wild dog that had terrified her and snapped at her bare feet.

The horror of what might have been robbed Jenny of any appetite. Her own supper sat untouched beside the tub she had ordered up to the room.

She wanted to shout and scream, wanted to beat the kid senseless. She wanted to point out that Graciela deserved the scares she had received and was damned lucky that nothing worse had happened. Through Graciela's bath, and throughout her recitation of the day's frightening events, anger and accusations burned on Jenny's tongue.

"Kid," she said, when Graciela's torrent of words shuddered to a halt, "I've got a lot to say, but first . . . you did fine out there. You handled yourself a lot better than I ever expected you would."

The praise came hard, but Jenny figured it would soften the kid for the harder discussion to follow. Besides, she conceded grudgingly, the kid deserved a word of praise. Jenny knew how hard it was on the streets. Earlier today, she wouldn't have given a centavo for the kid's chances to end her escapade relatively unscathed.

"How'd you know to kick that bastard in the . . ." she paused and coughed into her hand. "How'd you know to bite and kick him?"

Graciela pushed a long strand of wet hair away from her face and her chin came up. "I thought about what my mama would do." Her expression dared Jenny to scoff.

"Huh." Jenny tried to imagine Marguarita kicking some son of a bitch in the *cojones*. Impossible. "Well," she said finally, "your mother was a brave woman." That much was true.

Graciela's eyebrows lifted as if she hadn't expected Jenny's response. They studied each other. "How did you know I'd go to the train station?"

"That wasn't difficult." Jenny shrugged. "I guessed that you'd remember me saying your stinking cousins might show up on the seven o'clock."

The kid frowned. "I forgot you would be there too."

"It's damned lucky for you that I was."

"That's true," the kid admitted in a small voice. Sooty lashes came down on her cheeks as she closed her eyes and shivered. "I didn't want you to cut my hair."

"I figured." Jenny pushed a hand through her own sticky, matted hair. She wondered how long it would take for the bootblack to wear off. "Look, kid, it's good you got scared out there, because we can't go through this again, you understand? You wrecked our plan. I didn't find us a new hotel because I thought you might come back here. Now the clerk knows I've altered my appearance." Which meant that she'd rubbed bootblack in her hair for fricking nothing.

"Plus, you can't imagine what it was like when I didn't know where you were or what was happening to you." She looked out the window, up toward Marguarita's star. "I gave your mother my word. I promised that I'd take you to your father in California." She turned back to Graciela. "That's what I'm going to do, so you just make up your mind to it. The thing is, I need your help. You can't be fighting me every step of the way. That means we have to agree on a few rules. Such as, you don't run away again."

Graciela picked at the edge of the towel wrapped around her freshly washed body. "Why can't you just take me home to Aunt Tete? You don't want to take me to California, and I don't want to go there. I want to go home."

Lord, didn't she wish she could dump the kid on Dona Theodora's doorstep and ride away without a backward glance. "That isn't what your mother wanted. Look, kid, I gave her my word. I promised."

Graciela gazed down at her lap, pulled her napkin through her fingers. "Mama won't know if you kept your promise . . ." she whispered.

"I'll know!" Jenny glared. "When Jenny Jones gives her word, by God the thing is as good as done! This doesn't have anything to do with your mother anymore. Here's how it is, kid. After you give a promise, see, the person you gave it to is out of the deal. It's just you and the promise. If you keep the promise, then you're some-

body. You did right. But if you fail, then you might as well stick a knife in your gut because you aren't worth spit. You're a person with no fricking honor. Now that's how it is. And that's why your butt is going to California."

Graciela lowered her head and stared at her empty supper plate. A tear rolled down her cheek and plopped on the table.

"Now, you wrecked our plan, you worried me half out of my mind, and something terrible could have happened to you. This tells me that we need some rules. I want your promise that you won't run away again."

"I won't promise that," Graciela said in a low voice.

"Kid, I'm not going to cut your hair. I changed my mind. Look over there on the bureau. I bought some hairpins. We'll pin your hair up under a boy's hat. I should have thought of this before. If you don't take off the hat, it should be all right."

"Stop calling me kid! My name is Graciela. I hate it when you call me kid."

Jenny's eyebrows lifted in surprise. She had to stop thinking that Graciela was a miniature Marguarita. Etiquette and convention were making inroads on the kid, but they hadn't yet quenched her fire.

"All right," she said slowly, thinking over the request. "I can agree to that . . . if you'll agree to stop crying over every little damned thing."

They measured each other, weighing their negotiating strengths.

"I'll try," Graciela finally conceded. "But you don't think anything is worth crying over, and some things *are*."

"Maybe," Jenny said doubtfully. "At your age anyway. You've got to agree to dress like a boy. And you've got to stop asking 'why' all the time because you're driving me crazy."

"I'll dress like a boy if you'll stop threatening to hit me. It scares me."

Jenny considered. "Well, I can't agree to that," she said finally. "If ever I saw a kid who needs hitting, you're that kid."

"Why?"

"See? There you go with the why crap. Damn it!"

"I want to know."

"You need hitting because you're a superior, arrogant little snot and you think you're better than . . . other people." Color rose in Jenny's cheeks. "You don't do what you're told. You think you know everything when you don't know anything. You wish I was dead. You don't believe me or your mother about your greedy cousins. You have perfect manners and prissy ways. You don't know how to do anything useful, and your hankie is always clean. Of course I want to hit you."

Graciela's lips pulled down at the corners. "Well, you walk like a man, and you don't say please or thank you. You got in a *fight* with my cousins." She shuddered. "You're always angry, and you don't say your prayers at night. You talk bad, and you smoke *cigars* when you think I'm asleep. You don't know my father, and you didn't even know my mama. You have hair between your legs, and the hair on your head is ugly. You aren't a lady."

Jenny stood and looked out the window. The night was soft and hot; a million stars spangled the sky. She saw only one.

"I guess we know where we stand," she said finally. "That's good. But I've had about as much negotiation as I can stand for one night, and judging from those yawns, I'm guessing you have, too. So get your butt in bed, and we'll talk more about rules tomorrow."

"Why do I have to go to sleep before you do?"

"Because I want to read my dictionary and get my thoughts settled down. And because I'm the adult, and you're nothing but a kid. Listen . . . you promised to stop asking why."

"I didn't promise."

Kids ran a person around in circles. Jenny didn't know why any woman willingly became a parent. Prior to this journey she had believed that skinning carcasses was the worst occupation in the world. Now she was convinced that raising children made skinning carcasses look like a plum job. When it occurred to her that she might have to spend the next ten or twelve years raising Graciela, despair nearly knocked her to her knees.

"Put on your nightgown and get into bed." Scowling up at Marguarita's star, she waited until Graciela was ready to say her prayers, then she sighed and crossed the room to sit on the edge of the bed.

"You should kneel," Graciela reprimanded her.

"You're the one saying the prayers, not me. So say them and get it over with."

"At least close your eyes."

"All right! My eyes are closed. Say the damned prayers."

"Our Father, who art in heaven . . ."

Jenny heard a soft click and opened one eye, then she sprang to her feet in astonishment. The cowboy from

Verde Flores stepped into their room, nudged the door shut, then aimed a Colt at Jenny's chest. Her mouth fell open in disbelief.

"Unbuckle your gun belt. Slide it across the floor."

Graciela screamed, then scrambled up on the bed and pressed herself to the wall. Her eyes widened in fear.

"What the hell?" Jenny tried to sort it out. The cowboy? Here? Moving slowly in case he had an eager trigger finger, she lifted the hem of the poncho and reached beneath it to unbuckle her belt. "If this is a robbery . . ." But somehow she didn't think it was.

"You have a lot of explaining to do. Now drop the gun belt and slide it over here, or I'll shoot. Don't think I won't. Until I hear your story, I'm assuming the worst. Give me the gun."

The ice in his blue-green eyes told her that he meant it about shooting her. Reluctantly, she slid the gun and belt across the floor.

"How did you find us?" Her mind couldn't make the leap from meeting him at the Verde Flores depot to seeing him here. But clearly meeting him again was no accident. Her gut told her that he'd followed them, but she couldn't think why he would.

"I spotted you both out of the train window."

"Why are you so interested in us?" Jenny demanded.

But the cowboy was staring past her shoulder at Graciela. So that was it. "You filthy pervert!" Jenny's teeth pulled back in a snarl, and she lunged for him, catching him by surprise. Her head slammed into his belly like a battering ram, and the air ran out of him in a rush. When he doubled over, she brought her head up. The collision of head and forehead was harder on him than on her, and she knocked the Colt out of his hand.

Before she could snatch up his gun or her own, he grabbed her and they fell to the floor, rolling, hitting, and punching each other.

The fight was fair as fights went, and they were evenly matched. If Jenny hadn't jerked away to avoid a punch and banged her head hard on the side of the tub, she might have beaten him. But the head bang dazed her for a second, and that was all he needed to pin her.

For two long minutes, he sat on her, holding her wrists to the floor and they both panted hard, sucking in air. A hot trickle leaked from Jenny's cracked lip; his bloody nose dripped on her poncho.

"Jesus," he said, finally, staring down at her. "That's the first time I ever fought a woman." He stared at her bloody lip in disbelief. Then he stood and jerked Jenny off the floor. He slammed her down in a chair and pulled a length of thin rope from his belt.

"Graciela! Run!" Damned if she would make it easy for him. She twisted and thrashed and tried to break free.

He jerked her back hard and tied her wrists together. "Stay where you are, Graciela," he warned.

It wasn't that the kid chose to obey the cowboy over her, Jenny understood that. The kid was terrified. She cowered against the wall watching with huge eyes, too frightened even to cry.

The cowboy tied Jenny's ankles to the chair legs and looped a piece of rope around her chest and the back rails for good measure. Stepping backward to inspect his work, he wiped the blood from his nose, glaring down at her. He swore and shook his head.

"Don't you touch her!" Jenny warned, speaking through her teeth. Her gaze was as frozen as his. "I swear to you. If you harm that child, I'll hunt you down if it takes the rest of my life, and you won't die fast, you piece of scum."

"If I . . . ?" His mouth twisted in revulsion. "I'm not going to . . . my God! My name is Ty Sanders. Robert Sanders is my brother. I'm Graciela's uncle, for Christ's sake."

Jenny stared. Suddenly she saw the resemblance, the same blue-green eyes as Graciela's, the same wide mouth. Her mind raced backward, replaying Marguarita's story. Robert Sanders had not gone to Mexico with Marguarita; he had remained in California to ensure that his inheritance did not go to a younger brother. It struck her that the cowboy might be telling the truth.

After checking again to make certain that Jenny was securely restrained, he walked to the bed and stood by the edge of the mattress. "So you're Robert's daughter."

Jenny tried to read his expression, but she couldn't determine how he felt about his brother's daughter. The shortage of emotion suggested that he wasn't exactly overjoyed to meet his niece, and he didn't even know yet what a pain in the butt she was.

"I'm your uncle Ty. Your daddy is my brother," he said in a voice distinctly lacking enthusiasm. "I guess your name is Graciela."

"Don't talk to him!" Even if he was who he said he was, Jenny didn't trust his attitude.

The cowboy considered her, then he walked over and stuffed Graciela's napkin into her mouth before he returned to the bed.

"Your daddy sent me down here to find you and your mother and take you both back to California. He wants you to live with him."

Graciela was still pressed to the wall, but she was listening, not paying any attention to Jenny's rolling eyes or the noises she made behind the napkin.

"You know my daddy?" Graciela asked shyly.

"I've known your daddy all of my life." The cowboy wasn't cold to Graciela, but he wasn't particularly warm either. "I knew your mother, too, years ago. And I know your grandfather, Don Antonio."

Jenny stopped her futile struggle against the ropes to listen. Either the cowboy had done some research, or he was who he said he was. In either case, intuition told her that he was here reluctantly. He might indeed be Graciela's uncle, but he had no feeling for the kid.

"My mama is dead," Graciela confided in a whisper, tears brimming in her eyes.

"I heard about it when I went to fetch you at Dona Theodora's."

Graciela wiped away the tears and continued to stare at the cowboy. To Jenny's horror, she spied the beginnings of trust. Jenny renewed a furious struggle against the ropes that bound her to the chair. The minute Sanders had mentioned going to the no-name village to fetch Graciela, she understood his intention.

"You know my aunt Tete too?"

The cowboy smiled. "I met your aunt Tete years ago when she was visiting your grandpa Antonio. She and your mother were riding in their carriage and a wheel came off. I stopped to help, and your aunt Tete found fault with everything I did. She had a big fan, you know?" Graciela didn't move her eyes from the cowboy's face. "And she kept hitting me with it on the shoulder, right here. And she'd say, *'Con permisso, Señor,* but you are doing that all wrong.' "

Nodding and smiling, Graciela slid down the wall and sat on the bed, staring at the cowboy in fascination.

Realizing how easily the cowboy had charmed the kid made Jenny choke.

"Here's what we're going to do," he said to Graciela. "I'm going to take you to your daddy and your grandmother Ellen."

"I want to go home to Aunt Tete," Graciela said in a whisper. Singing the same tune she'd sung for Jenny.

"Your home is in California now." He studied the kid's expression. "But maybe you and your daddy can visit your aunt Tete or she can visit you. Going to California doesn't mean that you won't see your aunt again."

Jenny couldn't believe how easily he swept aside the kid's protest. Why hadn't she thought of that? She had only to glance at the kid's face to know Sanders had given her the perfect reassurance. The kid's face told her something else. With a sinking heart she realized that Graciela was going to go with the cowboy without a peep of a struggle, without a shred of regret, or a twinge of gratitude for what Jenny had gone through so far. The snot.

"All right, here's what I want you to do. You get dressed, all right? I need to talk to—" He jerked a thumb over his shoulder.

"Her name is Jenny Jones. She killed my mama."

Jenny squeezed her eyes shut and let her head drop forward. Damn it. She should have belted the kid when she had the chance.

"That's what I need to find out. As soon as Jenny and I have finished talking, we'll leave."

Graciela didn't hesitate. The disloyal, ungrateful little brat jumped off the bed and scampered to the bureau, removing the change of clothing Maria had packed for her. As modest as a full-grown lady, she stepped behind the dressing screen, and in a minute her nightgown flew past the side of the screen.

The cowboy removed the napkin from Jenny's mouth and sat down at the table, shoving Graciela's supper plate away from him. "Who the hell are you? And how did you get my niece?"

Jenny told him the whole story, starting with killing the bastard who had attacked her and ending with leaving Marguarita standing in her cell and Jenny hightailing it away from the compound dressed as a priest. She didn't spare any details.

Ty Sanders didn't interrupt, he listened quietly and watched her with cool eyes. "If you agreed to take my niece to her father, then what the hell are you doing in Durango?"

Jenny's lip curled in exasperation. "My primary concern was to get away from the cousins. How long did *you* hang around the Verde Flores depot waiting for them to wake up?"

"There are a lot of stops between here and Verde Flores. Why didn't you turn around and head north?"

"And risk having Chulo and Luis jump me again in Verde Flores?" Jenny snapped. "Untie me."

"Not a chance." The cowboy looked toward the bed, where Graciela had returned after getting dressed. The instant her head touched the pillow, she had fallen asleep.

He was silent for several minutes. "I'm inclined to believe your story."

"Listen, you son of a bitch. I don't ever lie. That's why Marguarita trusted me, a stranger, to take her daughter to California. That's why she asked me to raise the kid if your weak-spined brother couldn't or wouldn't."

The cowboy narrowed his eyes. "Looks like you bought your life cheap, Jenny Jones, because you don't have to take Graciela to California after all, and there's no chance that you'll be raising her."

"Yeah, well that isn't how Marguarita saw it." She yanked on the ropes, then gave it up. "Marguarita didn't say hand the kid to an uncle if one shows up. And she didn't say that you or any other family member could raise the kid if Robert couldn't or wouldn't. She told *me* to take the kid to California, and she told *me* to raise her if it was necessary." Leaning forward, she stared into his eyes, meeting glare for glare. "And that's how it's going to be. I promised. So, I'm not handing her over to you. I'm the one who's taking her to California."

He leaned forward, too, until their noses almost bumped. "No, you aren't. As of right now, you have no claim on my niece. Tomorrow you can go back to wherever you came from."

"Believe me, I'd love to do that. You can't even guess how much I'd love to dump that snotty kid in your lap and forget about her. But I gave my word. And I don't give a fricking spit if you're Graciela's uncle. It doesn't matter, not even a little bit. Because I promised Marguarita that *I* would take the kid to her father. We made a deal, mister, and I mean to honor my half of it."

The cowboy's gaze slid pointedly over the ropes bind-ing her to the chair, and a faint smile touched his lips. "It doesn't look like you're in any position to keep that promise."

Jenny decided that she hated his guts. "I'll admit I'm experiencing some unforeseen difficulties . . . but I will keep my promise. The kid is *my* responsibility."

"You're wrong. Marguarita didn't know it when she spoke to you, but circumstances have changed. She didn't know I was on my way to fetch her and her daughter."

"Yeah, well why didn't she know? Couldn't your lily-livered brother write a letter?" A sneer pulled at Jenny's lips.

"He did write. He wrote a hundred letters to Marguarita, letters she never bothered to answer."

"So you say. I happen to know Marguarita didn't get any letters from good old Robert. She sure as hell didn't know that Robert had sent for her. Do you think I'd be involved if she'd known you were on the way to fetch her?"

The cowboy stared at her with a thoughtful expression. "Dona Theodora," he said finally. "That's the only explanation. Dona Theodora intercepted the letters and kept them from Marguarita."

"Untie me, damn it!"

The cowboy stood and glanced toward the bed, where Graciela slept in a fashionable little traveling outfit. "I don't know why I'm bothering to say this," he stated, looking back at Jenny. "But what you said was correct. If Marguarita had known I was coming for her, you'd be shot full of holes. You would not be involved in a matter that doesn't concern you. The point I'm making is that you're out of this now. Graciela has family."

"Yeah, well Cousin Luis and Cousin Chulo are family,

too, and if they get their hands on Graciela, she's as good as dead," Jenny snapped, scowling up at him. "That's what family does for you."

"I've been thinking about this. You're right about Luis and Chulo being family. I don't think the cousins would kill a member of their own family. I think they'll go for ransom."

Jenny made a snorting sound. "Don't kid yourself, Uncle Ty. Graciela is the only thing standing between the cousins and the Barrancas fortune. You saw Luis and Chulo. Hell yes, they'd kill her. Why settle for ransom when they can inherit everything?"

"If they go for ransom, they can hit Barrancas *and* my brother. If they kill her, the only target is Don Antonio's fortune. That's too shortsighted."

"The cousins don't know your brother from a plate of beans," Jenny snapped. "I'll bet my mules and my rig that—" No, her mules and her rig were long gone. "But they do know about Don Antonio's wealth, and they know they're next in line once the kid dies. Count on it. If the cousins get Graciela, she's dead."

"You're a surprising woman," he said suddenly. "This conversation isn't at all what I expected."

"Untie me!" She jerked and yanked at the ropes.

Pulling her head back, he inserted the napkin into her mouth, then inspected his blackened fingers. "What the hell did you put on your hair?"

Shaking his head, he wiped his hands on his trousers, then walked to the bed and awkwardly lifted Graciela in his arms. At the door he looked back at Jenny. "By the time someone finds you, we'll be halfway to Verde Flores." Frowning, he hesitated, then spoke with reluctance.

"I deeply regret that it was necessary to hit you. And I'm obliged for what you've done for my niece," he said stiffly.

Jenny glared bullets. "Oo on a a itch!"

Suddenly he grinned and winked at her. "You were better looking as a redhead. Wash that black stuff out of your hair." He stepped into the hallway with Graciela in his arms and closed the door behind him. Jenny heard his boots receding down the narrow hallway.

Swearing and fighting to spit out the napkin, Jenny struggled furiously against the ropes. Twenty minutes later, she fell back in the chair, exhausted.

Letting her head fall backward, she stared up at the ceiling. *Marguarita, I heartily wish I'd never laid eyes on you. You couldn't help out a little, could you? Oh no. You've got to make this as hard as it can be. It wasn't enough to have the stinking cousins. You had to throw in an uncle. What the hell is this, a test?*

After a while her thoughts settled and it occurred to her that she had an idea where Ty Sanders was going, and, more importantly, she knew where he was not going. He wasn't going to Verde Flores. At least not immediately.

It irritated the bejesus out of her that he thought she was stupid enough to fall for a cheap trick. If you're running from someone, you don't tell her where you're going. Hell, she'd learned that dodge before she was Graciela's age.

Since there wasn't much else to do, since she was bound and gagged, she devoted the rest of the night to figuring out how she would get the kid back.

Chapter
Seven

Two minutes after Ty carried Graciela out of Jenny Jones's room, it struck him that he faced an uncomfortable problem which he had not anticipated. Where was he going to take her? After Jenny's offensive misconception, he felt distinctly uneasy about checking into a decent hotel with a young Mexican girl in his arms. A rowdy town the size of Durango had hotels where no one would blink at a man taking a young girl to his room, but the thought of anyone mistaking Ty for such a man twisted his gut in knots.

As he carried his sleeping niece down dark, deserted streets, he rejected the possibility of riding out of Durango tonight and avoiding the hotel problem. Even if Graciela were wide-awake and alert, he didn't know where he could buy a horse at this hour. He had to find a hotel. In the end, hating it, he settled for a fleabag where no questions would be asked.

Angry and embarrassed, he carried the child up a flight of stairs, wanting to smash a knowing smirk deep into the hotel clerk's sly face. There was a lesson here, he thought grimly. No more hotels. And his decision to avoid the train was correct. An Americano and a small Mexican girl were certain to draw attention and unpleasant speculation. The sickening roll in his stomach warned that his pride would not withstand that kind of prurient curiosity. He'd be setting himself up for a dozen fights.

Inside a shabby room, he laid Graciela on a bed that sagged toward the center, hesitated, then removed her hat. She roused slightly when he pulled off her boots, then she sank into the pillow, sighed, and again fell asleep.

After tossing his own hat toward a scarred bureau, he removed his gun belt, sat on a stool beside the window, flexed his shoulders, and let the enormity of tonight's business sweep over him.

The hotel problem underscored the sobering fact that he didn't know a damned thing about children. Especially girl children. Already it was evident that traveling with a young girl was going to present unique problems. Since he had assumed that Marguarita would accompany him back to California, he had also assumed that she would take care of her child. He hadn't wasted a single thought on Marguarita's offspring, hadn't anticipated that the child would have anything to do with him.

Lifting his head, he gazed across the room, frowning at a bar of moonlight drifting across the bed and illuminating Graciela's small features. Ty hadn't known Marguarita well; he didn't remember much about her. But he saw Marguarita in the child. Graciela's hair was soft brown and her skin was light, but no one would mistake her Mexican heritage. Aside from her eyes and mouth, she didn't resemble anyone in the Sanders family tree.

Leaning forward, he rested his forearms on his thighs and pushed a hand through the hair falling across his forehead.

Cal Sanders had refused to accept Robert's marriage because Cal could not bear the thought of Mexican grandchildren. That a Mexican might one day inherit the fruits of Sanders labor was an abomination too repugnant to contemplate. It was offensive enough that the Sanders ranch adjoined Barrancas lands; that the two families might intermingle was unthinkable to a man whose hatreds had been formed in his youth.

At age sixteen, Calvin Sanders had joined the American forces that invaded Mexico in '46. Ty's father had left his right arm in a bean field outside Mexico City, ending his brief role in the invasion and beginning a hatred of all things Mexican that until his death three months ago had burned as hot as the pitch used to cauterize his stump.

Ty pulled a hand down his jaw, then tossed one of his boots at a rat scratching at a corner of the plank floor.

That Robert had challenged their father's prejudice was one of life's ironies. Robert had been the amiable son, the son eager to please their father, whereas Ty had rebelled early. Long before he attained manhood, Ty had accepted that he and his father would never understand each other, could not share the same room without arguing. Each refused to bend. From childhood on, Ty's goal had been to leave the ranch and his father's dictates the minute he could support himself, and that's what he had done. His defection had wounded the old man, but he hadn't drawn blood.

It was Robert, the favorite son, who damned near killed

their father by marrying a *señorita*. And in the end, it was Ty who most resembled Cal Sanders.

Troubled, he stared through the darkness at the moon-lit face of his brother's daughter. Already this child was challenging assumptions Ty had picked up at his father's knee. Graciela wasn't a Mexican, as Cal would have dismissed her. This child was Ty's niece. His blood. The realization was throwing his thoughts into turmoil.

Leaning back, he stretched and turned his mind to something he could handle right now, Jenny Jones. An unconscious smile twitched his lips as he recalled his last sight of her, straining at the ropes, eyes flashing cold fire, swearing behind the napkin he'd shoved into her mouth.

It appalled him that he'd actually jumped into a punching match with a woman. A woman. Christ. But she'd given him no choice.

And what a woman she was.

Now that he didn't have to think about protecting his face and crotch from her flying fists and knees, he was free to remember the soft weight of her breasts pressing against his chest and the firm tautness of her buttocks filling his hands. Lord.

Her breasts were the only soft parts of her anatomy. The rest of her was as tight and firm as a new whiskey barrel. And she didn't lack for muscle, he thought, gingerly touching his sore nose.

In his time he'd met whores, workingwomen, a few rough numbers, but he'd never met anyone like Jenny Jones. She didn't fit into any category that he could nail down.

If she'd killed an attacker, then she wasn't a whore. She earned her bread, but not in a manner that any woman he'd met would have chosen. Unquestionably, she was a rough number, but he sensed that circumstance had shaped her, not choice. And he'd observed flashes of vulnerability at odds with her tough manner and tongue. Unaccountably, he also sensed a core of integrity and basic decency, qualities he didn't ascribe to the crude, unfeminine women who thrust their way into the male world.

The fact was, he couldn't get a fix on her. Certainly he didn't understand her position regarding his niece. Her tone and words convinced him that she didn't like Graciela. Yet he'd witnessed a touch of tenderness when he followed them back to their hotel. And she should have bowed out of the picture the instant she understood who Ty was, but she hadn't.

Everything about this strange woman fascinated him in a way few other women had. He felt a twinge of regret that he wouldn't see her again, would never learn what forces had formed her.

When he realized he was attempting to picture Jenny Jones dressed in a decent gown and with her hair grown out, he laughed softly. Usually, he tried to imagine a certain kind of woman in a state of undress. To his amusement, this was the first time he'd ever struggled to imagine a woman decked out in full Sunday flair.

Shaking his head and grinning, he folded his arms across his chest and leaned his back against the wall. He needed to get some shut-eye. Tomorrow was going to be a full day.

The first of several problems involved hairpins. Ty knew more about the outer universe than he knew about hairpins.

Frowning, he gazed down at his niece. The top of her head only reached his lower chest, but already he'd learned that short and small did not mean shy and quiet. "Say that again?"

"Well just look," Graciela insisted, her eyes glistening with moist frustration. "My hair keeps falling down. It isn't right. I need hairpins."

"Your hair looks nice," he said uncertainly, but it was the truth. Sheets of gleaming brown silk tumbled nearly to her waist. "I'd swear I've seen little girls with loose hair."

Her eyes flashed reproach. "Proper young ladies do not wear loose hair in public." She sounded as if this were so glaringly elementary that only a dolt could have failed to recognize the truth of it.

"If it's that important to you," he said, deciding to capitulate, "we'll buy some hairpins." He had to assume she knew where a person purchased hairpins. That thought led to another. "What else do you need?" He had carried her out of Jenny Jones's hotel with only the clothing on her back. "There's some paper in my saddlebags. Make a list. Can you write?"

"*Sí.*"

It was then that he realized she was staring at him with an uncomfortably urgent expression and had been for several minutes. "What is it?"

"I, uh . . ." she cut a desperate glance toward the chamber pot. Bright crimson flooded her cheeks and suddenly his own.

"Oh." There was no privacy screen in hotels like this one. Positive that his face was on fire, he stood so abruptly that his chair crashed over behind him. "I'll

just . . . I'll step into the hallway for a minute or two."
Abruptly he became aware of his own urgency. "Don't
leave the room until I return. Don't open the door to anyone but me."

Escaping, he rushed down the stairs, took care of business, then ran back up the staircase and halted outside the
door. How long did it take a child to pee? He couldn't just
barge inside thinking enough time had passed. Maybe it
hadn't. Cursing beneath his breath, he knocked on the
door.

"Come in," called a prim little voice.

"I told you not to open the door to anyone but me," he
snapped.

"It *is* you," she said reasonably, looking up from the
list she was composing at the table. "How do you spell
pantaloons?"

"You didn't know it was me. You should have asked."
He thought about locating a women's apparel shop, walking inside, and asking to buy a pair of small pantaloons.
Never in his life had he set foot inside a woman's apparel
shop. He'd never imagined that he would.

"I can spell corset," she said, chewing on the end of the
pencil, "but I can't spell pantaloons."

"Corset?" Blinking, he sat down across from her. By
effort of will he kept his gaze above her flat little chest.
"How old are you?"

"Don't you know?" she asked, looking hurt.

"Six? Six is too young for a corset. You won't need a
corset for several years." He could not believe he was
having this conversation. Discussing undergarments with
a six-year-old. He had never wondered when women began wearing corsets, but surely they waited until breasts

had begun to form. He couldn't be exact as to when this happy miracle occurred, but he thought it happened well beyond the age of six. Feeling the heat scalding his throat, he tugged his collar away from his neck before it choked him.

Betrayal filled Graciela's eyes, eyes so like his own. "Jenny said the same thing," she said accusingly, as if she'd expected better from him.

"Jenny is right." Now assured of being correct in his judgment, he repeated with confidence, "no corset. What else is on your list?"

She sighed deeply, then read out the other items. When she finished, Ty studied her in silence. To accommodate her requirements, he'd have to buy two trunks. He wouldn't have believed one small child could need so many things. And he didn't have the faintest idea what some of those things were. What in hell was a crimping iron?

"I'm sorry, but you can only take what will fit in the saddlebags." He'd pare his own things to the bare necessities and create as much space for her as he could, but it would be limited.

Interest gleamed in her eyes. "We're going to ride horses? We don't have to go on the train? Good. I didn't like the train."

"You can ride, can't you?"

She tossed her head. "Of course I can ride."

This information cast a new and encouraging light on the matter. If she had her own horse, it would be more comfortable than carrying her on the saddle behind him. But he'd need to find a horse that was well broken and gentle. Another positive was being able to accommodate an extra pair of saddlebags. This reminded him that he needed to buy an additional bedroll and provisions.

"I'll need a riding skirt," she commented, bending over the table to add another item to the list.

"We have a long way to go. Wouldn't trousers be more comfortable? Easier to ride in?"

She glared at him. "*She* wanted me to dress like a boy. I wouldn't do it. Young ladies do not wear trousers."

"I see." *She* was starting to sound like a very sensible woman.

"I ran away because *she* wanted me to cut my hair like a boy's." The story of yesterday's adventure poured forth. Ty listened and felt his chest grow tighter and tighter. Christ. His niece was lucky to be alive. But he finally understood the scene he had witnessed at the train station, why she had been so ragged and filthy, and why Jenny had appeared so furious. "You must have worried Miss Jones."

"I don't care," she said with a dismissive shrug. "I hate her. She killed my mama."

Ty felt he ought to say something, but he didn't know what. Anything he offered would sound as if he were defending Jenny, and he'd already figured how the wind blew on that issue. But her comment troubled him. If he understood correctly, Graciela was aware that Marguarita had chosen to take Jenny's place on the firing wall, she hadn't been forced. It was a long stretch to blame Jenny for her mother's death.

He cleared his throat and sidestepped the remark. "As soon as you're ready to leave, we'll find the corrals and buy two horses. We'll pick up the things you need, then we'll head north."

Her eyebrows lifted in dismay. "I wanted to buy my new things first. And when are we going to eat?"

"Can you wait to eat? We're getting a late start." Swiftly he ran some calculations in his mind. Any man who bought a horse in less than a day was taking his chances. A man who bought a horse based on only a few hours' observation was a fool. A man who bought a horse as Ty intended to, in about two hours, was desperate. It couldn't be helped. The most he could spare for the purchase was two hours. Then, say, another hour at the apparel shop. Considering how late they were starting, they wouldn't ride out of town before noon, which meant they'd depart in the worst heat of the day. And that was stupid and dangerous. On his own he would have risked it, but not with his brother's daughter.

"Never mind," he snapped, annoyed. "We'll have breakfast right away, and lunch before we leave. We'll figure on riding out about three."

Then she did something that paralyzed him. She studied his frown for a minute before she leaned forward, patted his hand, and gave him a dazzling smile. *"Gracias,* Uncle Ty."

"Oh hell, I'm hungry too," he said gruffly, irritated that the word "uncle" had struck with such impact. He'd been thinking of her as his niece, why should it surprise him that she would call him uncle?

He didn't figure it out until they were midway through breakfast. Referring to her as his niece was something of a cheat; in his mind he struggled with a lifetime habit of hating the Barrancas family, and of having let his father's intolerance of Mexicans sink barbs in his mind. But her "uncle" was honest and heartfelt; she unquestioningly accepted him as part of her family.

Ty hadn't often experienced shame, so he didn't immediately identify the discomfiting pressure pushing at the inside of his chest.

Jenny was wild with frustration.

She heard the nearest church bells peal nine times before a maid finally appeared to tidy the room and empty the chamber pot and discovered Jenny tied to the chair. The maid screamed and ran out of the room. Before the manager arrived to cut Jenny free the bells had sounded ten o'clock, and she lost more precious time while she persuaded the anxious manager that she didn't want trouble any more than he did; they didn't need to report the incident to anyone. All she wanted was to get the hell out of here and find Sanders and the kid.

By the time she burst out of the hotel doors and rushed into the street, the sun blazed hot overhead and she was sweating profusely and approaching panic. She didn't think Sanders had taken the northbound train, but the northbound had departed an hour ago, and now she couldn't be certain.

She had to pin her hopes on her belief that Sanders would go to the corrals. If she was too late and had missed him, she didn't know what she would do next.

As she trotted toward the edge of town, she reviewed her reasoning. Sanders had indicated that he would take Graciela on the train, so that meant he planned to leave by horse. Except, he didn't have a horse.

She had watched every passenger emerging from the train last evening, looking for Luis or Chulo, and she knew the cowboy had not been among them. He must have jumped off at the last minute.

But he must have had a horse in Verde Flores as horseback was the only way to reach the no-name village from the depot. Considering how a man felt about a good horse, he would have brought his horse with him on the train. But he wouldn't have had time to fetch it from the boxcars and still follow her and the kid back to the hotel.

Therefore, he now needed to buy another horse. And, therefore, sometime today he would show up at the corrals, probably sooner rather than later. As he'd want to leave Durango as quickly as possible, she figured buying a horse would be his first order of the day. The inevitable conclusion? Sanders had bought a horse hours ago, and she had missed him.

Damn. Biting her lips, she increased her pace to a run. By the time she reached the corrals her throat burned for air and daggers pierced her side. Already street traffic was thinning for siesta. Cursing, she fell against a tree trunk to rest and catch her breath, grateful for a spot of shade. When she could breathe without pain, she lifted her eyes toward the dust swirling above the animal pens.

She didn't immediately spot the cowboy and didn't expect to, but her gaze flew like a magnet to a splash of deep maroon. Relief sagged through her body, turning her muscles to straw. Thank heaven for whatever had delayed them.

Narrowing her eyes and peering through a haze of dust, she focused on Graciela. The kid was wearing a new riding outfit. And her hair was pinned up all proper and ladylike. She waited beside a pair of stuffed saddlebags, little gloved hands patiently clasped at her waist.

A humorless grin thinned Jenny's lips. Now she knew why the cowboy was late getting to the corrals, and she knew how he had spent his morning. Shopping. His aggravation, and she knew the kid well enough to guess the shopping excursion had not gone smoothly, was her gain. Good, and thank God.

After tugging her hat down to conceal her eyes and pulling the poncho away from her breasts, she slouched toward the enclosure farthest from the cowboy and Graciela.

She, too, needed to buy a horse.

They didn't ride out of Durango until almost four o'clock, by which time Ty was as restless as a herd before a storm. Everything had taken longer than he'd figured. She'd had to try things on at the apparel store, a seemingly endless process, and then a seamstress had been summoned, which ate up more time. Next came footwear, an item he hadn't considered, and the trying on and taking off and switching of tassels and discussion of colors. Through it all, he'd shifted from boot to boot, glaring pointedly at his pocket watch, which didn't expedite the shopping excursion by a single minute.

Following the purchase of undergarments, an experience he never wanted to repeat, they stopped to eat again although he wasn't sure why since Graciela mostly played with her food, sampling tiny bites between chatting happily about her new clothing. The food she had begged for stayed on her plate.

The time lost at the corrals was his fault. He'd insisted that she ride the horse he selected for her before he put down the purchase money. Then he'd had to buy saddles and wait while her stirrups were cut to size. This after a long discussion wherein Graciela insisted on a lady's sidesaddle, and he insisted on a regular. He had eventually prevailed, but she hadn't spoken to him since. Her silence irritated the bejesus out of him.

Grinding his teeth, he turned his head to glare at her. Immediately a long sigh emptied the air from his lungs. She looked so tiny and fragile seated atop the large mare that visions of disaster spun through his mind. She could fall off and break an arm or a leg. The horse might throw her, and she could break her neck and die. The mare could stumble and fall and crush her. He didn't know if the mare was easily spooked, but he could imagine it running off with the child and . . .

Well, damn it. Ty gave his head an irritated shake. He wasn't a man to borrow trouble, so why was he doing it now?

In fact, he didn't need to borrow, he had trouble enough already. She'd claimed that she knew how to ride, but that was only partially true. She knew how to stay on top of a horse as long as the horse walked. The one time the horse had broken into a trot, she had screamed and clamped onto the pommel, utterly terrified.

"Graciela," he said, moving his gelding up beside the mare, "we need to pick up the pace or it's going to take about twenty years for us to reach the border." At the present rate, she'd need that corset before they rode into California, and he'd be an old man.

She looked at him, then deigned to answer. "I've never been on a horse all by myself. Well, I have, but one of my cousins led it or walked along beside me."

Even though he'd quickly realized that her idea of being able to ride differed vastly from his thoughts on the subject, hearing her admission soured his disposition. He considered the problem for the next mile.

"Here's what we'll do. We'll sell your horse, and you'll ride behind me."

"You said this was my horse! You said I could ride her all by myself. That's what you promised!" Tears swam in her eyes.

My God, he had made her cry. Horrified, Ty watched the late-afternoon sun glisten in the water welling behind her lashes. The shock of it stunned him. He had made this tiny creature cry.

"Jenny wouldn't break a promise!" A tear ran down her cheek. "Jenny says a person isn't worth a fricking spit if he breaks a promise!" Another tear dropped on the bodice of her maroon riding outfit.

"Look, don't cry. All right?" A man was never so helpless as when faced with a woman's tears. A child's tears were even worse. "We won't decide anything right now," he heard himself say. "We'll talk about it later when you're calmer." Right now, he wasn't too calm himself. "Maybe you should wipe your nose."

To his great relief she managed to remove a snowy handkerchief from her cuff without dropping the reins.

"Jenny says a promise is sacred." Her voice muffled inside the handkerchief. "Jenny says anyone who breaks a fricking promise might as well put a gun to his head."

A little of "Jenny says" went a long way, he decided irritably. "Don't swear."

"I'm only telling you what Jenny said."

"I get the point, all right? Jenny Jones does not break her promises." Thin-lipped, he stared toward the sinking sun. In the future, he would be damned careful what he said and how he said it. Apparently children accepted every word as gospel.

Meanwhile, he didn't know how he was going to get around this obstacle, only that he had to.

He was still pondering the problem when they stopped to set up camp for the night, still thinking about how to pick up the pace while he tethered the horses, watered them, then dug a fire pit and unpacked provisions.

"I can fill your coffeepot."

"I'll do it," he said absently. She might fall in the small stream that ran near the campsite. When he returned from the stream, he noticed that she had unrolled the bedrolls.

"I can hang the coffeepot over the fire."

"I've already got it."

She pursed her lips, then sat down on her saddle and folded her hands in her lap. "I don't know how to cook," she informed him, watching as he set out the skillet. As if there was any way in hell that he would have allowed her to get that close to the flames. "Will you teach me how?"

"Aren't you kind of young to be cooking?" He shredded some boiled beef with his knife, added dried onion, and rolled the bits inside a tortilla before he placed them in the iron skillet and set the skillet on the fire to heat. He cut some more beef, more onions.

"Jenny says I should know how to cook by now."

He gazed at her above the flames licking the bottom of the coffeepot. "For someone who professes to hate Jenny Jones, you sure quote her a lot."

"No, I don't. She's not a lady. Did you know that she has hair between her legs?" Graciela shuddered. "Don't you think that's disgusting?"

Ty froze, and the tortilla dropped from boneless fingers into the dirt. Heat scalded his throat and jaw. Ducking his head, he stared at the tortilla, took his time picking it up and brushing off the sandy dirt. "Ah . . . well . . ." He cleared his throat with a strange-sounding cough.

And he wished like hell that he was anywhere on earth but here with this child. Silently he cursed Robert for asking him to undertake this errand. He cursed Marguarita for getting pregnant in the first place. He cursed himself for discovering a modest streak that he hadn't even suspected.

"Jenny says all grown-up women have hair between their legs." Her raised eyebrow conveyed enormous skepticism. "That's not true, is it?"

Oh God. Agony twitched his muscles, pulled down the corners of his mouth. The last time he'd squirmed like this, he'd been a schoolboy. Raising his knife to within an inch of his eyes, he inspected the blade with intense scrutiny.

"Ah . . . didn't you say that Jenny Jones never lies?" There was a nick that he hadn't noticed before. He'd have to fix that.

Graciela heaved a huge sigh, her shoulders dropped, and she directed a sad stare toward her toes. "So it's true," she said mournfully. "Well, *I'm* not going to grow hair between my legs."

He was dying, absolutely dying. When he could trust himself to speak, he cleared his throat with a choking sound and said, "A couple of these are hot. Fetch one of those plates." His voice sounded like it belonged to someone else.

And his treacherous mind flung visions of a naked Jenny in front of his eyes. Damn it, he could *see* a triangular patch as coppery as the flames blurring in front of his gaze.

"Look," he said, struggling against images no decent man should imagine in the presence of an innocent child, "we'll give the horse problem another day, all right? But we have to cover more ground. We'll trot and walk, trot and walk, until you're comfortable."

He'd known a redheaded whore in San Francisco. Her skin had been milk white, brushed with flame down there. Oh God, he couldn't think about this in front of his six-year-old niece. What kind of man was he? Sweating slightly, he poured a cup of coffee and watched her eat, making himself think about tomorrow's ride.

"Uncle Ty?"

"What?"

"I said I'd scrub the plates. Jenny showed me how. You rub them out with sand, then wipe them off with a wet cloth."

"Fine," he said absently, staring into the fire. He wondered if Jenny Jones's skin was milk white and brushed with flame down there.

"I'm tired. I'm going to go to sleep now." When Ty didn't respond, she made a little sound. "You have to turn your back, so I can undress and put on my nightgown."

"Oh." He spun on his heels so rapidly that coffee flew out of his cup. Damn Robert. Robert should have been here instead of him. Robert could have waited until their father's estate was settled; what difference would a few more months have made?"

"I'm ready to say my prayers now."

"Fine . . . is there something I'm supposed to do?" Tentatively he turned around and saw her kneeling beside her bedroll, dressed in a lacy white nightgown.

"You're supposed to kneel with me and listen."

"I guess I can do that." He supposed hearing a prayer wouldn't harm him. Might do him some good. But he was glad there was no one to see him going down on his knees.

"Fold your hands like this."

He dug his knees into the hard dirt and glared into the darkness. "Just say your prayers."

She said the "Our Father," then she asked God to bless a numbing list of people. It was sobering to hear how many Barrancas cousins there were. He wondered how many of them were searching for her right now.

Pausing, she opened one eye. "I don't know what to say about Jenny. She's gone now, so I guess I can stop asking God to kill her, but she still should be punished for killing my mama."

Shock narrowed his eyes. "You've been asking God to kill Jenny Jones?"

Graciela nodded solemnly. "But He hasn't done it yet."

He stared at her. "Does Jenny know you're asking God to kill her?"

"What should I ask God to do about punishing her? Should I tell Him some good punishments or just let Him decide what's best?"

"Graciela," he said slowly, inching into unknown territory, "now you know Jenny didn't kill your mother."

"Jenny was supposed to die, not my mama." Her chin lifted in a stubborn expression that inexplicably made Ty think of his father.

He studied the fresh onslaught of tears and decided he didn't want to get into this. "Why don't you just say amen."

She closed her eyes again. "God? You don't have to kill Jenny anymore, but you should punish her bad. You should make her cry and bleed a lot. She should feel very very sorry for killing my mama. Amen."

Ty blinked. His niece was praying for blood and death, and he'd thought she was an innocent?

"You can kiss me good night now," she said, smiling at him and lifting her cheek. He peered over his shoulder into the darkness, then brushed a hasty peck across her cheek. "Now you're supposed to tuck me in."

After pulling the blankets up to her chin, he rose to his feet and stared down at her. His bloodthirsty little niece looked like an angel with her hair flowing around her face and her lashes feathered on her cheeks.

Shaking his head, he returned to the fire and sat on a rock to finish the pot of coffee. This had been one hell of a day, and he felt the exhaustion in his shoulders, but he suspected he wouldn't fall asleep anytime soon.

It was after midnight before he crawled into his bedroll, and later still before he dropped into an uneasy doze.

The next thing he heard was the tiny click of a hammer being drawn. When he tried to sit up, a fist pressed him down, and he couldn't turn his head. His temple hit the barrel of his own Colt. Staring up at the first opalescent tints of dawn, he ground his teeth together and waited.

"I didn't figure you to be such a sound sleeper," said a cheerful voice whose husky tone he recognized all too well. "Put your hands on top of the blankets. Do it slow."

"You know I'll come after you," he said, narrowing his eyes at the sky. If she was a killer, he'd just advised her to shoot him now. Mexico had roasted his brains.

"If you do," Jenny said, whipping a rope around his wrists before he could make a grab for her, "I'll shoot you down like a dog. You just go on home to California and tell the sainted Roberto that me and the kid are on our way. You're not part of this anymore."

He hated himself for suggesting this, but it was a possible way out of a bad situation. "If you're so dead set on intruding where you don't belong, we could take her to California together."

"Do you really think I'm going to fall for that? The minute I relaxed my guard, you'd take Graciela and leave me behind faster than a fly can flap its wings." Once she had him trussed up like a hog, she woke Graciela. Ty couldn't see them, but he heard them shouting at each other. Eventually, Jenny dragged Graciela over to him and pointed.

"Take a good look at your uncle Ty," she said, leaning next to Graciela's face. "He's not taking you anywhere. I am. So get your butt dressed. We're going."

Graciela stared down at him with disappointment and contempt. "I trusted you." Having plunged this verbal blade into his heart, she spun in a billow of ruffled nightgown and flounced out of his line of sight.

Jenny leaned over him, her eyes narrowed into slits. "I made the promise. You didn't. Remember what I said. If I see you again, I'll kill you if for no other reason than the trouble you've caused me."

He lay on his side, tangled in his bedroll, as furious and mortified as it was possible for a man to be, listening to the sound of a horse receding in the distance.

One horse. Jenny Jones had solved the Graciela/horse problem in two minutes flat.

He stared at a tiny flowering cactus three inches from his nose and passed the time by imagining himself strangling a certain woman with milk white skin who was brushed with flame down there.

Chapter Eight

Jenny set a northern course midway between the Sierra Madres and the railroad tracks that rolled down the Central Plateau. If she could hold to a hard pace of twenty miles a day, she figured to make Chihuahua in about two weeks.

But two weeks was beginning to look like a wildly optimistic estimate. Three days out of Durango, the terrain gave way to rocky desert soil and deep arroyos that slowed her pace. Noonday heat blistered the ground, and they had to stop, seeking shelter where they could find it until later in the day.

As night approached, Jenny sought out the low shacks of the campesinos who labored to scratch a life from the poor soil. She knew she'd find a trickle of water near their pitiful patches and maybe a chance to buy fresh meat and milk for the kid.

"My face hurts," Graciela mentioned sullenly, staring with distaste at the chunk of goat meat roasting over the fire.

"Did you rub aloe on your skin like I told you?" The

smell of roasting meat made Jenny's mouth water in anticipation. The campesino's woman had sold her fresh tortillas, too, and a ripe squash. They would feast tonight. "Drink that milk," she reminded Graciela. "It cost the earth."

Graciela turned her sunburned face toward the campesino's shack, a dark smudge against the night. No light showed through the walls of mud and branch. Either the residents had gone to bed, or they sat around a flame too small to penetrate the chinks.

"Why can't we sleep in the house with them?" Graciela asked in a whiny singsong that had begun to grate against Jenny's nerves two days ago. "I don't like to sleep on the ground. I'm afraid bugs or snakes will crawl in my bedroll."

"Kid," Jenny said, striving mightily for patience, "That's no hacienda up there. Believe it or not, most people don't live like you did. Most people aren't rich and don't have servants, they don't have extra food or beds. Eight people live in that shack already. They don't have a square inch for you. Plus, no one up there is sleeping in a bed. They're either in hammocks or sleeping on the ground just like we are."

Graciela flung her the I-hate-you look. "You said you wouldn't call me kid."

After an interior struggle Jenny conceded that she deserved the accusing tone. "You're right," she snapped, leaning to inspect the chunk of roasting meat. "I'm sorry. If you find a bug in your blankets, squash it. If a snake gets in there, you get out." She stared at Graciela across the fire pit. "Complaining isn't going to change a damned thing. So just make up your mind that it's going to be a tough couple of weeks and keep your mouth shut about the inconveniences, all right? You aren't the only one who'd rather be sleeping in a bed, but you don't hear me complaining all the time."

The kid already looked a bit worse for the wear. Her fashionable maroon riding outfit was grey with dust and soiled by sweat. Part of the hem had torn loose. Since they had no water to spare for washing, their faces were dirty above fresh sunburns. Perspiration had blended with the dust near their scalps, creating a film of mud that eventually dried and began to itch and torment.

When a charred crust had formed on the meat, Jenny cut slices onto their plates and scooped mounds of hot squash on the side. "I know you're tired," she said to Graciela, "but you have to eat to keep up your strength. So clean your plate."

Graciela glared at her. "Uncle Ty didn't order me around."

"Huh! From what you've told me, you ordered him around." The goat meat was dry and on the tough side, but not bad, not bad at all. She'd eaten worse in her time. The tortillas, on the other hand, were thick and chewy and went down the throat the way she imagined ambrosia probably would.

According to her dictionary, ambrosia, a word she liked the sound of, was the imaginary food of the gods. Now that was something to think about. Before she ran across ambrosia, Jenny had never imagined God sitting down to supper. All day she'd been wondering who cooked the ambrosia. Surely God didn't prepare it Himself. Or maybe imaginary food didn't need to be cooked.

Graciela forked up a piece of goat meat, tasted it, and made a face. "Ack."

"It's not ambrosia, but it's all we've got, so eat it," Jenny said, pleased to have worked a new word into conversation.

"Uncle Ty wouldn't make me eat something I don't like."

Jenny narrowed her eyes. "I'm getting sick and tired of hearing what a swell fellow your Uncle Ty is."

"He's nicer than you are."

"Why? Because you wrapped him around your little finger? Because he waited on you and let you sit there like a useless bump on a rock?" She snorted. "Let me tell you something, kid. Sorry . . . Graciela. Since you and me hitched up, you've learned to make a halfway decent pot of coffee, you've learned how to lay a fire, you're dressing and undressing yourself, and you've learned to pin up your own hair. You can water the horses and fold up a bedroll. You can scrub out the supper dishes, and tomorrow, like it or not, you're going to cook most of our supper. You still don't know squat about most things, but you aren't as dumb as you used to be. Now you tell me . . . doesn't it feel good to know how to do something more than sit on your behind and watch other people take care of you?"

Graciela chewed another bite of goat meat and didn't say anything.

Now was as good a time as any to ask a question that Jenny had been wondering about. As casually as she could manage, she inquired, "Did your uncle Ty say anything about me?"

"He hates you because you killed my mama," Graciela answered, after she had swallowed and patted her lips with her handkerchief.

"He said that?" Jenny stared. "I told him what happened. He knows damned well that I didn't have anything to do with Marguarita's death! Did you explain to him that I don't lie?"

Graciela hesitated. "I told him what you said about promises."

"But he still thinks I had something to do with your mother's death?" She set her plate on the ground. "That son of a bitch."

She was still fuming after she got the kid into her bedroll and settled for the night. Sitting cross-legged on the ground, she stared into the embers of their cook fire and thought about Ty Sanders. It occurred to her that she was spending a hell of a lot of time thinking about Ty Sanders.

She couldn't look at Graciela without seeing the cowboy's blue-green eyes. Every time the kid mentioned Uncle Ty, and that was about two hundred times a day, she saw his lean wiry body in her mind. Remembered the hard muscle knotting his thighs and arms.

Jenny didn't seek out brawls, but she'd been in a few fights over the years. This was the first time, however, that remembering a tussle with a man had made her feel hot and strange when she thought about it afterward.

Worse, she knew what feeling hot and strange meant. Rubbing a hand over her forehead, she rose from the embers and walked toward the campesino's scraggly maize field, then turned and walked back to the campsite.

There had been a man in Yuma a few years ago, a man who for no reason that she could figure had made her feel hot and strange inside. Eventually she'd recognized it meant she had a hankering for him, and she had satisfied that hankering out behind Shorty Barrow's saloon in a wholly unsatisfactory coupling that had left the man smiling and her blinking up at the stars in bewildered disappointment.

Now here she was, having another hankering when she knew damned well that sex was a man's sport and there was nothing in it for a woman except a few bruises and two minutes of having someone's breath in your face. And, afterward, a feeling of loneliness as dry and empty as a desert. Never in her life had she felt as gut-bad lonely as she had that night out behind Shorty Barrow's saloon.

Until she met the cowboy, she hadn't had a hankering since.

Drawing back her boot, she kicked dirt over the embers in the fire pit, then strode over to her bedroll and crawled inside. Folding her hands behind her head, she stared up at the stars until she found Marguarita.

"I'm too fricking tired to tell you about today. Nothing happened anyway," she said. She squinted suspiciously. "Can you read my thoughts?"

That was a disconcerting possibility. She'd have to find a subtle way to ask the kid if people in heaven knew the thoughts of living people. She had a sinking feeling that dead people knew everything, especially those like Marguarita, who probably became angels. After worrying about it for several minutes, she decided that she didn't care if God knew she had a hankering for the cowboy. God was in the forgiveness business. She didn't think God wasted too much time thinking about Jenny Jones anyway.

But it made her acutely uncomfortable that Marguarita probably knew she liked to remember how good it had felt rolling around the hotel room floor with the cowboy on top of her. There had been one startling moment when she'd had a chance to knee him in the groin, but she hadn't done it because the hankering feeling had suddenly hit her hard and addled her brains.

Well damn. Her hands formed into fists behind her head. For all she knew Ty Sanders had a wife and family back in California. Not that it mattered. A man that good-looking wouldn't give Jenny a second glance in any case. He'd want some tiny little woman rigged out in lace and ribbon. Most men did. Men preferred birdlike women who smelled like flowers. Women who thought a callus was something unique to men.

Men turned their eyes away from rawboned women with a mule skinner's vocabulary. Women like Jenny might be good for satisfying a temporary hankering, but not for long-term company. There was no one out there wishing and pining to spend his life with a woman like Jenny Jones. There never would be. She'd learned that lesson a long time ago.

But it usually didn't hurt as much as it did tonight.

Much as she hated it, by late afternoon of the next day, Jenny recognized the need to find a room for the night. Graciela sat wilted on the saddle in front of her, sagging against Jenny's chest like a bag of hot rocks, too exhausted even to complain. The relentless white sun had severely burned the kid's face, and she felt feverish to the touch. They both needed a bath, especially Jenny. Her blackened hair was stiff and waxy, coated with dust and sweat. They needed some decent food and a real bed.

Knowing she'd run across a village if she angled toward the east and the railroad, she rode another four hours until she spotted smoky curls of burning chaparral, signaling cook fires ahead. Another few minutes brought the scents of food and smoldering refuse and animals and humans.

"*Buenos noches, Señora,*" she called to a woman standing beside a small yard garden at the edge of the village. "Where can I find a room, a bath, and a meal?"

The village wasn't large enough to boast a hotel, she could see that. But she had always found the Mexican people to be warm and hospitable. She and Graciela would not sleep on the ground tonight. Indeed, the senora walked them to the home of a daughter, who hurriedly moved two children out of a room and offered it to Jenny and Graciela.

"*Gracias, Señora.*" Exhaustion caused her voice to emerge from deep in her throat, sounding huskier than usual. If Jenny had been by herself, she would have said to hell with a bath and supper and fallen gratefully into one of the hammocks spanning the corners. But she had the kid to worry about.

Graciela stood in the center of the small room, one hand clasping the heart locket pinned to her chest, the other touching her fiery face. "I don't feel good."

"Senora Calvera is bringing a tub and something to eat," Jenny said wearily, sinking to a stool beside an open window. A warm breeze had appeared with the stars, and she jerked open her collar to dry the salty sweat slicking her throat and chest. The leaves of a courtyard tree blocked the night sky, and she couldn't see Marguarita's star. Good. She had begun to dread the night, as that was when Marguarita appeared in the heavens to gaze down and judge Jenny and the day's events.

Graciela bent at the waist and vomited on the floor. When the spasm passed, she pressed a hand to her mouth and raised stricken eyes to Jenny's openmouthed stare. "I'm sorry."

Stumbling, Graciela pushed a low stool against the wall and collapsed. When she fell back against the wall and closed her eyes, her lashes formed sooty crescents against white, white cheeks.

"Kid! What's wrong with you?" Jumping to her feet, Jenny clapped her hand on Graciela's forehead. The kid was burning up. Damn. She waved Senora Calveras's husband into the room. He carried a washtub dented enough to have belonged to the conquistadors an eon ago. "Okay, listen. A bath will cool you off."

Senora Calveras followed her husband, carrying two buckets of water, which she poured into the washtub. After glancing at the puddle of vomit, she pulled a rag from her pocket and tossed it to Jenny.

Jenny looked at the rag; she looked at the vomit. Well, crud on a crust, if that wasn't disgusting. But she could see how Senora Calveras would consider it Jenny's responsibility to clean up the mess. Graciela wasn't Senora Calveras's kid; she was Jenny's cross to bear. But first, she needed to get Graciela out of the heavy maroon riding outfit and into the tub.

Graciela opened her eyes and stared at the washtub with a dulled and miserable expression, as if bathing were a feat beyond comprehension. She sagged against the adobe wall like a rag doll.

"All right. Just this once I'll undress you. Stand up."

The kid not only looked like a rag doll, boneless and crumpled, she felt like a rag doll. Her arms hung limp as Jenny pulled them out of the maroon sleeves, and she swayed on her feet. When Jenny lifted her into the washtub, her skin felt as if a fire burned below the surface. She sat in the washtub, bent forward, staring glassy-eyed at her toes.

"Wait here." It was a stupid comment, like a naked, throw-uppy kid was going to run away. Reaching deep to summon energy, Jenny strode through the house and outside. She hesitated a minute, then explored the weeds encroaching on the kitchen garden. Thankfully, the moon drifted out of a cloud bank and she found a patch of cockleburrs almost at once, collected a generous handful, and carried them around the house to Senora Calveras's adobe oven.

"Por favor, Señora," she said in a worried voice. "Would you be kind enough to boil these in about this much water?" Spreading her hands, she indicated a quart. "Boil it down to this much." She narrowed the span to about a pint.

Senora Calveras placed a loaf of dough on her bread paddle and nodded solemnly. Lantern light gleamed along the center part in her hair. "For the little one," she said, handing Jenny a bowl of sliced onions and long strips of cloth.

Jenny blinked stupidly at the onions. "Is she supposed to eat them?"

"No, *Señora,*" Senora Calveras said softly. "For the bottoms of her feet. The onions draw out the fever." Lifting her own bare foot, she made a twirling motion with her finger indicating how Jenny should bind the onions with the strips of cloth.

"Oh." Well, what the hell. For all Jenny knew, the onions were as effective as cockleburr tea. Every woman had her own favored remedies. "*Gracias.*"

Graciela had not moved. Limp and crumpled forward, she still stared at her toes with fever-cloudy eyes.

"Kid, you're worrying me bad, and I don't like that." Wringing out a cloth, Jenny gently stroked the dust off Graciela's sunburned face.

"That hurts," Graciela whispered in a tiny voice.

"I know. I'll put some aloe on the burn as soon as we get you clean."

"I don't want supper. I just want to sleep."

"Fine. Stand up so I can towel you dry." When she lifted Graciela out of the washtub and set her on her feet, Graciela swayed in an invisible wind, her eyes closed. "Okay. Let me get your nightgown." She dropped it over Graciela's damp hair, then placed the kid in one of the hammocks, adjusted the pillow and pulled a light sheet to her chin.

Graciela gazed up at her. "I need my locket pin."

Jenny was practically dead on her feet, but the kid "needed" her locket pin. She ground her teeth. "Just a minute." After rummaging through Graciela's clothing, she found the locket and pinned it to the kid's nightgown. "Anything else, Your Majesty?"

"I didn't say my prayers."

"I'll say them for you. Our father who art in et cetera, bless all the rotten cousins and kill Jenny. Amen. Now lift up your feet so I can strap these onions on you."

Wordlessly, Graciela raised one small foot and let

Jenny bind the onions to her sole. Apparently she didn't think the remedy as strange as Jenny had thought it was. She did the other foot before she gently rubbed aloe on the kid's face and throat.

"Does that feel any better?"

Graciela gazed up at her, gratitude brimming in her blue-green eyes. *"Gracias,"* she whispered, her eyelids fluttering with fatigue. She lifted her cheek for a good night kiss.

The moment touched and softened Jenny for as long as it took to turn her attention to the vomit on the floor. Revulsion pulled down her lips. She had to do this. The vomit wasn't going to disappear on its own. Dropping to her knees, gagging and swallowing convulsively, she used the bathwater to mop up the puddle. God. She never would have believed she'd see the day when she would wipe up someone else's vomit.

No wonder her mother had been as mean as a snake. With six kids, she must have been doing this kind of cruddy thing all the damned time. In retrospect, Jenny found it admirable that her mother had not thrown her kids or herself down the nearest mine shaft. She must have wanted to about twenty times a day.

Reeling with exhaustion, she tossed the rag into a bucket, then contemplated the water left in the tub, wondering if she had the energy to wash herself. She decided it was either find the energy or scratch all night. Sighing, she stripped off her clothes and washed hastily, then she bent over the side of the tub and used a bar of hard brown soap to scrub her hair and scalp. Instantly, the water turned black. Getting rid of the bootblack was the first encouraging thing that had happened all day.

She longed to fall into her hammock at once, but she had to wait for Senora Calveras and the cockleburr tea, then she had to let the tea cool, then she had to rouse Graciela, which was no easy thing to do, and coax her to drink the tea.

"Tastes terrible," Graciela protested, shuddering.

"Just drink it. No, all of it."

At last, she snuffed out the candles and fell into her hammock, dropping like a rock. But as fatigued as she was, worry kept her awake. Straining, she listened for Graciela's breathing. Every time the kid moved, Jenny bolted upright and peered through the darkness. It was almost worse when the kid *didn't* move.

Hands folded behind her head, she stared at the ceiling as anxious thoughts pounded her brain.

It would absolutely ruin her life if the kid died on her watch. Graciela's illness was her fault. Who else's fault could it be? She'd kept the kid in the sun too long, in the saddle too long. She should have done this differently, or that, or something else.

If the kid bit it, then Jenny decided she might as well dig a grave and jump inside because if Graciela died, Marguarita was going to be truly and seriously pissed. If Jenny didn't kill herself, Marguarita would reach down from heaven and do it for her, and Marguarita would make it a horrible death, she knew that. If she let Graciela die, she would deserve a horrible death.

From now on, she vowed to slow their pace. Every other night, she'd rent a room for them. She'd make sure the kid ate three times a day and had fresh milk with every meal.

And from now on, she was going to start praying herself, begging God and Marguarita to keep Robert Sanders alive and in good health. The worst thing that could happen in her sorry life was for the kid to live but for Robert Sanders to die. Then she'd have the kid on her hands for the next fricking twelve years or so, and she'd be worrying herself half to death all the fricking damned time. Cleaning up vomit and God only knew what else that she hadn't run into yet. Damn, damn, damn.

Eventually, racked with guilt and inhaling the strong odor of onions, she fell into a restless sleep. In her dreams, she was a child again, being chased by the cowboy and her mother, who pelted her with onions.

"I don't know any stories," Jenny insisted for the fourteenth time. She drew a long, long breath, held it, then let the air seep through her lips. Once kids got an idea in their heads, nothing under heaven could dislodge it. "I haven't learned any stories in the five minutes that have passed since you last asked me. Look, I'll read you some of my favorite words out of the dictionary."

"We did that this morning."

"Was it only this morning?" It seemed like weeks ago. Maybe a lifetime. She'd been sitting on a hard stool beside Graciela's hammock so long that her tailbone ached, and so did her spine. The only time she had moved had been to mop up a new splatter of vomit. The rest of the time she'd watched the kid sleep and had struggled to amuse her when she woke.

Graciela unpinned the locket from her nightgown, opened the gold heart, and stared at the pictures inside. Tears gathered in her eyes.

"Let me see the locket." Jenny didn't care diddly about the pictures inside, but it was something to do to eat up a few minutes of this eternally endless day. And maybe if the kid wasn't staring at the pictures, she wouldn't cry.

After Graciela gave her the locket, Jenny hefted it in her palm, testing the weight and feel of real gold jewelry. It irritated her that a six-year-old kid was accustomed to wearing gold when she'd never owned any herself. Not that she wanted to. But every time she glanced at the gold-locket pin, it reminded her of the enormous gulf between who she was and who Graciela was. Sighing, she pried open the little gold heart and looked inside.

"So this is the sainted Roberto."

The tiny portrait revealed a good-looking son of a bitch dressed in a formal jacket and wide tie. He had dark hair and light eyes, but Robert was softer-looking than Ty. Jenny knew at once which brother had the *cojones* in the Sanders family. There was nothing tentative about Ty Sanders. Nothing indecisive in *his* gaze. Robert looked like a man born to whisper pretty poetry in the moonlight whereas Ty was a man created in the hard heat of the sun. She sensed that Robert bore ink stains on his fingers where Ty had calluses.

Aside from an anxious concern for his continued good health, Robert Sanders didn't interest Jenny.

Next she studied Marguarita's portrait. It seemed to her that Marguarita's lovely smile beamed encouragement. Guilt rocked Jenny's chest. Things were turning out pretty much as she had predicted. She didn't have a mother-bone in her body. But Marguarita had refused to believe it. Her unshakable faith in Jenny radiated up from the portrait. Jenny didn't imagine it. Marguarita was smiling at *her*. Sighing, she closed the locket and tossed it back to Graciela.

"You must know *one* story. Make something up."

"All right," Jenny snapped. "If it will stop you from whining, I'll try. Let me think . . . okay. Let's say there was—"

"You're supposed to start with once upon a time."

Jenny bit down on her back teeth. "You're pushing. But all right. Once upon a time there were six snotty little rich kids who were stolen as infants by a witch and her evil companion who took them to live on the side of a mountain."

Graciela fixed her gaze on Jenny's face. "Did the witch have red hair and blue eyes?"

Jenny's gaze narrowed into a long slitted stare. "You know, there are times when I'd really like to smack the crap out of you."

"What did the witch look like?" Not a flicker of fear or concern troubled the kid's gaze. Which made Jenny wonder if Graciela had noticed that Jenny did a lot of threatening and blustering without much follow-through. She'd have to think about that.

"Too fricking bad, but the witch did not look like me. She had gray hair and snake eyes."

"Oooh." Graciela clapped her hands together. "Snake eyes!" She shuddered happily. "Did one of the snotty little rich kids look like me?"

"There were three girls and three boys, and one of the snotty little rich girls looked exactly like you."

"What did she wear? Did she wear pretty clothes? Did she have tassels on her boots?"

Jenny cast a sly look toward the hammock. "What do you think she wore?"

While she listened to Graciela describe the little girl's dress, she decided telling stories wasn't as difficult as she'd imagined it would be. In fact, she might attempt this again. It was a good way to use new words and teach Graciela a few.

"The evil witch was a martinet. Do you remember what a martinet is?"

Graciela nodded solemnly. "A mean person with lots of rules, like you."

"That's exactly right, and don't you forget it." The kid had a good memory. They'd only learned about a martinet that morning. This story thing was going to work out very well.

On the third day, Jenny scoured the village and brought back some yellowed foolscap and a pencil stub. Graciela drew pictures most of the day. One of them made her laugh, and one of them made her cry. Later, Jenny examine the pages of foolscap. She couldn't make sense of the blobby pictures or figure out why they had made the kid laugh and cry.

She did know the delay necessitated by Graciela's illness made her feel frantic inside, and the pungent odor of onions had deadened her sense of smell for anything else. She was desperate to mount up and get moving again.

On the morning of the fourth day, thank God, the kid's forehead felt normal to the touch, and her eyes were bright and alert. Finally Jenny stopped worrying that Graciela might die and returned to wanting to kill her.

"We'll go for a walk," she decided, eyeing Graciela. "See how you do on your feet. If that works out, then we'll hit the road tomorrow morning first thing."

Graciela brightened immediately at the prospect of escaping the small, hot, onion-permeated room. She dressed herself more quickly than she had in Jenny's memory. Watching, Jenny was amazed. If she hadn't known better, she would never have believed the kid had spent the last three days in the hammock, sicker than a pup.

When they stepped outside into the morning sunlight, Graciela smiled up at her. "The black is all gone from your hair. It looks better. Nice and shiny and the real color again."

"I've been washing it every day," Jenny explained uncomfortably. Even bland compliments made her uneasy. She didn't know how to respond. By now she knew the kid liked to talk about hair and clothes and dumb topics like that, and some of the talk was even mildly interesting. But this was the first time the kid had said something remotely complimentary about Jenny's appearance. It annoyed her to discover how happy she was that the kid admired *something* about her.

Side by side, they walked along the main dirt road, keeping to the shade, nodding to people they passed. The village was small, with no reason for existing that Jenny could see. There was no industry. The railroad was miles to the east.

"I need an umbrella," Graciela remarked, squinting at the sun.

"Well, you aren't going to get one."

"Why not?"

Each time Jenny heard the word "why," her stomach cramped and her hands curled into fists. She was beginning to loathe that particular word. It curdled her brain.

"Cousin Jorje!"

"What?" Jenny broke from her reverie in time to grab the back of Graciela's cape and prevent her from running toward a man who had whirled at the sound of her voice and now stood in the center of the street glaring back at Jenny.

"Let me go!" Graciela struggled to break free. "That's Cousin Jorje. He's come to take me home!"

"Cousin Jorje?" Slowly Jenny turned her eyes back to the man in the street. He'd shoved his poncho over his hips to expose the guns at his waist. This was going to get nasty.

"Kid . . ." Jenny said, easing back the folds of her own poncho, "just how many fricking cousins do you have?"

The first bullet whizzed past her ear.

Chapter
Nine

Ty reined hard and jerked his head toward the sharp explosion of gunfire. If he hadn't heard the shots, he would most likely have ridden past the village, as it looked too small, too dilapidated, to have attracted Jenny's interest. A grudging respect for her judgment and abilities had soared since she'd tracked him and left him hog-tied in his bedroll. Now, when he puzzled where she had gone and what she was doing, he asked himself where he would have gone and what he would have done.

He would have camped where he could obtain fresh meat and milk for his niece, and that's what Jenny had done. Consequently, she'd left an easy trail to read. He was a couple of days behind her, and that made him crazy, but he could travel faster and longer than she could hampered by the child. He knew he'd catch up with her sooner or later.

When he did, it was going to be payback time. He'd had a lot of miles to brood about her getting the jump on him, about being trussed up and left for a day and a half with his nose in the dirt. He was feeling ornery and mean, spoiling for a good fight, just itching to get his hands on Jenny Jones.

Being in a brawling mood himself, the gunfire erupting from someone else's altercation attracted his interest. Touching his bootheels to the flanks of his horse, he trotted toward the village to judge if the fracas was worth getting involved in. A good fight would knock the edges off the tension between his shoulders, might allow him a restful night's sleep afterward.

He couldn't believe his eyes. Damned if the first thing he saw wasn't Jenny Jones standing in the middle of a dirt street shooting it out with a mean-eyed, mustachioed Mexican. Even wearing men's trousers and a shapeless poncho, there was no mistaking her. Her hat had flown off and lay in the dust at her feet, exposing a flaming cap of red hair.

If he'd missed the hair, and no man could, he would have spotted his niece. Jenny was shooting with one hand and fighting to hold Graciela behind her with the other hand. As Ty galloped forward, Graciela gave up trying to wrench free of Jenny's firm grip on her cape. She slipped out of the garment, darting around Jenny and straight into the line of fire.

"Graciela!" Ty shouted at the same time that Jenny did, sliding off his horse in a cloud of dust. "For Christ's sake, take cover," he snarled, then he shouted again at Graciela. Ignoring their yells, she ran toward the man shooting at Jenny and now at him.

"Don't shoot Jenny, Cousin Jorje," Graciela screamed. "It's all right. I'm here. You don't have to kill her!"

Swearing a blue streak, Jenny stamped her boot in frustration and waved her gun in the air. "Don't shoot," she warned Ty. "You might hit the kid!" The gun shook in her hand; she yearned to continue firing, but she didn't.

"Get your butt behind that tree!" After giving Jenny a shove, he dived toward the water trough and dropped into a crouch.

She leaned around the tree trunk. "Crud on a crust! There's more of them!"

Lifting his head above the trough, Ty spotted three men running toward the sound of the shots. Smiling and clapping her hands, Graciela called their names.

"More fricking cousins! My God. She's got a cousin in every jerkwater village in Mexico. They're everywhere."

Swiftly, he assessed the situation and reached a reluctant conclusion. "We're outnumbered." He glanced toward the tree and saw that Jenny had stepped away from the trunk. He shouted to her over the sound of gunfire. "Damn it, get behind that tree!" She had more guts than brains. "Listen to me. We can't win this fight. Hold your fire and let them go."

She whirled toward the water trough. "What are you saying, you son of a bitch? That we give up and let them take her?"

"We'll get her back. But not if we're dead."

She stared hard at him, then looked toward the street. Ty watched her face as she accepted the inevitable. Her shoulders slumped, her gun dropped to her side, and she covered her eyes with a shaking hand. A bullet chunked into the water trough; another pinged the dust in front of the tree. Cautiously, Ty raised his head, burning to return fire, but holding back because Graciela was happily running back and forth between the men. Frustrated, he made a fist and hit the trough hard enough to slop water over the sides.

Now the Mexes were retreating toward the cantina, the man at the rear firing back at Ty and Jenny. "Wait!" Graciela shouted.

She broke from the group of men and stood silently staring back at Jenny who had stepped into the street when she heard Graciela's shout. They looked at each other for a long moment, then Graciela wriggled her fingers in a shy wave, spun, and ran back to the men. One of the insolent bastards swung her up on his shoulders, arrogantly certain that Ty and Jenny wouldn't shoot, and the men moved swiftly toward the horses tied in front of the cantina.

Jenny sagged against the tree trunk, watching with dulled eyes as the men trotted out of the village, Graciela perched in front of Cousin Jorje. "They'll kill her. You know that, don't you?" she said, not looking at him.

Slowly Ty pulled to his feet and turned away from the dust kicked up by the Mexes' horses. He glared. "What the hell were you thinking about? Standing there in the middle of the street like some cocksure gunfighter with not a fricking thing between you and getting killed! You're damned lucky that Mex was a lousy shot. I'm amazed that you didn't take a bullet."

"I did take a bullet."

Swearing, he strode forward and ran his hands roughly over her shoulders, found the wetness just above her elbow. "Christ!" He stared down into her eyes. "Anywhere else?"

"Just the arm."

Shoving back her poncho, he gripped her shirt and tore

it open down the sleeve. She winced when he probed the wound. "You live right. The shot passed through the fleshy part. It didn't hit bone."

"We're wasting time, Sanders." She jerked away from him. "We've got to go after her."

"We will," he said grimly, wiping blood off his fingers. "First we get you doctored."

She made a snorting sound. "There's no doctor in this place. We need to go after them now."

"Were the cousins specifically looking for you, or was this shoot-out the result of an accidental meeting? Because if it was accidental, then nothing is going to happen immediately. Graciela is safe until they decide what they're going to do. It takes two Mexicans a full day of arguing just to agree the sky is blue."

Ty stopped, thinking about what he had just said, hearing the echo of his father. "Look," he said, frowning. "Four men, and that's what we've got here, are going to need two days merely to agree that they need a plan and another two or three days to decide what the plan's going to be."

Jenny tilted her head. "You don't think much of the Mexicans, do you, Sanders?"

He turned her toward the cantina and pulled her into step beside him. "For as long as I can remember, Don Antonio Barrancas has been trying to claim Sanders land as his, and he turns a blind eye when his men steal our cattle. His daughter split our family apart."

"That's one family, and it could have been anyone. Barrancas doesn't represent all Mexicans."

He frowned at her. "Maybe I'm starting to see that. And maybe you should mind your own business."

"I'm thinking about Graciela, and that makes it my business. Maybe your intolerance is one of the reasons I'm never going to let her go off alone with you."

They stood nose to nose, glaring at each other.

"Well, I take offense at that statement. I'm not so blinded by—certain things—that I'd dislike a child just because . . ." He was floundering here, starting to sputter. "If you're on some kind of mission to convince me that all Mexicans wear a halo—"

"I'm not on any kind of mission except to keep my promise to a good woman. I'd be the first to concede that the Barrancas cousins are rotten sons of bitches."

"That's the one thing in this world that you and I agree on." Taking her good arm, he pulled her into the cantina and ordered a bottle of tequila. "Sit there," he ordered, pointing to a stool in front of bare planks laid out as a bar. "Put your arm on the top."

"*¿Que esta?*" The man behind the bar stared at Jenny's bloody arm. He feigned surprise, as if he hadn't heard the shots in the street, hadn't watched the cousins jump on their horses right in front of the open-faced cantina.

"Your pals shot a woman. I'm going to clean her wound," Ty snarled. "You got a problem with that?" The man lifted both hands and moved backward a step. "How about you?" he asked Jenny.

She shrugged. "Has to be done."

Pushing back the edges of her poncho, he pulled open the halves of her bloody sleeve and inspected the wound at close quarters. A quarter of an inch to the left, and the bullet would have shattered bone, leaving her with a useless arm. A couple of inches to the right, and he'd be burying her right now. He poured tequila into a shot glass and shoved it toward her.

"Drink up. This is going to hurt like hell."

She tossed back the tequila without a gasp, suggesting she'd tipped a few in her time. "Been shot before. Outside El Paso." She wiped her good hand across her lips. "Some bastard tried to steal my rig and freight. He didn't get it. But he shot me just below the ribs." She looked up at him. "You ever been bored?"

"About five years ago. One of old man Barrancas's men winged me when I rode onto Barrancas land looking for the cattle they stole." He poured her another shot of tequila, watched her throw it back.

There wasn't a woman he knew or had ever known who would have sat there like Jenny Jones, bleeding on the bar and tossing back shots of tequila without a hitch in her husky voice, without a word of self-pity or complaint. Sitting there wounded, swapping tales about getting shot.

Shaking his head, he splashed more tequila into his glass and touched the rim to hers. "You know," he said, gazing at her cropped coppery hair before he let his glance slide to the clean angle of her jaw, "I can't explain this, but I have a powerful hankering for you. I beg pardon if that observation is out of line, but you strike me as a woman who's not averse to straight talk."

Her eyebrows shot toward her hairline, and her mouth fell open. "You got a hankering? For me? Why?" Disgust pinched her mouth, and for a bad moment he thought the disgust was directed at him, but then she apologized. "It's the kid. I'm so sick of hearing the word why, I swore I'd never use it myself."

He swallowed his tequila, watching her over the edge of the glass. "I can't answer that. I don't know why."

She wasn't remotely similar to the women he'd lusted after in the past. There was nothing dainty or even particularly feminine about her. But he never thought of Jenny Jones without thinking what a hell of a woman she was. If he didn't dwell on her peculiar hairdo and unfashionably tanned skin, she was even good-looking. When he recalled her breasts and small waist, sweat appeared on his brow.

She gave him a level look, turning the tequila glass between her fingers. "Graciela said you hated me for killing her mother."

"That's not true." He thought a minute. He didn't want to call his niece a liar, but she'd stretched the truth on this one. "Graciela must have misunderstood," he said carefully.

"That's good since it appears we need to work together to get her back." Eyes narrowed, she considered him with a thoughtful expression. "I was pretty damned pissed when I thought you hated me."

That was an encouraging sign, he decided, pouring her another tequila. "I was pretty damned pissed myself when you hog-tied me and left me in the dirt. I plan to even the score on that one." He shrugged. She was no tender greenhorn. She would understand the incident demanded a payback. "The thing is, I like your looks even with your hair whacked-up like that. It's a nice color. Better without the black."

She tugged on a short strand near her ear and frowned. "Lice."

"I figured something like that." A tall, strong-boned

woman wasn't to every man's taste, but he responded powerfully to the challenge she presented. "And I admire your style. Hell, who can explain a hankering. You aren't like any woman I ever met."

"That's for damned sure," she said with a laugh. For a moment he thought she might be blushing, but he decided her cheeks were more likely flushed with sun and pain.

Still, it impressed the hell out of him that she could sit there with a shot-up arm and laugh, paying no mind at all to the people gathered outside the cantina, staring in. She was an astonishing woman. And it hadn't escaped his notice that her arm was milky white down to her cuff line. He reckoned the rest of her body was white, too, except for the part brushed with flame. The part separating legs long enough to wrap around a man and guide him where he wanted to go. Imagination paralyzed him.

After a minute he swallowed and wiped a hand across his forehead. "It's time. Hold your arm steady." Shifting so she sat sideways to the plank bar, she extended her arm, made a fist and lowered her head. When he poured the tequila into her wound, she sucked in a sharp hissing breath and blinked rapidly. Her eyes swam, but no tears spilled over.

"It's all right to cry."

"No, it isn't," she muttered between her teeth.

After he'd washed the wound thoroughly and cleaned the blood off her arm, he poured the last of the tequila into their glasses and waited until she'd tossed hers back.

"Well?"

"Well, what?" Her voice was husky, and her eyes glistened with a damp shine, but Gawd a'mighty, she'd taken the pain like a man.

Ty decided he'd never wanted to bed a woman as badly as he wanted to bed this one. Since most women were docile creatures, he seldom thought in terms of taming a woman. But Jenny Jones was for damned sure not docile. She was prickly, stubborn, and exciting in a way he hadn't experienced before.

"Do you have a hankering for me, too?" He snapped the question, irritated that he had to humble himself by asking. He'd made a declaration here, and she owed him better than to leave him dangling and wondering. He'd revealed himself, and he deserved a revelation in return.

"I guess I do," she admitted after a lengthy hesitation, scowling up at him. "I don't fricking like it much, but now that you mention it, yeah, I guess I got a hankering for you, too." She glanced at the man behind the bar. "I need two thin slices of pork rind, *por favor*."

"And some bandage strips," Ty added.

"Listen. Just because we got a mutual hankering, doesn't mean we have to act on it." Her chin came up on a mulish angle. "Aside from the hankering, there isn't much about you that I like. So far, you've been a pain in the behind. And I might as well tell you, I've followed through on one hankering and getting shot was more of an enjoyable experience. I didn't like it."

That was disappointing news. The minute she'd admitted sharing his hankering, wild images had exploded through his mind like fireworks. Since she didn't seem to do things halfway, he'd figured her for a robust and enthusiastic partner. But somewhere along her trail, a man had treated her badly. That was a damned shame. Women were like fillies. Break 'em right, and they'd give a man pleasure every time he climbed in the saddle; break 'em

harsh or carelessly, and they were nothing but trouble forever after.

He'd have to think about this.

Taking the supplies from the bartender, he curved the
pork rind on both sides of her wound and bound them in
place by wrapping strips of cloth around her arm. Her
skin was warm and taut, and she had good muscle defin-
ition. If she hadn't been wearing the shapeless poncho, he
could have treated himself to a stolen glance at her magnificent breasts.

"I didn't say we had to act on the hankering," he commented casually. He wasn't positive that she'd stated an
outright rejection, but in case she leaned in that direction, he wanted her to know he hadn't made any firm
offer.

Standing, she touched her fingertips to the wrapped
arm. Her eyes were clear and her step as steady as his.
Looking at her, no one would guess that the two of them
had just topped half a bottle of tequila. Ty hadn't considered it until now, but holding her liquor was a good qual-
ity in a woman.

"How come you're blathering about hankering," she
demanded, striding to the front of the cantina, "instead of
planning how we get your niece back? Don't you care
about her? Or is she just some Mexican brat to you?"

His gaze snapped down hard. "How I feel about the kid
is none of your business."

"Right now, Graciela is my *only* business."

"Where's your gear?" When she talked about Graciela,
her face changed. A fierce determination tightened her
expression. She truly believed she was responsible for his
niece.

"Down a couple of blocks." When she turned, her face was half in shadow, half in sunshine. "I'm not going anywhere with you until I know how you feel about Graciela. If you aren't committed to getting her back, I need to know it right now."

Ty moved past her into the street, then stopped, forcing a man on a burro to ride around them.

"Here's how it is. I'm no happier about having a Barrancas in the family than my father was," he said, speaking between his teeth. "But Graciela is my brother's daughter, and I promised Robert that I'd bring her home to him. I also promised my brother that I'd take care of his wife and child if anything ever happens to him. I gave my word. You told me that you never lie, so you'll understand what that promise means. Graciela is part of my family, she's part of me, and she's my responsibility. I'm not leaving Mexico without her."

Jenny adjusted the sling he'd fashioned over her arm, then leaned toward him, her expression combative. "I have good news for you, mister. If something happens to Robert, you're off the hook because Marguarita asked *me* to raise Graciela and I gave her my word that I would. And I will."

"No stranger is going to raise my niece. Not you, not anyone else. She has my mother and she has me. She has family."

"She also has Don Antonio, and Marguarita didn't want *him* raising her daughter either. She picked *me*."

They stood close enough that he felt the heat rolling off of her, felt the power of her splendid body.

"The only reason you care what happens to Graciela is

because you made a promise to Marguarita," he stated flatly, staring at her mouth.

Her eyes blazed and her body tensed. "And I mean to keep that promise if it kills me. Or if I have to kill you. You are *not* going to raise Graciela. I *am*."

Never in his life had he wanted to punch someone as much as he wanted to punch the woman staring a challenge into his eyes. But if he raised a hand against her, she'd come right back at him, regardless of her wounded arm, and they'd be fighting and rolling in the dirt street of this tiny village whose curious population stood in doorways staring at them.

He had no idea how he could want to bed a woman and want to knock her senseless at the same time. It was a mystery to ponder some other time.

"The fact is," he snarled, opening and closing his fists, "neither of us has to raise Graciela. Robert will do that. As I've said before, your job is finished. Over. You'd do us both a favor if you'd ride out of here and forget about my niece."

Her lip curled away from straight white teeth. "Did the odds change when I wasn't looking? Did a few of the Barrancas cousins shoot themselves? Or do you plan to go up against four men all by your stupid self? You aren't that good, Sanders."

He flushed, remembering how she'd left him hog-tied in the dirt. His fists closed hard. She didn't know just how good he was, but his time would come, damn it. "You and I can't keep stealing Graciela back and forth. We have to work this out."

"There's nothing to work out," she said, spinning away from him and walking forward. "I'm taking the kid to

Robert. Me, not you. I gave my promise, and that's the end of it." She threw the words back at him. "If you want to tag along . . . well, I agree that's better than what we've been doing. It's up to you. I don't give a piss what you decide."

He didn't talk to her while she collected her gear and watched him saddle her horse; he didn't talk until they were a mile east of the village, following a clear trail left by the cousins.

"Your wound isn't bad," he commented stiffly, coming up alongside her mare. "You should be able to use your arm in a couple of days."

"I could use it now if I had to," she snapped.

Crimson shadows stretched before them, cast by a bloodred sunset. Ty judged they could ride another thirty minutes, then they'd have to set up camp for the night. "We can't make plans until we find out where the cousins are going and what they intend to do."

"They're heading toward the railroad, and they plan to kill Graciela. The only questions are when and how."

Her lack of doubt troubled him. "I want to play devil's advocate for a minute."

She scowled, then muttered, "Wait." After whipping a dictionary out of her roll, she thumbed the pages, held the book to the sunset light streaming over her shoulder, then she nodded grimly. "Go ahead. Be an advocate, you're a perfect devil."

"All you have is Marguarita's opinion that the Barrancas cousins intend to harm Graciela."

"They just rode off with her, didn't they?"

"From their point of view, they rescued Graciela from a stranger who stole her after her mother's death."

She threw up her good hand. "Mexicans are not as dumb as rocks!"

"I didn't say they were," he answered levelly, striving for patience. "I'm just raising the point that the cousins may have the same interest in Graciela as I do. She's family. You have no right to her, they do."

Jenny twisted in the saddle to glare at him. "By now everyone involved in this business knows that Marguarita died on the wall in my place. They know I sure as hell didn't force her to die; it was her choice. They know I didn't ride to the hacienda and steal the kid out of her bed; she was brought to me. They know Marguarita wanted me to take the kid to California. Count on it. From Dona Theodora on down, everyone knows exactly what happened and why."

"If this unfolds the way it's setting up, you and I are going to kill some Barrancas cousins," he said stubbornly. "I want some assurance that I'm not killing people without a damned good reason."

"Marguarita believed the cousins were murdering sons of bitches. She believed it enough to die rather than trust her daughter to one of them. That's enough assurance for me."

Ty reined in beside a shallow swale, then slid off his horse and walked down the incline to sniff, then sample, a thin puddle at the bottom. "The water's muddy but drinkable," he called up to Jenny. "We'll camp here." After he decided she wasn't going to argue, he returned to unsaddle their horses and handle the heavier items that she couldn't manage one-handed.

While he worked, he reviewed the scene he had witnessed in the cantina of the no-name village. His impression was that Cousin Emil had wanted Graciela for ransom. In retrospect, he recalled that Emil Barrancas had not actually said anything about a ransom. Perhaps the family loved the child and simply wanted her back home where they believed she belonged. That would explain the message from Dona Theodora Barrancas y Talmas. Dona Theodora expected the cousins to find and return the child to her. She didn't want to lose Graciela to a stranger *or* to the Sanders and California.

It troubled him that events could have a different explanation than the one Jenny put forward. It was equally troubling to consider that she might be right. Marguarita certainly had believed the cousins were capable of evil. She had died because she believed it.

After eating plates of beans and tortillas, they settled before the flames, drinking coffee as fiery stars burned holes in the desert sky.

"I'm a brawler and a fighter, a shooter when I have to be," Ty remarked, watching fingers of firelight dance across her strong features. "I'm not a murderer."

"If you're squeamish about killing, then head on back to California and wait for me and the kid to get there."

He laughed. "Now who's sounding stupid? You're going to face down four men? You aren't that good either, Jones," he said, enjoying dishing back her earlier comment.

She narrowed her eyes, then suddenly she laughed, ending in a smile. The smile transformed her face. With the firelight rosy on her cheeks and lips, and the smile curving her mouth and lighting her eyes, she was beautiful. Ty stared at her.

"I've got you figured," she said in that husky voice.

"You'll do what you have to because you promised your brother. You gave your word. You aren't going anywhere without the kid, so I'm not worrying about having to fight alone."

There was nothing to say. She was right, of course. She understood the power of a promise, saw a promise the same way he did.

"Do you have a family, Sanders? A wife and kids of your own?" Resting her coffee cup on her knee, she gazed at him across the flames, her expression unreadable.

"Hell no." The question made him laugh. "I'm not the marrying kind." When she continued to look at him, he leaned forward and poured more coffee into his cup. "A man like me can't live with anyone."

"Is that right?" She raised her coffee cup. "What makes you so ornery that no one could stand to live with you?"

"My ma said I was born mad." He shrugged and gazed into the flames. "Maybe she was right." He thought about it. "I never met a woman I could stand for more than a week." A grin curved his mouth. "I imagine they felt the same about me."

What began as charming feminine traits ended by irritating the bejesus out of him. Then came the naive and often silly or boring conversations. And the obsession with all the tiny nuances of etiquette with the inevitability of his forgetting something and offering insult. Not to mention the endless primping and smoothing and patting. The soft helplessness. And, most offensive, the ubiquitous efforts to change him. All women wanted to reshape a man into something other than what he was.

"So. What do you do with yourself when you aren't in Mexico? You a drifter?"

"I drifted along the coast for a few years."

"And then?"

"I always came home to the ranch." His father's ranch, and now his brother's. He frowned. "Why are you asking all these questions?"

"No reason." One shoulder lifted in a shrug that might have passed for indifference if he hadn't known her as well as he was beginning to. "Talking around the fire, that's all. Passing the time. No one says you have to answer."

"I have a place on the ranch. Three hundred acres my father cut out a few years ago. I run cattle, try to prevent old man Barrancas's men from stealing them. You could say we've been stealing each other's stock for twenty years." He'd tried his hand at other professions, but he always returned to the ranch. The land was in his blood. "You ever worked on a ranch?"

"Once, for about a year. The food was good. The pay was lousy. I suppose it's a satisfying life if you own the land."

"How about you? You ever been married?"

"Me? Oh hell no." Her laugh sounded rusty as if she didn't use it much. "I haven't had jobs that inspire romantic leanings. Cussing at mules, skinning carcasses, you get the drift." Yawning, she glanced toward her bedroll. "I'm like you. I never met a man that I didn't want to shoot after about three days." Standing, she adjusted the sling around her arm before bending forward to flex the stiffness out of her shoulders.

"Does your arm hurt?"

Incredulity widened her eyes. "What the hell do you think? Of course it hurts. Hurts like the devil."

Then she tilted her head and gazed up at the night sky. For several minutes she didn't speak. "Graciela is all right . . . isn't she?" she asked in a whisper, her eyes fixed on a distant star. "Make me believe they haven't killed her yet."

The raw anguish thinning her voice surprised him. This was the first flash of vulnerability and uncertainty that he'd glimpsed. For some reason seeing a vulnerable Jenny Jones made his chest tighten painfully. He cleared his throat and said what she needed to hear.

"Graciela hasn't been harmed," he stated firmly. "No one's going to kill her. We're going to get her back."

"I know we will." Turning her back to him, she faced the desert and the tall cacti standing guard like spiny sentinels. Her shoulders dropped, pulling her chin down.

"The kid asked Jorje not to kill me," she said in a low wondering voice, gazing down at her boots. "You heard her. I didn't imagine it." She stood in silence for a full minute, then she swore softly and kicked a rock toward a clump of scrub oak before she stalked toward her bedroll.

Ty cradled his coffee cup and studied the flames dying in the fire pit. He would have sworn that Jenny's only connection to his niece was her promise to Marguarita. Now he wondered. A minute ago she'd revealed a glimpse of something deeper that made him suspect he'd misjudged her.

"Sanders?"

Raising his head, he frowned toward her bedroll. "What is it?"

"I've got nothing to offer a man, and you've got nothing to offer a woman. So don't get any ideas about acting on that hankering. I've got my Colt in my blankets. You make a move in my direction, and I'll shoot your butt."

Indignation ruffled his brow. "Well, for God's sake. Do you really think I have so little conscience that I'd jump a woman with a shot-up arm?"

After a long silence, she called to him out of the darkness. "You just stay on your side of the fire."

Realization smoothed the anger from his forehead, and he laughed. She was thinking about him, thinking about those hankering feelings. Grinning, he gazed toward the saddle she used as a pillow.

"Darlin', when I'm ready to satisfy this hankering . . . you'll beg me to crawl in your bedroll. That's a promise."

Sputtering sounds of outrage erupted from her blankets, and she sat up. "That will fricking *never* happen!" she shouted furiously.

"Yeah. It will," he said softly. Smiling, he tossed the last of his coffee on the ground, then walked to his bedroll and kicked it open.

Whoever broke her had broke her wrong.

He was going to fix that. And she was going to enjoy the experience as much as he planned to. Thinking about it made his groin ache with anticipation.

Chapter
Ten

Joy and confusion alternated like twin beacons blinking across Graciela's expression. She was going home. Home to Aunt Tete and her own room and the comforts of the hacienda and the servants who staffed it, home to a secure life she understood.

But her mother would not be there. Home would never again be the place she had known. A shine of tears dampened her eyes.

Wrapping her arms around her knees, she sat in front of the campfire, shivering slightly as the sun sank behind the Sierras and the evening chill crept over the desert. Idly she watched Cousin Tito remove a tightly woven sack from a strap on his saddle and carry it toward the fire. At once her thoughts focused. Her neck prickled, and she sat up straight when she realized something moved inside the sack.

"Have you eaten snake before?" Tito asked, grinning at her. Eyes fixed on the sack, Graciela slowly rose to her feet. Nothing on earth frightened her more than snakes.

Holding the sack by his side, Tito swept a hard glance over Jorje, Carlos, and Favre, and abruptly Graciela became sharply aware of a strange unnerving tension that she had vaguely sensed all day. Now the tension leaped into her as well. Eyes wide, mouth dry, she tried to move backward a step as Tito knelt beside her and placed the sack on the ground, but her trembling legs would not obey.

"I'll release one of the snakes," Tito explained, smiling at her with a strange expression. "I'll club it. Then we'll skin it and roast it over the fire. The meat is white and juicy. You'll think you're eating chicken."

Graciela swallowed convulsively. She couldn't wrest her eyes from the horrifying sinuous movement slithering beneath the folds of the sack. Fear dried her mouth to dust and paralyzed her. Her heart thudded so loudly that she was only dimly aware the others had fallen silent.

Tito stood, inspecting the sliding movements within the sack before he flicked a look toward Cousin Jorje. Graciela didn't see what passed between them as she couldn't take her eyes off of the sack. She couldn't move, couldn't speak. All she could manage was a gasp when Tito grinned and upended the sack in front of her. Three large, thick rattlesnakes dropped to the ground in front of her feet.

Terror gripped her in paralyzing shock. She couldn't breathe; she thought surely she would faint. One of the snakes slithered past on her left, leaving an S-shaped track as it headed for the desert and darkness. One of the snakes lashed into a coil, its head raised, its tongue flicking and hissing.

Graciela knew the coiled snake would strike at any movement, so she fought to hold her shaking body still even though every muscle trembled and her brain screamed at her to run. Whispering through dry lips, she prayed that one of her cousins would shoot the hissing snake before it struck her. But none of them moved.

Shocked and dizzy with horror, she watched the third snake wind toward her. And she shook violently as it glided over the top of her shoe, then disappeared behind her. She desperately wanted to peer over her shoulder to make sure the snake continued toward the desert. Irrationally, she was terrifyingly certain that the snake would slip beneath her hem and twist up her leg before it sank its fangs into her flesh. She could only hope the snake wasn't sliding under her hem at this very minute, but she dared not look to see if it was. The movement would attract the coiled snake, the hissing snake that posed the greatest danger.

Striding forward, Favre shoved Tito out of his way, then shot the head off the coiled snake. Graciela jumped at the sound of the gunshot. Relief crumpled her bones and she fell to the ground as limp as a pile of rags. Almost at once, she leaped to her feet and shook her skirt furiously, then peered anxiously around her, frantically wiping at tears in order to see better. Knowing the other two snakes were out there, maybe just beyond the light cast by the campfire, made her shake with fear.

Favre stared at Tito, and his lip curled. *"El Stupido!"* Kneeling, he withdrew a knife from his belt and began to skin the snake he'd shot. One of the others laughed, then everyone returned to their tasks and finished setting up camp.

Deeply frightened, Graciela wiped her eyes and peered at Tito, expecting him to apologize for an accident that could easily have gotten her killed, expecting him to hug and pet her, hoping for reassurance. But he returned her gaze with cold eyes, and all he said was, "You are very lucky, *chica*."

Confused and still stunned, Graciela moved close to the fire and extended trembling hands toward the flames. She took care to stand well away from the dead snake.

After setting two forked sticks, Favre draped the skinned snake above the fire to cook. Graciela could not look at it. And when the time came to eat, her stomach rebelled. She tasted a few spoonfuls of rice and nibbled at a tortilla, but she didn't touch the lumps of roasted snake.

After the dishes were tossed aside, her cousins brought out a bottle of tequila and passed it among themselves. Occasionally one of them studied her with eyes kept carefully blank. The snakes were gone—she fervently hoped—but her fear remained.

Now that the incident had receded somewhat, Graciela found terrible thoughts creeping into her mind. As hard as she struggled to banish the thought, she felt a growing conviction that dropping the sack of snakes at her feet had been no accident. In the instant before Tito dropped the sack, he had looked at her with dark greedy eyes, and a small smile of anticipation had curved beneath his mustache.

None of the cousins had rushed to snatch her away from the snakes. None had drawn the pistol at his hip until Favre finally stepped forward. Shifting her gaze to his firelit face, she wondered if Favre had acted to save her, or if he had merely feared that the last snake would escape to the desert and they would have no meat with their beans and rice.

"Your bedroll is over there," Cousin Jorje said, jerking

his head toward the darkness. Twitching, Graciela turned large eyes to him, mute with silent terror. "The snakes are long gone," Jorje said impatiently. When she still could not move, he strode away from the fire, pulling her by the elbow. While she watched, trembling and quiet, he turned out her blankets to show her nothing fanged or poisonous waited within. "Go to sleep now," he ordered in a voice she recognized. It was the voice grown-ups used when they wished to discuss adult matters that children should not hear.

"Good night," she whispered, feeling abandoned as Cousin Jorje strode away from her, returning to the safety and companionship of the campfire.

Before she crawled into her bedroll, she walked on top of it even though she had watched Cousin Jorje shake out the blankets. When she felt nothing snake-shaped beneath her shoes, she reluctantly slid inside and turned anxious eyes toward the fire.

For the first time in her young life, Graciela Sanders did not feel safe in the presence of relatives. Something was very wrong. These men were not cousins she saw frequently, like Luis or Chulo, but she remembered the men around the fire as being talkative and boastful, teasing and gay.

No one had laughed tonight. There had been no jests or merrymaking along the trail or around the fire. They had not petted her or heaped lavish compliments on her as they had at Aunt Tete's hacienda. They had treated her like an unwelcome stranger.

After murmuring hasty prayers, she wrenched her mind from disturbing thoughts and let herself recall the softness of her bed at home and the row of vividly clad dolls on her shelf. Her books, her slate, the small box of treasures she hadn't thought to see again. These memories cheered her.

But when she remembered that she would never again run to her mother's room to share cups of morning chocolate, would never say her prayers with her mother kneeling beside her, would not ride in the carriage breathing her mother's perfume or hear her mother's voice, a rush of pain crushed her chest.

Her mother was dead, and she was afraid of the men at the campfire.

Burrowing deeper into the blankets, struggling not to cry, Graciela sought something good to think about. She thought about telling her friend Consuelo about her recent adventures.

Consuelo had never ridden a train or seen a town the size of Durango, she was sure of it. Certainly Consuelo had never had a day alone with no duenna or family in attendance. Nor had she dressed her own hair or bathed in a stream. Consuelo's eyes would widen and she would gasp when she learned that Graciela had exchanged clothing with a street urchin and that Graciela had eaten food cooked over an open fire and had slept on the ground.

"Is she asleep yet?"

When Cousin Jorje came quietly to look at her, she squeezed her eyes shut and pretended not to know he stood over her gazing down. After she heard the chink of his spurs retreating, she returned her thoughts to Consuelo, trying to decide how she would explain Jenny to her friend.

Jenny had killed her mother and Graciela hated her for

that. But it was also true that Jenny had cared for her when she was ill, and Jenny had taught her good things to know. She resented that Jenny treated her like a servant, yet Jenny's approval had become oddly important to her.

Conflicting views confused her, so she turned her mind to Uncle Ty instead, wondering if she would ever see him again. Here, too, her mind tugged in differing directions. Uncle Ty had been nice to her, and she liked him well enough, but she had an uneasy sense that Uncle Ty didn't particularly like her in return.

This suspicion upset her badly. All her life she had been fussed over, petted, loved. Without a doubt, she knew that she had been the center of her mother's life. She was her aunt Tete's favorite. Until tonight, she had unquestioningly believed that she was loved and adored by all her cousins.

That she might not be loved by all the people in her life was a new and frightening thought that shocked her deeply.

Brushing a tear from her cheek, she closed her eyes tightly and wished the day's exhaustion would carry her into slumber. But as her thoughts quieted, she became aware of low, tense voices rising and falling around the campfire.

"We know what has to be done," she heard Jorje say. The harshness underlying his voice sharpened her attention. "Since the snakes didn't solve our problem, I say we do it ourselves."

"For the love of God. She's just a child!" This was Favre, who had shot the snake before it struck, who had danced with Graciela on her last name day.

"Not so loud."

"Luis and Emil have decided a certain person has to die," Favre said, speaking so quietly that Graciela had to strain to hear. "So let them kill her."

"And let them inherit all of Don Antonio's money?" Tito said sharply. "Is that what you want?"

Graciela's breath stopped and gathered around a pounding heart. They were speaking of her grandfather Antonio. And herself. Jenny had been right. Her cousins wanted her dead.

The idea of this was too devastating, too enormous and unthinkable to comprehend. Stiff with fear and fresh shock, she lay in the darkness, gripping her blankets and shaking.

"You're fools if you think we'll ever see a centavo of Don Antonio's wealth." Carlos rose to his feet, silhouetted by the dying flames. He waved his arms in an angry gesture. "Already Luis and Chulo are planning their journey to Norte America to tell Don Antonio that his daughter and granddaughter are dead. Who do you think Don Antonio's new heirs will be? You're loco if you think Luis and Chulo will remember to mention us."

Jorje also stood. "That's why I say we take care of this problem." He cast a glance over his shoulder toward Graciela's bedroll. "And we insist that one of us goes with Luis and Chulo, then they can't cut us out. We found her. If we"—he shot another glance over his shoulder—"dispose of this problem, then we have Luis and Chulo right here." He pounded a fist in the palm of his hand.

"She's a Barrancas," Favre snarled. "Like you. Like me. You would kill a member of your own family? I spit on all of you."

In the sudden silence, Graciela heard the thunder of her

heart knocking against her ribs. A torrent of tears streamed down her cheeks, and the hands gripping her blankets shook like dry twigs. Panic and fear squeezed her chest accompanied by an ache that she was too young to recognize as the pain of betrayal.

What could she do? There was nowhere to run, no place to hide. Wiping frantically at the tears wetting her face, she tried to think of a way to escape, but no answers came.

"Help me," she whispered, curling her fingers around the locket pinned to her chest. She could not have said to whom she addressed the urgent plea. To God? To the tiny portrait of her mother? Or did she hope that Jenny would find her again as she had in Durango?

When dawn tinted the sky with streaks of pink and blue, she rose reluctantly and silently, her eyes dull and bruised from lack of sleep. Now she, too, held herself distant and withdrawn. Now she refused to meet her cousins' eyes for fear they would glimpse how profoundly frightened she was.

"Time to *vamoose*," Jorje announced after they had eaten and packed the saddlebags. He extended his arms to lift her onto his horse, but Graciela shook her head.

"I want to ride with Favre," she whispered.

"As you wish," Cousin Jorje agreed with a shrug. He gave Favre a long, narrowed look before he mounted his horse.

With a flourish, Favre bowed before her, then lifted her onto his saddle and swung up behind her. Graciela longed to thank him for his words on her behalf, but she feared admitting she'd overhead part of their conversation. She could almost hear Jenny saying: protect your backside, give nothing away.

When they stopped at midday to seek shelter from the blazing sun, Graciela shaded her eyes and anxiously scanned the rolling, empty horizon. Buzzards circled a cluster of cacti to the north, and she spotted a hawk diving through wavy shimmers of heat floating near the ground, but she saw no riders.

"Are you worried that the red-haired witch is following?" Cousin Jorje asked, handing her a goatskin filled with water.

"A little," Graciela said, not looking at him.

He laughed and puffed out his chest. "They won't follow." When he said "they" she remembered that Uncle Ty had joined Jenny. "Us," he said, thrusting forward four raised fingers. "Them." Two fingers lifted on the other hand, and he laughed again.

Slowly, Graciela nodded. Her heart sank beneath the weight of his words. Before she stepped into the shade, she again searched the horizon, lingering on the dips and rises.

Her cousins smoked or dozed beneath the shade of their sombreros. Occasionally they spoke in low voices among themselves. Made drowsy by the heat and a lack of sleep, Graciela found a spot near a low bush and had drifted into a light, restless slumber when two hands closed around her throat.

Her eyes flew open and she struggled to sit up, grabbing at the fingers circling her neck.

"It would be so easy," Carlos murmured near her ear.

His fingers tightened steadily, pressing into her flesh and Graciela choked, fighting to draw a full breath. Black dots spun in front of her eyes and her lungs burned before a blur flashed across the side of her vision.

Favre's body crashed into Carlos, knocking him away from her. She toppled backward and lay where she had fallen, gasping for air. When she could breathe again, she sat up, swallowing gingerly, and stared at the two men rolling and fighting in the desert dirt. Jorje and Tito stood across from her, also watching, hands on the pistols at their hips.

Graciela didn't know what happened because she turned away, her stomach churning, and she didn't look at the fighting men again until she heard a gunshot. When she dared to look, Favre lay in the dust, his bloody face unrecognizable. Carlos sprawled on his back, Favre's knife buried to the hilt in his chest.

Gasping, choking on horror and tears, Graciela doubled over and vomited in a clump of low cacti.

Jorje swore as Tito checked both men, then looked up shaking his head. He snarled something at Graciela, but her ears still rang from the shot and she didn't hear.

She was too frightened to look at him or Jorje, and her throat made no sound when she tried to speak. She darted one last horrified glance at the blood soaking into Favre's poncho, then she ran a few steps onto the desert and stood with her back to the camp, shaking as if the hot breeze were a gale.

She felt as she had when she was ill, hot and cold at the same time. Her teeth chattered. These were not the laughing cousins who had danced with her and teased her at the hacienda. She didn't know these men; they might have been strangers. Gingerly she touched the bruises beginning to appear where Carlos's fingers had circled her throat, and she swallowed the dark taste of bile and fear.

Without Favre, she was at the mercy of Tito and Jorje. Sooner or later they would kill her. She sensed this. She *knew* this.

Deeply frightened, she scanned the empty land baking in the midday heat. Jenny had promised, she told herself, and Jenny never broke a promise. Jenny would come and save her. She had to believe this. Jenny must be out there. Somewhere.

When she turned dragging footsteps back to the campsite, Jorje and Tito were hacking shallow graves out of the hard desert floor. She clung to thoughts of Jenny whenever she noticed Tito or Jorje studying her with hooded, speculative eyes.

She prayed that Jenny would arrive while she was still alive.

"There!"

Ty followed Jenny's pointing finger, nodded, and they both urged their horses forward and down into the next dry gulch. Jumping to the ground, they crawled up the far side of the arroyo, and Ty wrestled a spyglass out of its case.

He spotted them at once, resting in the thin shade of some stunted scrub oaks. Silently, he handed over the glass. "She's unharmed."

"So far," Jenny muttered. Stretching out on her stomach, she propped one elbow in the dirt and steadied the glass. A minute later her forehead dropped against her arm. "Thank God!" Lifting the spyglass again, she peered intently. "I only see two men." She returned the glass to Ty.

"But four horses," he said. "The other two are somewhere nearby."

Ty slid down the incline and lifted a canteen from his saddle. After a long swallow, he wet his throat and face. The temperature must be near one hundred degrees. His shirt was soaked with sweat. Not speaking, he watched Jenny break twigs from the scrub oak and construct a shaded area by draping her saddle blanket over the twigs, which she had driven into the ground.

Sensing that an offer to assist would offend her, he waited and watched her try and fail until the shelter was constructed. The view wasn't unpleasant. Sweat molded her trousers around shapely buttocks, and her wet shirt outlined two handfuls of breast.

Swallowing images as hot as the scorching air, he joined her beneath the shade she had created and gave her the canteen.

"We take them at night," he said. Her throat arched when she tilted her head back to drink, offering a long clean line that he wanted to explore with his fingertips.

Jenny nodded and wiped a hand across her lips. "Has to be tonight. They'll reach the railroad tracks tomorrow."

"Are you thinking dead? Or are you thinking incapacitated?"

She scowled then whipped out her dictionary. A minute later she said, "I'm thinking incapacitate, like in tied-up and their horses run off. Unless they give us no choice, then we kill them." Slapping shut the dictionary, she pushed it into her back pocket. "Incapacitate. That's a good word."

"So far we agree." Ty jerked open his collar. The air hung hot and motionless at the bottom of the arroyo. Nothing stirred. Sitting this close to her, he could feel the heat rolling off of her, could smell the pork rinds drawing out any infection beneath the bandage on her arm. He mopped his face and throat. "Want me to take a look at your wound?"

"I checked it this morning. It's coming along." She shifted, brushed some small rocks out from under her, leaned against the saddle at her back. "Don't worry, I'll hold my own tonight."

"I'm not worried." But of course he was. Two against four weren't the preferred odds, especially as one of the two was one-handed.

As if she'd read his mind, she slipped out of the sling. Grinding her teeth, she extended her arm, winced, folded it back near her breasts, then extended it again.

"Stop looking at my chest, damn it."

"I'm looking at your arm."

"No, you aren't."

"All right, I'm not."

"So stop it."

She stared until he lifted his gaze to her eyes, then she extended her arm again, working out the stiffness. It had to hurt like hell.

Since he'd grasped how she thought by now, Ty knew they wouldn't risk leaving the arroyo until after midnight. A long sweaty afternoon stretched before them and most of the night.

"We aren't going to sleep tonight, so you should try to catch some shut-eye now," she said, working her arm.

"Can't. Too damned hot." He considered kicking off his boots, then decided the effort required more energy than he was willing to waste. But he stretched out, propped his head against his saddle, and lit a cigar. When he noticed Jenny inhaling the smoke, he offered it to her, not really surprised when she took the cigar with a sigh of pleasure. He lit another for himself.

"How come you're so dead set against satisfying a hankering?" he asked when she paused to rest her arm against her thigh and enjoy the cigar.

"I told you. I gave it a try, and I didn't like it. More important, I sure as hell don't want to get pregnant." She exhaled a perfect smoke ring, watched it widen and slowly dissipate. "Who's going to hire on a pregnant woman or one with an infant hanging around her neck? I figure the worst thing that could happen to me would be to get myself knocked up."

"There are ways to make sure a woman doesn't get pregnant." He released his own smoke ring and sent it wobbling into the still air.

"Yeah, and if those ways were always successful, there would be a whole lot less people in this world." She tossed him a look of contempt. "You said you aren't the marrying kind, Sanders. You're the walking-away kind. You use women to ease your hankering and then it's *adiós*. Well thanks for offering to use me, I'm fricking flattered, but I'm plain not in the mood to be used and abandoned. Too damned bad we didn't hitch up during one of those times when I was yearning to be used and kicked away." Leaning to one side, she spit in the dirt, cutting her eyes toward him to make sure he hadn't missed the gesture.

Ty stared at the horse blanket over his head, searching for a defense. "That's one way of looking at it," he said finally.

"That's the *only* way I'm ever going to look at it. I'm never going to throw myself on some son of a bitch and beg him to use me, get me pregnant, and then walk away. No hankering is worth the consequences."

"My brother didn't abandon Marguarita after he got her pregnant," he said, studying the faded pattern zigzagging across the horse blanket.

"You aren't your brother," she snapped, working her arm again. "And he's nothing to hold up as an example if you ask me. He married Marguarita but he was never a husband to her or a father to the kid. He let his wife be sent away in disgrace rather than give up his precious inheritance."

She spoke around the cigar gripped between her teeth, looking down at her arm. Sweat trickled along her hairline. Ty watched her and decided he liked a woman who appreciated a good cigar. Occasionally his mother smoked, on her birthday and after the annual branding.

It surprised him to suddenly realize that Ellen Sanders would take to Jenny like shine on a nickel. Like Jenny, his mother defied convention by wearing men's trousers around the ranch, she enjoyed a drop now and then, and she didn't put on female airs. She, too, would have said "pregnant" rather than search for a polite or vague euphemism.

"Would you walk away from three thousand acres of prime California land?" he asked, half-wishing she'd stop moving her arm. Sweat stood on her brow, and she'd bitten into the cigar.

"The point is not what I would do," she said, stopping to exhale a stream of smoke into the motionless air. "The point is, Robert chose his inheritance instead of Marguarita and the kid."

Ty laughed without amusement. "You'd understand if you'd known my father."

"What about your father?"

"Three things. No one said no to Cal Sanders. Second, he didn't want me to inherit his ranch. And he would have done whatever he had to do to keep Robert from running after a Mexican wife. It wasn't only the threat of disinheritance. He would have destroyed Robert, and Robert knew it. No one crossed Cal Sanders without paying a heavy price."

She wiped a sleeve over her forehead and started working her arm again. "How come your father didn't want you to inherit the main ranch?"

"Maybe because I told him I didn't want it." That was the only way he'd known to hit back at Cal Sanders, by rejecting the one thing his father cared about. "Seems to me that we've strayed a far piece from the subject at hand. Which is, what are we going to do about this mutual hankering?" Raising a hand, he touched his fingertips lightly to her cheek.

"We're going to forget about it," she said, jerking her head away from his touch. "We're going to incapacitate it." A grim smile touched her lips. "I like to use new words."

"I noticed."

She frowned at her arm, then slipped the sling back on. "Don't want to overdo." Leaning back, she rested against her saddle. "There was a woman in El Paso who let me borrow her books. When I had a steady team, I could read while I was hauling. If you can read, you don't ever have to be lonely, and I can read," she finished proudly, watching him.

"Very admirable." Ty settled his head against his saddle and tilted his hat brim over his eyes so he wasn't tempted to stare at her breasts.

"The thing is," he said, speaking around his cigar, "*my* hankering isn't incapacitated." Looking down, he could see the spot where her thighs met. A damp stain outlined a V at her crotch like an arrow pointing to heaven. A stirring occurred in his own trousers, and he closed his eyes.

She sat up abruptly and lifted his hat brim so she could stare down at him. "Is there something wrong with your ears? How many times do I have to say this? You and me can hanker till the moon falls out of the sky, but nothing is going to come of it. Now, that's how it fricking is, Sanders, so you just make up your mind to it. I might have to raise one kid, and I don't know how in the hell I'm going to do that. I sure don't want *two* kids dragging me down. So you just forget any hankering thoughts."

She slammed his hat down on his face hard enough to knock the cigar out of his mouth. Sitting up, he slapped at the sparks on his shirt, found the cigar, and flipped it out from under their makeshift lean-to.

"You're starting to irritate me," he said, fighting to hold his voice level. "I keep telling you that Robert is going to raise Graciela himself. But you keep hearing that it's your job and yours alone. I'm telling you for the tenth time, Robert is alive and well and he *wants* his damned daughter."

She had a way of leaning into him to make a point, thrusting her face forward until their noses almost touched. At the moment, being so close made him want to grab her and cover her mouth with punishing kisses until he felt the fight drain out of her stubborn bones, until he felt her slip trembling into surrender.

"The kid is half-Barrancas."

"You think that's going to surprise Robert? Robert's been in love with Marguarita Barrancas since we were all children. I'm the brother with the Barrancas problem, not him." His mouth twisted in disgust. "Right now, he's trying to put an end to the animosity between our two families."

They had argued about old man Barrancas before Ty left for Mexico. Robert didn't want Marguarita caught between her husband and her father. He wanted to end hostilities that had existed for twenty-five years. Ty strongly disagreed. Too much water had flowed beneath this particular bridge. There were too many stolen cattle, too many property skirmishes, too many wounded men and harsh exchanges on both sides of an ongoing dispute. Ty wasn't willing to forgive and forget, and he didn't understand how Robert could even consider it.

Jenny drew back and her eyes narrowed. "You're really something. You must have been dancing in your boots when you learned that Marguarita Barrancas was dead."

"I wasn't happy to hear that she'd died," he said after a minute. "But I wasn't sorry either. She tore our family apart." Anger tightened his jaw. "My father was never the same after Robert married a Barrancas. From then on he treated Robert with the same contempt as he treated me. He started drinking, letting the land and the ranch go to hell. Robert spent the next six years hating himself for not having the guts to defy the old man. My mother was caught in the middle of it."

"It was Robert who caused the trouble in your family, not Marguarita." Jenny sneered. "If Robert had kept his parts in his pants, there wouldn't have been a problem." Leaning forward again, she jabbed a finger against his chest. "I'll bet there wasn't a night went by during the six years Marguarita waited that she didn't wish she'd said no when your brother mentioned he had a hankering. Huh! That's not going to happen to me."

Stretching out, she settled her head on the saddle, then flounced onto her side, presenting her back to him. "I'm through talking. I'm going to get some sleep."

If that wasn't just like a woman, Ty thought, angrily staring down at her. She had to have the last damned word. Lying back down, he crossed his arms on his chest and glared up at the horse blanket.

After a time, he concluded they had made some progress. The obstacle preventing a mutual hankering from ending satisfactorily had been defined. Now a solution could be considered. Meanwhile, he would begin the wooing process. That decision made him think of Mrs. McGowan, and he smiled.

Mrs. McGowan had taken him into her bed when he was sixteen and randy as a stallion. The farrier's wife had taught him wondrous things, things his feverish young imagination hadn't yet dared to dream. In retrospect, everything he knew about pleasing a woman had come from Alice McGowan, and she had given him some of the best advice he'd ever received.

"Treat all women like they was fine ladies," Alice had

advised before he dragged her down between the sheets. "Treat every woman like she was the last woman on earth and you was one of the million men trying to get her."

Considering the state he'd been in at the time, it was nothing short of miraculous that he remembered her advice. But he did, and he'd put it to good use over the years.

Yessir, Jenny Jones didn't know it yet, but she was going to surrender. Idly, he wondered if she knew the word capitulate.

All her life Jenny had wanted things she didn't or couldn't have. Usually she shrugged and got past the wanting. But this time fate was playing the trickster.

Destiny had thrown her together with a hard-eyed, hard-muscled, good-looking cowboy, the very sight of whom tied her innards in hot knots. If that wasn't enough torture, fortune's imps had given him a powerful hankering for her, then upped the ante by inflicting her with a mighty hankering for him.

The mutual hankering secretly thrilled her and pissed her off at the same time because she couldn't follow through on it.

She'd have to have grits for brains to risk a pregnancy by a man who announced first off that he was a user. It wasn't that she was angling for marriage. Hell, she was no more marriage material than he was. No way would she ever expect or even hope that the son of a prosperous rancher would choose an uneducated, crude, and rude mule skinner for a wife. That wasn't the problem.

She would have dropped her trousers in an eye blink if she could have known for absolute positive certain that she wouldn't turn up pregnant.

Worrying how she was going to support and raise Graciela was enough to keep her awake nights. Adding another kid would finish her. And before the three of them starved or froze to death, Jenny would have fallen through all the stages of degradation that it was possible for a woman to experience.

She didn't deserve that, and she didn't want Graciela and a new kid to witness it happening to her.

Thinking about the horror and misery of watching two kids starve because she couldn't find work made her so mad that she rolled over and kicked Ty.

Instantly he came out of a doze and glared at her. "What the hell was that for?" Leaning forward, he rubbed his shin.

"I keep telling everybody that I'm not the mother type! But you all seem to think I can work miracles and pull food out of the fricking thin air! Well, I'm not going to be used, and I'm not going to prostitute myself or beg in the streets. And no kid of mine is going to starve in front of my eyes. Do you hear me?" She made a fist and hit him on the shoulder. "I don't even like you."

If she'd had the full use of both arms, she would have built another lean-to and moved her saddle. The heat squashed any idea of giving it a try. The best she could do was lie back down and move as far from him as she could.

A minute passed, then she heard him stretch out again.

"Has anyone ever told you that you have beautiful eyes?"

"Shut up!" She stared at the saddle horn. "Why the hell did you say that?"

"Well, it's true," he said in a lazy voice. "I'm just making an observation. You have beautiful eyes, beautiful breasts, beautiful hips."

Oh God. The hankering feeling came over her strong. No man had ever said such words to her. And she had a weakness for pretty words. The feverish heat curling in her stomach suggested she also had a weakness for handsome cowboys. Crud on a crust.

"Wake me when it's time for supper," she said, in a strange husky voice.

To warn off the hankering, she tried to imagine herself holding a squalling infant with her red hair and the cowboy's blue-green eyes. The image was amusing, horrifying, frightening, and . . . something else that made her stomach roll over and dissolve into mush.

Groaning in disgust, she turned her face into the crook of her arm. If Graciela didn't get her killed or ruin her life, Ty Sanders would.

Chapter
Eleven

Contrary to expectations, the Mexicans did not break camp and move on. When Jenny checked through Ty's spyglass, the two men appeared to be arguing. Judging by their gestures, it appeared one wanted to leave the campsite while the other remained indecisive. There was still no sign of the missing men. Graciela, thank God, seemed unharmed.

Because it worried Jenny and Ty that the missing two men had not returned by sunset, they decided to wait until dawn to make their move. The delay would provide the absent cousins the greatest opportunity to reappear, and would give Jenny and Ty the greatest assurance that the missing men would not suddenly arrive in the midst of their attack.

The night passed slowly, with little conversation. Finally, to Jenny's relief, the time arrived to shake the drowsiness from their heads, mount, and ride across the dark desert.

A hundred yards from the Mexican's camp, they tethered their horses, then Jenny moved stealthily to the left and Ty silently circled the camp from the right. They came together again near a stunted cactus not far from where they had left their horses.

"There's no outlying guard," Jenny reported in a whisper, her lips nearly touching Ty's ear. His muscles were taut, communicating his readiness for the fight to come. She shared his edginess. She, too, resonated with the need to release the tension of having spent so many feverishly speculative hours alone with him. The pressure of unrequited hankering jangled her nerves and unsettled her thoughts. The way she figured it, a righteous fight would do them both good and clear the air.

Ty cupped her chin in his palm and turned her head to position his mouth near her earlobe. A flow of warm breath and whispered words made her thighs tense.

"I think the missing men are dead. Looks like two fresh graves about twenty yards from the fire."

Now it was again her turn. When she moved her head to whisper a reply, her lips grazed his chin and her breasts pressed lightly against his upper arm. "If they're dead, then our odds just improved."

Pulling back, he glared into her eyes. "What are you doing? You're going to get our butts killed."

Frowning, she peered through the darkness. "What the hell are you talking about?"

"You know damned well what I'm talking about. These."

His hand moved up between them and he cupped one breast, lifting the rounded weight in his palm. His unexpected touch exploded through her body like an invisible beam that instantly dissolved her bones.

The strength shot out of her legs, and Jenny dropped hard to her knees, which placed her at eye level with his thighs. She stared straight at his crotch. It was a damned fine crotch in her opinion, impressive, really, but right now she was too amazed to devote much thought to a crotch that had occupied her mind for most of the day.

At this moment, the impact of Ty's warm hand cupping her breast rocked her mind like a small earthquake. She flat would not have believed that a man's casual caress could drop her to her knees. Of course, no man had actually caressed her before. Based on her experience, men grabbed, mauled, pummeled, and kneaded. They didn't gently cup, stroke, or caress.

"Je-zus," she whispered, as he knelt down beside her.

"What's wrong? Is it your arm? Something with your legs?"

"Don't touch my breast again, or I'll kick you in the groin," she whispered angrily. Gripping his hand, she pulled herself to her feet, then shook off his fingers as if his touch were lethal.

"Then don't go rubbing up against me like you did," he snapped, speaking an inch from her lips. "Not when we're about to start a fight. You have lousy timing." He spread his hands and released an exasperated sound between his teeth. "All the damned day and all night, I've been waiting and hoping you'd show some interest. And when do you do it? Two minutes before we're going to go in and risk getting ourselves killed—goddammit, Jenny."

A rush of heat flushed her face. "I wasn't rubbing on you! I was only leaning close to whisper in your fricking ear." Defensive, she instantly forgot the thrill of pressing against him. "Are we going to do this, or are we going to stand here arguing until the sun comes up?"

They stood boot tip to boot tip, hat brim to hat brim, scowling at each other in the darkness of predawn, fighting a powerful backwash of hankering.

"One of the men is sitting up, asleep in front of the fire," Ty whispered, frowning down at her mouth. "The other one is wrapped in a bedroll, sleeping on this side."

"Graciela's in the middle," Jenny added. His gaze was narrow and cool, but his body radiated enough heat to scorch a woman's hide. She was positive that his hard eyes burned an imprint on her lips. Swallowing, she thought about stepping backward, but her legs wouldn't move away from him. "We have to figure the kid is going to get in the way, that she's going to try to protect her fricking cousins."

"How's your arm?" A light touch brushed her shoulder. "Are you going to be able to use it?"

"It's sore, but it won't be a problem." At least this time she didn't humiliate herself by falling to her knees when he touched her. "I'll take the cousin in the bedroll, and I'll grab the kid. You take the cousin dozing by the fire. He's the one most likely to give us trouble."

They stared into each other's eyes. "I'd like to kiss you for luck," Ty said finally.

"Oh God, don't do it." She placed both palms on his chest and gave him a push. "You saw what a touch did to me. So don't go trying for a kiss. Turn your butt around, and let's get this fight over with." Even the thought of kissing him made her stomach lurch into a long hot roll. Her legs had that boneless feeling again. "Damn it, Sanders. You've been tormenting me for hours with teasing remarks," she whispered fiercely, getting angry. "I'm telling you for the last time . . . *stop it.*"

"What about you? For the first time in my life, I'm going into a fight with an erection! That kind of distraction can get a man killed."

"See how you are?" she demanded, leaning into him, her eyes flashing. "There you go with more suggestive remarks."

He swore softly, staring at the front of her poncho like he could see through it, then he pulled out his gun. "You've got me so worked up I can hardly think straight. Christ! Wait for my signal. We'll strike at the same time."

She couldn't help it. She strained through the darkness, trying to see if he really did have an erection. When he noticed where she was looking, he groaned and shook his head. Another rush of color heated her cheeks.

"Well, you could have been lying," she snapped. But she was pleased to notice that he was not. In fact, she felt wildly flattered and slightly astounded that he was in the same agitated state of arousal as she was. Flipping open her pistol, she ran her thumb over the chamber, double-checking the load of bullets. "Forget hankering and start thinking about that cousin dozing by the fire. Let's go."

"Concentrate. Focus," he hissed before he ran a hot finger down her throat. An instant later he had faded into the shadows.

She tried to concentrate on the matter at hand, but her thoughts kept flipping around erections and kisses and touches and feverish speculation about a hard-eyed cowboy's body and intentions. She would have sworn that her throat burned along the line he'd drawn with his fingertip.

"Well crud on a crust." After giving her head a vigorous shake, she dropped into a crouch and moved up toward the embers glowing in the cousins' fire pit, darting from one clump of low cover to the next. She promised firmly that she would not jeopardize this action by getting stuck on distracting memories of his hand curving around her breast.

Before she managed completely to thrust the recollection out of her mind, she found herself inside the campsite, practically on top of the sleeping cousin. Glancing up, she saw Ty rise behind the cousin dozing before the fire. His hand clapped over the man's mouth and he dragged him backward.

The noise of the scuffle between Ty and the first cousin was slight but enough that when she gazed down at the man in the bedroll, his eyes flicked open, instantly alert. An explosion ripped through his blankets. If she hadn't dived to the side when she saw his eyes, the son of a bitch would have plugged her. Rolling up on her knees, she fanned the hammer of her pistol and fired. To make sure she'd hit her mark, she jerked back his blanket, tossed his gun into the darkness, then slapped a hand on his throat and checked for a pulse.

"Good riddance."

The force of a small body flying out of the darkness knocked her on her back in the dirt. Swearing, teeth bared, she freed her arm and jammed the barrel of her pistol into . . . Graciela's ribs. "Kid! Damn it, I almost shot you."

Struggling to sit up, she tried to shove Graciela aside, but Graciela wouldn't budge. A full minute elapsed before she understood the kid was not fighting her. Graciela had wrapped her arms around Jenny's neck, and she clung like paint on a fence, sobbing and babbling hysterically. After a hasty check to reassure herself that Graciela was unharmed, Jenny felt like babbling herself. Getting the kid back in one piece made her almost feel like weeping.

Ty loomed out of the darkness, grimly satisfied, shoving his gun into his holster. Jenny met his glance, returned his hard-eyed nod, then turned her attention to the kid.

"Kid! Kid, slow down. I can't understand a word you're saying."

Graciela pulled back an inch and rubbed both hands against wet eyes. "My fricking cousins tried to *kill* me!" Jenny didn't grab her fast enough to prevent her from shifting to look at the dead cousin in his bedroll. But the kid didn't flinch. The tears rolling down her cheeks were not for the dead cousins.

Turning back to Jenny, she talked a hundred words a minute, waving her arms, her eyes huge. "They turned snakes loose on me!" A shudder of remembered horror trembled down her body. "Snakes this big!" Her arms flew open wide. "Then Carlos tried to choke me, but Favre wouldn't let him, and they got into a fight and killed each other. And I was so scared and so afraid you wouldn't come, but I knew you would, but you didn't, and I thought they'd kill me for fricking sure!"

She threw herself into Jenny's arms, sobbing again, clinging like a burr. Jenny waved her hands in the air, then patted Graciela's back awkwardly, amazed by how deep down, damned good it felt to have the kid's little warm body in her arms. "It's finished now," she murmured over and over. "I'm here and you're safe. No one's going to hurt you."

When she glanced up, Ty was standing over her, fists on his hips, scowling.

"What?" she asked, frowning up at him.

"Did you hear what my niece said?"

"She said she finally believes that her rotten cousins were trying to kill her, just like I've been telling her all along." She didn't understand his angry expression.

"She said her 'fricking' cousins were trying to kill her for 'fricking' sure."

"Well, thank God they didn't get the job done. It sounds like they tried, the bastards. Did you hear what she said? The sons of bitches turned snakes loose on her. Snakes!"

"Jenny, my niece said 'fricking.'" He stared at her, then cast a meaningful glance at Graciela's heaving back.

"Graciela, you've got to stop crying now." Jenny tried to peel the kid off her chest. "You got my bad arm caught between us, and it's hurting like hell."

Reluctantly, Graciela released her grip and edged backward a step. She cast anxious glances between Jenny and Ty. "Are they all dead?"

"Those men aren't going to hurt you ever again," Ty said gently. Kneeling, he sat back on his heels and studied the kid's face. "Are you all right?"

This time the kid flung herself on the cowboy's neck and burst into fresh sobs, interspersed with an incoherent story involving snakes as long and thick as a fence rail. Ty looked as surprised as Jenny had when Graciela had jumped into her arms, then he did the same thing she had done. He held Graciela's sobbing body, awkwardly patted her back, and murmured soothing sounds deep in his throat.

"I was so scared of the fricking snakes! One of them tried to crawl up my leg, and—"

"Honey, wait. Listen a minute." Ty eased her away from his shoulder so he could gaze into her eyes. "Nice little ladies don't say words like fricking."

So that's what he was irked about. Pulling to her feet, Jenny knocked the dust off her hat, then settled it on her head.

Graciela looked at Ty, then at Jenny. "Jenny says fricking all the time."

Now they both looked at her. Jenny glared back.

"You know your mama wouldn't want you to say words like that," Ty said. Lifting a hand, he tucked a strand of loose hair behind Graciela's ear. "And I know your father and your grandma Ellen sure wouldn't want to hear a pretty young lady cuss and say bad words." He paused and sent Jenny a scathing stare. "I'll bet Jenny doesn't want you to say fricking either."

Sucking in her cheeks, Jenny tilted her head and gazed up at the sky. The stars were fading, but not Marguarita's star. Marguarita's star was always the last to go. A cold, steady beam glared down at her.

Okay, Marguarita, Jenny thought, *so she's starting to talk like me. What did you expect? You knew I wasn't any fancy-talking bluestocking when you chose me. Mule skinners are famous for cussing; it goes with the job. This isn't my fault.*

Yes it was. Marguarita knew it. She knew it too.

"Jenny?" Ty called to her in a voice stiff with righteous indignation. He had her pinned in a corner. No way was he going to let her squirm out of this.

Jenny lowered a scowl to the kid. "He's right. Don't

say fricking anymore. Next time I hear you cuss, I'm going to wash your mouth out with soap. You hear me?"

Graciela's chin lifted, and her eyes flashed blue-green outrage. "That's not fair. *You* say it."

Ty grinned, watching her shift her weight from boot to boot.

Red dots flamed on her cheeks, and she kicked dirt at the embers in the Mexicans' campfire. She narrowed her eyes to slits and hissed at Ty. "You think you're so superior and self-righteous. Well take a look around you, cowboy." She flung out her good arm. "We got two dead cousins here. Are you worried about your precious niece looking at two dead and bloody bodies? No, you're all worked up like some prissy preacher because she used a cussword. Maybe your frick—" She slid a frown toward the triumph spreading over Graciela's smug expression. "Maybe your stupid priorities aren't where they should be. Even *I* know kids shouldn't be sharing a campfire with two dead bodies."

She had him there, all right. One look at the color in his face told her so. He came to his feet like a shot and spun Graciela so she faced away from the dead cousin in the bedroll.

"All right. This isn't the best situation. But listen and hear me good. You are never in your life going to find a man less like a prissy preacher," he snarled. "If my niece wasn't here, I'd show you the kind of man you're dealing with."

The smoldering stare he swept over her body shot a hot shiver straight to Jenny's toes. My God, he was a fabulous man. As hard as a railroad spike. She couldn't believe that a man like this had developed a hankering for *her*.

Almost dizzy with pleasure, she swaggered toward Graciela and clasped her arm. "Time to go, kid. Let's ride."

The kid gazed up at her with teary, reddened eyes, and Jenny guessed she hadn't slept more than an hour since the cousins snatched her. "Are we going to bury Jorje and Tito?"

Jenny considered. "You think we should?"

"Hell no," Ty snarled.

"I didn't ask you." She looked down at Graciela. "It's your call. But before you decide, I have two words to say. Snakes. Choking."

Ty strode forward. "You can't ask a child to make that kind of decision. It's too much responsibility."

"No it isn't." She tapped a finger on top of the kid's head. "What's it going to be?"

Graciela lifted her chin, squared her little shoulders, and walked toward the horses.

"Wrong horses," Jenny called. "Ours are over there." Graciela spun and marched back toward her. As she passed, Jenny gave her shoulder an approving pat. "Good choice."

"*You* say fricking." Graciela glared, then continued toward the horses.

Jenny frowned. This was going to be a problem. Glancing up at the pale sky, she imagined she spotted Marguarita's star still gazing down at her. If it was possible for a star to look pissed, this star did.

All right. I've lost the kid a couple of times. I'm sorry about that. But I've got her back, haven't I? She narrowed her eyes on the sky and thrust out her chin. *Now, about this cussing. I am what I am. You can't expect me to change my ways just to please a kid. Hell, you must have said fricking a time or two, didn't you?*

She couldn't imagine it. No cussword had ever tainted Marguarita's lovely ladylike lips. And Marguarita would have dropped into a swoon at the sound of a cussword scorching her small daughter's tongue.

A heavy sigh whistled up from deep in Jenny's chest, and she smacked a fist against her thigh. She just hated being responsible for a kid. It changed everything. And problems kept popping up like dogs in a prairie village.

When she reached the horses, Ty had already mounted, holding Graciela on the saddle in front of him. "If we set a good pace, we'll reach the railroad in time to flag down the next northbound."

"And if we miss it?" she asked sourly, shading her eyes against the glare of dawn.

He shrugged. "Then we hole up in the nearest village and catch the morning train."

"Someone back in that village will have let Luis and Chulo know that the dead cousins snatched the kid."

"Possibly. But they won't know that we have her back."

He was right again. She hated that too.

If they'd been traveling without a child, they would have reached the railroad tracks with time to spare before the northbound came whistling through. But Graciela slowed their pace.

When it became obvious they had missed the train, Ty dropped back beside Jenny's mare. He tilted his hat brim toward a smoky haze rising in the distance. "Must be a village up there. I say we find a place for the night. Agreed?"

Her gaze fixed on Graciela's flushed face, and she nodded. "The kid could use a bath, a decent meal, and a good night's sleep."

"So could I," he said, flexing his shoulder muscles. He and Graciela were pasted together by sweat. He was mildly surprised by how fatiguing it was to ride for hours with her leaning against his chest. "How are you feeling?" he asked her.

"Sad," his niece answered in a small voice.

He didn't know what to say to that. Adults were not as frank about expressing feelings as he'd discovered his niece was. Pulling his scarf off his neck, he wiped perspiration and dust from his face, searching for a comment.

"I'm sorry you're sad," he said finally. When that didn't seem adequate, he added, "I can see how you would be." People she'd trusted and loved were dying all around her.

"Uncle Ty?" she asked in that same small voice. "Do you love me?" Shifting on the saddle, she turned huge blue-green eyes to study his face.

"Well," he said uncomfortably, staring into a sober gaze so like his own. Frantically, he searched his conscience, weighing truth against a glib equivocation. When he cut a glance toward Jenny, she was watching with a smirk on her lips.

In the end, there was only one possible answer. Any other reply would have been unnecessarily cruel.

"Yes, I do," he said, the words sticking to the roof of

his mouth. This was the answer Robert would have wanted.

"Could you say it?" she asked after a hesitation, tears brimming between her lashes.

Oh God. He drew a breath, ground his teeth together, then mumbled, "I love you." If Jenny uttered one word, made a single choking noise, he'd kick her off her horse and ride off without her. When he shot a scowl in her direction, she was gazing straight ahead, sucking in her cheeks. But she wasn't laughing, and she didn't make a sound.

"I love you, too, Uncle Ty." Graciela kissed his jaw, then nestled back against his chest.

His grip tightened on the reins and he stared at a point in space, trying to figure out what had just happened.

He wasn't a man who frequented places where children were likely to be. Consequently, his exposure to children had been severely limited, and that's how he'd preferred it. When he did encounter children, he generally ignored them, irritated by the noise they made, their interruptions, the difficulty of trying to converse with undeveloped minds.

Therefore, he was totally unprepared for the unaccustomed emotions aroused by one trusting declaration and one innocent kiss.

Frowning, he reminded himself that Graciela Sanders was half-Barrancas. She was the living proof of his brother's folly, his brother's lack of judgment. A mistake. Ty's original plan had been to fetch Marguarita and her child, deposit them on Robert's doorstep, and from that moment encounter them only at a distance and at infrequent family gatherings. He had been unable to imagine any circumstance under which he would willingly share the same room with a Barrancas.

Suddenly he could.

And that was disturbing. He couldn't sort out how he felt about this abrupt and mystifying change. When he became aware that Jenny had spoken, he blinked and turned his head. "Are you talking to me?" He thought she'd muttered something that sounded like "ungrateful snot," but that didn't make sense, so he must have heard wrong.

"I said let me do the talking. You're such a rude bastard that if you inquire about a room, we'll spend the night sleeping in cactus spines."

He gave her a tight-lipped smile, recalled his wooing campaign, then replied in English rather than Spanish. "I'll leave the arrangements in your capable hands, darlin'. No one could resist your dulcet charm."

Out came her dictionary and the rifling of pages. And then a suspicious frown. "Do you mean to say dulcet or was that a mistake?"

"Honey, you're the sweetest thing this side of the Rio Grande." A grin twitched his lips, and he felt better. Mrs. McGowan's advice had been smack on target. If nothing else, he'd just knocked Miss Jenny Jones off-balance and left her reeling with the confusion he read in her eyes.

She checked the dictionary entry again, then shoved it back into her pocket. Her face flickered through a half dozen emotions as she struggled to glue the word dulcet on herself. Ty almost laughed, guessing that she didn't find the fit too comfortable.

Graciela shifted against his chest. "Jenny is not sweet and she is not charming."

"You speak English?" he asked, blinking at the top of her head.

"My mama taught me," she said proudly. "So I would be ready when my papa came for us."

"What a smart little girl you are."

"Yes I am."

"Smart enough to recognize horsesh—" Jenny paused and swallowed. "To recognize nonsense when she hears it. Dulcet, my butt." Touching her heels to the mare's flanks, she galloped away from them, leaving Ty and Graciela to eat the dust kicked up by her horse's hooves.

By the time Ty's gelding walked into the sun-baked little village, Jenny's horse was tied in front of a sod-roofed shack, and she'd already arranged for food and a washtub.

As he dismounted and lifted Graciela to the ground, he examined a few of the brown faces drawn by curiosity to watch him. He couldn't visualize any of them offering a room if he'd been the one asking.

"Buenos tardes," he said, forcing his lips into a curve.

A chorus of smiles and greetings returned his salutation.

Son of a bitch. Maybe Jenny was right. Maybe he was a rude bastard. On the other hand, it was also possible that these people didn't deserve his courtesy. Very likely someone from this village was already riding toward Verde Flores to inform Luis and Chulo that a gringo couple had ridden in with a Mexican child.

Jenny was unpacking her saddlebags when he and Graciela entered the one-room shack. The furnishings were primitive but included three hammocks, a rough-hewn table, and several stools. Privacy and shelter from the sun improved Ty's spirits immediately.

"Senor Armijo is going to hang a red rag on the pole near the tracks. The morning train will stop when the engineer sees the signal. That's taken care of." Jenny's gaze dropped to Graciela. "We'll have bathwater in a few minutes and something to eat. Afterward, you need to rest and get some sleep."

"It's still light out. It isn't even night yet."

"A few days ago you were sick enough that I wondered if you were going to make it. And you look like you haven't slept since then. You can hardly keep your eyes open. You need some sleep."

As far as Jenny was concerned, the matter was settled even though Graciela stamped her feet and continued to argue. Jenny ignored her.

"It would help if you'd see to the horses," she said to Ty. "So do it."

Dropping his saddlebags next to hers, he narrowed his eyes. "Let's get something straight right here, right now. You want something from me, you ask. You don't order."

Flipping back the hem of her poncho, she placed her hands on her hips and leaned forward. Her lips pulled back from her teeth. "It would be fricking dulcet of you if you'd condescend to unsaddle our horses, water and feed them. Would you please turn your butt around and go do it?"

"See?" Graciela shouted. "*She* said fricking."

He leaned forward too. "That is not the proper use of the word dulcet."

"I don't fricking care."

Her chin came up next to his, and she stood so close

that her breasts almost pushed into his chest. If his niece hadn't been watching, Ty would have grabbed Jenny and kissed her senseless. He wanted to conquer her, wanted to crush the challenge in her eyes, wanted to drive into her and leave her whimpering for more.

"Yeah, you care." The color streaking up her throat confirmed it. She didn't like to use a word wrongly. A tight smile thinned his lips. "Do you like to fight in bed too?"

She threw a glance over her shoulder. "Shut up."

"Do you scratch and bite?" he asked softly, staring at her mouth, enjoying the crimson rushing into her cheeks. "Do you like it rough? Or do you prefer long gentle strokes?"

Her mouth dropped open, and she sputtered. "Are you crazy? Get out of here. Go! Right now." Shoving at him, she pushed him toward the door and almost into the man carrying a large washtub.

Grinning, Ty tipped his hat to Senor Armijo, then stepped into the late-afternoon sunshine.

She was weakening. She was going to topple and fall. When she did, he'd be there to catch her in his arms. By God, he thought with relish, this was going to be one coupling that he'd never forget. Neither would she.

Chapter
Twelve

Jenny was so rattled that she undressed Graciela without even tossing a hint that the kid should do it herself. Sanders was a crafty bastard. But she recognized his game. She'd heard enough about courting to recognize wooing when she saw it. The darlin's and honeys. The unexpected touches. The outrageous flattery and the suggestive remarks. It was all calculated to get her out of her trousers and into his bedroll.

"Dulcet, my butt."

"Jenny!" Indignant, Graciela drew wet knees up to her chest and stared out of the washtub. "You aren't listening. I'm telling you about the fricking *snakes*."

That caught her attention. Rocking back on her bootheels, her wrists hanging limp over the edge of the washtub, she stared at the bruises around Graciela's throat and felt her heart sink.

"Hand me the soap."

She didn't want to do this. But she was only as good as her word. That was all she had.

Graciela's eyes widened as Jenny grimly rubbed the soap between her palms, working up a lather. "No!"

"Oh yeah," she said firmly. The soap smelled rank and stung her hands. But either she washed the kid's mouth out, or she threw away everything she was. Her credibility, her self-esteem, herself.

It was a fight. The kid was slippery and full of spit and vinegar. By the time Jenny won, enough water had splashed out of the washtub that she was soaked and exhausted. Sitting on the dirt—now mud—floor she rested her back against the washtub, caught her breath, and examined her hand.

"You bit my finger, you little snot."

Crying and still spitting soap suds, Graciela shouted at her. "I hate you!"

"Your precious uncle Ty would have done the same thing." She rubbed the teeth marks ringing her forefinger.

"No, he wouldn't!"

"Listen, I don't give a rat's ass what falls out of your mouth. It's your uncle Ty who insists that you act like a lady." She hesitated, then turned around and said the rest of it. "And he's right. You started out prissy enough. All you have to do is go back to being what you were."

Graciela stood and snatched the towel Jenny held out to her. She wiped her wet eyes and nose. "*You* cuss."

"I know it, and I've been thinking about that." She grabbed back the towel and dried the kid's back, trying not to rub snot on her. Then she lifted Graciela out of the tub and stood her on one of the stools so she could drop a thin shift over her head. The shift had come from Senora Armijo. Anticipating the next demand, she automatically removed the heart-shaped locket from Graciela's jacket and pinned it on the shift. This done, she tucked the kid under her arm and dropped her into one of the hammocks.

Pulling up a stool, she sat down and wiped sweat off of her forehead. "Look, kid."

"Graciela. You promised."

"Graciela. I cuss. I don't talk nice, you're right about that." She looked into the kid's eyes. "But you don't want to be like me." A pang pierced her heart. She hadn't known it would be so hard to say this. "I'm everything you don't want to be." She drew a long breath and held it a minute. "I'm uneducated, crude, mean, mad at the world." Dropping her head, she examined her large, callused palms, remembering Marguarita's soft, smooth hands. "Until now, it didn't matter what I was or how I talked or what I did." She lifted her head again and frowned. "See, nobody ever cared what I did before."

She hadn't dreamed a time would ever come when someone might want to emulate her talk or behavior. Consequently, it made her feel tight and strange inside to hear her words on the kid's lips. A small part of her was astonished and secretly flattered. But a larger part was appalled. Now that Ty had called her attention to the problem, it struck her as jarring and offensive to hear cusswords on a child's lips.

Graciela sat up in the hammock and leaned over her knees to rub a spot of mud off her toes. "It's not fair that you can say things that I can't," she insisted stubbornly.

A long silence stretched between them while Jenny tried to concoct an argument against fairness. Actually, she came up with several winning rebuttals, the best being: Adults can do and say things that kids should not. But she could guess how well that would go down with the kid. She wouldn't have bought that argument either if their positions had been reversed.

"I don't know how we solve this problem," she admitted, frowning. "But I can tell you this." She jerked her head back at the washtub. "I don't want to go through *that* again. You have to stop cussing."

Graciela's chin came up, and that one irritating eyebrow arched. "I'll stop if you will."

A short bark of laughter burst from Jenny's lips. "Me? I've been cussing since I was your age. It's one of the things I'm good at." Looking at the kid's freshly scrubbed face, it was hard to believe she was capable of uttering a cussword. But she was, and the problem would get worse because cusswords were what she was hearing. Jenny's shoulders slumped. She didn't like the direction or the inevitable conclusion of this conversation.

"Uncle Ty doesn't cuss."

"He doesn't do it in front of you, that's all."

And that, of course, was the solution. Seeing a partial reprieve, she immediately brightened. She didn't have to change her whole person to accommodate the kid. All she had to do was make a few changes when the kid was right in front of her. Probably she could do that. The more she considered, the better the compromise seemed. It answered the fairness problem, and that was the largest stickler.

"All right," she said slowly, "here's the bargain. Neither one of us says fricking anymore." Silently she added, *in front of each other*.

A mixture of triumph and disappointment gleamed in Graciela's eyes. "We can't say hell or damn or crud or Christ or son of a bitch either. Uncle Ty wouldn't like it."

Uncle Ty could jump in a tub of scum for all Jenny cared right this minute. Thin-lipped, she considered, then nodded with great reluctance. "This is going to be a pisser."

"We can't say piss either."

"Well my God." Jenny stared. "I'm not going to be able to talk. What did your mother say when she was really piss . . . irritated?"

Graciela pursed her lips in a prissy moue. "When Mama was angry, she said she was displeased."

"Huh!" She would have rolled her eyes and said Je-zus, but Je-zus was undoubtedly prohibited also. "Listen, I'm going to forget occasionally. You have to accept that up front. I've been talking like I talk for a long, long time. A person doesn't change overnight. So don't go thinking I'm breaking a promise if a cussword or two slips out."

Graciela cast her a sideways glance and a small smile. "If you forget and cuss . . . do I get to wash your mouth out with soap?"

Jenny blinked, then threw back her head and laughed. Every now and then there were moments when she enjoyed the hell out of the kid, and this was one of them.

"If you try I'll be very . . . displeased. Besides, I'm bigger than you are." They grinned at each other. "You know," she said softly, "when you're not being a snot, you aren't too bad."

Pink flooded the kid's face, and she leaned forward, rubbing at her toes. "I'm hungry."

"Senora Armijo is fixing us something right now." She touched Graciela's shoulder blades, gazed at the bruises around her throat. "There's something I want to say. I'm sorry you had to learn that your cousins," she paused, searching for acceptable words, "are rotten, greedy people. But it's good that you finally know it. Because Luis and Chulo are still out there, and they're still looking for you. They're dangerous, Graciela. Maybe worse than the cousins we left in the desert."

Graciela's lip trembled. "Cousin Tito dropped the snakes right in front of me! He wanted them to bite me!"

"You were very brave, and I'm proud of you. It's hard to be alone and scared and have snakes poured on you."

The pink deepened in Graciela's cheeks and her eyes shone. It astonished Jenny how much the kid seemed to value her approval. And it worried her, too. As far as she knew, nothing she'd ever said had affected anyone. Now it seemed that Graciela absorbed her words like a sponge. It was a sobering thought, a little frightening to wield that much influence on another person.

"I'll bet you were never scared of anything."

A smile curved her lips. "Well, you'd lose that bet. I've been scared plenty of times."

One of the things that scared her opened the door and swaggered inside.

"Senora Armijo is right behind me with supper," Ty announced, tossing his hat toward a wall peg. "What happened here?" Frowning, he inspected the muddy floor.

"Nothing," Jenny said, noticing the anxiety fade from Graciela's eyes when the kid realized she wasn't going to reveal the soap incident. "Put the food on the table," she instructed Senora Armijo.

They didn't speak until Jenny had thanked the senora, and she had withdrawn. Then Ty lifted Graciela out of the hammock and placed her on a stool in front of the table.

"Looks like beefsteak cooked with tomatoes and onions," he said cheerfully. He brought up a stool for

Jenny and one for himself. "Are you ladies as ready as I am for something besides beans and tortillas?"

Slowly, Jenny seated herself and tucked a gaily colored napkin inside the collar of her shirt. It felt strange to be sitting down to supper with a man and a child. Suddenly she recalled a picture she'd seen in a catalog of a family sitting at a table together. They had been dressed better than she and Ty and Graciela, and the furniture was a hell of a lot nicer, but Jenny had studied the picture and she'd known the man and the woman and the child were a family. Not a family like any she had known, but a family like her heart wanted a family to be.

"You're supposed to put your napkin in your lap," Graciela commented. "Like this."

"Well la-de-da." Now she noticed that Ty had placed his napkin in his lap, too. A dull throb of color heated her cheeks. "I like my napkin tucked in." Reaching with her fork, she speared a chunk of meat and dropped it on her plate. "What are you doing?" she demanded when she noticed Ty leaning toward the kid.

"What's it look like? I'm cutting my niece's steak."

"She's not crippled. She can cut her own damned meat."

"You're not supposed to say damn." Graciela gave her one of the superior smiles that Jenny detested.

"Jenny, she's six years old."

"Which is plenty old enough to feed herself."

"I'm not allowed to use knives," Graciela said, turning a charmingly helpless look on Ty.

Jenny lowered her fork. The little snot liked being waited on. "Let me ask you something. If someone," she squinted at Ty, "didn't cut that meat for you, what would you do? Pick up a hunk and gnaw on it?"

"No!" The kid looked appalled.

"Would you sit there and starve?" Graciela glared at her. "If you were hungry enough, I'll bet you'd figure out how to cut your own meat. So," she said, deliberately issuing a challenge, "are you hungry enough?"

Ty placed his knife and fork on his plate, dropped his napkin on the table. Scowling, he rose to his feet. "I'd like to speak to you outside."

"We're eating."

"Right now." Turning on his bootheel, he strode to the door and stepped into the fading light of sunset.

Jenny pulled her napkin from her collar and threw it on the table. She glared at Graciela. "Figure out how to use that knife. And be careful. I'll be back."

The ramshackle collection of shacks looked picturesque in the dying light of the day. Two boys and a dog ran down the rutted lane toward the smell of frying chilies. Laughter rose from the shack next door, and a woman's voice singing the slow, sweet notes of a lullaby.

Jenny walked across the dirt yard to a wooden cart with a broken wheel. "What do you want?"

Ty placed both hands on his hips and gazed at her in silence. The coppery twilight bronzed his skin and emphasized the hard, clean lines of cheek and jaw. Looking at him made Jenny feel weak inside, which she hated. They had hardly started this confrontation, and already she felt at a disadvantage.

"You expect too much of her."

"Well, you don't expect enough." Leaning against the cart's side slats, she crossed her arms over her chest.

"When is she supposed to learn how to cut her own food? When she's twenty? Fifteen? Twelve? She has to learn to do things for herself."

The sunset reflected in his eyes like points of flame. He'd washed for supper, but trail dust still lay in the creases of his shirt and waistcoat. He smelled of leather and horse and sweat, the scents she associated with the best of men. He was lean and taut, a whiplash of a man. Ruthless enough to do what he had to without a pang, confident enough to touch a woman with gentle fingers.

Frowning, Jenny turned her face away from him.

"She's an heiress. Graciela will inherit more wealth from Don Antonio Barrancas than she'll be able to spend in a lifetime. And she's also my brother's heir. For the rest of her life she'll be surrounded by servants. They'll dress her, dress her hair, prepare her food, see to her every need."

She jutted her chin. "Yeah, well suppose it doesn't work out that way. Suppose that pretty world goes to hell and she has to survive on her own." A sound of disgust rattled the back of Jenny's throat. "What chance would she have? A kid who can't even cut her own meat."

Leaning forward, Ty placed a hand on each of her shoulders and gazed into her eyes. "Listen to me. What happened to you is never going to happen to Graciela. She's never going to be abandoned and alone."

"If I have to raise her—"

He placed a finger over her lips, then tilted his head and considered the sky for a moment. "All right. That's not going to happen, but let's say that it did." Impatience sharpened his tone. "You've got Graciela, and you're going to raise her. Where do you start? Where would the two of you go?"

"Is this a serious question?" Suspicion narrowed her eyes. When she realized she couldn't think straight with his large, warm hands resting on her shoulders, she shrugged away from him.

"Where would you take her, Jenny?"

"I don't know." Frowning, she tried to focus on the question. "I suppose I'd go to San Francisco since it would be the nearest town of any size. I'd find work there."

"And what would you do with Graciela while you worked?" Withdrawing a thin cigar from his waistcoat pocket, he lit it and waved out the match, exhaling slowly.

Jenny had considered this problem a hundred times already but had found no satisfactory answer. The kid was not street-tough enough to leave alone, but Jenny couldn't think of any job where an employer would permit a child on the site unless the child was also working. "I'll figure out something," she snapped.

"Where would the two of you live?" He glanced at the glowing end of the cigar, then studied the sagging lines of the shack they had rented for the night.

"If you have something to say, just say it." Anger boiled in her chest. She didn't like the dismal situation he was trying to make her admit.

He lowered his eyes to her face. "Do you really believe that Marguarita wanted you to take Graciela away from a life of comfort and ease? Do you think she would have chosen deprivation and hardship for her daughter?"

Silence rang in Jenny's head. Swinging around, she searched the sky for Marguarita's star, needing reassurance.

"She said if Robert couldn't or wouldn't take the kid, I was to raise her. That's what she made me promise."

For the first time since this whole thing began with the kid, her voice didn't ring with confidence. "Damn it." He was trying to confuse her.

"Marguarita was dying, Jenny. She was frightened for her child and for herself. Is it surprising that she wasn't thinking as clearly as she might have? Plus, if you're right, and she didn't receive Robert's letters, then she didn't know that my father was dead. If she'd known Cal Sanders was dead, I doubt she would have experienced a single qualm about trusting Graciela to my mother's care. It was my father she feared and worried about, and with good reason.

"My mother is prepared to welcome her granddaughter and love her. She would have done the same for Marguarita, because that's the kind of person she is. Ellen Sanders was my champion when I was growing up, and she'll be Graciela's champion, too. She stood up for me more times than I can count. To help her boys, she fought my father, the elements, the world at large. Robert would have told Marguarita about Ma. He would have told her that our father would never welcome her, but she would find support and a fair, clear mind in our mother.

"Had Marguarita known the true situation as it is now, she would have asked you to take Graciela to Robert and that's all, confident that my mother would raise the child if for some reason Robert could not. I'll never believe that Marguarita wanted her daughter to grow up as a street urchin roaming the back alleys of San Francisco." His gaze hardened. "Would you do that to Graciela, Jenny? Would you deprive her of safety and comfort? Of an education? Would you deny Graciela her birthright and condemn her to hardship? Simply to honor a promise that was asked and given based on incomplete information."

Jenny stared. "This conversation has strayed a far distance from whether or not you should cut the kid's meat for her," she whispered.

"What you're trying to do would be laudable in different circumstances," he continued, speaking in a quiet voice. "Your independence and resourcefulness helped you survive. But Graciela isn't you. Once we take her home, Jenny, she'll never be alone again or forced to fend for herself. She'll never be hungry, will never have to work for bed and board."

"That's *if* Robert wants her," Jenny whispered stubbornly. But her words lacked force. Deep inside, Jenny was beginning to accept that Robert would be a father to Graciela.

Yet she continued to worry about a future that might include the kid. Lowering her head, she rubbed her temples. Everything Ty said made sense. And yet . . .

"Let Graciela be a child, Jenny. Stop flogging her because she isn't a six-year-old adult."

Her head snapped up, and she leaned into him, flashing eyes catching what remained of the dying light. "What the hell makes you such an expert on kids?"

"I don't know crap about kids. But I know this," he said, matching her glare for glare. "I grew up too fast, and so did you. Neither one of us had much of a childhood. I was doing a man's work by the time I was eight; you were fending for yourself at an age when most girls are still playing with dolls. That's not how it's going to be for Graciela. So ease up on her. Let her have her childhood."

Narrowing their eyes, they studied each other in the deepening shadows.

"I wish you'd never found us," Jenny snarled in a low, harsh voice. "I wish it was just me and the kid. Things were simpler then."

Needing to get away from him and the confusion he planted in her head, she returned to the shack, stopping abruptly just inside the door.

The first thing she noticed was the table. The meat she and Ty had left on their plates was now cut into ragged bite-sized pieces. A grim smile thinned her lips. Either the kid had known how to use a knife, or she'd learned in a hell of a hurry.

Reaching for the table lantern, she carried it past the washtub and looked into the hammock at Graciela's sleeping form. The kid had climbed onto a stool and then into the hammock. The light from the lantern outlined a faint milk mustache tracing her upper lip.

When Jenny heard Ty enter the shack, she said softly, "Looks like she can manage just fine when she doesn't have someone to do for her." Calling his attention to the cut meat and the fact that Graciela had climbed into the hammock unassisted should have given her a glow of smug pleasure, but it didn't.

Instead, she gazed down at Graciela and wondered how it would feel to know with absolute certainty that you would never again go to bed hungry. That you would always have a pillow under your head and clean sheets. To know you would never be alone. How would it feel not to fear tomorrow?

"I could use some light over here," Ty called from the table.

Lowering a finger, Jenny touched the gold locket pinned to Graciela's shift. Then she carried the lantern back to the table and sat in front of her steak. The first bite was cold and stringy.

"Senora Armijo brought a jug of pulque. Do you want some?"

She nodded, then pushed the bite-sized pieces of meat around her plate. Whatever appetite she'd had was gone. Giving it up, she shoved her plate away, then swallowed a generous swig of the pulque. The liquid scalded down her throat and brought a shine of moisture to her eyes.

"So what are you going to do when this journey is over?" she asked, watching Ty eat.

"I'll help Robert operate the ranch . . . run some cattle on my own place."

"Ranching is a demanding life," she commented, "but a good one. Don't have to worry where the next beefsteak is coming from."

When he finished eating, he leaned back in his chair and crossed an ankle over his knee. "Cigar?"

"Don't mind if I do." To her surprise, he leaned forward and lit it for her. It was pleasant sitting at the table, smoking, listening to the village quiet down for the night. She had feared it might feel awkward to sit without talking, but it didn't. That, she thought, was the measure of true companionship. Not that two people could talk, but that they could be comfortable just sitting together in silence.

"You look pretty in the lamplight."

Jenny choked and burst into a fit of coughing. "Damn it, Sanders. I've asked you a dozen times not to say that kind of crap to me."

"Why not? It's true." Squinting, he watched her through a curl of smoke. "You've got strong good features. You're the kind of woman who's going to get more handsome as the years go by. Long after more conventional beauties have faded, you'll still be turning men's heads."

She stared at him, then laughed with genuine amusement. "Funny how you're the only man who's noticed how all-fired pretty I am."

"Oh I doubt that. I might have the distinction of being one of the few who's mentioned it, but I'm sure as hell not the only man who's noticed."

Her cheeks turned scarlet, and her ribs suddenly ached. This kind of talk embarrassed her, made her deeply suspicious, and she didn't know how to respond. "Shut up," she said finally, focusing intently on the end of her cigar.

"Have you ever been kissed? I mean, really kissed?"

The question and the husky timbre of his voice made her twitch and feel strange inside. Her skin suddenly felt hot and itchy. "I've been kissed," she said defensively, scowling at him.

He grinned. "Must have been a brave man."

"What the hell is that supposed to mean?"

"You're an intimidating woman." His gaze traveled lazily over her face and throat. "I imagine most men would back away from a challenge like you."

"Huh!" Instead of patting her hair as she had a sudden idiotic desire to do, she blew a smoke ring toward the shadows in the corner. "Most men don't even see me. Which suits me just fine."

"If they don't see you, it's because you don't want them to. That's why you hide yourself under that shapeless poncho and wear an old hat pulled down to your ears." He released a stream of smoke and watched it drift into the darkness. "If you'd grow out your hair and wear a pretty dress, you'd have men lined up to get at you, darlin'."

Jenny wet her lips and swallowed. "Like that's what I want." When she realized this conversation was making her hands tremble, she stubbed out her cigar in disgust and made a face. "I don't want to talk about this."

"Instead, you wear that chip on your shoulder and dare anyone to pay you a compliment. You talk and act like one of the boys, so you don't have to deal with being one of the girls."

"Just shut the hell up."

"If I were to kiss you . . ." He paused, dropping a lazy lingering glance to her mouth. "Do you know how I'd do it?"

Her heart lurched and knocked against her rib cage. She gripped the edge of the table and squeezed her eyes into a warning squint. "I'm telling you for the last time . . . *shut up.*"

He kept his gaze on her mouth, studying her through eyes that seemed to smolder in the depths. "I'd start out slow. Real slow, so's not to spook you. I'd put my hands on your waist, low, almost on your hips. Then I'd draw you up against me. Let you feel what I was thinking." A smile touched his lips.

She understood the reference. Jenny tried to swallow, but her mouth was suddenly as dry as a desert bone. Eyes locked to his, unable to move a muscle, she held her breath and waited, wanting him to stop but helplessly wanting to hear more.

"I'd rub against you, slow like, getting the feel of you, letting you get the feel of me." His eyes narrowed, and his jaw clenched hard before he made it relax. "Then, I'd move my hands up your waist, under that poncho, right up your rib cage until I could feel the soft heat of your breasts resting on the tops of my hands."

"Shut up," Jenny whispered, staring at his mouth.

He flipped his cigar out the door of the shack and dropped his hands to his thighs. "I'd lean over you and put my mouth down next to yours, but I wouldn't kiss you yet." They stared at each other in the lamplight falling over the table. "I'd breathe you first. I'd sip your breath and hold it inside. Then I'd touch my tongue to your bottom lip."

The air ran out of Jenny and her shoulders collapsed. Her arm slid off the table, and her cigar dropped out of boneless fingers. "Oh my God," she murmured. Her heart slammed against her ribs and she heard her pulse thundering in her ears. The night gathered around her, dry and hot, and she felt as if she were strangling.

His gaze fastened on her mouth. "I'd run my tongue around those lips, tracing the shape and size. And then . . ." He rose to his feet, his face moving out of the light and into shadow. "Stand up, Jenny."

"I can't," she whispered, staring at him. Her knees had turned to soup. This time he hadn't even touched her. This time he'd melted her bones with words. Helpless to resist whatever would happen next, she gazed up at him with fear and confusion widening her eyes.

Ty took her hand and pulled her to her feet. Instantly,

she felt the heat of his body and her own quickened response. Eyes fastened on his firm, hard mouth, she licked her lips nervously and tried to speak. "Don't." The word emerged as a croak, totally lacking conviction.

She blinked and swallowed hard. She saw the smoldering desire in his narrowed gaze, and she thought he would kiss her. Thought she would surely die if he didn't. Instead, he raised a hand and drew his fingertips along her jaw, then slowly down her throat.

Jenny gasped. Pinpoints of fire sparked on her skin, lanced deep into her body. A tremor began in her toes and swept upward, shaking her as if she had the ague. Nothing like this had ever happened before.

She could easily have repulsed crude talk or a rough direct grab. God knew she'd done so plenty of times in the past. But she had no experience with and no defense against gentleness and seductive words.

Holding her hand, not speaking, Ty led her outside into moon-washed shadows. Helplessly, Jenny followed on trembling legs, not resisting when he leaned her against the wall of the shack. Unable to utter a word, she gazed up at him with large round eyes, waiting for whatever would happen next.

He placed a hand on the wall on either side of her face, then slowly, he leaned in to her, enveloping her within his heat and scent. The solid weight of his hips meeting hers made her suck in a sharp deep breath, and she closed her eyes on a low groan. He moved against her deliberately, pressing her against the wall, letting her feel the full power of his arousal.

Dropping his head, he murmured next to her ear, his voice thick and husky. "I wanted you the first time I saw you." His breath was warm and heavy, the pressure of his body hot against her. "I saw you go after Luis and I thought, there is a magnificent woman, a woman worth taming."

She wanted to object, wanted to laugh and tell him that no man would ever tame her. But she couldn't speak. Her heart slammed in her chest. Her skin was on fire. Hot weakness pervaded her body, and she felt a warm dampness spreading between her legs.

A sound almost like a sob caught in her throat. And she felt her hips moving against his as if imbued with a will of their own. His lips grazed her forehead, searing her nerve endings, and still the words murmured against her skin, but she scarcely heard.

Touch overwhelmed other sensations. She was blind to the white moon suspended in warm darkness, deaf to the hoarse whisper against her temple. Dimly she sensed the scent of him, hot and male, but it was touch that kindled a blaze in the pit of her stomach. His lips whispering against her temple, the pressure of his hips pressing her against the wall, the power of an arousal so hard that she felt the outline on her own flesh.

"Please," she whispered, lifting parted lips. His words, his touch created a wild need inside her, stripped her emotions raw, and crushed any thought of resistance. Unable to live another minute without his mouth on hers, she grabbed his shirt and pulled his upper body toward her, then circled his neck with her arms.

Instantly, his hands dropped to her waist and he shoved her roughly against the wall. When she gasped in surprise and pleasure, he ran his hard callused hands up her rib cage, holding her against the wall with his hips.

His mouth hovered an inch above hers. "Slowly," he whispered, his breath flowing across her lips, hot with the sweetness of pulque and the torment he inflicted on her.

Panting, squirming under the heat of his hands, Jenny let her head fall back against the wall as his thumbs caressed the underside of her breasts. She trembled violently, her hips returning the insistent pressure of his, her hands tugging and releasing in convulsive movements on his shoulders. She couldn't breathe, couldn't think; all she could do was feel the wildfire his touch sent shooting along her skin.

"Jenny." His voice was a hoarse, tortured command.

Swallowing hard, feeling the sweat trickling between her breasts, the wetness between her legs, she opened helpless eyes.

And finally, finally, his mouth came down on hers—hard, deliberate, possessive. Her arms tightened around his neck and she pulled him in to her, wrapped so tightly against his body that she could feel his heart pounding against her breasts, could feel the hard grind of his hipbones.

Wild and crazy with wanting, she opened her lips to his tongue and thrust back with her own. Her fist closed in his hair, and she pulled him harder against her. Beneath her poncho, his hands closed over her breasts, and the sudden heat through her shirt scalded her and made her gasp and break from his kiss. His lips trailed down the arch of her throat, then returned to her mouth to conquer and ravage and leave her breathless and panting and mindless with need.

Then he was holding her, whispering against her ear, his hands stroking warm circles on her back. Gradually her violent trembling subsided and her breath quieted. She rested her head on his shoulder and wondered what in the hell had happened to her.

"I think we should get some shut-eye. We didn't have much sleep last night," he was saying when his words began to sort themselves out and make sense.

Easing back in his arms, she blinked at him, too dazed to fully grasp his words. When she did, she didn't understand what had happened. She had felt his powerful desire, had expected him to drag her to the ground and take her. As crazed as she had been, she wouldn't have resisted. He must have known that.

Stumbling, trying to steady her mind, she moved back into the shack and checked on Graciela. The kid was sound asleep, unaware that minutes ago the world had tilted and spun out of orbit.

When she turned, Ty was standing in the doorway, a dark silhouette with the moonlight sharpening his lean angular form.

Jenny licked her lips, tasting him there. "Why?" she whispered.

He knew what she was asking. "It has to be your decision," he said in a voice still raw with desire. "When you're ready, you'll come to me." A match flared, and he lit a cigar. "Get some sleep."

Suddenly she felt bone tired, as limp as a washrag. "What are you going to do?"

"Have a smoke. Do some thinking."

For a long moment, she didn't move. Then she sat on the edge of a hammock and swung herself inside, listening as he sat at the table and poured another tumbler of pulque.

"Ty?"

"Yeah?"

She stared up at the dark rafters. "I was wrong. Until tonight, I'd never been kissed."

"I didn't think so," he said softly.

Chapter Thirteen

In the morning, nearly thirty people accompanied them to the railroad tracks. Although the train steamed past every day, it seldom stopped; therefore, the villagers made a festive event of the occasion. Women wrapped themselves in their best rebozos, and the men wore starched white shirts and embroidered sombreros. While Ty and Jenny's horses were being loaded into a boxcar, a boy ran alongside the train holding an armadillo up for passengers to see. Women sold husk-wrapped tamales through the train windows and tortillas folded around hot chorizo. Someone strummed a guitar, and two men danced around their sombreros, puffs of dust following the rowels on their spurs.

Once the horses were loaded, Ty led Jenny and Graciela into one of the middle cars and found seats for them and a place to store their saddlebags.

"I hate the train," Graciela stated. "It's hot and it smells bad." Making a face, she shoved a chicken off the end of the bench seat. "When will we get there?"

Jenny used the end of a newly bought shawl to fan her

face. The air was stifling and stank of roosters and dogs and greasy food and old sweat. "You don't even know where 'there' is," she said, looking out the window at the villagers waving at the faces peering back from inside the train.

Before he sat down, Ty scrutinized their fellow passengers. Most were women and children. Two old men sat together at the rear of the car, three men appeared to be traveling with their families. They looked hot and uncomfortable, but not dangerous. No one displayed more than a cursory interest in the new arrivals.

Once the train got under way, he leaned to pull up the window against the soot and cinders that flew inside and speckled the clothing Jenny had purchased from Senora Armijo. Beneath a grey shawl she wore a white blouse tucked into a faded blue skirt. The clothing was worn, but clean and pressed, and attracted less attention than her trousers and poncho would have. Graciela's new clothing was similar; both wore untrimmed straw hats.

"You look beautiful," he said, smiling at them after settling his lanky frame on the hard wooden seat.

Graciela returned his smile and patted the thick bun pinned on her small neck. Jenny glared, then returned her gaze to the window.

She'd been strangely subdued this morning, tossing him quick glances that he couldn't read, hastily looking away when he caught her studying him. He suspected she was remembering last night, just as he was.

Lighting a cigar, Ty smoked and watched the desert roll past the streaked window. Occasionally the horizon revealed glimpses of distant mountains, but largely the short grass and dry shrubs pocking the Central Plateau offered little distraction.

His thoughts drifted from the hot light of day to feverish moonlight kisses. He didn't regret kissing her. Considering the level of tension between them, kissing had been inevitable.

What had surprised him most was Jenny's innocence. She was a tough, skeptical woman who had lived an unconventional life. He doubted there was much that she hadn't seen, hadn't experienced. As a result, she had learned to place a distance between herself and others, had learned to shield her emotions and the central kernel that was herself. She was a loner, asking nothing, expecting little.

But when it came to lovemaking, Jenny Jones was a babe in the woods, as vulnerable as an adolescent. Drawing on his cigar, he studied the clean firm line of her profile.

Even before he led her outside the shack, he had sensed that she would surrender. There was no guile in her, no coyness. In the seduction arena, she possessed no defense; she wore her emotions like a beacon pointing the way. Her wide eyes and trembling lips had informed him that she would follow where he led. Instinctively, he understood that Jenny had been taken, but never wooed or seduced. She'd experienced sex, but not lovemaking. He would have wagered his horse that she'd never been fully aroused before last night.

The question raised by the light of day was why hadn't he pressed his advantage? God knows she had been willing, as wildly and wonderfully responsive as any woman he had known. Fully aroused, she had been ready and eager to give herself, so why had he pulled up short?

Frowning, he listened to the ratchety click of the wheels and the din reverberating inside the car. The squawk of chickens, the cries of children, the sawing buzz of conversation.

God knew he'd wanted her, had been hungry for her. His desire had been powerful enough that he'd ached for hours afterward. Even now, sweat slicked his brow at the memory of her heavy breasts resting on top of his hands. He didn't dare let himself recall how she'd twisted her hips against him, wild and uncontrolled, hot with promise.

Leaning over his knees, he crushed his cigar under his bootheel, then pulled the scarf from his neck and blotted sweat from his throat and face. When he saw her watching, he commented defensively, "It's like a Turkish bathhouse in here."

"You ever been in a Turkish bathhouse?"

"Once. In San Francisco."

"What is a Turkish bathhouse?" Graciela asked. She sat next to Jenny, as prim and proper as a tiny schoolmarm, her hands folded in her lap, her spine straight against the seat.

Today he saw Robert in Graciela's eyes, in her chin, in the curious way she tilted her head. He also recognized an echo of his mother, his father, perhaps himself. He wondered what old man Barrancas would see in this child, the thought surprising him. Would Don Antonio see Marguarita in the shape of Graciela's mouth? When he noted the child's aristocratic carriage, would he rediscover the wife he had buried? Would he glimpse himself?

Ty flexed his shoulders in an effort to find a comfortable spot against the hard wooden back of the seat bench. Cigar-smoke circled his head, expelled by a man sitting directly behind him.

"The train's going to stop at Verde Flores in about three hours," he said quietly, looking at Jenny. She met his gaze and pressed her lips together. "Maybe we should talk about that."

"What's a Turkish bathhouse?" Graciela asked again.

"People go there to take baths," Jenny snapped. Shifting on the seat, she adjusted her shawl, letting Ty see the pistol shoved in her waistband. He also saw the shape of her breasts curving beneath gathers of thin material. Christ. She had breasts to haunt a man's dreams.

"I figure the cousins are going to have someone checking every northbound that rolls through."

The first time he'd seen her, he had thought she was attractive in an untraditional, rawboned sort of way. The memory now impressed him as strange. It seemed impossible that he could have overlooked her beauty.

Her mouth was wide and firm, the lower lip lushly full. Coppery brows capped eyes as blue as a summer sky, fringed by thick, pale lashes. Her face and throat were tanned, but that no longer seemed unusual. Instead, the rose and gold tones enhanced her vitality and the richness of her coloring. Although he'd grown accustomed to her short hair, he could imagine it long, flowing down her back like a sheet of silken flame.

"Sanders?" She glared at him. "What the hell's the matter with you? Are you listening?"

Graciela elbowed her in the ribs. "You said hell."

"Sorry." She rolled her eyes, then narrowed them into a squint. "What are you thinking about?"

There was so much accusation and warning in the question that he almost laughed. The sudden color in her cheeks confirmed that she had guessed his thoughts.

"We need a plan," he said, speaking to her mouth. She raised a hand and covered her lips, the self-conscious gesture making him smile. The warning in her stare didn't mask a flash of helplessness opening at the back of her eyes.

Suddenly he understood why he hadn't pressed his advantage last night. He didn't want her feeling helpless or confused, not this particular woman.

The night she had left him hog-tied in the desert with his nose in the dirt, he had sworn that he would find her point of vulnerability and use it to punish her.

Well, he'd found her soft spot, and he'd proved that he could level her with seductive words and a little tenderness. It surprised and irritated him to discover that he was loath to do so. He wanted her helpless from a point of strength, not helpless from ignorance. He wanted her to surrender to *him*, not merely to skill and experience.

"You make me feel crazy inside," he said softly, staring at her. Sunlight slanted through the dirty window turning her eyes almost translucent. A light sheen of perspiration lay on her flushed face like dew. It continually surprised him how different she could look from day to day, from minute to minute.

"She makes me feel loco, too," Graciela said happily. Hero worship shone in her eyes and the pleasure of a shared opinion. Startled, Ty frowned at her, then looked back at Jenny.

She clasped her hands in her lap so tightly that the knuckles turned white. "We need to stop thinking about— other things—and devise a plan," she said tightly, speaking through clenched teeth.

"Can you stop thinking about—other things?" he asked. He sure as hell couldn't.

"What other things?" Graciela demanded, looking back and forth between them.

"Nothing important," Jenny said sharply, her cheeks turning crimson.

Ty laughed softly. He would conquer her helplessness kiss by kiss. Though he suspected he would live to regret it, he would teach her who controlled events between men and women. When she understood her power, that's when her surrender would be the sweetest.

The sun was directly overhead when the train chuffed into the Verde Flores station. The terrain had altered and softened. Trees flanked the river that tumbled through town, clumps of mesquite and creosote bush flowed away from the village perimeters.

An hour earlier, according to plan, they had exchanged places with a family in the last seats across the aisle so Graciela wouldn't be framed in the window on the depot side of the train.

As soon as the train lurched to a stop, Ty glanced at Jenny who nodded grimly, then he walked down the aisle and stepped outside onto the platform between the cars. He quickly glanced across the sagging depot porch. People rushed to greet passengers getting off, others stood, gathering belongings prior to boarding. Leaning out, Ty looked up and down the length of the train, then, scowling, he returned inside and slid into the seat next to Jenny.

"Three men," he said quietly. "One's on the platform. One just boarded the car directly behind the locomotive. The other is checking the cars at the rear."

She nodded. "They'll walk through the cars, working toward each other."

"That's my guess." He touched Graciela's shoulder, gazed into her wide eyes. "We discussed this, remember?" She nodded solemnly. "If one of them gets past us, you run outside and make a hell of a noise. We'll see you or hear you. Otherwise, stay right here. Don't move."

When he finished, Jenny placed her hands on Graciela's shoulders and peered into her face. "Don't go having any second thoughts. Don't start thinking your cousins want to take you back to Aunt Tete. You know what they want." Graciela bit her lips and nodded. "Say it."

"Money," his niece whispered. "They want to hurt me."

"That's right," Jenny stated firmly. "If you get some crackbrained idea about joining up with a cousin, say this word: Snakes." She stared into Graciela's eyes. "We have to trust you, kid. Graciela. We're trusting you not to run off. Tell me you won't."

"I won't."

"Your word is your bond."

Ty touched Jenny's shoulder. "She understands. We're losing time." When she stood and straightened her shoulders, he watched her gaze harden as she shifted her thoughts toward the men searching for them. "You go forward, I'll take the back."

He wasted another minute gazing deep into her eyes, fighting a protective urge. The straw hat and skirt made him very aware that she was a woman. It impressed him as crazy to send a female off to fight a man.

Hell, what was he thinking? He'd known men who couldn't throw a punch as hard as she did. "How's your arm?"

"Like new. Get moving." She glanced at Graciela again, then turned smartly in a swirl of skirts and strode toward the door at the front of the car without a backward glance.

He frowned, watching her go. He would have felt better about this if she'd been wearing her usual trousers and shapeless poncho.

"Don't worry," Graciela said calmly, not a doubt in her voice or demeanor. "Jenny is very strong and very brave."

"Yes, she is." Leaving Graciela alone concerned him. "Don't move."

But she did. Before he had taken two steps, she changed seats, moving forward to sit with a Mexican family. He nodded. She was a clever kid.

Moving quickly, he walked through the next crowded passenger car, then the next. The cousins weren't leaving anything to chance. The man he'd spotted at the tail end of the train had started with the boxcars first. Once Ty was certain the man hadn't yet entered the passenger cars, he dropped to the ground and sprinted to the closest boxcar. The doors were open and he pulled himself inside, almost colliding with a man preparing to jump out.

Ty didn't give the bastard a chance to collect his thoughts. Springing to his feet, he came up with an uppercut that sent the Barrancas cousin flying back among the horses and mules.

Pressing his advantage, he jumped forward and took a fist in the gut. Hammering at each other, the two of them rolled in the bedding, trying to avoid stamping hooves.

Jenny walked swiftly through the forward car, stepped onto the platform, then peered through the window into the next car. Immediately, she ducked out of sight. Chulo moved slowly down the middle aisle, scanning each face he passed.

Leaning out of the platform enclosure, she tried to judge how close they were to departure. She noticed the officials were already aboard before a cloud of steam obscured her vision. The whistle shrieked overhead, then the cars lurched and clashed together.

As the train rolled forward, she grabbed an iron handle to steady her balance, then withdrew her pistol and waited for the door to open. When it did, she let Chulo step past her and reach for the door to the next car before she moved up and jabbed him in the spine with the barrel of her pistol.

He held his gun at his side, against his leg. She twisted it out of his fingers and smiled when he swore. "Put your hands flat against the door," she ordered crisply, tossing his pistol off of the train.

Already Verde Flores receded behind them and the train was moving faster. Hot wind blew across the platform, caught Jenny's straw hat and snatched it away, fluttered her skirt around her ankles. She waited for the train to reach top speed, idly listening to Chulo swear and threaten and tell her what he and the Barrancases were going to do to her. She couldn't steal their little cousin. They would kill her. They would take their pleasure on her first. And et cetera. Jenny liked the word, et cetera. It covered a lot of ground.

"All right, pig, here's what we're going to do." She shoved the pistol barrel tight against the roll of fat at his waist. "You're going to take one step backward, turn right, and you're going to jump off this train. If you even think about hesitating, I'll shoot." She moved back, opening a space between them so he couldn't grab her. "Move, you son of a whore. *Jump.*"

Wind whipped her hair and skirt, the platform swayed back and forth beneath her boots. And Chulo was fast.

He spun with a snarl and she didn't see the knife in his fist until it had slashed across her waist and the bloodied blade flashed in the sunlight.

She staggered backward toward the door of the forward car, firing as she fell. Chulo doubled forward, grabbing his gut. Jenny didn't see him fall off the train. She was frantically grabbing for a handle, trying to keep her hem from snagging in the coupling. When she felt safe, she looked up. The platform was empty. The son of a bitch had gone over the side.

Now she peered down at herself, inspecting a red stain seeping across her white blouse. Damn it. The wound didn't hurt yet, but it would. Swearing between her teeth, she shoved her hot pistol into her waistband. Pressing a hand against the wound, she shrugged her shawl into place to conceal the blood, then jerked open the heavy door, walked through the passenger car, across the next platform, and into the following car.

Ty stood up beside Graciela and strode toward her,

glaring and kicking chickens out of the aisle. He gripped her shoulders. "What the hell took you so long?"

"Do whatever it takes to move the people sitting across the aisle from us. We need privacy."

When he lifted a questioning eyebrow, she opened her shawl enough to reveal a glimpse of blood. "Christ!" His eyes returned to her face. "How bad?"

"Don't know yet," she said through clenched teeth. The pain was beginning. "My guess is, I'll need some stitching."

"I'll get that family moved."

He managed it faster than she would have imagined, changing sullen resistance to smiling acquiescence with a handful of pesos. Jenny pressed her hand to the wound, feeling the blood well between her fingers, and hoped her weaving steps would be attributed to the motion of the train. By the time she reached the last seat, sweat gleamed on her forehead and her face was ashen. Dropping onto the seat, she closed her eyes.

"Jenny?" Graciela stared at her.

"Your son-of-a-bitch cousin Chulo knifed me."

Leaning over her, Graciela tugged at the edge of the shawl, then gasped and covered her mouth. She twisted away, one hand pressed to her stomach, one hand against her lips.

Ty sat across from them facing forward, watching to make sure no one paid them any attention. "Let's see how bad it is," he growled.

Jenny swallowed, then removed her pistol and handed it to him. Clamping down a groan, she eased her blouse out of her waistband and raised it to a point beneath her breasts. "You tell me. How bad?" she whispered, watching his face.

He met her eyes. "About four inches long. Looks shallow at the ends, deeper in the middle. You're right. You need stitches." Reaching beneath the seat, he pulled up a set of saddlebags, then swept a look down the length of the car. "Any ideas on how we're going to manage this?"

"How long before we reach Chihuahua?"

He shrugged. "Assuming a minimum of stops, probably not until midmorning tomorrow."

It was too long to wait. She needed tending now. "All right." Concentrating, she tested the pain for bite and depth, decided she could bear it. There wasn't much choice. "You carrying any liquor in those saddlebags, cowboy? I could sure use a drink."

He removed a bottle of tequila, pulled the cork with his teeth, then handed it across to her. "Obliged," she muttered, before taking a long pull. Liquid fire roared toward her belly. "All right. Find Graciela's nightshift. It's probably the cleanest thing we've got. Tear it into bandage strips, and we'll need a couple of mop-up rags."

Graciela sat on her knees on the seat, staring at Jenny with tears running down her cheeks. "I forgot to tell God not to punish you."

"God didn't do this. Your fat pig of a cousin did," Jenny spit. A look of satisfaction hardened her eyes. "He won't do it again, that I can promise you."

Graciela's hands fluttered, reaching, withdrawing, wanting to touch but afraid to. "I'm sorry, Jenny. I'm sorry."

"It's not your fault, kid." The tequila helped, so she took another long swallow, watching Ty rip the hem off

Graciela's nightdress. "What happened to the other bas-tard?"

"He's lying in the desert somewhere between here and Verde Flores, waiting for the vultures."

"Good." She took the length of hem from him and wadded it, then soaked the cloth with tequila. "I need your help," she said to Graciela. "Hold my blouse up out of the way."

The wooden seat back shielded them from the rest of the car. Anyone looking in their direction would see only the back of Jenny's head, would see Ty smoking and glaring at them.

Jenny drew a breath and exhaled slowly before she pressed the tequila-soaked cloth against the wound. White-hot pain chewed a path to her brain, and she sucked in a hissing breath, blinking against a scald of tears. "Je-zus! Sorry, kid, but . . . oh my God."

Smothering sobs, Graciela slid down the seat and curled into a ball, shaking and twitching. She covered her head with her shawl.

When she could make herself do it, Jenny held the bloody rag tightly beneath the wound like a dam and poured tequila directly into the wound, catching the over-flow with the cloth. Her hands shook, and she ground her teeth together so hard that the grinding sound was all she could hear.

"Lord a'mighty, that smarts." Gasping, she tried to draw a full breath. "What about the third man? Did he get on the train?"

"I don't know," Ty said gruffly.

When she finished cleaning the wound with the liquor, she fell back against the seat back, closed her eyes, and swallowed a long draw from the tequila bottle. Panting, she rested a minute. When she opened her eyes, Ty was staring at her with an unreadable expression.

"This feels worse than getting shot," she said, testing the steadiness of her voice. A little quavery, but better than she'd expected it would be.

He passed her a lit cigar, and she filled her lungs with hot smoke, then exhaled. Ty waited a full minute. "Here's where it gets sticky," he said in a low voice, watching her. "I can't stitch it without getting down on my knees in front of you." They both knew that would certainly attract unwanted attention. "And you can't do it yourself . . ."

Jenny nodded. She dropped a hand on Graciela's shaking body. "Kid? Graciela? Stop crying and sit up. We have to talk."

Graciela pulled the shawl away from her tear-stained face and stared up. "Are you going to die?"

"Well hell no." She bit her lip. "Make that, shoot no. But I'd have to say that I'm mighty . . . displeased right now. And I need your help." Forcing her mind into a narrow channel, she concentrated on the kid. She had to be careful here; the damned kid would remember every minute of this. What was said, what was done, how it was said and done. It was a fricking pain in the butt to be responsible for a kid, to have to set examples.

"You need *my* help?" Bewildered, Graciela sat up, clutching the shawl to her chest. She glanced at Ty's frown, then back to Jenny.

Jenny licked her lips and thought about the kid instead of the pain. "You told me you could sew, remember?"

Graciela nodded solemnly, not yet understanding.

Jenny gazed into her eyes. "Graciela . . . I need you to sew the edges of the wound together. Can you do that?"

Horror screwed the kid's expression toward the center of her face. Little gasping sounds bleated out of her chest. "I . . . I can't."

"Jenny." Ty leaned forward, staring in disapproval.

"Who else have we got?" she snapped, cutting him off, not looking away from Graciela's white face. "You can do this. It's just like sewing a seam. All you have to do is sew the edges up against each other. I'd do it myself except I can't see the wound." Her breasts were in the way.

Graciela shook her head back and forth, wrung her hands. Tears gushed down her face, and the usual snot. "I can't, I can't."

"Wipe her nose, will you?" Jenny said in disgust. She took another deep swig from the mouth of the tequila bottle.

"For Christ's sake, Jenny. This is too much to ask of a kid. I'll do it," Ty growled, fumbling in the saddlebags for the sewing kit.

"Fine," she said, glaring. "Give the kid your pistol and let her serve as lookout. Tell her to shoot the third cousin if he comes in here looking for us." She knew she'd made her point by the frustration drawing his face.

"If the man on the depot platform boarded the train, don't you think we'd have seen him by now?"

"Maybe. Or maybe he's biding his time, waiting for the next stop."

His face darkened, and he turned his gaze to Graciela. "I'm sorry, honey. I don't like this any more than you do, but it looks like you'll have to do the sewing."

Graciela had both small hands clamped to her cheeks and was crying and shaking her head. "I can't! I can't!"

"Listen to me," Jenny said, speaking quietly. Gently, she pulled one of the kid's hands into her own, leaving a bloody smear. "If we don't stitch the wound, it won't stop bleeding. It won't start to heal." She gazed into Graciela's wide wet eyes. "If we don't stop the bleeding, I'm going to be in real trouble. Do you understand what I'm saying?"

"I can't stick a needle into . . ." A shudder twitched down the kid's body. Her face had turned the color of whey.

"Yes, you can. Hide is tougher than cotton, it's like stitching leather. But you can do it. You just have to push the needle a little harder."

Graciela dropped her head on Jenny's shoulder. Her back shook. "It'll hurt you."

"Oh yeah. It's going to hurt like a son of a . . . gun. I'll try not to scream if you won't."

"The train is shaking too much!"

Jenny lifted a hand and stroked the kid's hair, wondering what had happened to Graciela's hat. "I trust you to do the best you can."

Graciela pulled back and stared into her eyes. "You trust me?" she whispered.

"I'm trusting you with my life, kid." Jenny stared back. "And that's okay. See, I figure you owe me. I took care of you when you were sick, now it's your turn to do something for me. I was there for you, now you have to be here for me. The fact is, you've got it easy. I'd rather sew a few stitches any day than mop up buckets of vomit. God!"

Graciela wiped her eyes and nose on her sleeve, something she wouldn't ordinarily have dreamed of doing, then she slid a glance toward the sewing packet Ty was kneading between his fingers. "Can I have a taste of tequila?"

"Hell no." Jenny scowled. "If you start drinking next, so help me I'm going to have to smack you bad." She closed her eyes, took a couple of deep breaths, then looked at Ty. "Give her the sewing packet." To Graciela, she added, "Pick the strongest thread and double it. Tie off each stitch. And Graciela?"

The sewing packet was shaking in her hands. "Yes?"

"If I should faint, don't stop sewing. In fact, if I faint, you sew as fast as you can, understand?"

Ty muttered a string of curses, then stood in the aisle with his back to them, his angry stance daring anyone to approach. Jenny flicked a glance at him, then motioned to Graciela to kneel in front of her.

It took several tries before Graciela picked up the rhythm of the train's sway and was able to thread the needle. Her hands shook so badly that the thimble continued to fall off her finger. Jenny took a long hit from the tequila bottle, then she and Graciela stared at each other.

"We've been through a lot," Jenny said quietly. "What we're doing now is just one more thing. No harder than anything else."

"Does it hurt?" Graciela whispered, her eyes wide, the needle trembling between her fingers.

"Hurts a lot." The wound hurt like a son of a bitch, and she wanted to say so, but she didn't. She was as proud of her restraint as she was of anything she'd ever done.

Marguarita, I hope you are fricking paying attention. If I ever had reason or provocation to spit out some choice cussing, now's the time, by God. I hope to hell you're noticing what a good example I'm setting here.

"Are you going to cry?"

"I might. I would hate for you to notice, so don't look up." She peeled back the bloody tequila-soaked cloth to expose the wound and heard Graciela suck in a sharp, hissing breath. "When you're finished, pour more tequila on it." Closing her eyes, clutching the blouse up out of the way, she leaned against the seat back and tried to hold her breathing steady and regular.

The first jab was no more than a pinprick, enough to get her attention but too tentative to penetrate skin. So was the second jab.

Jenny pried open her jaws. "For God's sake, are you going to sew or are you going to just torture me? Do it and get it over with."

On the kid's fourth try, the needle went in, and Jenny fainted.

Chapter
Fourteen

Ty made a pillow out of the saddlebags, then covered Jenny with her shawl when she curled down on the seat. Kneeling beside her, he studied her flushed face, hoping she wasn't feverish. "Is the bandage too tight?"

"Feels like a corset."

"Do you want more tequila?" He smoothed a length of sweat-damp hair back from her forehead. "We have more tortillas if you're hungry." She shook her head. "All right, get some rest. Sleep is the best healer."

He eased back on the seat beside Graciela and lit another cigar to occupy his hands. Outside, the light was starting to shade toward evening. Long shadows pointed away from the cacti, which were taller now than those growing deeper in the wastelands. If he'd been on horseback, he would have noticed the northern incline of the land, but the motion of the train distorted such observations.

Smoking, seething with anger and concern, he studied Jenny's pale face. The way her lashes curved in a coppery crescent on her cheek, the way her lips parted slightly.

It should have been him. Not her. Hell, she'd already been shot. If someone had to get wounded, it was his turn. Frowning, he glared out the window over Graciela's head.

Marguarita might have chosen her daughter's protector hastily, but she had chosen wisely. She must have sensed Jenny's fearless persistence, her stubborn and dogged commitment to a promise once given. So far, she'd received a blackened eye, a cracked lip, a shot-up arm, and a slashed stomach. And they weren't yet out of Mexico.

Gradually he became aware of Graciela's low murmur beside him. "What did you say?"

"I'm praying," she answered in a choked voice. "I'm telling God that I didn't mean it about making Jenny bleed."

"Listen." He dropped an arm around her shoulders and let her burrow into his side. "What happened to Jenny wasn't your fault."

"I asked God to punish her," she mumbled against his waistcoat.

Instantly the conversation tumbled into deep water. Ty drew on the cigar, searching for answers as ephemeral as smoke, not sure if he could shape them into the form his niece needed to hear. If someone had inquired, he would have said he was a spiritual man but not religious. To him, God was a spark within every living thing, an artist who painted with sunset clouds and ocean mist, a sculptor shaping human clay, earthly soil, and distant stars. The way he saw things, God was the creator. Any dogma beyond that was nit-picking.

Never would he have believed that he might be called upon to interpret God for a child. He wondered if Robert had any inkling of how parenthood was going to change his life.

"Well, God doesn't grant unjust requests." All he could do was hope for the best. "You wanted Jenny punished for killing your mother, and that was wrong. So God ignored that part of your prayers."

Graciela peered up at him. "But she *did* get punished. She got shot, and she got knifed."

"Well, I know that," he said, floundering. "All right, just for the sake of discussion, let's suppose that God punished Jenny because you asked him to." Now what? "Did you tell God that you'd changed your mind? You did change your mind, didn't you?"

She nodded solemnly, her gaze fastened on his face.

"Well, then. There you are. God turned things around by letting you be the person to save Jenny's life."

Graciela's eyebrows soared. "I saved Jenny's life?"

"She would have bled to death if you hadn't sewed her up."

She relaxed against his body like a dog he'd had once, going hot and limp on his chest. After several minutes of silence, she lifted her head. "Uncle Ty?"

"What?" He gazed at Jenny over her head.

"Sometimes I like Jenny," she whispered.

"So do I." The object of their discussion was snoring slightly, moaning softly every now and again. Smiling, he decided that any man who hankered after Jenny Jones lusted for reality, not fantasy.

"When I like her, it makes me feel bad inside because of my mama."

With one sentence, she tossed him back into the deep water. Awkwardly, he patted her shoulder to soften his words. "Honey, you know Jenny didn't kill your mother. You *know* that. Your mother explained it, Jenny's explained it, I've explained it. You've got to stop blaming Jenny. It isn't fair to her." Oh God, he'd made his niece cry again.

"Listen, it's all right for you to like Jenny." Pulling off his scarf, he pushed it into her hands. "Wipe your eyes. And your nose. It's better if you like Jenny, because . . ." His mind jumped around like spit on a griddle, searching for a reason. "Because you own her now. She's your responsibility." And he'd been the one telling Jenny not to expect too much of a kid. Damn.

"What?" Wadding up his scarf, she pressed it against her wet eyes.

In for a penny, in for a pound. He drew a breath. "Not far from the ranch where your daddy lives, there's a big town called San Francisco. In San Francisco, there's a lot of Chinamen."

"What's a Chinaman?"

"Men who used to live in China. Across the sea. Never mind that part. These Chinamen believe if you save a person's life, then you're responsible for that person forever after, sort of like you own them." Maybe it wasn't the Chinamen who believed that, he wasn't sure, but he'd heard it somewhere. "The important thing is, it's good that you like Jenny. It's all right to like her. It's a lot better that way since you own her now."

She hid her face behind his scarf, and he could almost hear her thinking. When she lowered the scarf, she was frowning. "Do you and Jenny own me? Because you saved me from my cousins with the snakes?"

This was getting complicated, and he wished he'd

never mentioned it. "I suppose we do," he conceded uneasily, irrevocably linking the three of them in her mind. This was a problem he'd worry about later.

When the train stopped to take on more passengers, he bought bowls of fiery stew for their supper, a loaf of fresh dark bread, and he refilled their canteens. After the train moved out again, Graciela wet a strip of her torn nightgown and gently wiped the sweat from Jenny's face. Jenny roused briefly, murmured something, then slept again. Ty watched his niece adjust the shawl around Jenny's shoulders and decided Jenny had been right and he had been wrong. Six-year-olds were capable of much more than he would ever have believed.

Graciela lifted his arm and nestled beneath it, resting her head on his chest. "Tell me a story."

His eyebrows rose toward his hat brim, and he cleared his throat. "I don't know any stories."

"Tell me about when you and my daddy were little boys."

"You don't want to hear about that." But she did, so hesitantly at first, then with growing pleasure, he told her about the time he and Robert had tried to steal Don Antonio Barrancas's prize bull and how he'd gotten gored for his trouble. "Right in the butt," he said, laughing. "Couldn't sit for a week." Then he told her how his mother had always baked an extra cherry pie because she knew her boys would steal one, and about the time he and Robert had sneaked out their bedroom window to sleep in the haystack but Cal caught them and blistered their behinds. He might have talked until midnight, remembering himself and Robert, except he noticed that she'd fallen asleep.

Trying not to wake her, he lit another cigar and gazed

out the window as the train rolled through the desert night. Graciela was not his daughter, and Jenny was not his woman. But it felt good to watch over them while they slept as if they were his. He would have torn the limbs off anyone who came near them.

For the first time in his life, Ty glimpsed why a man might choose the aggravation of a family.

Jenny struggled to sit up, blinking at the morning sunlight. Across from her, Graciela still slept, her head in Ty's lap, but Ty was awake, watching her.

"Mornin'," she said, pulling her shawl down over her bloodied blouse. "Did you get any sleep?"

"Some. How are you feeling?"

"I'd have to say I've felt better. This damn train is shaking me to pieces. Can I have some water, please?" Their fingers brushed when he handed her the canteen, and she glanced at him, frowned, then poured water on a strip of Graciela's nightshift and washed her face and hands.

The desert outside the window was a sun-baked sand and alkali plain, but here and there she spotted a few bony, mean-looking cattle. She wondered what they found to eat out there.

After running her tongue around her teeth she drank deeply from the canteen, then replaced the cap. "We're almost clear of the wastelands. We'll start seeing farms and ranches soon." Leaning, she scanned the western horizon, spotted towering cacti and low brown hills curving against the morning sky. She'd made the El Paso–Chihuahua freight run enough times to recognize the terrain.

"We need to hole up for a few days," Ty announced quietly, watching her comb her fingers through her hair. "Give you a chance to mend and get your strength back."

Slipping a hand beneath her shawl, she gingerly explored with her fingertips, tracing the bandage that Ty and Graciela had wrapped around her waist. She couldn't decide if the pain was less or about the same as yesterday. Pain was a hard thing to remember, hard to define by degrees.

"The cousins are going to find the bodies we left behind," she pointed out, resting against the hard seat back. "Luis is still out there. He's going to come after us."

"Chihuahua is big enough that we could stay there a month, and they'd never find us."

That was true. Nearly two hundred years old, the city of Chihuahua rose like an oasis among roses and orange groves. Gone were the mining shacks and narrow lanes of the Colonial era. Now the city boasted broad, clean streets and an aqueduct three miles long. A profitable trade system flourished between Chihuahua and Texas, which had contributed to Chihuahua's growth and importance. By comparison, Durango was a mere whistle-stop.

"The cousins are going to dog us all the way to the Rio Grande, aren't they?" Jenny murmured, closing her eyes.

"The way I figure, the worst is behind us. When you can travel comfortably we'll take the train to El Paso, then change to the Southern Pacific. The Southern Pacific will take us all the way to San Francisco. We'll buy a wagon and team in San Francisco and two days later we'll be drinking coffee in my mother's kitchen." He paused. "You don't have to go all the way, Jenny. You can say good-bye in El Paso."

She made a snorting sound, then gasped and placed a

hand against her waist. "You know better than that. I'm sticking until the end. I'm not saying good-bye until I hand the kid over to your sainted brother. Besides, there's nothing for me in El Paso anymore."

"Good," he said softly, his eyes clear and intense in the early light.

Good? That was a change. Turning her face to the window, Jenny pretended to peer outside, but slid her gaze back to the cowboy. Just looking at him turned her insides to liquid. He sat wide-legged, one hand on Graciela's back, the other hooked on his belt. Dark stubble shadowed his jaw. Far from being unappealing, the new whiskers hardened his features and made him look dangerous. Her lower stomach tightened, and she remembered his mouth hot on hers. Lordy. How could she be hankering when she was hungry, weak, and wounded?

Being kissed—really kissed—must have knocked loose some kind of craziness in her brain. All day yesterday and first thing today, the only thing she could think about when she looked at him were those wild erotic kisses in the moonlight. All of her life she'd laughed at romantic notions of moonlight and endearments and something as stupid and awkward as a kiss. But that was before. Now it was after.

She licked her lips and saw his jaw tighten as he watched. "All right, I can't stand it. Why did you say 'good' when I said I'm staying until the end?"

His hard gaze devoured her, moving slowly over her face and throat. "Because I'm not ready to let you go," he said in a husky voice. "You and I have unfinished business."

A light shiver of dread and anticipation trailed down

her spine, and she bit her lower lip, staring at him, trying to catch her breath.

Suddenly, she knew it would happen. Her and Ty. It wouldn't matter that in her heart she knew sex was nothing more than three minutes of dry pain and disappointment. It wouldn't matter that she was scared to death of catching a baby. She met his gaze and felt her heart lurch, and sensed an emptiness she'd never known before. Filling that emptiness was tied to him, and it would drive them both loco until they gave in to it. And they would, because the hankering quivered and flashed between them like lightning sizzling along invisible wires. Unless they answered the hankering, the lightning would burn them both to crisps.

"I'm hungry," Graciela said, sitting up and rubbing her eyes with both fists.

Jenny held Ty's narrowed gaze for another minute, then turned to Graciela with relief.

From the window of their hotel room, they could see the twin spires of the Church of San Francisco rising above the rooftops of Chihuahua. The street below was broad and lined with fragrant orange trees. In addition to the usual wagon traffic and burro carts, a smart black carriage spun over the cobblestones.

Jenny let the curtain drop and turned back to the room, casting longing eyes toward the two beds. All she wanted to do was curl into a ball and sleep.

"When will Uncle Ty come back?" Graciela sat on one of the beds and bounced up and down, testing the resiliency of the mattress.

"He returned to the depot to fetch our horses. Since

we've decided we won't need them again, he'll arrange with a stable to sell them." The water in the painted pitcher on top of the dresser was cool, and she filled a tumbler. She couldn't seem to drink enough water. "Get off the bed. I need to lie down."

"I'll help you take off your boots."

Jenny blinked in surprise. "Well, that would be right nice." Sitting on the mattress with a sigh, she extended her feet and Graciela tugged off her boots. Jenny wiggled her toes and sighed. "Feels good."

"What can I do now?"

"Something quiet. All I know is that I need to lie down and rest." The trip from depot to hotel had been short, but carriage wheels bouncing over street stones had shaken her so badly that she'd worried her stitches had broken loose. Pulling up her blouse, she checked for wetness on the bandage, relieved to discover the wrappings remained dry.

"I don't have anything to do," Graciela said in a whiny pout. "I wish you'd tell me a story."

"I'm too tired. Go look out the window." Crawling beneath the blanket, Jenny pushed her face into a soft feather pillow. Pillows were the epitome of luxury. If she could sleep on a soft pillow every night, she'd think she was living the life of a princess.

She was almost asleep when she felt a slight pressure on the mattress. When she opened her eyes, Graciela's face was only a few inches from hers. The kid knelt beside the bed, her arms folded on the sheets. She rested her chin on her hands, studying Jenny.

"What the hell—dickens—are you doing?"

"I own you."

"What?" Jenny sat up and stared. "Nobody owns me."

"Yes I do," Graciela insisted solemnly. "Uncle Ty explained it."

After Jenny heard the story, she frowned. "I knew a Chinaman in Denver when I was working in a washhouse, and he never said anything about owning someone if you saved their life."

"It's true. Uncle Ty said so." Graciela fluffed the pillow, and told Jenny to lie back down. Jenny stared, then did so. "I saved your life all by myself, so now I have to take care of you until you die. Owning someone means you have to be responsible for them. Do you know what responsible means?"

"Kid, I know more words than you will ever know in your whole life," Jenny said in disgust. "And you don't own me, and you aren't responsible for me." Graciela continued to kneel beside the bed, observing her. "Stop looking at me."

"You and Uncle Ty own me too. Because you saved my life."

"Now listen." Jenny sat up again. "Nobody owns you either, and they never will. You own your own self. You're responsible for yourself, and you take care of yourself. You can't depend on anyone but yourself."

Her words hung in the air, giving her time to reach the appalled conclusion that they were not true. She and Ty had depended upon each other almost from the minute they had joined forces. She had depended on Graciela to stitch her up and stop her wound from bleeding.

"All right, sometimes you have to depend on other people," she amended feebly. After years of being totally self-sufficient, she was suddenly depending on others. The realization shocked her. How had this happened?

Graciela wore the superior little smirk that Jenny hated. What did she know? She was a kid. Kids had to depend on adults for everything.

"It's time we changed this bandage," Jenny decided. "Find your nightshift in the saddlebags, and we'll tear up some more strips. And bring me our little mirror. I want to see these stitches."

When she peeled off the old bandage, carefully, painfully, she noted there had been some seepage, but no serious bleeding. That was good. She rested a minute against the headboard of the bed, then, when she thought she could stand the sight, she lifted her blouse and adjusted the mirror against her waist.

"Well, that's some cut all right," she said finally. Graciela waited with an expectant expression. "You did a good job. Those are nice neat stitches. If I didn't know better, I'd think you made a living sewing people up."

Pride glowed on the kid's face, and her eyes sparkled brightly. "This one was the hardest." She pointed to the last stitch.

Jenny smiled. "The way I remember, the first one was the hardest."

Instantly Graciela's face caved in on itself and tears swam in her eyes. "I didn't want to hurt you," she whispered.

A thumb pressed on Jenny's heart. They'd traveled a long way from Graciela asking God to strike her dead. A long, long way. An embarrassing dampness pricked the back of her own eyes.

"That's the nicest thing anyone has ever said to me,"

she murmured when she could speak past the lump clogging her throat. She hesitated, then patted the bed beside her. "Come up here."

Graciela climbed on the bed and leaned against her shoulder. "It was so hard, and I was scared. There was all that blood!" A shudder trembled along her body. "And the train was shaking."

Jenny put her arm around Graciela's small shoulders and held her. "Sometimes you have to hurt someone to help them. And you're right. It's awful hard. But you did it, and I'm proud of you. It looks like you really did save my life." She paused. "But you don't own me." Resting her cheek on the kid's head, she inhaled the warm dusty scent of her hair. It was a nice scent, a uniquely kid scent. It surprised her how much she enjoyed holding Graciela, smelling her hair.

"Jenny?" Graciela murmured against her chest. "Sometimes I like you."

Oh God. The admission made Jenny's throat close, and she thought she might be strangling.

"Do you like me sometimes, too?"

"Sometimes I do," she conceded in a strange, thick voice. "Not too often, but sometimes."

That's how Ty found them, snuggled together on the bed, sound asleep.

Graciela woke when he entered the room and he placed a finger over his lips, tipping his hat brim toward Jenny. Graciela nodded, then carefully eased away and slid off the bed.

"How is she feeling?" Ty asked quietly.

"Tired," Graciela whispered. "I think the wound still hurts her."

He stepped to the bed and gently placed the back of his

hand against her forehead. Her skin felt hot but dry, feverish. Careful not to wake her, he raised her bloody blouse and inspected the wound. He'd seen worse. The edges were a little red, but his niece had placed the stitches as well or better than he could have. He thought a minute, then motioned Graciela toward the door.

She hesitated, looking back at Jenny. "Where are we going?"

"I never met two females who lost as many clothes as you two. We're going to go buy you both a new rig." Immediately Graciela brightened and placed her hand in his, ready to go.

She led him from shop to shop, spending his money as happily as a full-grown woman, buying so much for herself and Jenny that he had to purchase a trunk to pack it in. Then she imperiously announced that he needed new clothing, too, and they embarked on another round of shops and leather stores. By the end of the afternoon, Ty decided that a day in the saddle rounding up strays was less exhausting than shopping with a female, even a six-year-old.

After he threw up his hands and announced that he'd had enough, he took her to a café for orange juice and a slice of sweet Mexican pastry.

A dazed feeling stole over him as he watched her daintily pick the frosting off the pastry and eat it a crumb at a time. When he'd come through Chihuahua on his way to Verde Flores and the no-name village, he hadn't noticed any family places like this one. He'd stayed the night in a low-ticket dive, and he had passed the evening drinking beer in a rowdy cantina on the rough side of town off the far end of the plaza.

That night seemed a lifetime ago, his thoughts so different from his attitude now, that he might have been a different man. Since then, he'd covered a lot of ground. He'd bought four horses, killed two men, and—this amazed him—he'd purchased women's undergarments and outerwear, and he was sitting in a café with a child instead of tossing back beers in a cantina, and—this also amazed him—he no longer saw only a Barrancas mistake when he gazed at his niece. When he looked at her now, he saw a beautiful child with eyes as blue-green as his own. He saw her spirit and her smile and the absolute trust when she placed her hand in his.

And there was Jenny. The stranger who had earlier ridden through Chihuahua hadn't known women like Jenny Jones existed. That man had seen women as soft vacuous creatures whom a male courted to satisfy a physical need. That man would have laughed at the idea of respecting a woman for qualities such as courage, loyalty, or integrity. He would have sneered in disdain if someone had suggested that he'd ache for a woman who could outcuss and outfight him, and who could hold her liquor like a man.

He sensed that this trip, which had begun as a grudging favor to his brother, would end by changing his life. Frowning, he realized he was never again going to see things the same as he had before he undertook this journey. Something was happening to his perspective. Long-held ideas and opinions were sloughing off like flecks of rust.

"Uncle Ty?" She had finished the juice and pastry and impatiently waited for him to emerge from his reverie. "We should check on Jenny now. We've been gone a long time. She might need us."

What worried him was the suspicion that *he* was beginning to need *them*.

*   *   *

Jenny slept until the first delivery boy pounded on the
door. After that, deliveries arrived every few minutes and
she gave up trying to sleep. During a lull, she ordered a
bath and something to eat. After bathing, she opened
packages and let her mouth drop in amazement at the
array of clothing she found, holding up petticoats and
shimmys and stockings and nightgowns and skirts and
blouses and two traveling ensembles complete with
matching hats and string bags. She had never owned such
fine clothing in her life.

Graciela had made the selections, of course. Jenny
doubted Ty knew anything more about women's clothing
than she did herself. Her guess was confirmed a minute
later when she began unwrapping the parcels containing
Graciela's new apparel.

She sat hard on the side of the bed clutching a miniature version of the same traveling ensemble she'd just
held against herself to check for size. The small ensemble was the same cut and color as the adult version.

She had seen matching outfits like these in catalogs.
When she and Graciela boarded the train wearing their
smart new traveling ensembles, they would look like
mother and daughter.

Leaning forward, she covered her eyes with a shaking
hand.

Marguarita, I'm in trouble here.

It wasn't as satisfactory to think the conversation as it

was to talk to Marguarita's star, but she couldn't wait for
evening.

*Something's happening between Graciela and me. I'm
not trying to take your place, you have to know that. I
didn't mean for her to get attached to me, especially now
that I know your precious Roberto is waiting for her and
wants her.*

She hunched over farther and pressed a hand to her
waist. Her stomach hurt.

*It's not good that Graciela and I should form an at-
tachment because I'll have to leave her in a few weeks.
She doesn't love me like she loves Ty, but she likes me
sometimes, she said so. And I . . . I like her, too, Marguarita. It didn't start that way, and I sure never expected
to like her, but I do. It took me a while to see it, but she's
everything you said she was. She seems awful smart for a
kid her age, clever as hell when she wants to be. She's
beautiful and well-mannered, and she knows lots of
words. And brave. My God, she's brave. Did you see how
she sewed me up?*

Good Lord, she even sounded like a parent. Tossing the
small ensemble aside, she walked to the window, pulled
back the curtains, and stared up at the sky.

*Marguarita, you have to help us. Don't let her like me
too much. I've been saying good-bye to people all my life,
but Graciela hasn't. It's hard for her. This isn't very admirable, but I'd like it if she felt sad to see me go. But I
don't want her to hurt over it. She's had enough hurt. I
don't know what the answer is to this. I sure hope you do.*

"We're back!" Graciela ran into the room. "Uncle Ty,
she's awake! Did you see all our new clothes? Mine are

the same as yours. We even have earrings. Did you find them?"

"I didn't find any earrings," she said in a faint voice. While Graciela tore through the remaining packages, she looked at Ty. "You had a shave, and you bought every article of women's clothing in Chihuahua."

He laughed and handed her a paper packet. "This is a fever powder. The chemist said to mix a tablespoon in hot liquid and take it three times a day." Stepping close to her, he cupped her chin in his palm and lifted her face. "Your eyes are a little bright and your skin is flushed, but you look . . . beautiful. Did you wash your hair?"

She closed her eyes and swallowed, swaying toward him. "I had a bath," she whispered.

Would she ever get used to his touch? Was it possible to imagine a time when he would touch her, and her bones didn't melt? When that look in his eyes didn't pour warm honey down the inside of her skin? Would the time ever come when she could stand this close without wanting to wrap herself around him and dissolve into his warmth and strength?

Stepping back, she touched her fingertips to her temples and shook her head. "Maybe I should take some of that powder now. I am feeling feverish."

Graciela tugged on the wrapper Jenny had found in the packages and put on after her bath. "Look. These are our earrings. They're real turquoise and silver!"

The kid was so pleased that Jenny didn't mention that she had never had her ears pierced and wouldn't be able to wear the earrings.

"The shop had earrings with blue stones that weren't

real turquoise, but Uncle Ty said, 'not for his girls.' Uncle Ty bought us the real ones."

"I'll be horn-swoggled," Jenny said softly. Bright color infused the cowboy's face. She would have sworn Ty Sanders was incapable of a blush. A slow grin curved her lips.

"It was a stupid comment," he said irritably, turning away.

"Your girls, huh?"

"I'm going out for a drink. When I'm ready for supper, I'll bring back food for us." He jammed his hat on his head and slammed the door behind him, then opened it again and peered inside. "I'll send someone up with hot water for the fever powder."

"Much obliged," Jenny said, grinning at his glare. After the door slammed the second time, she gazed at the two beds and wished she hadn't been knifed, wondering. *Maybe* . . .

"Did you try on the hats?" Graciela called, holding up a straw heavy with silk flowers. "I like this one best."

Jenny wrenched her gaze from the bed. What the hell was she thinking? Even if she'd been healthy as a horse, nothing was going to happen between her and Ty. Not in this room. Not with Graciela a few feet away. Sighing, she sat down at a small table and watched Graciela try on the hat. She could understand how a man and a woman made one child. What was more difficult to grasp was how they found the privacy to make a second.

When she realized she was worrying about things she had never in her life expected to even think about, she laughed out loud and shook her head. It must be the fever.

* * *

Long after Graciela had fallen asleep beside her, Jenny lay awake listening to Ty toss and turn in the bed next to theirs. Eventually, he threw back the blanket and walked through a wash of white moonlight to the waistcoat hanging over a chair. A minute later she saw the flare of a match and smelled cigar smoke.

"Bought new long johns, too, I see," she commented softly, smiling in the darkness. The long johns pulled tight across his shoulders and chest, sagged a little behind. He didn't have much of a butt. Must have pounded it off galloping after cows.

"Why aren't you asleep?" He returned to his bed, mounded the pillows against the headboard, then leaned against them, smoking in the darkness.

"I've done nothing but sleep for almost twenty-four hours."

"How are you feeling? Did the fever powder help?"

"I think it must have. And my stomach doesn't hurt like it did. Hell, I'm as tough as an old hen. Always did heal fast."

"Jenny . . . come over here."

Her heart rolled over in her chest, and she caught a quick breath. But she hesitated, fighting the siren call of temptation. "No sir, I'm not getting in a man's bed with a kid in the room," she said, as prim as a preacher's wife. Except for the hint of regret.

"Just what kind of low bastard do you think I am?" She couldn't see his glare, but she felt it and almost laughed. "Nothing's going to happen in this bed except some kissing and some touching and a whole lot of frustration on my part. Now get on over here."

Temptation won. Actually, it wasn't much of a contest. "Well . . . I would like a puff off that cigar."

Easing away from Graciela, she carefully slid off her bed and tiptoed around his. Lifting the hem of her new white nightgown, she crawled up beside him. "Give me one of those pillows."

"Can't do it, I need them both. You'll just have to snuggle on me." He opened his arm and she drew a breath, then slipped in beside him and rested her head on his shoulder. Oh Lord, it felt so *good.*

"You're like cozying up next to an oven." But she didn't move away from the hard heat of him. Reaching up, she took the cigar from his mouth and put it between her own lips, drawing the smoke out slowly. "Ahh, that's wonderful. I've been wanting a smoke all day."

After she exhaled again, he took the cigar from her fingers and stubbed it in a dish on the table between the beds. "Why didn't you get a cigar out of the saddlebags?"

"I just . . . you know, I just . . . I wasn't certain when you and Graciela were coming back. I don't like to smoke in front of her. It sets a bad example." She couldn't believe she was managing to speak coherently when all she could think about was his hand dangling so near her breast.

"You're something, you are," he said, laughing softly. "As hard and brittle as an eggshell on the outside, soft as yolk inside."

"Are you going to talk nonsense all night, or are we ever going to get to the kissing part?" When he laughed again, his lips in her hair, she shivered in anticipation. "Do it quietly. We don't want to wake Graciela."

"Kissing doesn't make too much noise." Sliding down,

pulling the pillow with him, he brought his head next to hers. Then he caressed her face, gently teasing a thumb across her lips. "Do you know what I wish we could do?" he whispered in a thick voice.

"We can't," she said, her mouth dry. Already her heart was pounding so hard that she could hardly breathe, and her skin was flushed with fire. He'd moved close, not pressing against her, not risking causing her pain, but close enough that she could feel the rigid length of his arousal. She sucked in a breath and closed her eyes.

He kissed the corner of her lips, his hand hot on her throat. "I'd like to skin that nightgown off of you and run my tongue all over your body," he murmured.

"My God!" Jenny eased back and blinked at him. She'd never heard of such a thing. The idea of someone licking her body should have been disgusting . . . but, strangely, it wasn't. Oh, it wasn't. Imagining what such a thing would feel like made her tremble and feel hot and shaky inside. If she hadn't already been lying down, she would have fallen flat the way she did the first time he touched her breast.

He kissed her eyelids and his hand moved in a light caress over the top of her bosom. "I'd like to kiss you here," he whispered, dropping his hand farther to stroke her nipple through her nightgown. She gasped and felt her rib cage swell. "And here." His fingers passed lightly over the bandage at her waist and stroked her lower belly.

"Oh my God." Panting lightly, she squirmed against his hand. She couldn't have remained still if her life had depended on it. How was he thinking of these things? These strange, erotic things that she had never even imagined.

"And here."

"*There*?" Her eyes flew open and her mouth dropped in amazement. His hand cupped her most private part, scalding her right through the thin material of her nightgown. "You want to kiss me *there*?" She thought she might faint just thinking about it.

He laughed softly against her lips. "Right there. Give me your hand. I'll show you what thinking about kissing you there does to me."

She knew what he was going to do, and she didn't resist. She let him draw her hand down between them, down to where his long johns tented out.

"My God," she murmured again, curving her fingers around the length of him. When he groaned, she snatched her hand back, but he caught her fingers and pressed them back around him. Tentatively at first, then with growing curiosity and assurance, she explored the power and maleness beneath her hand.

To her astonishment, she discovered she could create a baritone symphony of groans and moans and low, tortured whispers. If she did this, his body arched and quivered. If she did that, he kissed her so fiercely that her mouth burned. When she did this and this, he went limp and groaned.

He held the power to kindle a fire in her belly and drop her to her knees with a caress. But she had power, too. The realization astonished her.

"Wait," he begged, his voice a hoarse rasp. "Stop for a minute. This is torture."

"I like torturing you," she whispered wickedly, covering his face with kisses, teasing him with her hips to see what might happen.

A groan of pain rumbled in his chest. "I might have known you'd learn fast." Then he slid down and opened the top of her nightdress, his mouth and tongue finding her breasts. "I'll show you what torture is."

When Jenny staggered back to her own bed near dawn, her lips swollen and her breasts aching, she decided he'd kept his promise. She burned for him, was on fire for him. Never had she experienced anything even remotely similar to this kind of arousal and desire. He had brought her to explosion after explosion with nothing but his hands and his voice in her ear. And she had discovered she could do the same for him. It had been wild, erotic, exhausting, and delirious. And informative.

When she crawled into bed beside Graciela, she cast the kid a glance of resentment and grudging affection. If Graciela hadn't been here . . . but then, if Graciela hadn't been here, she and Ty wouldn't have been here either.

"Ty?" she whispered, leaning forward to look across at him.

"Hmmm?"

"Before tonight, I never had an . . ." She didn't know the proper word. Lordy, Lordy. She hadn't even suspected that a woman could erupt like that. "Ty? I thought I knew about—you know, men and women—but I didn't know a damned thing."

"Well, you sure do now," he said softly. A low chuckle groaned from his side of the room. "You sure know now."

Chapter
Fifteen

Uncertain if the Barrancas cousins were searching for them in Chihuahua, Ty and Jenny stayed off the streets as much as possible, seldom venturing outside their hotel room. Jenny decided being cooped up in the room was the worst part of her healing process. She would go stark raving mad if she heard Graciela whine, "What can I do now?" one more time.

Staring blindly at the pages of a Mark Twain novel that Ty had bought for her, she considered her situation regarding Graciela. She didn't want to be a parent, had sworn never to be a parent, and she hated being forced into the responsibilities of a parent. She didn't like kids, had never liked kids, didn't believe that she ever would like kids.

But, much as she detested it, she was starting to sound like a parent. This astonished her as greatly as hearing parental-type admonitions and cajoling fall from Ty's handsome mouth.

If their circumstance hadn't been so wearing and worrisome, it might have been amusing. She and Ty were two people who disliked children and had never expected to have to deal with any. But here they were, struggling with parental problems such as lack of privacy and setting an example, arguing over a six-year-old and expectations of her capabilities, and, at the moment, trying to hang on to their sanity while confronted with a bored and irritable kid.

Given the same situation, would actual parents have taught their child to play poker and twenty-one? Jenny had to believe they would, even Marguarita.

"Should I raise, call, or fold?" Graciela asked impatiently, tipping her hand toward Jenny while shielding her cards from Ty's sharp glance.

Jenny sighed and looked up from her book. She'd read the same paragraph ten times. "I told you. I make it a practice never to advise a man how he should play his hand."

"I'm not a man. I'm a kid. Fold, right?"

Jenny looked into Graciela's disappointed eyes and nodded. "I'm not telling you what to do, but," she leaned over the corner of the table to whisper, "you only have a pair of fours. If it was me, I'd fold. Now don't interrupt me again."

Graciela tossed her cards on the table with a look of disgust, and watched Ty grin and pull a pile of matchsticks toward his chest. "Let's play again."

"Can't," Ty said, counting his matchsticks. "It's almost time for supper."

Jenny considered abandoning any attempt to read. "Teach her how to play solitaire, will you?" she suggested. "That will give us a break."

"I don't want to learn another game, I want to play

poker," Graciela insisted, pushing her mouth into a pout. "And I want to win. Mama and Aunt Tete let me win at games."

Jenny laughed, and even Ty grinned. "Well, you can forget that. Nobody here is going to 'let' you win. The day you win a pot from me or your uncle Ty, you can pat yourself on the back because you'll have won it honestly. Until that distant and improbable day, you are going to lose, so just make up your mind to it. Now stop talking, I'm trying to read."

"Why don't you read out loud while Uncle Ty and I play another game of poker?"

Jenny narrowed her eyes and sighed. "I read to you this morning. Now I want to read to myself. Maybe I'll read more to you on the train, but not now. So, shut up."

Graciela let her shoulders slump and did her best to look utterly dejected. Jenny studied her a minute, then slammed her book shut.

"Since you already feel rotten, this is a good time to remind you that your uncle Ty and I are going out tonight. I don't want any grief from you about this."

Graciela's mouth dropped in exaggerated astonishment, and she stiffened in outrage. "You're going out without me?"

Ty shuffled the cards and eased them back into the box. "I hired the hotel owner's wife—you know her, Senora Jaramillo—to stay with you while we're gone. You won't be alone."

"I hate Senora Jaramillo. She's fat, and she has a mustache. I won't stay with her, I won't!"

"Yeah, you will," Jenny said calmly. "You can scream and shout and cry all you want, but you're staying here. I told you about this three days ago when I showed you my new gown."

"I'm going, too!" Her hands formed into fists on the tabletop, and tears streamed down her face. "We own each other. We're responsible for each other. You have to take me too!"

"Oh for heaven's sake." She frowned at Ty's stricken expression. "I know what you're thinking," she snapped. "But just remind yourself who the adults are and who the little snot is. If we let her get away with this crap, then she's right. She owns us." She turned a glare back to Graciela. "And that isn't going to happen."

"I hate it when you talk about me like I can't hear you."

"Graciela, honey," Ty said in a coaxing voice. "Senora Jaramillo knows how to play poker."

Jenny noted that the kid didn't give in right away, but she brightened a little. Pride insisted that she string out her sulk and make it abundantly clear that she'd been hideously betrayed. By now, Jenny recognized the ploy, and she almost laughed. She wondered if she had tried to manipulate the adults in her life when she was Graciela's age. If so, she had been as certain of failure as was Graciela.

Ty stood, guilt writ large across his face. "If I take you out for supper while Jenny is getting dressed, will that make you smile?"

Jenny rolled her eyes. "And you said I'm an egg yolk. Look at you. She has you wrapped around her little finger."

"I'll get my cape," Graciela said happily. Shooting Jenny a triumphant glance, she slid off her chair.

"Sucker."

Ty laughed and settled his hat on his head. "We'll be back in about an hour. Will that give you enough time to bathe and dress?"

He had performed his ablutions earlier and stood before her tall and heart-stoppingly handsome, wearing tight-fitting black suede pants and a black velvet Mexican jacket over a starched white shirt. The flowing red tie at his collar caught her eye, as she hadn't seen him wear a tie until tonight.

"You look wonderful," she said softly, letting her gaze travel along the taut muscle swelling at shoulder and thigh. A light shudder thrilled down her spine as she thought of the nights they had shared during this week. Now, they were familiar with each other's bodies. She knew he could shatter her with a kiss or a touch. And she knew she could direct him or stop him with a whisper. A glint of fledgling power shone in her eyes. "Where are we going?"

"It's a surprise," he answered gruffly, narrowing his gaze on her lips. "I hope you'll enjoy what I have planned."

He wouldn't say more, but the hard promise glittering in his expression spoke volumes. Wherever he planned to take her, she wouldn't be disappointed.

She wet her lips and swallowed, smiling when she noticed his jaw tighten. "While you're out, would you check the train schedule? I'm feeling right as rain and ready to head for Texas tomorrow. Graciela? You remind him. It's time to go."

Because she was buoyed by the prospect of an evening alone with Ty, it struck her as amusing that Ty soothed Graciela's fits of temper by offering her a treat whereas

Jenny aimed for the same result by assigning a task. The kid, she suspected, was clever enough to see through them both.

After they departed, she ordered up a bath and carefully laid her new gown on one of the beds, letting her fingers linger on the whispery apricot-colored satin. A month ago the calluses on her palms would have snagged the smooth, embroidered fabric. Now that she wasn't driving every day or wrestling cartons of freight, her calluses had faded. Yesterday, for want of something to do, she had even borrowed Graciela's file and shaped her nails. Smiling, she decided that hell had frozen over the minute she applied a file to her thumbnail. Henceforth, sinners would shiver instead of sweat.

Graciela being Graciela, and knowing about such things, had bought a cake of rose-scented soap, and Jenny borrowed it for her bath, working the fragrant lather against her skin and scalp.

One nice thing about short hair and dry desert air, she decided while toweling off, was how quickly her hair dried. Standing naked before the bureau, she leaned to the small mirror on top and combed her hair back from a center part so it would dry close to her head.

Next she examined an item of clothing she had vowed would never touch her body, a corset. Laughing at an image of Ty buying such an intimate contraption, she held it up for inspection, flexed the steel bones, and studied the lace and ribbon trim. At least it hooked up the front. Even so, she doubted she would have worn the evil thing except that Graciela had insisted her gown wouldn't fit properly without a corset to nip her in here and push her up there.

Once she had assembled and donned her undergarments, she returned to her hair, pleased that it had dried slicked back from her face. Here her fingers moved with certainty. Though she would have submitted to a whipping rather than admit it, over the years she had secretly experimented with comb and brush. Hair, her own hair, was a feminine item that she understood. In a flash, she had pinned a circlet of flowers near the nape, creating the illusion of a bun on her neck.

Next came a spritz of Graciela's rose cologne, then she hesitated. How foolish would she feel if she patted powder over her cheeks and bosom? Just a slight dusting. Before she could change her mind, she applied powder to her face, throat, and shoulders, then leaned to inspect herself.

My Lord. She looked like a different person. The powder muted her tan, her slicked-back hair exposed a broad, rather noble forehead, she decided, shyly pleased. Tonight her eyes appeared as blue as a shining spring sky. Caught up in a transformation she had never worked before, she plucked a rose petal from the flowers in the window box and rubbed it over her lips, leaning to the mirror to judge the effect.

With only minutes to spare before Ty and Graciela knocked, then opened the door, she carefully stepped into the apricot-colored satin gown and hooked the side closing, wishing for a full-length mirror so she could admire the poufs of pale green cascading down the back of the gown. The pale green matched the swirls of delicate embroidery adorning the slim front of her skirt and repeated in a wide ribbon bow at her breast.

Staring down at herself, she imagined a newly emerged butterfly, a splendid creature heretofore hidden inside

awaiting exactly the right moment and the right acces-
sories to shine forth. Or maybe she merely looked like an
elegantly gowned lady of the night. She didn't know.

Ty and Graciela stopped in their tracks when they saw
her.

"Jenny!" Graciela breathed, staring. "You look beautiful."

Crimson circles flared on her cheeks as she raised her
eyes to Ty, and she smoothed trembling fingers over her
hips. Only when she noticed that his gaze smoldered with
a fire no woman could fail to mistake did the tremor in
her hands alter from uncertainty to pleasure. Still . . .

"Do I look like a whore?" she whispered, wondering if
she should have avoided the powder and rose petal lips.

"You look . . . like a vision," he murmured hoarsely.
"That gown fits like a second skin, and the color is wonderful with your hair."

Her throat warmed with a rush of delight. But he was a
man; she couldn't fully trust his response. Therefore, she
turned an appeal to Graciela. "Is too much bosom hanging out?" Never in her life had she exposed this much
flesh. When she glanced down, a mountain range of pale
mounds met her gaze.

Graciela walked around her, giving a tug here, straightening a fold there. "That's the fashion," she announced
sagely, sounding as knowledgeable as an experienced
shopkeeper. When she had completed a full circle, she
stood back and, eyes wide with disbelief and admiration,
and she said softly, "Oh Jenny. You look so beautiful. You
look like a princess."

"Oh my. Well, thank you." She cleared her throat, then

darted a glance toward Ty, who hadn't moved. He stood as if rooted to the floor by the sight of her.

"Jenny?" Graciela bit her lips in indecision, then nodded and touched the locket pin on her chest. "I . . . would you like to borrow my pin for tonight?"

The shy offer blindsided her. During the entire time they had traveled together, through all their travails, Graciela had worn the locket. Always. Day and night. It was her most prized possession, the only tangible memory of her mother.

Oh Lord. Jenny blinked hard and swallowed the sudden lump in her throat. "I would be honored to wear your pin," she murmured in a husky voice. Sitting on the side of the bed, she waited while Graciela removed the locket from her chest then carefully pinned it to the bodice of Jenny's gown. They gazed at each other for a lengthy moment, then Graciela leaned forward and brushed a hasty kiss across Jenny's cheek before she darted away to the window.

Openmouthed, Jenny lifted a hand to her cheek and stared. If nothing else happened tonight, already it had become an evening she would remember for the rest of her life. Graciela had kissed her.

"Well," she said, dropping her head and blinking hard. Were there tears in her eyes? No, of course not. "Where is my fan and bag? And where is Senora Jaramillo?"

"I hear the good senora on the staircase," Ty said. He hadn't taken his eyes off of her. "My God, Jenny," he said softly, his voice thick. "I wish you could see yourself. You look . . . amazing."

Hot with pleasure, she stood and collected her fan and bag from the top of the bureau, and dropped an apricot satin shawl over her shoulders, feeling the pale green fringe brush the crook of her arms. To cover a sudden bout of nervousness, she focused on Graciela while she tugged on her gloves, but she was acutely aware that Ty watched each small movement she made.

"Mind what Senora Jaramillo tells you. Don't play poker for real money, only matchsticks, and go to bed when the senora tells you to. I better not hear that you were smoking, cussing, or drinking up here."

The kid didn't smile. She was getting pissy again. "You didn't used to care when I went to bed."

"I do now. Now I understand the responsibilities of this job. Whether I like it or not, I have to think about your best interests. If it's any comfort to you, I'd rather think about my best interests instead of yours. Frankly, thinking about you first and always is mostly a pain in the . . . neck."

Ty removed his hat with a flourish, bowed before his niece, then kissed the top of her head. "Here's Senora Jaramillo now. We'll see you in the morning." When Graciela crossed her arms over her chest and spun around to present her back to him, he frowned at her a moment, then pressed his lips together and turned to greet Senora Jaramillo.

After a few minutes with Senora Jaramillo, Jenny took his arm and they stepped into the corridor. The instant the door shut behind them, they halted. "Put your ear against the wood and see if you can tell if she's crying," Jenny whispered.

Ty pressed his ear to the door. "They're talking."

"You're positive that she isn't crying?" She pressed her fingers together. "I can't believe how rotten I feel about leaving her. I *know* she's deliberately trying to make us feel lousy. I *know* this. But damn it, her tactic fricking works."

Instantly, she wished she hadn't cussed. Instinct insisted that cusswords didn't sit well on the lips of a woman wearing apricot-colored satin and matching shawl and slippers. For the first time in her life, Jenny felt an urge to beg pardon for talking the way she had talked for most of her life.

Stepping away from the door, Ty framed her face between his palms and kissed her deeply and without haste, cutting off her dazed apology. When their lips parted, he gazed down into her wide eyes. "We are not going to talk about Graciela tonight, or the Barrancas cousins. We are not going to flog ourselves for leaving her. Tonight is ours. It belongs to us."

Already her heart was slamming against the bones of her corset. "Where are we going," she asked breathlessly, more for something to say than from any real curiosity. As long as she was with Ty, as long as he continued to look at her with that slow smolder lighting the back of his eyes, she didn't care where they dined.

Dined. Well la-de-da. A length of satin, some ribbon and lace, and wasn't she the grand lady? It would be wise to keep in mind that she had skinned buffalos, had washed other people's dirty laundry, had driven a team of foul-smelling jacks. No apricot-colored satin was going to change who she was.

"Come with me," Ty said, taking her gloved hand.

At the staircase landing, Jenny turned to descend, but he laughed softly and tugged her toward the stairs leading up. A question leaped into her eyes, and he smiled, and said, "You'll see."

When he stopped to fit a key into the door of a room on the top floor, Jenny burst out laughing. "You dog," she said, pressing her gloved fingers beneath eyes damp with laughter. "For this I needed an expensive new gown? And a corset?"

But the room Ty led her into was not just another hotel room. Having never seen a suite before, Jenny gasped, and her gloved hands flew to her lips.

It was as if they had stepped into a small, opulent house. Through a doorway, she glimpsed an elegant four-poster, but they stood in a beautifully furnished living room.

Smiling, Ty took her arm and led her toward a circular stairway. "We're dining *al fresco*. Do you know what that means?"

"I don't have a fricking idea what that means," she whispered, too awed to be irritated as she usually was when he used words she didn't comprehend.

"It means in the fresh air, outside."

The staircase circled up to a rooftop courtyard so lush and lovely it took Jenny's breath away. What seemed like hundreds of potted plants created a tropical riot of shade and color, winding up trellises, trailing along the stone railings. Moving to the railing, Jenny peered down at the distant street to remind herself that she couldn't be standing in a real garden.

Then she gazed out at a stunning view of the city bathed in sunset tones of russet and gold. Beyond the city stretched the desert rangelands, and in the distance she identified the dusky silhouette of the Sierras. Jenny had never been high enough to view such a panorama and the beauty of it stopped the breath in her throat. Floating above the city on a blossom-laden cloud, she decided if nothing else occurred tonight, this was already an unforgettable evening.

It wasn't until she turned to breathlessly thank Ty for showing her the city from above that she noticed a linen-clad table, lit by candles and set with colorful Mexican crockery and gleaming silver.

"I . . . you . . . this is just . . ."

Ty laughed, carefully observing her openmouthed wonder. Pleased that she was stammering, he nodded to someone behind the trellis, and the soft strumming of guitars filled her ears. Kicking back her train, Jenny spun in a swirl of satin and spotted three Mexican musicians positioned at a discreet distance from their table. They tipped wide-brimmed sombreros to her, bowed, then continued playing.

"Ty!" She wet her lips, feeling overwhelmed. "This is . . . astonishing. Wonderful." Wringing her hands together, she gazed up at him. "When did you . . . It's just so . . ." Words failed her.

Smiling, he offered his arm and she accepted it self-consciously, letting him lead her to the table and extend her chair. Caressing fingers brushed her bare shoulders when he removed her shawl and placed it on a bench with his hat, and she shivered lightly at his touch.

The moment he sat across from her, a waiter appeared out of the foliage and served wine in cut-crystal glasses that trapped the candlelight inside a dozen small surfaces.

"To you," Ty said softly, touching his glass to hers.

"This is . . . I've never . . . I feel like I've been poleaxed," Jenny whispered, glancing over her shoulder to see if the musicians could observe them through the roses climbing over the trellis. The waiter also appeared to have vanished, although she suspected he hadn't really.

"Do you like it?"

"Oh my heavens, yes. It's like . . ." But she couldn't draw a comparison because nothing remotely like this courtyard or this evening had formed any part of her experience or imaginings. "Oh Ty," she breathed, staring at him. "Thank you. I will remember this evening all the rest of my days." A tiny frown marred the smoothness of her brow. "When I saw you opening the door to another hotel room, I thought . . ."

He moved his chair closer to hers, then reached for her hand and brought it to his lips. The heat of his mouth penetrated her glove, and she was thankful that she was seated. No man had even kissed her hand before, and she would have laughed herself sick if one had tried. But she wasn't laughing now.

"Jenny, there are two paths this evening can take. It's your choice. We can enjoy a pleasant meal, some conversation, and then return to Graciela and our room on the second floor. Or, we can enjoy a pleasant meal, some conversation, and then explore the bedroom in the suite below . . ."

Her hand trembled in his and she swallowed hard, thinking of the wild kisses they had exchanged this week while Graciela slept. "I think you know what I want to do," she whispered. She didn't seem able to speak in a normal volume.

"I don't want any misunderstanding, Jenny. That

wouldn't be fair to either of us," he said, gazing at her lips. "I think we both know how things stand, but a review wouldn't hurt."

She drank her wine, watching him intently over the rim of the glass. "You promised that I wouldn't catch a child."

"You won't." Lifting his hand, he stroked his knuckles along her jawline. "I'm very fond of you, but we've sworn that neither of us is the marrying kind. Whatever happens tonight, there is *no* commitment on either of our parts either fancied or implied. Are we agreed on this point?"

"You son of a bitch," she murmured, closing her eyes and arching her throat to his fingertips. "How many times have you snookered some poor female with this speech?"

"I'm thinking of you. I don't want to mislead you. Tonight is an interlude between two people who enjoy each other, that's all it is. Or am I wrong? Have I misunderstood your position?" he murmured, his voice husky with desire.

She caught his hand before his fingers reached her cleavage, raised it to her lips and lightly nipped his forefinger between her teeth, tasting salt and soap. The sound of his groan pleased her enough that she could clear her thoughts a little and focus on the business at hand.

Lifting her glass, she tossed back the wine then jumped slightly as the waiter appeared out of thin air to refill their glasses. After he vanished, she leaned forward, deliberately displaying her bosom to test his reaction. "Can the musicians or the waiter hear what we're saying?"

Ty stared at her breasts, and she smiled at the perspiration that appeared on his brow. "No."

"All right, cowboy," she said briskly. "I'm here to satisfy a powerful hankering that has driven me half fricking insane, especially during the last few days. The only promise I'm looking for is that I don't catch a baby, that's all. Consummating this hankering isn't going to place your freedom or independence at risk. All I want from you is tonight." She waited until his gaze lifted from her breasts to her eyes. "Once this journey ends, you and me are going to part company, no strings attached. Satisfied?"

Without warning, the jolting reality of her future blotted the sweetness of the guitars and the perfume of the flowers.

They were going to say good-bye. She stared at him, the defiance fading from her eyes. In about two weeks, they would suddenly turn awkward with each other and struggle to find words to say *adiós* and farewell. He would step out of her life as suddenly as he had jumped into it, leaving her a different person trying to fit into her old existence.

It occurred to her that all she would ever have of him had to fit within the next two weeks.

"I'm glad we understand each other," he murmured, gazing deeply into her eyes and toying with her fingers.

Jenny wet her lips. "Just don't go planting any seeds, hear me? I don't want a kid to ruin my life."

His laugh was soft and confident. "You are so lovely tonight. You look just as I imagined you would. Magnificent."

"Well," she said, feeling the tension grow hot on her skin, "now that everything's settled, let's go downstairs and do it." Taking her napkin out of her lap, she started to rise, stopping only when she noticed his grin. "What?" she asked, frowning.

"Oh Jenny, there's never been another like you. Sit down." As she slowly sank back to her chair, he took her hand, peeled off her glove, and covered her palm with kisses. "We're going to make love, I promise you. And I promise that you're going to enjoy it." The intent smoldering look he gave her stopped the breath in her chest. "But first, we're going to eat our dinner. Then we're going to linger over coffee and cigars in the candlelight. I promised myself a long time ago that nothing would happen until you begged." The sudden hard look narrowing his gaze sapped the strength from her bones, and she couldn't breathe. "That's going to happen," he promised softly, dropping a hungry gaze to her lips, to her breasts.

Yeah, Jenny thought, shaking inside, it would happen. Probably long before they reached the coffee and cigars. Since the evening was apparently designed to torture them both, she drew a hitching breath and decided she might as well get into the spirit of things, now that she understood.

"Signal the waiter to hurry up and serve the food," she whispered. Then, feeling foolish at first, but with growing confidence as she keenly studied his reaction, she drew her fan from her throat to the top of her breasts before she dropped the leaf open. Tormenting him was such a pleasure that she continued the game throughout the meal.

Over dinner they spoke of their childhoods, of books they had read, places they had gone. They talked about music, which neither of them really understood, and about ranching, which they did know—and neither of them could recall a word of the conversation a minute after it passed.

Fingers caressed crystal stems, teasing mouths kissed silver forks. Knees brushed beneath the table linen, fingertips grazed above. Food appeared, then vanished, and they could not have said whether they ate or if the waiter whisked away plates as fully laden as those he had served.

By the time fragrant cups of coffee materialized before them, they were feverish and shaking with need, burning for each other. Jenny vibrated inside, resonating to each teasing touch, each penetrating glance. The scent of him, the look of him, every small gesture he made plucked an inner string directly connected to a hot damp center.

"I'm begging, Ty," she whispered hoarsely, squeezing her trembling eyelids shut. "I'm begging you to take me before I die of wanting you."

"Say it again," he demanded, his voice harsh with desire.

"Please. Please, please, *please.*"

These were the words he had waited to hear. Standing so abruptly that his chair crashed behind him, he pulled her to her feet, then tossed her over his shoulder. With one hand stroking her bottom, he carried her down the staircase, ignoring her helpless laughter, and set her on her feet next to the four-poster. When she saw the fiery heat blazing in his eyes, saw the hard, intent line of his mouth, the laughter died on her lips and a tremor swept from her scalp to her toes. Swaying, she placed a hand on his chest to steady her balance, letting the heat of him flow into her palm and rush to her pounding heart.

"Oh my God," she whispered, gasping. "I'm shaking so badly that I—"

"Don't move," he commanded, his voice thick with urgency. "Let me undress you."

She swallowed hard and struggled to breathe. "Are you . . . are you going to lick me all over like you said?"

Deft fingers opened her gown while his lips set fire to her throat. "All over your body," he promised huskily. His head dropped to her breast, and she felt his tongue explore her cleavage.

Jenny dropped to the edge of the bed as if she'd been gut shot. Lava bubbled in her belly, and she felt certain that she was strangling. Dazed, she stared up at him, dimly aware that candles burned around the bed, not cognizant enough to wonder who had lit them or when.

"I'll lick you all over, too," she promised, deciding fair was fair. The thought of such strange doings made her light-headed, or maybe her swirling head was a result of the teasing nips and feverish kisses that spread over her shoulders as he pushed down her tiny cap sleeves.

Jenny decided she'd had enough teasing, tormenting, and fiery torture to last a lifetime. All week long they had touched and caressed and stroked and inflamed. She could not stand another minute of it. Squirming away from him, she wiggled out of the apricot-colored satin and flung it away from her. "Hurry up, hurry up," she panted, jerking and yanking at her undergarments.

When she looked up again, cussing and frustrated because the corset hooks would not yield to boneless fingers, Ty was naked. "Oh my Lord." A long, moist gasp broke from her throat, and her fingers flew to her cheeks.

Never in her life had she expected to admire a naked man. But he was so beautiful. Utterly splendid. So lean and hard and wiry-muscled, so pale beneath the dark feathery hair narrowing from chest to rampant need. "Oh

Ty." She spoke his name mindlessly, like a sigh, like a plea. "Ty."

Flinging her arms around his neck, she locked her mouth to his in a long, hot, ardent kiss that made her mind sing and her body quiver. His hands roughly circled her waist like a brand, claiming her, possessing her, and she nearly sobbed with the relief of knowing that tonight, this time, she would not have to return to her own bed without truly knowing him. This time they would not have to be quiet or circumspect in movement.

And they weren't. They toppled onto the bed, wound tightly together from lips to thighs, rolling and thrashing, unmindful of squeaking bed ropes or their own gasps and groans. Ty's fingers were more nimble than hers, and he had her corset opened in a moment, flung aside the next. And then, oh Lord, and then his lips were on her breasts, sucking, licking, driving her mad with waves of sensation that crashed one over another like stormy tides, drowning her in hot pleasure.

There could be no waiting, not when their bodies trembled at fever pitch. They came together in panting, gasping, titanic need and urgency, and Jenny cried out his name when he entered her and she rocked up to meet his first deep thrust.

She expected a few thrusts, and then it would end, but it didn't happen that way. Her eyes flew open in surprise and her fingers tightened on his damp shoulders when he kissed her again and again as their bodies meshed and thrilled to an exciting rhythm that built rather than diminished. And it was unlike anything Jenny had ever known. There was no pain, no thought for anything but Ty and the sensations he aroused with his mouth and body. There was only the rapture of awakening to her own body and to his, the fainting tension of feeling inner forces build and build and build until she could no longer contain the earthquake that gathered between her thighs.

When the blissful eruption ended, she collapsed beneath him, only dimly aware that he withdrew before his shoulders convulsed, and he gathered her to his chest with a low groan. "Jenny . . . Jenny."

For a long while they did not move, but held each other close, waiting for pounding hearts to quiet. This, too, was new to her. In her experience, the man took his pleasure, withdrew, and buttoned up as he left. And that was that. But not tonight, not with this remarkable, hard, and splendid man.

After a time, they roused and Ty lit cigars for them both. They smoked in contentment, her head on his shoulder, and she didn't even wonder that they lay together naked and unembarrassed. She didn't let herself think past the moment, and the moment was one of the best in her life.

"Would you like anything?" he inquired, his voice heavy with satisfaction. "Coffee? Tequila? Wine?"

"No," she said after deciding there was nothing on earth that she needed this minute except to be here, with him. "Good cigar." She wasn't sure if it was or not, and she didn't care.

"You're like I imagined you would be," he murmured against the top of her head. "Milky white where the sun hasn't been, and brushed with flame down there. Am I what you expected?"

"Oh yes, you're beautiful," she said matter-of-factly, puzzled when he laughed. "But . . ."

"But what?"

"Well, I guess I'm a little disappointed that we didn't do the licking all over. I was kind of looking forward to that," she admitted, squirming against him. Every time she thought about the licking all over, she couldn't remain still. "It's such a peculiar and strange thing that I'm sort of glad we didn't do it, but at the same time, I never licked anybody or had anybody lick me and I guess I just—"

"You thought we were finished?" His low chuckle cut off her words, then he took the cigar from her fingers and stubbed it out. "Jenny, honey . . . we're just getting started," he promised gruffly, kissing her temple. "There's going to be licking all over. And kissing in places you haven't even thought about."

"There is?" Her eyes widened and her heart leaped into her throat before diving toward her stomach. "*All* over?"

"*All* over," he said hoarsely, turning her to face him.

He started with her lips, teasing with his tongue, not letting her kiss him when she frantically tried. Then he tasted her throat before his head dropped to suck and tease at her breasts. "I love your breasts," he murmured before his head dropped lower. And lower. And then lower. She thought she was going to die from the shock and pleasure of being licked and kissed *all* over. And when it was her turn, she thought sure that *he* was going to die when she kissed and licked him all over.

When dawn crept over the city, they returned to their own room, dazed and stumbling, gazing at each other with awe and wonder and the puzzlement of blissful new emotions both denied feeling.

At the door of their room, Ty cupped her face between

his hands and kissed her gently, tenderly. "Thank you for an evening I will never forget."

"I look like hell, don't I?" she whispered, trying to smooth her hastily assembled clothing.

Grinning, he leaned to insert the key in the lock. "You look like a woman who has been well loved."

It was the first time the word "love" had appeared in any conversation, and they both ignored it. Once inside the room Ty shook Senora Jaramillo awake and saw her to the door. Then, wonderfully unselfconscious, he stripped, donned his long johns, and gave Jenny a light kiss before he dropped onto the bed. In a moment, he was snoring.

Smiling, she moved in the pearly predawn light, hanging up her gown, folding her undergarments, searching for her nightshift. Before she climbed into bed beside Graciela, she moved to the window and glanced up at the sky, seeking Marguarita's star before it ceded to the dawn.

I did you wrong, and I apologize. I thought you were an idiot to give yourself to Robert and risk catching a baby. I figured you got what you deserved for being so stupid. I thought I was better than you because I had more sense than to ever do such a damned fool thing.

Well, I was dead wrong. I didn't know how it could be between men and women, Marguarita. If Robert made you feel like Ty made me feel tonight, I can see why you'd risk everything to be with him. I'm sorry I judged so harshly. I didn't know.

She started toward the bed, then returned to the window and Marguarita's star.

Marguarita? I hope Robert licked you all over. It's just

the damnest thing! I'd hate to think you became an angel without first getting licked all over. It's probably not proper to talk about this, but I think you would have liked the licking a lot.

She yawned and stretched. *Good night, my friend. Tomorrow night I'll talk to you from El Paso. From there we start the final leg of the journey.*

As she climbed into bed, she wished she hadn't mentioned that last part. Curling protectively around Graciela's small body, she inhaled the clean sweet scent of the child's hair, and smiled at the sound of a light baritone snore emanating from the other bed.

She wished it could be like this forever. The three of them together. Suddenly her stomach cramped and her throat closed, and she felt a sting of sadness behind her eyes.

Chapter
Sixteen

Even if the train ran late, which was likely, they would arrive at the rail terminal in El Paso Del Norte before supper. "We'll cross the Rio Grande and find a hotel in El Paso on the American side," Ty explained to Graciela. "Tomorrow morning, we'll board the Southern Pacific bound for San Francisco. And we'll be home in about a week."

While he answered the next hundred questions from his niece, he gazed at Jenny, who sat across from him and Graciela. Her head rested against the window, and she dozed despite the heat and noise inside the car. Pride and amusement softened the look he swept over her molded traveling jacket. He liked seeing evidence that he'd plumb worn her out last night. Except she'd worn him out too. He wouldn't say no when it was his turn to catch an hour or two of shut-eye.

God almighty, but she was a magnificent woman. He enjoyed just watching her sleep. And last night she had been everything he had hoped she would be and more. Passionate, enthusiastic, uninhibited, and eager to give back what she learned. He'd never had a woman with a body as superb as hers, lush, curvacious, taut, well muscled, and built for endurance. And responsive? Remembering her wild abandon made his groin tighten painfully. He had to figure out how they could be together again tonight.

"Uncle Ty?" Frowning, Graciela tugged at the pocket of his waistcoat. "You aren't listening."

"You're telling me about your friend, Cordelia."

"Consuelo!"

He couldn't hire just anyone to stay with his niece while he trysted with Jenny. The problem was finding someone on short notice, then establishing reliability. That he should be pondering such a dilemma impressed him as frustrating, exasperating, amusing, and there was another feeling he couldn't quite identify. Something warm and protective, something that touched him inside whenever he observed the trust in Graciela's gaze.

Oddly, he suddenly recalled a saying of his mother's. "A boy becomes a man the day he holds his first child in his arms." It took a child to make a man, he thought, frowning down at Graciela. And a woman, a very special woman.

Strange new ideas were still prodding his emotions two hours later when all hell broke loose.

He felt the explosion beneath his feet a second before the blast of dynamite roared through his ears. The train wheels locked, the cars clashed together, and Jenny was flung from her seat to his, coming awake with panic in her eyes. Screams sounded around them. People, animals, boxes, and baskets flew through the inside of the car.

Trying to hold Jenny and Graciela as the car shuddered and rocked up on one set of wheels, Ty ground his teeth and swore viciously. Clouds of grey-and-white steam billowed up past the window, but not before he spotted horses and riders. When Jenny's fingers dug into his thighs, he knew she, too, had spotted Luis Barrancas through the glass and steam.

Up ahead, the engine ran off the ruined track and plunged down the track bed, plowing into sand and cacti before crashing on its side. The following car twisted and toppled, forcing the next car to the opposite side of the track bed. When the hellish din diminished and the cars lurched to a stop, Ty thanked happenstance that they had boarded toward the rear. The car they were in tilted high on one side, but it hadn't fallen.

Pushing Jenny aside, he found his saddlebags and ripped open the pocket. "Here." He thrust a pistol into her hands and a pouch full of cartridges. She shoved her hat out of her eyes and loaded the gun with steady hands, her mouth grim.

"We need horses," she snapped.

He nodded. It didn't surprise him that she tracked his thoughts as if he'd spoken aloud. "Stay here," he said to Graciela, who pushed up her hat brim, then stared around them with frightened eyes and a white face.

"Wait until we come for you," Jenny finished. She struggled to stand, kicked a terrified chicken out of her way. "Let's go."

As if they'd discussed it, she turned toward the back door of the car, leaving him to run through the debris-laden aisle toward the front. As he burst onto the crazily canted platform between twisted cars, he heard her first shots and saw a rider go down. Rolling steam made his eyes water, but offered some cover. Unfortunately it obscured the Barrancas cousins as well.

Jumping to the ground, he ran through hissing white billows, firing at forms looming out of the steam. Three men on this side. He winged one, sent one to hell, and the other wheeled, then spurred toward the back of the train.

Spinning, Ty climbed back onto the platform, crossed to the other side, and vaulted down. In the midst of spiraling dust and gusts of steam, he spotted Jenny, fighting to hold the reins of a dun and a black horse while firing at a rider bearing down on her. Hot steam scalded his eyes as he ran up beside her, fanning his pistol. The rider veered and dropped, his boot catching in the stirrup. The horse raced toward the desert, dragging the man.

"We told you to stay inside!"

By the time he turned, Jenny was tossing Graciela up on the dun, struggling with her skirts to mount behind the child. When she threw the reins of the black to Ty, he caught them, jumped in the saddle, and shouted, "Ride!"

They were a mile from the wreck before he noticed two significant events. Graciela had disobeyed and left the train, but she had brought his saddlebags; he recognized them hanging across the dun mare.

And he'd been shot in the side.

The first thing was to create some shade. When she spotted two tall cacti, Jenny shouted his name and pointed before she rode toward them.

"How badly is he hurt?" Graciela asked for the hundredth time, shifting to lift anxious eyes to her face.

"I don't fricking know, all right? Please, Graciela, I'm as worried as you are, but I don't know. We'll find out in a few minutes."

But it was bad, she knew that. The knowledge boiled in her brain, searing and frightening her.

Though it appeared they weren't yet being pursued, they had ridden hard for the last two hours, heading north across arid ground that hadn't tasted rain in months. Now it was clear they could go no farther.

Blood caked Ty's right side. Thirty minutes ago, he had slumped in the saddle. Jenny kept watching him, fearing that he would fall off the black at any moment. The sound of the train wheels continued to vibrate in her head, but instead of clickity click, the sound she heard was, Oh God, oh God, oh God.

Please, please, don't let him be dying. Please, no. I'll do anything you want, just let him live. She repeated the litany again and again, unaware that she did so.

Swinging out of the saddle near the cacti, she lifted Graciela down and tossed her the reins. "Give me a minute, then tether her." Shaking fingers fumbled at the girth strap and buckle, then she had the saddle on the ground and dragged it toward the twin cacti. Once she'd draped the horse blanket over the cacti to create a block of shade, she pulled the saddle beneath the canopy. There was a canteen, thank God, but precious little else on the horse that would be of use to them.

The black, with Ty sagging on his back, would have walked past her if she hadn't run to grab the bridle and one of the reins that dragged the ground. She shouted at Graciela to tether Ty's horse, too, then caught him as he clumsily tried to dismount, falling heavily against her.

"This way." Dropping his arm over her shoulder, she led him to the pitiful lean-to she'd constructed. It wasn't until she had him beneath the horse blanket and resting against the saddle that she realized her heart was slamming against her ribs and she could hardly breathe. He was badly wounded. Very badly.

"What can I do?" Graciela asked in a thin, high voice.

"See if there's another canteen on the black. Bring everything you can reach."

Ty opened his eyes, placed a hand against his side. "This one's bad, Jenny."

"I know, cowboy. Let's have a look at you." Pressing her lips together, she helped him out of his waistcoat, drew a deep breath, then opened his shirt and steeled herself. "It's not a flesh wound," she said after a minute. "Lean forward, let's see if the bullet passed through."

It hadn't. And that was bad. Lowering her head, she swore steadily for a full minute, not stopping until Graciela returned and pressed a second canteen into her shaking fingers.

"Here." Graciela curved her hand around the neck of a bottle of mescal. Mescal packed a powerful punch and she was glad to have it.

Jenny pulled the cork with her teeth and handed the bottle to Ty. He nodded gratefully, took a long pull, then wiped the back of his hand across his lips. Graciela knelt on one side of him, Jenny on the other.

"This one could get me. It won't . . . but it could."

"It will," Jenny said flatly, "unless we get some help."

Graciela stared at him. "I'll sew you up!"

Jenny's chest rose and fell before she spoke. "Honey, this is different. That bullet has to come out."

Graciela wrung her hands, and tears and snot rolled down her face. "We'll take it out!"

Jenny gazed into his eyes. He knew what she was going to say. They held each other's gaze. "We'll talk about it, but I don't think so. If I make one tiny mistake, I'll kill him." What she didn't say, what made her wild and frantic inside, was knowing that even if she got the bullet out, he'd already lost too much blood to ride. Ty wasn't going anywhere.

Graciela clawed at her arm. "You have to try! Jenny, you have to cut out the bullet! I'll help!"

Ty held Jenny's gaze for another minute, then reached for Graciela's hand. "Honey, you and Jenny can't stay here. Luis was one of the men who blew up the train. We didn't get him. He'll be coming after us."

"We won't go," Graciela wailed. "We won't leave you!"

"Graciela, we've got two canteens. Only enough water to last until tomorrow, a couple more days if we ration. And no food. Even if Luis wasn't after you, you'll die if you stay here."

Oh God, oh God, oh God. The words clicked through her mind, drowning the scream stuck in her throat.

She made herself speak in a low calm voice. "He'll need nursing, Graciela, constant tending for at least a week. But we don't have food or water to keep us alive for a week. If we stay, it's suicide."

Graciela made a choking sound. "But if we leave, he'll die!"

Reaching across Ty's bloody shirt, she caught Graciela's hand and squeezed it gently, swallowing the scream bubbling in her throat. "I'm going to ask you to do something that I know you don't want to do."

"What?"

"I want you to go stand by the horses and let me and your uncle Ty speak privately."

"I don't want to." But she slowly pushed to her feet and dragged her feet toward the horses, where she stood, looking back at them, wringing her hands together.

Jenny accepted a slug from the mescal bottle, passed it back to him. She took his hand and held it firmly. "Drink up, cowboy. I want you drunk as a skunk before I go poking around your insides. Least I can do is give that bullet a try. Better I kill you than let the desert or Luis do it."

He squeezed her hand. "No sense putting either of us through that." His steady gaze told her that he saw his future. "You need to get her somewhere safe. Leave me a canteen and a loaded pistol."

Oh God, oh God, oh God. She gazed into his eyes. "I don't know if I can do this, Ty. Just ride away and leave you here," she said in an unsteady voice, blinking hard.

"Listen to me, darlin'. There's no sense all three of us waiting for the vultures. Now you know I'm right." He clenched his jaw, waited a minute, then continued talking. "How close is the next village, do you figure?"

"You've been through these parts. There isn't much of anything between Chihuahua and El Paso Del Norte. No place where they'd have a surgeon or a doctor. Best we can hope for is a local healer and some luck."

He nodded. "You'll have to see to it. I can't ride. Couldn't get back on that horse in a month of Sundays."

She stared at him through a film of tears. "I can't do it,

Ty. I can't ride out of here and leave you to die alone in the sun and the desert. I cannot fricking do that."

His grip tightened when she would have snatched her hand away. "Listen to me. If you stay here, Graciela dies right along with you and me."

"Someone might come along and—"

"And they might not. Or it might be some more god-damned Barrancas cousins. Luis is still out there unless you killed him, and I missed seeing it."

She shook her head, cursing Luis Barrancas.

"Jenny? Look at me. You made a promise. You gave your word to take her to Robert. Now get on that horse and go. Right now. You think I want you and Graciela sitting here watching me die? Get the hell out of here."

Moaning, she leaned forward and beat her fists on the ground. If she stayed, she might be able to save his life. Maybe. Maybe someone would happen along with food and water.

"Jenny," he said quietly, "there aren't any promises between you and me. But you made a promise to a woman who died in your place."

She lifted her head and screamed at him. "Just shut up about that! Don't you think I know it?" Right now, she hated Graciela. If it wasn't for the risk to Graciela, she'd stay here with Ty and take her chances. But she couldn't do that. She had made a promise to a dying woman, and now a dying man was telling her that she had to honor that promise.

"And I made a promise to my brother. I'm depending on you to keep your promise and mine."

"I know it, I know it. Oh Ty. Oh God." Hands gripping desert sand, she dropped her head and felt the scald of tears burn her eyes. "Don't die," she whispered. "I'll send someone back for you. Just don't die. Hang on."

"That's my girl," he said softly, tipping the Mescal bottle to his lips. "Jenny? I have no right to ask this, but . . . wait at the ranch for a month. Will you do that?" A painful lopsided grin twisted his mouth. "I'm feeling lucky. I'll come for you."

She lifted her head, tears glittering in her eyes. "You stupid son of a bitch! Why'd you have to go get yourself shot?" Raising on her knees, she leaned forward and kissed him hard on the lips. Then, staring into his eyes, she shouted for Graciela. "Come over here and say goodbye to your uncle. We're leaving."

Graciela ran forward and dropped to her knees beside him. "No! I won't leave you! We have to stay together!"

Ty touched her cheek. "You go with Jenny. I'll meet up with you both at the ranch."

Graciela dashed tears from her eyes. "Please don't die, Uncle Ty. Please don't die! I'll pray real hard for you."

Jenny stood and looked down at him. "Is there anything you want me to tell Robert or your mother?" The talking was making him weaker. And looking at him was killing her by slow degrees. His pale face, the sweat on his brow and upper lip, the blood drying on his shirt. Oh God, oh God, oh God.

"Tell them . . . oh hell, just tell them to take care of my girls." His eyes urged her to go, then flickered with pain when Graciela threw herself on him, sobbing.

"Do you have everything you need?" Jenny whispered. She picked Graciela up and slung the kid over her shoulder. She saw the canteen and pistol in his lap, and the bottle of mescal before her vision blurred. She'd also seen the effort he made to appear alert, to remain conscious.

"Just go," he muttered, his voice starting to slur.

"Ty?" she whispered, drinking in the last sight of him. "Thank you for . . . for everything. I love you."

His head dropped and she didn't know if he'd heard. Every instinct screamed at her to stay with him. He needed her. He needed nursing, needed that bullet out of his body. He was a good man; he deserved better than to die alone on the Mexican desert.

"I'll find a village. I'll send someone back. I promise!"

I promise. Never had she detested two words more. Blinded by tears, she threw Graciela up on the black, pulled her skirts to her thighs, and swung up behind her. Because she couldn't bear to look at him again, she cantered away without a backward glance.

Fighting to hold his eyelids open, Ty watched until all he could see of them was a small plume of dust floating against the horizon. By then he had dulled the pain in his side by drinking most of the mescal. Silence settled like a shroud.

His chances weren't good. He knew that. With a full canteen, and if he didn't move much, he figured he might have four days. As weak as he was, as much blood as he'd lost, he probably had less. But he was a determined bastard, and tough. He wouldn't go easy.

Shifting his back against the saddle, he opened his eyes and spotted three buzzards circling a spot about two miles in the distance. His hand tightened on the grip of the pistol.

He had enough bullets to stave off predators, at least for a while. The night chill would be a problem and the heat of the day, but no worse than the lack of food.

Closing his eyes, he let his head drop toward his chest.

Damn it. He should have told her that he loved her. He should have told them both.

Because when he'd watched them ride away, he'd recognized the truth. The same thing had happened with his father. The old man had to die before Ty realized that he'd loved him. Now it took his own dying to make him recognize what he'd been fighting for weeks.

Damn it. He should have told them. He should have said the words.

The gun slipped from his hand, and he slowly rolled onto his side.

Jenny rode through the sunset and into the night, Graciela limp and sleeping against her chest. Sometimes exhaustion won, and she dozed, waking with a panicked jerk and wondering how long she had slept. Finally, near dawn, she smelled a village and veered east toward the ripe scents of habitation.

There were only a dozen huts arranged around a weed-clogged plaza and a cracked fountain, which had long ago ceased to function. That was enough. Reining before the first shack she came to, she stumbled toward a rawhide door, reeling with fatigue.

"I need help, *por favor*," she whispered to a man who peered through the stitching at the edges of the rawhide. "I have *dinero, Señor*. I can pay, but please . . . help me."

He studied her reddened, exhausted eyes, scanned her rumpled, bloodstained jacket and skirt. Then he glanced toward Graciela slumped on the horse in front of his house.

He opened the door. *"Mi casa es su casa, Señora."*

"Gracias, Señor, gracias. My child," she said, collaps-

ing against the doorjamb, her gaze grateful. The man called to someone behind him, and a woman stepped past Jenny, sliding her a look of curiosity before she rushed to help Graciela off the horse and into the house.

First, Jenny saw to it that Graciela washed and ate. Before she touched the food Senora Gonzales offered her, she drew Senor Gonzales into the yard and the early glow of sunshine.

She told him about Ty, her voice urgent and shaking. "He's out about a day and half's ride. He'll need a healing woman and a carrying litter." Senor Gonzales rubbed the money she had pressed into his palm. Then he nodded and turned away from her, heading toward the plaza, which looked more desolate in full daylight than it had in the faint hints of sunrise.

For a long moment Jenny considered waiting for Senor Gonzales to return with Ty. That's what she wanted to do. Then her head cleared and she realized that imposing on the hospitality of these people for three days would strain the resources of the village.

Regardless, if she had truly believed the village men would bring Ty in alive, nothing on earth could have induced her to leave.

But she couldn't bear to be here if what they brought back was his body. She wanted to remember him as he had been, vividly alive, larger than life, a man whose eyes danced with pale fire, a man whose hot touch could send her crashing to her knees. A hard, dangerous man capable of surprising tenderness, a thief who had stolen a love she hadn't know she possessed.

"Damn it!" He would have laughed at the moisture in her eyes, would have ridiculed her weakness. Raising her hands, she ground the heels of her palms against her eyelids. She had to be strong for Graciela. Graciela had loved him, too.

After she ate food she felt too numb to taste, she and Graciela climbed into the same hammock and held each other until Graciela cried herself to sleep. Eventually Jenny slept, not waking until the heat of the day had passed.

She bought fresh clothing from Senora Gonzales, and a wagon from an old man who looked dazed by the number of pesos she dropped in his hand. She hitched the black to the wagon, loaded jugs of water and a basket of food, and she and the kid drove away from the village that would become the grave for her heart.

Two days later, hollow-eyed and trembling with fatigue, Jenny and Graciela crossed the Rio Grande and entered El Paso, Texas.

The next afternoon, wearing hastily purchased traveling ensembles, they boarded the westbound Southern Pacific, holding tickets for San Francisco.

The accommodations on the Southern Pacific were so far superior to those aboard the Mexican National Railway it seemed impossible the two railroads could occupy the same universe.

No dogs, chickens, or piglets roamed the aisles of the Southern Pacific. The scent of food baskets and an overflowing latrine did not permeate every breath. Seats were upholstered. There was a separate dining car and private compartments.

The funds Marguarita had supplied were running low, but Jenny splurged for a private compartment with sleeping shelves rather than subject herself or Graciela to sleeping sitting up.

"I'm sad," Graciela said quietly, leaning her head against Jenny's shoulder.

"I know." Jenny took her hand and held it in her lap.

They stared unseeing out their compartment window as New Mexico rolled beneath the wheels of the train. The desert wasn't as sparse here. There were clumps of chaparral, more varieties of cactus. Stands of piñon and desert pine.

By now, they would have found Ty's body in the Mexican desert. Perhaps they had buried him there. Or maybe they had brought him back to the village. If the village had a name, Jenny didn't know it. That upset her, and she worried and fretted about it all day. Not until they donned their hats to go to the dining car did she decide it wasn't important that she didn't know the name of the village. He was gone. That's all that mattered. She had found him, and now he was gone.

Long into the night, she lay on her sleeping shelf, gazing at the curved roof, wincing when Graciela moaned in her sleep, listening to the ratchety click of the wheels carrying them into a starry void. She should be considering what she would do after she left the Sanders ranch, but her mind wouldn't function. She hadn't yet accepted Ty's death; she couldn't, wouldn't. How could she bear to think about saying good-bye to Graciela, too?

It wasn't until the third day that she noticed Graciela was not wearing the gold locket pin. "Wait here," she said anxiously, standing abruptly and reaching to pin on her hat. "You must have lost it at supper. I'll go back to the dining car and search."

"I didn't lose it," Graciela said, turning her face to the window. "I'm not going to wear the locket anymore."

Frowning, Jenny looked down at her. "Why not?"

"Because I don't want to look at her picture. I don't want to be like her. I want to be like you." Graciela stared up at her, the words tumbling over each other in a rush. "My mother was weak. She cried about everything. And she didn't know how to do anything. *She* didn't know how to shoot a gun or make a campfire! *She* couldn't have driven a wagon across the desert." Her eyebrow lifted, and her mouth twisted. "If I'd been with *her,* I'd be dead now. And so would she."

Jenny's arm flew up and she slapped Graciela hard enough to knock her off the bench seat. When she hauled her back to the seat, her fingers bit deep into the kid's shoulders.

"Don't you *ever,* not *ever,* say anything against your mother! Do you hear me?" Her eyes blazed down at the handprint flaming on Graciela's cheek. "Your mother was the bravest woman I've ever known. The most loving and selfless person you will ever know in your whole life. She loved you more than anything else in this world, and don't you *ever* forget it. Whoever you are, whatever you become, you owe it to her. If you grow up to be half the woman she was, you can count yourself proud. So you talk about her with respect, and you honor her and you love her."

Graciela jerked free and backed against the window. "She died."

"Don't start that again," Jenny warned between her teeth. "I didn't kill your mother."

"You didn't kill her. I did!" Graciela screamed. "*I*

killed her! She died to save me." Her expression crumpling in agony, she sank to the rocking floor and covered her face. "I killed her!" she sobbed. "She died for me. It's my fault!"

"Oh my God." Jenny stared in shock. Of course. She should have looked deeper, should have guessed. She should have asked why Graciela was so insistent that Jenny had killed her mother. It was because she could not bear to confront what she truly believed. Marguarita had died to give Graciela a chance to live. Marguarita would not have explained it that way . . . but the kid possessed a keen intelligence. She would have grasped the underlying meaning of what Ty and Jenny told her about her cousins, she would have sensed the desperation beneath her mother's plea for a promise from a stranger. "Oh my God."

Dropping to the floor, Jenny reached for her. "Graciela! You didn't kill your mother. No. Never." Jerking the child into her arms, she held her hard against her pounding heart. "Honey girl, your mother was dying of consumption. Taking my place only hastened the inevitable by a few days. She was very, very ill, you must have seen that."

Graciela clung to her, sobbing against her shoulder. "She died to make you promise to save me. It's my fault!"

"No, no, darling." Jenny smoothed her hair with shaking hands. "She just ran out of time. It was no one's fault."

"If it wasn't for me, she would have died in her own bed. I killed her! They shot her because of me!"

Jenny held her, staring over her shoulder at the desert beyond the window. Echoes bounced in her mind. "He wouldn't have died if you'd watched over him like I told you! It's your fault that Billy's dead!" And her own agonized cry, "But Ma, he ran away from me! I didn't see him fall in the lake!" My fault, my fault, my fault. She had been nine years old. Billy had been seven. Jenny shook her head sharply. How many times had she relived the day of her brother's death?

"Graciela, your mother did not go to the firing squad for you." She drew a breath and felt tears gather at the back of her eyes. "She did it for me." Graciela clung to her, sobbing quietly, listening. "I . . . your mother and I knew each other. We were friends." She stared out the window at the desert.

"Marguarita knew I'd been wrongly accused. And she knew she was dying. She asked me, as her friend, to take you to your father because she no longer could. It was an easy promise for me to make. See, I'd planned to go to California with you and Marguarita all along. The three of us were going to go together. I . . . I was going to watch out for your killer cousins. That's what Marguarita wanted me to do."

Was she babbling? Would this story hang together? Was she any good at this?

"Then I got arrested, and they were going to kill me, so I couldn't go to California like we planned. And Marguarita got so sick. I told her we should have gone earlier, but she . . . her aunt Tete needed her, and you know how kind and generous your mama was, so we kept putting it off, and then it was too late because she was too ill to travel."

There wasn't as much cactus outside the window now. Low bushes and scrub grass had begun to appear. But it looked hot, so hot. As hot as hell out there.

"So she came to me in jail, and I begged her to save my life. She was dying anyway. But I could take you to your father. I could protect you from the Barrancas cousins. We could each do something for the other. Graciela, look at me."

She eased the child away from her body. "I was selfish because I wanted to live, and I saw a way to do it. I promised your mama I'd take you to California just like I'd planned to do anyway. And your mama, well she loved me because we were friends, and she wanted to save my life. Your mother didn't trade her life for yours, Graciela. She exchanged her life for mine. Because we were sister-friends. Because I wasn't sick, and she was. Because she knew I'd honor our friendship and take care of you. I didn't kill her, Graciela. But I might as well have. She died to save my life."

"Is that true?" Graciela whispered, wiping her eyes to peer hard into Jenny's.

Oh God, oh God, oh God. "As God is my witness, I've told you the truth. Have I ever lied to you? Or to anyone else? If anyone is to blame for your mother's death, it's me for being so stupid as to get myself arrested and sentenced to a firing squad. And it's her fault, too, for being so brave and wanting to save a friend who could help her daughter. But you are not to blame. Not you. Never you."

"Oh Jenny." The kid's arms came around her neck, choking her, holding on tight. But this time her sobbing was softer; a torrent of grief, not blame. Deep sorrow, not fault.

"There's something else," Jenny said after a long time, speaking softly, stroking the child's back. "Don't go thinking you're to blame for what happened to Ty." She waited until her voice steadied. "Your uncle Ty is an honorable man who would help any two people who needed him. Remember how we met him? How he jumped into the fight at Verde Flores? He didn't know us then. His conscience pointed him toward that bullet, Graciela, not you. If Ty dies, and I refuse to believe that he will, it won't have anything to do with you."

"I thought it was my fault that he . . . are you sure?" Graciela murmured against her damp shoulder. Her agonized whisper told Jenny that she had guessed right.

"I'm very sure. Now. Let's find that gold locket and pin it on your jacket so we can honor a fine and courageous woman who was my friend and who loved you as much as any mother ever loved a daughter."

"Jenny? I love my mama. But I love you too."

Oh Lord. Her arms tightened around Graciela's body and she buried moist eyes in the child's hair. She was strangling. She thought she might die. "It's all right," she whispered finally. "That doesn't mean you love your mama less. It just means that you care for me too." She swallowed hard, hearing her heart crack in her chest. "It doesn't mean you're being disloyal to your mama. I think she'd like it that you care about me a little."

That night she didn't try to sleep. She sat beside the window, watching moonlight shadows slide across the desert miles. She didn't regret lying to Graciela; she would do it again in the same circumstance. But she felt the empty space where she'd taken a chunk out of herself. And she ached with the sweet pain of a child's love.

Toward morning, she raised her eyes to search for Marguarita's star.

I hit her, Marguarita. Funny, isn't it? All the times I

threatened to smack her, but I never did. Then she stopped wearing the gold locket and I . . . well, you know what happened.

Was lying the right thing to do? Or did I throw away the one good thing about myself? I don't know anymore. I just know I couldn't let her go on hating herself for believing that you died to save her, that your death was her fault. I didn't think you'd want her sitting around at my age hurting herself with blame and fault during the lonely times.

And I guess you heard her say that she loves me.

Oh Marguarita. This is so fricking hard. I just didn't know anything could be this hard.

How can I say good-bye to her?

Chapter
Seventeen

San Francisco was the largest city Jenny had ever set foot in. There was opportunity here for a woman who didn't shy from hard labor and wasn't afraid to get her hands dirty. She didn't look like that kind of woman now, wearing a trimmed hat and driving gloves and the rumpled skirt and jacket of her traveling ensemble, but soon she would.

She drew the wagon on a rise and narrowed her gaze on the frenzied activity occurring down below at the wharves, listening with half an ear to Graciela's awed babble about the ocean. The only thing Jenny knew about oceans and harbors was that wharf rats were always in short supply, and the pay would be enough to keep her alive.

Satisfied that at least she had a plan of sorts, she clicked her tongue at the mule and returned to the road cutting inland from the coast.

"When will we reach the ranch?" Graciela asked, lowering the dictionary she'd been reading aloud.

"I expect we'll arrive tomorrow. Keep reading. And stop leaning on me."

She rolled her eyes in affectionate exasperation when Graciela ignored the instruction not to lean. It remained a mystery as to the exact moment when she had turned into such a pudding. And a mystery as to how the kid knew it had happened.

"Jenny?" Graciela kept her gaze fixed on the dictionary. "I'm scared."

The air ran out of her lungs, and her chest hurt for a moment before she dropped an arm around Graciela's shoulders. "Sooner than you believe it's possible you're going to feel like you've known your daddy and your grandma forever. And they're going to love you. Have you ever met anyone you couldn't charm?"

"I like it when you say nice things." Tilting back her hat brim, the kid cast her a tiny grin. "Do I charm you?"

"Huh! Not very likely." She laughed. "Well, maybe sometimes. But I'm a hard case. Your daddy and grandma Ellen will be pushovers for a manipulator like you. Remember that word?"

Graciela laid her cheek on Jenny's shoulder. "What about Grandpa Barrancas?"

Jenny had also been thinking about Don Antonio. None of her conclusions were fit for a child's ears. "For the moment, at least, you should probably just wait and see if he sends for you." She glanced at the top of the kid's hat. "He might not, Graciela. He was mighty displeased with your mama, and that might extend to you. I wouldn't set my hopes too high if I were you."

"When I get really scared about meeting all of them, I just pretend I'm you and think about what you would do."

Jenny bit down on her back teeth and stared at the mule's ears. "And what would that be?"

"You'd be polite and say *por favor* and *gracias,* but inside you wouldn't give a cuss if they liked you or not."

"Well, I guess that's right," she said, holding her gaze on the mule's head. Her innards went to mush. "It doesn't matter if anyone likes you as long as you like yourself. Yessir, that's all that's important. You find one good thing about yourself, and you hang on to that."

"I have lots of good things."

Jenny laughed. "Yes, you do, you little snot." She tightened her arm around Graciela's shoulders. "You're smart and pretty and brave and loyal and you sew better than anyone I ever did see."

"I don't cry much anymore either. You forgot that. And you and me, we stopped cussing. That's a good thing, too."

"Oh Graciela." She couldn't speak for several minutes. "Tonight you'll need to polish those boots and we're going to wash your hair until it squeaks. Send our clothes out to be brushed and pressed."

Graciela pressed her face against Jenny's shoulder, and a light tremor rippled down her small body. "Jenny? They're going to like me, aren't they?"

"Honey girl, you hold your head high when we drive up to the ranch house. You just remember that you're Marguarita Barrancas's daughter, and your mama didn't bow her head to anyone. And you don't need to either. *They* should be worrying if *you* are going to like *them.*"

Frowning, she glared at the road. If anyone dared to look askance at Graciela, Jenny would tear through the Sanders ranch like a tornado.

* * *

They arrived at the ranch shortly after noon the next day. Jenny hauled up on the reins in front of the gate. "Well," she said quietly, "we've come a long way, but there it is."

The main house sat back from the road about a quarter of a mile. Ty had described the circular veranda, and she knew to expect two stories, but he hadn't mentioned how large the house was. The impressive size, coupled with a multitude of well-maintained outbuildings and stock pens, suggested the extent of the Sander's prosperity. Seeing the spread, she better understood why Robert had been unable to reject his inheritance. And Ty's rebellion now assumed larger significance.

"Smooth your skirt and sit up straight," Jenny said absently, studying the layout. Eucalyptus and cedar shaded the house, but the lush pastures were clear of trees and brush. The cattle were fat and shiny. The Texans Jenny knew would have trampled their grandmothers to own a spread as green and picture-perfect as this.

Nervously, Graciela touched the gold locket pinned on her chest, then straightened her hat. "We look beautiful," she stated in a shaky voice. "Do you have a clean hankie?"

"It's still in my sleeve, right where you put it this morning." She gazed down into Graciela's face, noting the smooth light brown skin and brilliant blue-green eyes, the abundance of dark hair pinned on her neck. "You're the loveliest little girl I ever knew or ever saw," she said in a light, choking voice.

Their long journey together would end when the door of the ranch house opened. New people would enter Graciela's life and swiftly become important to her. They would take Jenny's place. When that door opened, another door would begin to close.

"Graciela?" she whispered.

But how could she say, "You are the child of my heart that I will never have, and I love you." Was it fair to grab this precious child and hold her close when the time had come to let her go?

"What?"

"I just . . . nothing." Clicking her tongue, she flapped the reins over the mule. "Kiss your daddy and your grandma Ellen even if they're ugly as sin, hear me? And don't go blabbing about Ty. Let me tell about him. And don't ask about Don Antonio, not yet."

No one came out to greet them, as no one expected a woman and a little girl. Jenny had to knock at the door, then ask a pleasant-looking Mexican woman if she might have a word with Ellen or Robert Sanders.

Though she had never met Ellen Sanders, she recognized Ty's mother when she came to the door, smiling politely and wiping sugary hands in a white apron. Ellen Sanders had the same blue-green eyes as Ty and Graciela, the same lean carriage. Sun and weather had carved fine lines in her face, but so had character. Jenny released a long breath. She liked this woman at once.

Drawing a deep breath, she pulled back her shoulders. "Mrs. Sanders? My name is Jenny Jones." She waved a hand toward the small figure waiting anxiously on the wagon seat. "And that is Graciela Elena Barrancas y Sanders. Your granddaughter."

"Graciela Elena," Ellen whispered, staring. "Oh my God. Marguarita named the child after her mother and me." Then she ran past Jenny, crying and laughing and shouting for Robert and a dozen others. "Maria! Ring the yard bell. Bring everyone! Quickly, quickly! My granddaughter has come home!"

In the melee that followed, Jenny was forgotten.

Bits and pieces of Jenny's story emerged throughout a day of rejoicing tempered by sorrow. Robert, enough like Ty that her heart ached at the sight of him, understood at once that Marguarita would not have sent Graciela alone if it were possible to accompany her. Hearing his fears confirmed extinguished the light in his eyes. When he learned that Ty, too, would not be coming home, he walked away from the celebration.

Ellen bore the news in stoic silence. "We'd hoped to end the feud with Don Antonio for the sake of Marguarita and the child. I don't know if that will be possible now that a Barrancas has killed my son."

"He might make it," Jenny insisted stubbornly.

Ellen peered into her eyes, then walked toward the west pasture, where she stood for almost an hour before rejoining the impromptu barbecue in her granddaughter's honor.

It was one of the longest days in Jenny's memory. She ate when she was handed a plate, drank buckets of lemonade, listened to a cowboy fiddler, exchanged polite conversation with people whose names she promptly forgot. She remained in the background, watching Graciela until she understood from Graciela's flushed excited expression that it was going to be all right. With a child's generosity, Graciela opened her heart to the new family, who were so obviously prepared to welcome and cherish her.

Jenny had no doubt that she witnessed the beginning of a strong and loving bond between grandmother and granddaughter. Ellen Sanders had loved Graciela on sight. Henceforth, Ellen would step into the breach. She would serve as Graciela's example and her champion. Ellen would raise her, teach her, reprimand her, praise her, and love her.

She also hoped that, in time, Robert would love his daughter. Right now, Robert was deeply wounded, smothered by the death of dreams so recently resurrected. But eventually, she hoped he would draw close to the child who had proudly shown him the small portraits within the locket she wore.

Jenny lowered her head. Never had she hated anyone as fiercely or as passionately as she hated Robert Sanders right now. In some secret darkness of her soul, she had hoped to find him dead. The admission shamed her, but Robert's death would have allowed her to fall back on her promise to Marguarita and she could have taken Graciela to raise with a free conscience.

She would have taken Graciela from the big, richly furnished house. And the thousands of fat cows. And the beautiful bedroom and the wonderful life that awaited her here.

She would have taken Graciela from all this to live in a shack by some stinking wharf? Was her love that selfish?

Stomach cramping, head splitting, she stumbled through the day, happy for Graciela, miserable for herself. Missing Ty with a painful ache that cleaved her in two.

Finally, at ten o'clock, at Graciela's insistence, she oversaw Graciela's bath in a room set aside for that purpose, listened to her prayers, and tucked her in bed. Tonight new people appeared in the list of please-blesses.

Graciela kissed her, then fell back against a plump pillow and gazed up with shining eyes. "They aren't ugly as sin. Daddy is as handsome as Uncle Ty. And Grandma Ellen is pretty, don't you think so?"

"Yes, she is," Jenny whispered, pulling a linen sheet to Graciela's chin. "Where's your locket?"

"I let Daddy keep it. He wanted to. Daddy's sad now because of Mama, but he said we'll get acquainted later. I like Juana, too. And Grizzly Bill."

"Who the hell is Grizzly Bill?" When Graciela lifted that one irritating eyebrow, she recanted the cussword.

"He's the foreman. He says he has a little horse just my size. Oh Jenny, everyone likes me!"

"Well, of course they do." Standing, she gazed down at a tumble of dark hair spilling across the snowy pillow and tried to smile. "Are you too excited to sleep? Would you like me to punch you in the jaw and knock you unconscious? I'd be happy to do it."

Graciela laughed. "I love you, Jenny. Good night."

"Good night, kid." Leaning, she blew out the light, then hesitated in the doorway, observing the room in which Graciela would grow to be a woman. A light breeze ruffled lace curtains at the windows. Braided rugs cushioned the floor. Flowered wallpaper climbed the walls, the colors repeating in quilt and bedskirt. It resembled a picture in a rich man's catalog.

Expressionless, Jenny closed the door and walked toward the staircase.

Robert and Ellen waited for her at the foot of the stairs.

They sat at a heavy claw-foot table in the kitchen because Ellen shared Jenny's opinion that kitchens were the best place to hear news, good or bad. By the time she finished telling her story, the grandfather clock in the parlor had chimed midnight.

Robert pushed to his feet, his face pale. Jenny didn't think he'd heard much beyond the sound of bullets hitting a wall and a woman's frail body. "I'm much obliged to you, Miss Jones. This family owes you a great debt. You're welcome to stay at the ranch for as long as you like. When you leave, you'll leave with a sizable purse."

Jenny frowned. "I don't want your money, sir. Bringing Graciela home wasn't a job. It was a promise."

She and Ellen watched him stumble into the night, letting the door bang behind him. Then Ellen sighed heavily.

Turning her head, she gazed out the window. "I guess you don't understand a lot of this."

"It's none of my business."

"Are you a drinking woman, Jenny Jones?"

"I've tipped a few in my time," Jenny said cautiously.

"Good." Ellen went to a cabinet, moved some sacks and boxes, and returned to the table with a bottle of bourbon and two tall tumblers. "I'm sensing there's a lot about you and my son that you haven't told," she said, when the tumblers were full. "I need to hear it."

Jenny tossed back a swallow of liquid courage and let it burn down her gullet. Then she talked about Ty.

When she finished, Ellen shared out the rest of the bourbon. "Last time I drank this much was after I buried Cal." She studied Jenny's face in the lamplight. "You loved my boy," she said softly.

"It doesn't matter anymore."

Ellen leaned back in her chair, away from the light. "Of the two boys, Ty was most like Cal, only neither of them ever saw or admitted it. Stubborn and hard as nails, them two. Neither would bend an inch." She smiled down at her tumbler. "When he was a tadpole, Ty used to say he wanted to fight outlaws and rescue pretty women when he grew up. If a man's got to die, it's good to face it doing what he always wanted to do." She lifted her eyes. "I like you, Jenny Jones. You got real promise. That was my mama's highest praise. She'd say, 'Ellen, you got real promise.' "

"Thank you, ma'am. But you don't know me."

"You think I don't?" Ellen laughed before her face sobered. "You won't tell a lie to save your own hide . . . but you'll lie to spare a child's feelings?" She smiled across the table and spoke softly. "I know you, all right. You have a heart as big as your courage, and you love that little gal upstairs."

Jenny gazed into her tumbler. "I have to leave. Tomorrow." The words fell out of her mouth, pushed by the pain of liking Ty's mother, of sitting at a table where he had sat. He had walked through these rooms, maybe used this glass. Everywhere she looked, her heart saw him. And Graciela.

"Honey, I know you want to put things behind you and move on. And I know a clean cut hurts the least. But that little girl don't know that. And that little girl still needs you. So I'm asking you to stay a while until she don't feel she's surrounded by strangers." She reached to cover Jenny's hand. "Saying good-bye isn't going to hurt less a month from now than it will tomorrow."

Jenny thought about it, then nodded reluctantly. "I guess you're right. And I promised Ty I'd wait a month." Tilting her head back, she gazed at the ceiling and blinked at moisture swimming in her eyes. "But it's so hard."

"Loving is, honey. Loving is."

She made herself useful by helping with the wash and cooking, and she surprised Grizzly Bill and the boys during branding week by working as hard and as well as a man. She put up jelly, made pickles, joined Ellen at the mending basket.

And slowly she withdrew from Graciela.

Now it was Ellen who listened as Graciela chattered through her nightly bath. And it was Ellen or Robert who heard her prayers and tucked her in at night. During the day, Jenny made certain there were always others present, and they weren't alone together. It hurt that Graciela didn't appear to notice.

One day, thinking she could bear it now, she borrowed a horse and rode to Ty's house. The house was silent and boarded up, but the clean strong lines reminded her of him. This was the house he had chosen and built for himself. She sensed him here.

Sinking to the porch steps, she gazed out at the land Ty had ridden and loved, opened herself to the air he had breathed, and finally she let herself grieve. A tear spilled down her cheek, then she covered her face in her hands and sobbed as she had not sobbed since childhood, not since her favorite brother had drowned in the lake. She wept for Ty, and for herself, and for dreams that had died before being born.

Stumbling, she reeled about the yard, shouting fury at the sky, dashing tears from her eyes and screaming her pain for God's ears. It wasn't fair. It wasn't right. He should have lived.

Eventually she returned to the porch steps and sat there, rocking in anguish, remembering every word Ty had spoken to her, every small gesture he had made. In agony, she recalled every detail of the night they had spent together, the long kisses and feverish caresses, the whispered words, the soft laughter.

Despite everything, during the long days of silence with no word from him, a tiny corner of her heart had continued to hope. That was what hurt the most, that little flame of hope when there was no hope. Today, she tried to kill it. It got smaller, but her hope was as stubborn as she was. It wouldn't die entirely.

At the end of the long afternoon she returned to the ranch house with reddened swollen eyes and trembling lips. Ellen studied her then gently touched her arm. "Did it help?"

"No."

"Jenny? Would you ride with me today? Jake's been teaching me. You'll be surprised how well I can ride now. All by myself!"

"Good idea," Ellen agreed before Jenny could think of an excuse. "That will get you both out of my hair while I finish these pies."

"There's someplace I want to go," Graciela confided, lowering her voice.

"Oh? Where's that?" Removing her apron, she hung it on a peg.

Graciela slid a look toward Ellen bustling around the kitchen. "It's a secret. I'll tell you later."

"Give me a minute. I'll change into riding duds."

"No, what you're wearing is fine. All you need is a hat."

Jake, whom Graciela had firmly wrapped around her little finger, had the horses saddled and waiting. "Pretty sure of yourself, weren't you?" Jenny asked, swinging up into a lady's saddle with a frown. She could ride sidesaddle, but she hated it. "All right. What's the secret and the big rush? Where are we going?"

Once they reached the main road and Graciela reined her pony to the right, Jenny figured it out. "Wait a minute. Hold up there, kid." She leveled a stare at Graciela's flushed face. "Do you think we're going to just ride up to Don Antonio Barrancas's place without an invitation or a by-your-leave?"

"He's my grandpa."

"Yeah, well he isn't beating a path to your door to acknowledge that fact, now is he?"

Graciela tossed her head. "Maybe he doesn't know I'm here."

"After three weeks? If even I have heard about Don Antonio's new stud bull, then you can bet your butt that he's heard about you. News travels fast around here."

Graciela gave her the superior schoolmarm look. "I want to meet my grandpa Barrancas. I know the way to his ranch, Jake told me. But I'm afraid to go by myself."

Jenny considered. She knew Robert and Ellen would

disapprove, but . . . why not? Maybe it was time Don Antonio met his granddaughter. Plus, as hardheaded as Graciela could be, the kid would go there sooner or later regardless of instructions to the contrary. Better that she went with a champion at her side. Reluctantly, Jenny moved her borrowed horse up beside Graciela's pony.

"All right, but this goes against my better judgment. And if Don Antonio tosses us out on our butts, don't say I didn't warn you."

The day was warm, and a light breeze carried a tang of the distant sea and the scent of nearby blossoms. It was the kind of bright spring day that made the heart sing just to be part of it.

"Jenny? Do you still like me?"

"What?" She snapped her head to the right and stared. "Of course I still like you. Why would you ask a dumb fool question like that?"

"You've been acting all strange since we came here. First, I thought you were hurting over Uncle Ty. But then I thought—"

Now was the time, there would never be one better. All she had to do was find the courage to announce that soon she would be leaving. "Look, kid," she said, fixing her gaze straight ahead as her chest tightened. "You've got family now. You don't need—"

But she didn't finish the speech that she endlessly rehearsed every night. Two men rode out of the brush beside the road and ordered them to halt. "You're on private property," one of them said in thickly accented English. "This is Barrancas land. Turn back."

"We've come to call on Don Antonio Barrancas," Jenny stated coolly. She nodded to the second man and switched to Spanish. "Please inform Don Antonio that his granddaughter wishes to pay her respects." The men stared at Graciela, then both wheeled and galloped up the road.

Jenny waved at the dust settling atop her hat and shoulders. "Well, we'll know in a few minutes if we're welcome or not."

"Mama said Grandpa Antonio is very strict," Graciela confided anxiously. "I don't think he likes little girls."

"Then you were very brave to come here."

The Sanders ranch suggested prosperity, but the Barrancas spread shouted wealth. Jenny sucked in a breath when she spotted the tile-roofed hacienda through a feathery stand of cedar. If she hadn't know this was a private residence, she would have assumed it was a government seat. The outbuildings were easily twice the size of those on the Sanders ranch, and she had never imagined so many stock pens could exist in one place.

Straightening her shirtwaist with an unconscious gesture, she gazed at the hacienda and wished she'd worn a jacket and a better hat. "I'm thinking this wasn't such a good idea, kid."

"Stop calling me kid," Graciela whispered, staring.

"At least they aren't going to throw us out right away."

A man, a woman, and a boy stood waiting beneath a porte cochere. The man silently assisted them to the ground, and the boy led away the mare and the pony.

The woman gasped and covered her mouth when she saw Graciela. She cast an anxious glance at Jenny, then returned her stare to the child. "This way, *por favor*," she murmured, leading them inside.

Everything was massive. Huge beams supported the

ceiling. A wide staircase led to a shadowy second floor. The furniture was large and gleaming, sitting atop carpets as fine as tapestry.

Graciela edged closer to Jenny and gripped her hand as they followed the woman through the great hall, down a short tiled corridor, and into a cool, beautiful room with cream-colored walls and brightly upholstered furnishings.

"*Café, señorita?* the woman murmured, not taking her gaze from Graciela. "Perhaps something cool?"

"*Nada, gracias,*" Jenny answered, transfixed by the two portraits above the fireplace mantel.

One of the women was Marguarita, young, glowing with health, and breathtakingly beautiful. The other woman, obviously Marguarita's mother, was older but equally as lovely. Both women had dark eyes; otherwise, Jenny might have been seeing Graciela at age sixteen and again at age forty.

"Hello, Grandpa. I'm Graciela."

Spinning, Jenny confronted a tall handsome man, younger than she had assumed he would be. Grey streaked Don Antonio's dark hair at the temples, and an outdoor life had weathered his face, but she doubted he was much older than Ellen Sanders, whom she knew to be forty-six.

He stared at her over Graciela's head, no trace of welcome in his cold black eyes. "Why have you come here?"

She cleared her throat and straightened her spine. "Senor Barrancas, I am Jenny Jones. I've brought your granddaughter from Mexico to California. I have news of your daughter if you wish to hear it."

He lowered a frown to Graciela and clasped his hands behind his back. "I have no daughter," he said harshly.

"Yes you do, Grandpa. Don't you remember?" Graciela whispered. "See? That's Mama in the portrait. But Mama died and so did Uncle Ty." She moved a little closer to Jenny. "Cousin Jorje and Tito tried to kill me. So did Cousin Luis and Chulo. Chulo cut Jenny, but I sewed her up."

Don Antonio's head snapped up and his black eyes flashed. "What nonsense is this?" Jenny believed she had observed an instant of pain at the mention of Marguarita's death, but now she saw only fury. "Did you bring this child here to insult my family in my own house?"

Jenny's gaze narrowed, and her back went ramrod straight. "Apparently your relatives south of the Rio Grande believe they are more entitled to your fortune than your granddaughter. They did their damnedest to kill us both. They did kill Ty Sanders."

"If I had a granddaughter, no member of my family would dare harm her. If you are referring to Sanders's bastard"—he flicked Graciela a look of contempt—"your lies become ridiculous. Sanders's bastard has no claim to Barrancas property."

"I have your daughter's marriage papers, *Señor*. Graciela, named for your late wife, is not a bastard." Dots of color flamed on Jenny's cheeks, but her voice emerged as steady as rock. "Your daughter was not the fool that perhaps you believe she was. She confirmed that Graciela is indeed your legal heir, *Señor*, whether or not you accept her. And you have my word that it's only luck that prevented your family from killing your granddaughter."

Rage stiffened his jaw. "You are not welcome here,

Señorita. Take this child, whoever she is, and leave my lands at once."

Graciela's chin came up and her posture unconsciously mimicked her grandfather's. "Jenny does not lie." Her shoulders pulled back and indignation burned in her eyes. "And neither do I! Tito poured snakes on me, and Luis blew up our train and killed Uncle Ty. They did, too, try to hurt your granddaughter. That's me, Grandpa!"

He turned on his bootheels and had almost reached the door when a sharp voice called his name.

"Senor Barrancas."

Jenny turned to see Ellen striding into the room, wearing a hastily donned jacket and hat. She threw Jenny and Graciela an exasperated glance, then walked forward and seated herself on the only piece of furniture that was not upholstered.

"Perhaps some refreshments?" she said in Spanish to the woman hovering in the doorway. "Coffee for the adults, lemonade for Don Antonio's granddaughter."

The woman cast a quick glance at Don Antonio's frosty rage, then hastened away.

Ellen's smile did not touch her eyes. "Forgive me for assuming the role of hostess, but it appears you have several guests today."

"*Señora* Sanders," Don Antonio said icily. "Please accept my condolences for the loss of your husband."

"I have suffered new losses," Ellen answered softly, beckoning Graciela to come sit beside her. "My son and my daughter-in-law."

Hardly daring to breathe, Jenny stood beside the fireplace and watched the frigid but carefully polite interplay between the representatives of two families who bitterly hated each other. And her respect and admiration for Ellen Sanders grew by leaps and bounds. Ellen had seized upon Mexican courtesy and used it to manipulate Don Antonio.

Moreover, Ellen had guessed Graciela's destination, had followed, and was bent on holding her own while sitting in the lion's den.

"I pray you will forgive a blunt observation, but I doubt the loss of your alleged daughter-in-law pains you any more than the loss of a Sanders pains me."

Ellen met his eyes. "You are wrong. I was deeply sorry to learn of Marguarita's death. I intended to welcome my son's wife to my home, and I was prepared to accept and love her. The Barrancas and Sanders women were never part of the feud between you and my husband."

"I have business to attend," Don Antonio said stiffly. "When you have finished your coffee, Chala will see you to the door."

"You have lost a daughter, and I have lost a husband and a son," Ellen said quietly. "Let it end, Antonio." She placed her arm around Graciela. "Let our beautiful granddaughter serve as a bridge of truce between your family and mine. She came to you of her own free will and against my wishes because she wants to know her mother's family, too. I was wrong. She is as much yours as mine. She was right to come to you. You sent one chid away. Will you harden your heart against this child, too?"

When Ellen sent Jenny a glance, she read it at once. Without a word, she moved forward, took Graciela by the hand, and led her out of the room.

For the next hour, she and Graciela wandered the grounds surrounding the hacienda. No one approached them. No one spoke to them. When they spotted the boy leading their horses toward the heavy carved front doors, they hastened to the porte cochere.

Ellen emerged grim-lipped and hard-eyed. She mounted her horse without speaking, waited for Jenny and Graciela, then rode out in front. She didn't drop back beside them until the horses had trotted off Barrancas lands.

"Will he accept her?" Jenny inquired softly.

"Damned if I know! That is the proudest, stubbornest, most unbending man I ever met outside of Cal Sanders. But at least he knows the whole story now. I don't think the old jackass believes half of it, but I gave him an earful to think about." Her gaze narrowed. "Speaking of jackasses . . . what the *hell* were you two thinking of to go busting in there like thieves rushing to a lynching? I ought to whup the both of you for being so dad-burned stupid."

It was Graciela who began. First she looked astonished, then surprised. "Jenny. Grandma sounds just like you!" She burst into delighted laughter.

Jenny gazed at Ellen and fought to hold her expression steady, struggled to look contrite. But Graciela's infectious laughter grabbed the tensions of the last two hours and transformed them into giggles. Jenny's mouth twitched. Her shoulders shook. And then she was roaring helplessly. "We must have lost our minds," she shouted, laughing so hard she thought for certain she would fall off her horse. "You'll have to whup us."

"You sure as hell did lose your minds!"

"Grandma, you can't cuss. Me and Jenny quit cussing. You have to stop cussing, too!"

And then Ellen was slapping her hat against her thigh and laughing until tears streaked down her cheeks.

Every time they looked at each other throughout the rest of the week, one of them would chuckle, and then they would all burst into laughter until they had to hold their sides and sit down.

And each day of work and laughter, each walk with Robert, each task shared with Ellen and Maria, each trip to sit on the porch of Ty's house, each time Graciela slipped her small hand in Jenny's, made it harder for her to think about leaving.

But she had to leave soon while at least part of her heart still belonged to her. She kept giving chunks of it away, to Ellen, to old Grizzly Bill, to the boarded-up house, and a small slice even went to Robert who held himself aloof in his pain and grief, lost in despair that she understood only too well.

Tomorrow the month she had promised Ty would end. The day after, she would ride away, as hollow and scooped out as a person could be and still claim to be living.

Chapter
Eighteen

"Grandma? Can we bake a cake today? Maybe a cake would make Daddy smile."

Every time Graciela looked at her daddy, his sad expression made her chest hurt. When she'd given him her gold-heart locket, she had hoped her mama's portrait would help him feel better, but it didn't seem to. She didn't think her presence helped either.

Of all the people on the ranch, she was most shy around her father. He held himself aloof and distant, wrapped in misery. Sometimes she guiltily wished Uncle Ty was her daddy, and she liked to daydream about her and Jenny and Uncle Ty being together. That would have been so wonderful and perfect.

Graciela watched Grandma Ellen exchange a glance with Jenny before she wiped sudsy hands on her apron. "We'll bake a cake tomorrow, honey. But this morning, Jenny wants you to go riding with her."

"Oh good!" She clapped her hands. "Just you and me? No one else?" This was a far better treat than baking a cake.

"Just you and me," Jenny confirmed in a strange husky voice.

"Can we go to Uncle Ty's house?" They visited his house regularly, pulling weeds away from the front steps, sweeping off the porch. Graciela liked to go there because she liked to think about Uncle Ty, and because she could see the rooftops of her grandpa Barrancas's hacienda from Uncle Ty's porch.

"Put on your split skirt because we aren't going to ride those sissy ladies' saddles," Jenny said. "Hurry up, now. I'll fix us a lunch basket while I'm waiting for you."

Before she skipped up the staircase she heard Grandma Ellen suggest that Jenny carry a gun. "A couple of the boys mentioned seeing strangers yesterday and the day before. At first Jake thought they were new Barrancas hands, but he did a little checking and they aren't. Jenny, you know I don't feel good about you and Graciela going up to Ty's place alone. I wish you'd take Jake or Grizzly Bill with you."

"This will be the last time."

There was an odd silence and Graciela overheard soft whispery sounds as if Grandma and Jenny were hugging. Something about them today made her feel uneasy. She had that strange prickle of dread and anxious anticipation like she sometimes felt just before a lightning storm.

Stopping on the landing she sucked in a breath and held it, thinking about the long glances between Jenny and Grandma Ellen and the way they'd both been fussing over her during the last week. And yesterday, Jenny had given Grandma Ellen the documents they had brought from Mexico. Last night her daddy had said something about having Jake drive Jenny somewhere. These small events came together and suddenly she understood.

Whirling, she leaned over the bannister and hot tears blinded her. "No!"

Jenny couldn't leave. She wouldn't let her. She loved Jenny and they owned each other. If Jenny left the ranch, then she would go too. It would be a hundred times less painful to say goodbye to Grandma Ellen and the others than to let her Jenny go. She couldn't do that.

Angry and upset, she struck the bannister with her fist. She wished Uncle Ty would hurry up and come home. He wouldn't let Jenny leave them. Uncle Ty would be furious if Jenny left, she just knew it.

Covering her face, she scrubbed her palms against the tears burning her eyes. It was so hard to be a helpless kid. There was so much she didn't understand and couldn't control.

Please, please God. Don't take Jenny away from me too.

Jenny couldn't figure out what had happened between the time Graciela left the kitchen and when she reappeared with reddened eyes and accusation pinching her expression.

"You got a burr up your tail?" she asked after they had ridden to Ty's house in heavy silence. "I don't remember you ever being this quiet for so long." She looped her mare's reins around the hitching post and watched Graciela do the same before she lifted down a picnic basket and carried it to the porch steps.

Graciela sat on the step above her. "Why are you wearing a gun and those pants?"

"I'm wearing a gun to humor your grandma. It was either wear a gun or bring along Jake or Grizzly Bill, and I didn't want to do that. I want today for just you and me." She pulled a chicken leg from the lunch basket and offered it, but Graciela shook her head. "Suit yourself. Anyway, the gun is just a precaution."

"I know why you're wearing pants again. You're getting ready to leave, and you're getting used to work trousers."

Jenny froze, then lowered the piece of chicken she'd brought to her mouth. She kept forgetting how bright Graciela was. Nothing got past the kid's sharp little eyes and mind. She had hoped to delay their private good-bye for a while yet, had hoped for one last lovely afternoon to remember before they got into fare-thee-wells.

Lowering her head, she wiped her fingers on a napkin. "The Sanderses aren't my kin, honey girl. I've imposed on their hospitality long enough. I've seen that you'll be loved and taken care of... I've waited the month I promised Ty." She raised her head and gazed into Graciela's swimming eyes. "Honey, I have to go now."

"Uncle Ty is going to come home and he's going to be really mad when you aren't here." Angry tears rolled down her face.

Jenny sucked in a deep breath before she answered. "I've tried to accept that Ty is dead even though a little part of me"—she touched her heart—"refused to believe it. But, honey, if Ty was alive, he would have sent word." It hurt so much to give up hope. That was the hardest part of it. The ache was constant, her sense of loss as fresh as daylight. "You and me... we're the only ones who thought he might make it, but that was just wishful thinking because we loved him. I think we've got to accept the worst."

The kid's tears drowned her, just fricking killed her to see and made her want to cry, too. She felt as if she were strangling on salt and bile, and she wasn't prepared when Graciela jumped into her lap and wrapped her arms tightly around her neck. For a moment they teetered within a gasp of falling off the porch.

"If you have to go, then I'm going with you!"

"No, honey girl, you can't." Jesus Lord, this was driving a knife through her heart. She'd rather have relived Chulo's blade slicing her belly than have these little arms clinging around her neck and feel a child's sweet tears on her cheek. "These are your people. They love you, and you love them, too. You'll have a good life here."

"I'm *your* people! I love you, and you won't say it, but you love me, too, I know you do, Jenny! You have to take me with you. Who'll give you clean hankies? Who'll sew you up?" Her arms tightened, holding on. "Who'll teach me new words and new things? If you go, who'll teach me how to be like you?"

"Oh Graciela. God." She held on so tight that she feared she might hurt the child. When Graciela pushed back to peer in her eyes, she had to force herself to loosen her grip.

"Jenny! You're crying! Oh!"

They clung together and let the tears come, sobbing until their eyes were dry, until all they could do was sit together in combined misery. Jenny adjusted Graciela's weight on her lap and rested her cheek against the kid's hair. She would never forget the fragrance of Graciela's hair and the weight of her small, warm body. That weight had started off mighty heavy; now she welcomed it. How was she going to live without this child? Losing Ty had already carved away half of her heart; she would leave the other half behind when she rode away tomorrow.

"I do love you, Graciela," she murmured hoarsely. "No, don't look at me. I have some things to say, and it'll go easier on me if you don't look while I'm saying them."

"I'll follow you when you go. You can't stop me."

"I don't want you to do that."

Marguarita? If you're listening, I beg you . . . please. Please, help us both.

"Honey girl, believe me. I've tried to think of some way that we could stay together, but there is none."

"You could marry my daddy."

She had considered this possibility herself. And had concluded that even if Robert accepted such a doomed proposal, it would end in disaster. She disliked him intensely for keeping himself a stranger to his daughter, felt contempt for his weakness, past and present. "Your mama is the only woman your daddy will ever love." Graciela would grow up motherless and mostly fatherless, and there wasn't a fricking thing she could do about it.

"But *why* can't you take me with you?"

She fought the hot lump threatening to strangle her. "Because I love you enough to give you the life your mama wanted for you. I don't want you growing up on the streets like I did. I want to know you're safe and happy and loved. I want to know that you're clean and eating good food and sleeping in a bed with a pillow. When I think of you, and Graciela I will think of you every day until I die, I want to think of you here. If you want to make me happy, then stay here with your daddy and your grandma Ellen, and be happy yourself."

"I can't—"

A shot exploded through the quiet sunny spring morning. Splinters flew from the post above Jenny's hat.

Before the slivers of wood hit the porch floor, Jenny had tossed Graciela over the railing and dived after her, drawing her pistol as she fell. Easing her head up, she peered through the porch rails, scanning the shrubs and underbrush. "Did you see anyone?"

Graciela peeked, then gasped and ducked down again. "It's Luis! And my cousin Emil, and I think I saw the Cortez brothers."

Jenny released a stream of silent cussing that would have curdled a preacher's eyes. Now she saw the forms slipping through the trees and brush, maybe six men, and she spotted a man who looked enough like Luis Barrancas that Graciela had to be right. It was Luis. Her first shocked thought was: It can't be. Followed by: Yes, it can. The bastard had followed them and found them in California.

She fanned a barrage of shots toward the trees and underbrush, her mind racing. Ty's place was too far from the Sanders ranch house to hope that anyone there would hear the shots. She could expect no assistance from that quarter. But without help, the outcome was predictable. She was outnumbered, outgunned.

"Kid, listen to me. We've got one chance." And it was probably a slim one. She squeezed off a shot, felt Graciela's wide, frightened eyes fixed on her face. "When I stand up and run toward that low rock wall, you run as fast as you can in the other direction, to the hitching post. Follow me so far?"

Graciela nodded. "You want me to ride back to the ranch."

"No, honey, that will take too long. Ride like hell for your grandpa Barrancas's place. You tell him these are his fricking relatives and his fricking problem, only say it nice, no cussing." A bullet tore through the brim of her hat, knocking it off her head before she ducked down, face-to-face with Graciela.

"What if Grandpa won't come?" Graciela asked anxiously.

She touched the kid's cheek. "If he's decided to accept you, he'll come. If he's still being a jackass, he won't. It's that simple." But Graciela would be safe. Ellen had told Jenny enough about Don Antonio Barrancas that Jenny believed him to be a man of pride and honor. Ellen had hinted that the hostilities between the families had originated with Cal Sanders, not Don Antonio. There was not a doubt in Jenny's mind that the cousins had to be here without Don Antonio's knowledge. "Use some of that charm you're always telling me you have, or my butt is dead. Now give me a kiss for luck, and let's do it."

Graciela kissed her hard on the lips, then they looked at each other for a long minute.

"All right, on the count of three. One . . . two . . . go!"

Fanning her gun and running in a crouched zigzag, she dashed across the yard, bullets shaving weeds all around her, but somehow she made it to the stone fence with all her parts intact. She leaped over the stones, then dropped flat to the ground. Behind her, she heard Graciela's pony crashing through the underbrush and prayed there were no Barrancas cousins on that side of the house. If she had guessed right, that the cousins were here without Don Antonio's knowledge, she didn't think they would risk exposing themselves to being sighted from his hacienda. But who could tell what the crazy bastards might be thinking?

Rolling on her back, she reloaded, then flipped onto her stomach and got off a couple of shots, narrowing the odds against her by one Mexican, who fell out of the brush, twitched, then lay still. But she didn't celebrate.

This shoot-out was not going to end well. Not this time. Somehow it seemed fitting that her luck would run out here, as close to Ty as the ranch could offer.

A hail of bullets whizzed over the wall and she waited, wondering if the cousins were creeping up on her, hoping for a lull so she could lift her head and fire a few more shots.

She was on borrowed time anyway, she told herself, easing up for a peek over the wall. A head darted out from the corner of the house, ducked back. They had reached the house.

She should have died a couple of months ago in front of a firing squad. The time since then had been a gift and she silently thanked God for it. She had used her extra time well. She had known Ty and she had known Graciela; she had known love. She had kept her promise to Marguarita. Her house was in order, she had no future and no regrets, and she supposed she was as ready as a person ever was to meet her maker.

Firing steadily, she peered over the wall to see how close they were now. Then a fiery impact struck her shoulder and she flew backward with a gasp. Damn.

Touching her fingertips to her left shoulder, she felt the wetness, blinked at the blood on her hand. Grinding her teeth together, she hoped the bastards weren't cheering yet, because it was going to take more than one bullet to kill Jenny Jones. Crawling on elbows and stomach, she moved up to the wall again then eased onto her back to reload.

The firing was intense enough that she didn't hear the horse riding down on her, didn't see the man until he leaped down next to her as his horse jumped the stone wall. Rolling, he knocked the gun from her hand and was on top of her in one smooth motion.

"Why is it that every damned time I run into you, you're in the middle of a fight? What's wrong with you, woman?"

"Ty!" Her eyes flew open and she went limp, halting her effort to knee him in the groin. Struck dumb, she just stared at him. She couldn't believe it, but there he was, grinning down at her, his blazing blue-green eyes as beautiful and dangerous and full of Old Nick as she remembered. "Ty!"

Her arms flew around his neck and she dragged him down out of a rain of bullets, kissing him hard over and over and over. Then she stared at him again, made a fist, and punched him with her uninjured hand hard enough to lay him out in the dirt beside her.

"You no-good inconsiderate stinking piece of cow flop! You selfish unthinking bastard!" A bullet parted her hair before he gave his head a shake and jerked her down into his arms. "Haven't you ever heard of a fricking telegraph? Do you have any damned idea what you put us through? We thought you were fricking dead!"

"I *told* you I'd be home in a month. Do you think you're the only one who keeps a promise? And besides, I wanted to surprise you." Gently, he touched the bloodstain widening across her shoulder. "I swear, darlin'. Are we ever going to know each other when one of us isn't shot or cut?" His grin widened.

"We are outnumbered here, you idiot. There's two of us and four or five of them. What are you blathering about? We are going to *die*." She covered his face with kisses. "Oh God, I'm so glad to see you!" Tears of joy blinded her. "Now haul your sorry butt up here and shoot some cousins, so at least we don't die in disgrace."

"Honey, you just stay right where you are, here in my arms because I had plenty of time to think and I've got some things to say to you. Help is right behind me, and you won't believe who's leading the posse."

The words were hardly out of his mouth when a dozen riders galloped through the trees and brush. Ty pulled Jenny out of the path of Don Antonio's horse seconds before the black stallion flew over the stone wall, followed by a stream of riders and horses.

"He came," Jenny whispered, closing her eyes and slumping on Ty's chest. "He came for Graciela."

"You need to talk louder," Ty said, pulling her on top of him. But the gunfight was moving away from them now. Only an occasional stray bullet smacked into the stone wall.

Using a fat bottom stone on the wall as a pillow, he settled his head against it and gazed into her eyes. "I love you, Jenny Jones. Now hear me out and don't interrupt. I know you and me aren't the marrying kind, but we have to get over that and get married anyway."

She blinked down at him in amazement. "You're proposing marriage in the middle of a fricking gunfight? With me bleeding all over you? Ty Sanders, you left your brain back there in the Mexican desert."

But he loved her. Oh God, he loved her. He'd said the words. He loved her. And suddenly that was the only important thing in the world. If the gunfight was still going on, she didn't hear it. She heard only his voice, saw only his gorgeous tanned face. The only thing she felt was his hard body, tight and hot beneath hers. That, and the fierce pounding of her heart singing in her ears and mind. He loved her.

"Get down here and put your head on my shoulder. I'd be real pissed if you got yourself killed at this point in my proposal, and especially after all I went through to get here before the month was up."

She pressed her head on his chest, smiling foolishly, listening to the rock-steady beat of his heart. It belonged to her. His heart was her heart now. "Well, get on with it, then. Why do you think we have to get married?"

"Because I want to bed you down again and marriage answers the problem of you maybe getting pregnant. Because I need a woman in my bed and in my house. Because I love you, and you love me. And, finally, because Ma said if I didn't marry you, I didn't have the sense God gave an ant." He laughed. "She sent me up here after you and told me not to come back unless you said yes." Gently, he lifted her enough to gaze into her glistening eyes. "Say yes, Jenny. Promise you'll marry me. Promise you'll still be here, driving me crazy and loving me when we're little and old and surrounded by grandchildren. Promise that you'll let me love you until I take my last breath. Promise."

"Oh Ty. I promise. With all my heart, I promise!"

Oblivious to everything but each other, they lay together behind the stone wall, touching, kissing, both talking at once until a shadow fell across them. Blinking, surprised to notice the absence of gunfire, they came to their feet, exchanging embarrassed and self-conscious glances.

Don Antonio removed his hat and swept it across his body in a bow. "Welcome home, *Señor* Sanders."

Ty hesitated, then thrust out his hand, and Don Antonio Barrancas clasped it. The two men gazed into each other's eyes, silently reviewing past grudges, measuring what a different future might hold.

"I have a gift for you both." Not looking away from them, Don Antonio raised a hand, and one of his men led a horse forward. Luis Barrancas lay draped across the saddle. He had not died peacefully.

"This gift does not erase my family's shame. Nor will any apology ease the insult of doubting you, *Señorita* Jones." Pride stiffened his neck, and Jenny saw how difficult the moment was for him. "To my shame I rode here in response to a distraught child's pleas, but I did not believe her story or yours until I saw Luis with my own eyes." His cold gaze flicked toward the two cousins who had survived the gun battle. Don Antonio's men held them at gunpoint. "I will know the full extent of my family's treachery by nightfall."

"And Graciela?" Jenny asked, beginning to feel the pain throbbing in her shoulder. She leaned into Ty's arm, drawing on his support.

Don Antonio fixed his eyes on Luis's body. "Perhaps I have been mistaken about many things, *Señorita*." He turned to look at Ty. "No Barrancas will ever again ride onto Sanders land in anger. If you agree, the hostilities between our families end here."

Ty hesitated, then nodded. "Agreed." The two men shook hands again.

"Give Graciela a chance, *Señor*," Jenny said softly. "She wants to love you." She suspected Graciela's self-proclaimed charm had begun to dent his resistance. If he gave the child half a chance—and she saw now that he would—Graciela would have him wrapped around her little finger in no time flat.

"The child will dine tonight at the hacienda," he announced abruptly. "One of my men will return her to the ranch before darkness."

"*Bueno, Señor,*" she whispered. Before he sipped his after-dinner coffee or lit his cigar, he would belong to Graciela. Lowering her head to hide a smile, she noticed the blood dripping down her arm and off her fingertips. "Well, damn." Glaring, she scowled into Ty's eyes. "I have to say, cowboy, as husband material, you aren't working out too well so far. You didn't send me a telegram like you should have, and it's going to be a long time before I stop being pissed about that, and now you're standing here talking while any fool can see that I'm bleeding to death right in front of your sorry eyes. I just might have to rethink hitching up with you."

Laughing, he lifted her in his arms and grinned down at her. "Too late. You promised to marry me, and I never saw a woman hang on a promise like you do. So, you're stuck with me, no-good that I am."

Smiling, she rested her head against his shoulder while

he carried her to the horses. "Well, I guess I am. Course, you're stuck with me, too. And maybe I like that a lot."

Cradled in his arms, bleeding all over his chest, she decided this was the happiest day of her life.

Uneasy undercurrents flowed beneath the party his mother gave to celebrate Ty's homecoming and his engagement to the woman he had thought of every minute of every day during his long difficult recovery in the Mexican village and then his journey north.

The Barrancas men and the Sanders men stayed on opposite sides of the barbecue pit, eyeing each other with suspicion and mistrust. His mother and Don Antonio exchanged guarded pleasantries and treated each other with frigidly exaggerated courtesy. Only the presence of other guests prevented the discomfort between the two families from flaring openly.

But today marked a beginning. Time would bring other gatherings and eventually pleasant encounters would outweigh the memory of past hostilities. Graciela, who ran happily from one group to the other, would draw both families toward a shared future.

When the women stole Jenny away from his side, Ty walked to the pasture fence to join Robert and looked back at all he loved best. The land, the home where he had grown to manhood. And now the woman who would soon be his wife, standing in the twilight holding the hand of a child. This precious woman and child had opened his mind, had changed his attitudes and finally his life. His chest tightened when he looked at them, and he had to swallow hard.

"She's a fine woman," Robert said quietly. "You're a lucky man."

He nodded, pride squaring his shoulders. "I've never known another like her."

She looked beautiful tonight, flushed with happiness, her eyes shining when she waved to him. Her hair, below her ears now, captured the flaming light of sunset and reminded him of the feathery fire between her strong thighs. The dress she wore molded her magnificent breasts and flared over hips meant to bear a man's babies. Someone, probably Graciela, had pinned a bouquet to the sling that cradled her wounded arm close to her body. God a'mighty, but he loved her. He couldn't believe his good fortune that he'd found her and that she loved him.

By the end of the week she would be healed enough to travel, and he intended to take her to San Francisco, away from his mother's watchful eyes and insistence on separate bedrooms until the wedding. He would make love to her until she was dizzy with laughter and desire and weak with satisfaction, then he would buy her a trousseau and an apricot-colored wedding gown.

"I should have gone with Marguarita to Mexico," Robert said softly. He, too, watched Jenny. "I'll never forgive myself that I didn't. And the ranch—it should have been yours."

"I'm happy with my three hundred acres." He lit two cigars, handed one to his brother.

"I don't love the land like you do. I never did." Robert smoked in silence for a moment. "That's what I can't live with. I let her go to please Pa, maybe because I didn't want you to have what I thought was rightfully mine." Disgust and self-loathing twisted his mouth. "I didn't even have the backbone to go fetch my own wife and daughter. I asked you to do it because I was ashamed to face Marguarita. And, God forgive me, a part of me is glad that I didn't have to. How does a man live with that?"

There was no answer he could give. Robert was his brother, and he loved him. But they had never understood each other, had never walked in the same set of boots.

"You have your daughter," he said finally. "Give her a chance, Robert. I've only been home three days, but I can see that you aren't letting Graciela be part of your life. She deserves better."

"Yes. She does," he said, his gaze fixed on Jenny and Graciela. "I've done a lot of thinking in the last few days. I've concluded that one of the things I can do to atone for the mistakes I've made is give my daughter a loving family and the happiness she deserves." He exhaled slowly, watching a curl of cigar smoke drift toward the pasture. "I'm leaving, Ty. I'm going to Mexico to say good-bye to my wife. Afterward, I think I'll go to South America. Maybe I'll end up in Mexico City, who knows?" He shrugged. "All I can say for sure is that I'm never coming back here."

"And Graciela?" Ty asked sharply.

"It won't surprise you when I ask you once again to take on my responsibilities and make them your own."

For a moment Ty didn't speak. He could guess what was coming, and sadly, Robert was right. It didn't surprise him.

"The ranch should always have been yours. Now it will be. As for my daughter . . . you and Jenny can give her a real home. I can't. Every time I look at her, I see Marguarita and my failure as a husband, as a father, as a man. That's not fair to her, and it's not something I can live with. Will you do these last things for me? If Jenny agrees, will the two of you take the ranch and my daughter and make them your own?"

"You know the answer." He didn't have to discuss it with Jenny. He knew how she felt.

"You found something in Mexico that changed you," Robert said, studying Ty's face. "Maybe I'll find something there, too."

Ty smoked in silence, watching Jenny across the yard, and remembering the weeks of healing in the Mexican village on the edge of the desert. By then he was a changed man, but he hadn't yet examined those changes. With time to think, he'd realized that Mexico had birthed his father's prejudices but had buried his own. He owed his life to the good people in that desert village. Without their kindness and generosity, without their compassion for a stranger, he would be dead. Mexico had given him his life. Mexico had given him Jenny and Graciela.

"What will you tell Graciela?"

"That I'm going away for a long time. When you judge the moment is right, tell her that I'm dead. It's better that way."

"I care about you, Robert, but right now I'd like to punch you in the mouth."

His brother's smile was painful to see. "That's the difference between us, Ty. You're a fighter, and I'm not. If it helps any, I'll feel guilty about my daughter for the rest of my life."

"Then stay here and be a father to her."

"I can't." Robert lifted a chain from around his neck

and dropped Graciela's gold-locket pin in Ty's hand. "Give her this after I've gone and tell her that I love her. Maybe someday she'll understand that I loved her enough to give her the best parents to raise her."

Ty slipped the locket into his pocket. "Is there anything I can say to change your mind?"

"No."

He nodded in final and reluctant acceptance. "I'd like you to stay until after the wedding. I want you to stand up with me. And Robert, write to Ma occasionally. Let us know that you . . ." Swallowing, he gripped his brother's shoulder. "You can always come home. You know that."

"I know," They looked into each other's eyes. "Think of me sometimes. The way it used to be when we were kids, before things got so damned messed up."

And then Jenny was walking toward them, the promise of heaven shining in her blue eyes, and he forgot everything except the miracle of knowing this splendid woman was his.

Meeting her halfway, he caught her in his arms, then led her around the side of the house into a pool of shadow beside the azaleas and pulled her against his body. "My God, you're a beautiful hunk of woman."

Pink bloomed in her cheeks and she laughed, winding her uninjured arm around his neck. "Cowboy, I hope you never believe this, but you're the only man in the whole world who thinks so."

"Have you looked in a mirror, darlin'?" He kissed her, a teasing nip at her earlobe that he hoped would drive her crazy with wanting him. "You've changed since I first laid eyes on your sorry self. Course the essentials are the same," he said with a grin, sliding a palm up her side to her breast. Her soft moan sent an aching hunger to stiffen his desire.

She pressed her chin against his and stared into his eyes. "Ty? Sometimes . . . I just . . . am I going to make a good wife?"

"There'll be some rocky periods, I imagine," he murmured, adjusting her hips against his. "But you've got promise, Jenny Jones. I expect you'll grow into a fine wife. You've already learned the most important part."

She laughed softly, deep in her throat, and closed her eyes as he covered her beautiful strong face with increasingly ardent kisses. Then she caught his hand and cupped it around her breast.

"Do you think anyone would miss us if we rode over to your house?"

She'd learned her lessons well. Now it was she who teased and tormented. "Everyone will miss us," he said, kissing her eyelids, the corner of her mouth. "This is our party."

They gazed into each other's eyes and laughed. Neither of them had ever cared a tinker's damn about what other people thought.

"I don't want to wait for San Francisco, cowboy," she whispered huskily, pressing against him. "I've waited long enough for you to get your butt back here and into my bed."

"I'll race you to the stables," he said in a voice hoarse with his need for her. "Last one there has to take my boots off."

Holding hands and laughing, they ran toward the first

stars appearing in the night sky, toward the stables, and toward the promise they had found in each other.

Later he would tell her that Robert was going away and had asked them to start their life together with a six-year-old daughter whom they both loved. He would hold her while she wept with happiness. Right now, all he could think about was being with her.

Jenny. Whispering her name had kept him alive in the desert. She would make the rest of his life worth living. Jenny.

Epilogue

After the wedding, the guests helped move the furniture out of the living room and parlor and pushed the chairs against the walls. Musicians tuned their instruments, sampled the punch, then the dancing began. A hundred smiling guests drifted between the dance floor and the refreshment tables or strolled about the torchlit yard.

Jenny stood beside the parlor archway, watching Graciela waltz in the arms of her handsome new husband, her face pink with happiness, her eyes shining as she gazed up into his adoring dark eyes. They moved to the music, but she doubted either of them heard a note. They saw and heard only each other.

An arm slipped around her waist and she started, then relaxed against Ty's chest. "I like him very much, don't you?" she asked softly, smiling as Diego leaned near Graciela's ear and whispered something that made her blush and laugh and stumble in his arms. Grinning, he caught her, then spun her in a circle, holding her as safe and secure in his arms as he would hold her in their life together.

Ty wrapped his big hands around her waist and rested his chin atop the curls she had so artfully arranged. "She'll make a fine doctor's wife," he commented in a husky voice. "If Diego isn't careful, she'll shove him aside and perform all the surgery herself. Do a good job of it, too."

Jenny laughed, leaning into him. Her gaze skimmed the other dancers, noticing Don Antonio and Ellen, Grizzly Bill and the widow Parker, other neighbors she cared about. But always her gaze returned to Graciela and Diego. How beautiful they were tonight. So young and happy and filled with each other and visions for their future.

"When do you plan to dance with the mother of the bride, cowboy?" The warmth of his chest against her back felt solid and familiar and so damned good. Suddenly she wished the wedding was over and they were upstairs in bed, wrapped in each other's arms.

"Now you know I hate to dance."

"You looked real fine dancing with the bride," she teased.

"That's different. I *had* to do that. But I'm hoping an understanding woman like yourself will let me off the hook."

Graciela ran up to them when the waltz ended and laughed. "I hope Diego and I are still cuddling in corners when we've been married as long as you two."

Ty grinned and leaned to kiss her on the cheek. "I have to keep my claim fresh or some bastard with a discerning eye might move in on my territory." When Jenny and Graciela laughed, he said softly, "Honey, you look beautiful tonight. You plain take my breath away. The only woman more beautiful than Doctor Candeleria's new wife is my wife, and maybe, just maybe, it's a toss-up."

Graciela took their hands and the three of them stood linked as they had always been linked. "I love you both so much," she whispered, her lovely eyes glistening. Leaning forward, she kissed Jenny's cheek, then Ty's. "Oh Mama. Papa. I'm so happy."

"I know, honey girl. I see it." Dropping Ty's hand, Jenny straightened the gold-locket pin on the bodice of Graciela's wedding gown, touched her daughter's hair, and kissed her cheek. "Well, shoot. Will you look at me? I've always hated weepy women, but Lord, I've wept a bucket of happy tears today."

"Darlin', you better go back to that new husband of yours. Already he's looking lonely." Ty embraced her, holding her for a long moment. "If he doesn't treat you right, you just tell me and I'll have your mother beat the piss out of him."

Laughing, Graciela kissed and held them both, then lifted her skirts and ran across the dance floor. Standing with their arms around each other's waists, Jenny and Ty watched her go.

"I'm going to miss her like life itself," Jenny whispered, leaning her head on Ty's shoulder. "How did she grow up so fast?" When he didn't answer, she tilted her head to look up at him. "Ty Sanders! Is that a tear in your eye?"

"Well, hell no," he said gruffly. "Must be a cinder."

"Guess that would be the same cinder that gave you so much trouble when you walked her down the aisle and put her hand in Diego's." She smiled, loving him so much that she thought her heart would burst. "When's the last time you saw Robby, Billy, or Ty Two, by the way? Our boys wouldn't be outside sampling the men's punch, now would they?"

"Wouldn't surprise me. That's what Robert and I did when we were their ages." He kissed her long and hard, not caring who noticed. "Send these people home so we can go to bed," he said against her lips.

"Soon, cowboy. Meanwhile, check on our boys and find out what mischief they're up to." She nipped his lower lip, then laughed. "You can threaten *them* that their mother will beat the piss out of them if they're misbehaving."

Ty grinned and gave her a quick pat on the fanny. "How did a tough *hombre* like me turn into such a softie? Damnest thing ever happened in my whole life."

"You held your babies in your arms," she said softly, touching his cheek.

"That might have done it," he agreed, smiling. "Come with me. We'll beat the piss out of those rascals together. Show the young hellions who's running this outfit."

"They know who's running this family, and it isn't us," she said, giving him a smile and long kiss. "I'll meet you on the front porch in five minutes. There's someone I need to speak to first."

He nuzzled a kiss against her palm, then went in search of his sons, and she followed him with her gaze, her heart overflowing with the emotion of the day. After watching Graciela and Diego open the next dance, Jenny touched her handkerchief to damp eyes, then slipped into the kitchen and out the back door.

It was dark in the backyard. Cicadas sang in the bushes, competing with the music and conversation floating through the windows and around from the front of the house. But the celebration wasn't so loud that a person couldn't talk to an old friend.

She sat on a tree stump and folded her hands in her lap, then she tilted her head and gazed up at the spangled sky. Tonight, Marguarita's star seemed the brightest in the heavens.

It's been a while since we talked, my friend. But now that you have Robert with you, I figure you haven't missed me too much.

Today is our Graciela's wedding day. Before I pinned your locket on her gown, we looked at your portrait and said a prayer for you. I've felt you near all day, so I guess you heard.

Diego's a fine young man, Marguarita. I think you would approve. He loves our Graciela, and he'll make her happy. I hope you can see how beautiful she is tonight. She's like a flame blazing with joy. She loves him so much.

"Here she is! I found her, Papa." Robby, her youngest boy, came barreling around the side of the house, running toward her. His good white shirt had worked out of his waistband and one suspender hung off his small shoulder. "Mama, Mama! There's going to be fireworks! Come see!" He caught her hand and pulled her toward the light.

Laughing, she bent and dropped a kiss on his tousled hair. "You go on. I'll be right behind you."

When he had gone, tearing back the way he'd come, she lifted her face to the starry sky, blinking at quiet tears of happiness. *Marguarita? Everything I have and love, you brought to me. Ty, my boys, my home . . . and most of all our daughter, the daughter of my heart.*

She's a wonderful and very special young woman, your daughter and mine. She's beautiful and honest and strong. Her heart is courageous and true. She's the best of you and me. We can both be proud tonight.

Go to sleep now and rest. Our job is done. You kept your promise, and I kept mine . . . And, Marguarita? You were right. Mine was the easiest promise. She has been my joy and my treasure. She was so easy to love.

Good-bye old friend. Thank you for the precious daughter we shared and the life you sent with her.

After wiping her eyes, Jenny gazed up at Marguarita's star for the last time, then she lifted her skirts and ran toward the front of the house and the fireworks showering the night sky. She ran toward her husband and her sons and new promises to keep.

DON'T MISS THESE
BREATHTAKING ROMANCES
FROM
MAGGIE OSBORNE